CW01471679

Souls Run Wild

The Untold Journey of a Soldier Through War,
& Determined Survival

David Payne

DISCLAIMER & COPYRIGHT

Copyrights © 2025 By David Payne

All rights reserved. No part of this publication may be reproduced, stored in a retrieval system, or transmitted in any form or by any means — electronic, mechanical, photocopying, recording, or otherwise — without the prior written permission of the author, except in the case of brief quotations used in critical articles or reviews. This book is a work of biographical fiction. While inspired by true events and real-life experiences of the author, certain names, locations, and identifying details have been changed to protect the privacy and safety of individuals. Dialogue, events, and characters may have been adapted for narrative clarity and dramatic effect.

The views and opinions expressed are those of the author and do not necessarily reflect those of any military institution, government agency, or affiliated organisation. This book does not claim to provide an official or historical account of military operations or political events.

The author bears sole responsibility for the contents of this book. Any resemblance to actual persons, living or dead, or actual events is purely coincidental unless explicitly stated. The events and conversations in this book have been set down to the best of the author's ability, although some names and details have been changed to protect the privacy of individuals.

For lists included in this publication every effort has been made to trace or contact all copyright holders. The publishers will be pleased to make good any omissions or rectify any mistakes brought to their attention at the earliest opportunity.

For permissions, media inquiries, or rights, please contact:

Davidpaynechurt@aol.com

Acknowledgement & Dedication

Well, I could fill another chapter with those who have helped over the years; however, that said, I will keep it to those who have their names etched upon my soul. Jimmy, to whom I must give credit for his weaknesses, which gave me encouragement to support him.

Jeff and Rita, without their friendship and help, I do not think I would ever have been able to put pen to paper and recall this history. To Min-Jun, Ha-Un, and Joe, they know without saying anything how heartfelt my thoughts are toward them.

Finally, to my dearest friend Anne Marie, the past memories we have shared have inspired me not only to fight for my existence but also to write this manuscript. I must not forget Saqib for his encouragement in bringing it all together for print. Many thanks to all.

TABLE OF CONTENTS

SOULS RUN WILD

By: **David Payne**

PREFACE

My story is a testament to a life experience that many people may have had the misfortune of experiencing fragments. However, I have yet to meet anyone who has experienced a journey so extraordinary. It has become a legacy, a cautionary tale to be observed but never replicated, which is now my right to leave, hoping that it is viewed but never re-enacted. Too many lives have been lost or shattered while performing the same duties I once did. Ultimately, I realised it was all futile, a tragic waste.

As a young man, I served in the British Army, where my story starts. Subsequently decorated for my contributions to Special Operations in Northern Ireland, where both Overt and Covert operations were conducted. I can never go back to that Island for reasons that will become apparent. This experience started me on a treadmill that I could never get off; it led to more terrorist hideouts. Ultimately, taking me all over the world, analysing, lecturing, and warning me of the terrorist threat that we all face now and in the future, culminating in me eventually returning home after five years of forced exile. I can only say in my twilight years, "They are still out there."

After my life's worst five years' experience, I told my story to a dear friend, who, honestly, did not believe it. Although she told me you must write this down, it is dynamite! I laughed. That night, I sat in my apartment and thought about what I had been told; she was right to ask me to put pen to paper and see what would happen.

I must thank my dear friend Anne Marie, whose memories kept me going over those last five years. To my daughters for not having a father during their teenage years and for supporting me after such a lengthy period of absence from their lives, when they did not know if I was alive or dead.

As all serving soldiers do, I signed the Government's Official Secrets Act for reasons I will not elaborate on, and this has restricted me from telling this story as fact, so it has been written as a biographical novel. Names have been changed; however, it has been inspired by actual events.

Chapter One
Arrival

I arrived at Belfast docks at 7:00 a.m. on a freezing January morning in 1976. I had never been to Ireland before, though I had heard plenty from soldiers who had served there in previous years. Many of their stories seemed too far-fetched to be true. Tales of ambushes in the dead of night, of ghostly figures melting into alleyways, and of an enemy always watching but never seen.

Soldiers love their war stories, a blend of bravado and warning, often exaggerated, often laced with dark humour. Some were meant to impress, others to unnerve, giving the impression that in this conflict, they held the power over life and death. And in the case of Ireland, and my own story, they did.

I had given little real thought to the situation. Still, I had read about Ireland's long and troubled history—the rebellion against English rule stretching as far back as 1147, the siege of Dublin Castle, the doomed resistance at the GPO building, and the executions that fuelled further unrest. That history had fed into the tensions of 1969, leading to riots, barricades, and the occupation of Northern Ireland by British forces. This was now known simply as "The Troubles."

Back then, I had no idea how deeply I would become entwined in that history.

The voyage across the Irish Sea had been long and trying, the cold air from the open deck whipping through the ferry. We had set off from the dreary port of Liverpool on what could only be described as a flat-bottomed cattle barge, packed with Guinness-swilling Irishmen, their voices raised in song and slurred conversations.

At last, I stepped onto Irish soil, taking in the grey, rain-soaked dockside, the air thick with salt and diesel fumes. A short walk led to a covered section of the dock, where all arrivals were funnelled into a basic search area. There was no grandeur, no welcome—just a stark concourse where bags were dumped unceremoniously for inspection. Posters lined the walls, bluntly listing what could and could not be brought into Northern Ireland.

Officials, both men and women, carried out the inevitable searches with practised efficiency. I dropped my two heavy cases in front of an officer who looked at me with a sharp, assessing eye.

He was a typical Irishman, or so I had thought. Many outside Ireland imagine them as red-haired, broad-shouldered men with a fondness for whiskey and brawls. How wrong that is. A typical Irishman, I soon learned, was simply a man with an Irish accent—sharp-witted, tough, and resilient, with no need for lucky charms or tame leprechauns.

Only now do I fully appreciate why.

The officer looked at me with an inquisitive eye before speaking, his tone sharp and authoritative.

"Are you in the Army?"

I hesitated. I was still wary of whom I should tell. But this was a uniformed security officer, so surely, it was safe to answer.

"Yes," I replied.

His entire demeanour shifted in an instant. Without another word, he emptied out my cases, sifting through my belongings with an air of deliberate scrutiny.

I'm a fairly pleasant chap, but I tend to take offence when a stranger decides to treat me like a criminal.

"What the hell do you think you're doing?" I snapped. "You won't find any bombs in there."

It was meant sarcastically. A harmless remark. A mistake.

Could he not tell I was a soldier? I had short hair, an Army-style suitcase, and was clean-shaven, unlike most of my travelling companions, who looked as though they had just walked off the M6 motorway, carrying more than their fair share of tar.

Then came the prickle of unease—that feeling of being watched. I didn't see them at first, but I soon did. Two uniformed police officers, both built like butchers, appeared at my side.

Before I could process what was happening, I was grabbed, spun around, and shoved against the nearest wall. Then came the search—rough, thorough, and utterly humiliating.

One of them must have had a sudden thought because he barked, "Identification?"

I produced my ID immediately, my protests growing louder at the rough treatment.

"This is bloody ridiculous! Get me a British Army officer!"

It was as if my demand had been wired straight to headquarters.

A Second Lieutenant entered the enclosure, flanked by two soldiers in combat gear, their flak jackets bulky, their FN SLRs held with a quiet but unmistakable authority. Their eyes constantly scanned the room, taking everything in.

The officer took my ID card from the policeman, glanced at it, and exchanged a few quiet words. Then he turned to me.

"Sir, you have much to learn about Ireland. Let the first lesson be this—you never joke about bombs."

I exhaled sharply. Of course.

I muttered an apology to the police, who were already turning their attention elsewhere.

With my luggage finally cleared and my treasured ID returned, the soldiers led me out of the reception area and towards a blue and white bus.

Inside, six to eight men sat waiting—clearly soldiers. One of them handed me a cigarette without a word, which I accepted.

The Lieutenant, however, wasn't done with me yet.

"Wise up—and fast. Make everyone your enemy. Think of everyone as a gunman or a carrier."

His voice was flat, matter of fact—and then came the words that truly sank in.

"If you don't, the next time I see you, it'll be in a pine box."

I felt embarrassed, to say the least.

But he was right.

I had never met such a young officer who was so thorough and capable. He could not have been in the Army more than a year or so, yet he already had the sharp instincts of a seasoned soldier.

As soon as the other soldiers who had arrived on the ferry joined us—three of them bound for Londonderry as well—we were told to board the bus.

I passed the young officer, my head slightly bowed, feeling somewhat like a scolded schoolboy. As I walked by, I glanced up and said, "Thanks."

He gave a slight nod, his voice casual but carrying weight.

"Come on, sir. It happens to us all, so don't worry. Maybe I'll see you again. Stay lucky. Soldiers aren't very pretty dead."

I took in his words. That kid had just given me the best advice I would receive that day.

And as you'll come to see, he was absolutely right.

For those who have never been to Ireland, there is no better time to witness its raw beauty than in the early morning. The land is soaked in mist, rolling over the green lumps and bumps they call fields, lending the countryside an almost dreamlike quality.

It was like stepping back in time—a glimpse of a world that seemed untouched by the chaos I knew lurked beneath the surface. Old women wrapped in heavy shawls trudged along narrow roads, horses pulled weathered carts, and elderly men stood in the doorways of cottages, their trousers tied at the knees with cords, watching the world with quiet patience. The cars that passed were museum pieces, held together more by willpower than mechanics.

It was peaceful. Too peaceful.

I knew better than to trust the illusion.

The journey to Londonderry took about an hour and a half without stopping. Eventually, the bus turned into the old naval barracks, coming to a halt just inside the heavy iron gates.

As I gathered my thoughts, the driver turned to me, offering a brief farewell.

"Goodbye," he said. Then, after a pause, "God be with you."

Those words lingered in my ears, hanging in the cold air.

They would stay with me for the next two years, which now—standing at the threshold of a new reality—felt like a lifetime.

The guard at the gate looked incredibly young, barely old enough to be in the Army, let alone carry a submachine gun.

I approached him cautiously, sliding out my ID card—I was learning fast.

He took it without a word, glancing at the details before asking,

"Number, rank, and name?"

I answered without hesitation.

Out of the corner of my eye, I noticed a second guard, his rifle trained straight at me—just in case.

The first guard nodded slightly, then called over to the Guard Room, summoning another soldier.

"Been expecting you, sir. I'll get you sorted out."

Gesturing towards my cases, he added,

"Leave your luggage here, sir. I'll have it taken to the Officer's Mess for you."

I thanked him, and with that, we were off.

When we arrived at Brigade Headquarters, my escort pressed a bell on the wall.

It reminded me of something out of an old film—like trying to get into a dodgy nightclub, half expecting a burly doorman to demand a password.

Instead, a small window in the door slid open, revealing two watchful eyes.

"Who are you?"

For the third time that day, I produced my ID card.

Satisfied, the eyes disappeared, and the door unlocked with a heavy metallic clunk.

I stepped into a narrow corridor, which led through to an inner office.

The space was filled with maps, documents, and endless streams of information.

For the first time since setting foot in Ireland, I felt a semblance of security.

But that feeling wouldn't last long.

On the wall hung a massive map of the entire province, its surface covered in markings—strategic lines, unit positions, and operational sectors. Adjacent to it was a large scale map of Londonderry and its surrounding counties, every road and checkpoint meticulously plotted.

I studied both maps intensely, my eyes scanning the familiar military symbols and notations. It didn't take long to recognise what they signified. This was a war zone.

I had seen these kinds of maps before and used them myself in briefings and operational planning. The coded symbols, the movement patterns, the areas marked for heightened security—they told a story of constant conflict, of a land teeming with military activity.

A voice from behind broke my focus.

"Hello, Dave."

I swung around, startled.

Standing before me, as large as life, was a familiar face.

"Alec," I gasped.

It had been nearly two years since I last saw him—back when he was going through Depot training while I was instructing. He looked almost the same, though a little stockier, his mop of dark hair just as untamed. He stood about 5ft 8ins, solidly built, every bit the good soldier I had remembered.

We shook hands firmly, exchanging the usual reunion pleasantries—family updates, unit movements, the kind of small talk that softened the otherwise rigid formalities of military life.

Alec had been expecting me. So had my new Officer Commanding.

Alec led me to my new company lines, housed in an old naval building.

The place had a central staircase, its stone steps worn smooth with time. The walls were coated in blue gloss paint, a colour that did little to hide the age and wear of the structure.

When we reached the first floor, we stopped in front of a door immediately opposite the staircase. The bold letters on the nameplate left no doubt as to whose office it was—

Regimental Sergeant Major (RSM).

Alec motioned for me to go in, stepping aside.

I rapped on the door, though it was already fully open, and was met with a firm but polite "Enter."

I stepped inside in proper soldier like fashion, coming smoothly to attention before my new RSM.

I knew him—long before I had even been commissioned.

Mr Kerr, the Regimental Sergeant Major, was not at all the type one might expect from his rank. Unlike the usual gruff, drill square voiced RSM, Kerr was a pleasant, well-mannered chap, his presence commanding but not overbearing.

"Welcome, sir," he said, offering a nod. "And congratulations on your commission."

"Thank you," I replied.

He studied me for a brief moment before continuing.

"Welcome to your new company; however, I don't think you'll be here long."

The remark struck me as odd, but I let it pass without comment.

Before I could dwell on it, Kerr gestured towards an adjoining office.

"I'll take you in to meet the Major," he said. "He will explain more."

With that, he led me through the door to meet Major Peter Cameron—my new Officer Commanding, who dismissed the RSM and commanded me to sit, so I did.

Major Cameron began by reciting my past 15 years of service, his tone neutral, but the level of detail caught me off guard.

I sat there, mildly astonished—not because I had forgotten my own history, but because he seemed to know it inside out. Every posting, every operation, every commendation—it was all laid bare before me.

There it was, in black and white—close protection work for Government Ministers, both foreign and British heads of state. Then, the mention in dispatches, glaring from my record as part of a citation I had never paid much mind to.

He continued, listing my time in Berlin, where I had conducted a thesis and study on the formation of the Red Army Faction — more commonly known now as the Baader Meinhof Group. My research had covered their tactics, structure, and ideological motivations, a study that had somehow become part of my official file.

Then came my training and instructional roles, the many diverse areas I had worked in throughout my career.

Finally, Cameron looked up at me, closing the file with a decisive motion.

"Impressive," he said.

I wasn't sure if it was a compliment or merely an observation, but I gave a small nod in response.

Then, his tone shifted.

He outlined a plan, one that seemed vague in detail but undeniably important.

A new experimental task force was being formed in a particularly challenging area along the border with the South.

Because of my diverse background and operational experience, I was selected to establish and lead it.

This initiative wasn't Cameron's—it came from higher up the chain. A high ranking officer had conceived it, and I would be briefed in full shortly.

Cameron made a quick telephone call, speaking in low, clipped tones.

When he finished, he turned to me and said,

"We're off to see the officer in charge in ten minutes."

We left his office and made the short walk to Brigade Headquarters, passing through the now familiar routine of ID checks and security procedures.

Every checkpoint, every pair of watchful eyes, and every repeated demand for identification reinforced the high-stakes atmosphere.

Eventually, we arrived outside the office of the Brigade Commander, Brigadier Howard Woodford.

The name wasn't new to me—I had served under him before.

A staff officer greeted us, providing a brief but precise rundown on how the meeting would proceed. We were even instructed on where to sit when called in.

It felt like preparing to enter the lion's den.

The door opened, and we stepped inside.

The Brigadier was a well-built man, about forty-five years old, his sandy coloured hair beginning to silver at the sides.

He wasted no time.

"Thank you, Peter. I will continue from here; you may go."

The sudden dismissal caught me off guard.

Cameron, unfazed, simply saluted and left without hesitation.

I was beckoned to sit, which I did.

The Brigadier regarded me for a moment before offering a slight, knowing smile.

"Don't let this extra pip frighten you," he said casually.

I recognised the remark for what it was—a reference to our past service together, back when he was a Colonel.

Then his expression darkened, the tone of the room shifting instantly.

"I made sure you were posted here for a reason."

That got my attention.

Up until now, my transfer from Berlin had felt abrupt and unexplained. One moment, I was stationed in Germany. The next, I was in Northern Ireland with barely a week's notice—no reasoning given.

Now, at last, I was about to learn why.

The Brigadier exhaled deeply, leaning back slightly in his chair.

He looked older than I remembered. The lines on his face had deepened, and there was an undeniable weight in his expression.

"Before I start this briefing," he said, his tone measured, "I will say this—nothing we discuss today will leave this room. Do you understand?"

"Yes, sir," I replied.

His sharp gaze held mine for a moment before he continued.

"We have a big problem here in Ireland, Captain," he said, his voice taking on a harder edge.

I could feel the gravity of the conversation shifting.

"It's an intelligence problem—or, more accurately, a lack of intelligence."

He leaned forward, his tone becoming more forceful.

"The IRA is more organised than we are. Far more organised. The fact is, they're beating us hands down. Politically, that is a disaster. Militarily, it's unacceptable. And I will not stand for it."

His face reddened slightly, frustration creeping into his voice.

I had anticipated a serious conversation—but this? This was much bigger than I had imagined.

Then came the words that confirmed it.

"Therefore, the General Staff at the MOD level have agreed on a plan I have put forward to them as a possible way to achieve eventual success over the terrorist activities."

His tone was sharp and decisive.

This wasn't some vague policy discussion—this was a direct strategy already in motion.

And I was now a part of it.

The Brigadier's voice remained firm, unyielding.

"The IRA (Irish Republican Army) and UVF (Ulster Volunteer Force) have become extraordinarily successful in moving supplies of arms and explosives into the North. These are ending up in the hands of the bomb makers and gunmen in Belfast. It must cease!"

I sat upright, listening intently as he continued.

"We intend to stop this flow from the South and abroad by forming a small task force—to arrest the terrorists and, at the same time, retrieve the flow of supplies on its passage to Belfast."

Then came the words that hit me like a hammer.

"You have been selected to form and lead this task force and to achieve our objective."

My mind reeled. How the hell did I manage to get into a situation like this?

But there was no time to process it—the Brigadier was already pressing on.

"Over the next few weeks, you will be instructed by both our Military Intelligence and the Ulster Constabulary on the hot spots and all the known terrorist personnel—IRA, UVF, and the various splinter groups."

His tone left no room for doubt—this was not just another routine assignment. This was warfare in its most unpredictable form.

"You will be equipped with everything you need to succeed and will eventually have a great deal of power to command the security forces in the North to act on the information you pass to them."

He paused, eyeing me closely.

"Understood so far?"

I straightened. "Yes, sir, but—"

He cut me off with a swift hand gesture.

"No questions yet."

He reached across the desk, picking up a Manila envelope marked in bold lettering:

"Secret – For Officers' Eyes Only."

He slid it towards me.

"The way I want you to go about this is to form a handpicked team of around twenty soldiers. Major Cameron and I have drawn up a list of possible for you to select from."

I picked at the sellotape, sealing the envelope, peeling it off in one smooth motion. Inside was a single sheet of paper—a list of thirty names.

I studied it carefully.

A wave of unease settled in my gut.

I either knew or had heard of nearly every man on that list.

They were hard men, like Blackthorn—seasoned, ruthless, and capable of working in the most demanding situations. Some were ex-SAS, some were former Paratroopers, others had backgrounds in police close protection units.

They were the kind of men you trusted with your life.

And if the devil had cast his net over this lot, he would have reaped one hell of a harvest.

A tingling sensation crawled up my spine, followed by a slow, sinking feeling in my stomach.

The Brigadier spoke again, drawing my attention back to him.

"Your area will be based in South Armagh. You will operate out of the security forces base at Newry."

He stopped there, waiting.

For a moment, I wondered if he expected me to say something.

He wasn't going to get a response—not yet.

I took a deep breath, exhaling slowly through my nostrils, making sure he heard it.

Then I lifted my head and locked eyes with him.

By now, he must have known exactly how I felt. Terrified.

He stood, pacing a few steps before slipping both hands into his trouser pockets. He pulled out a packet of cigarettes, shaking one loose before lighting it with deliberate ease.

He took a sharp inhale, exhaled slowly, then turned his gaze back to me.

What he said next nearly choked me.

"You will gain the confidence of the people of Newry, Bessbrook, Crossmaglen, Fork Hill, Ross Trevor, and Warren Point."

His eyes narrowed slightly.

"You will take whatever action you need to in order to ensure this flow of arms and explosives is stopped. Finally."

One thing I had learned from my study of Northern Ireland—and from the stories I had heard from those who had served before me—was that these towns were the worst hotspots for terrorist activity in the entire province.

Even the Ulster Constabulary, the very force tasked with maintaining order, refused to go near them.

The Brigadier continued, his tone unwavering.

"Your information will be treated in strict confidence, and action upon your request will be carried out without question."

His eyes locked onto mine, making sure the gravity of his words settled in.

"You will liaise only with the company commanders whom you require assistance from and report progress directly to my office. You have a twenty-four hour a day contact should you need my authorisation."

He leaned back slightly, his voice steady.

"All company commanders in your area will be briefed regarding your presence and my instructions accordingly."

I absorbed his words in silence. This was not a task for the faint-hearted.

Then, as if switching gears, he gave a slight nod, a trace of a smile appearing at the corner of his mouth.

"How about starting the training on Monday?"

He spoke casually, but the weight of what he was saying hung in the air like lead.

"You can have your band of merry men start with you. They are all in theatre, warned and available, and any vehicles and weapons you require will be issued."

His voice carried a tone of finality.

"Major Skinner, my staff officer, will be your contact for anything you need. He will also be my linkman regarding your training and progress at the Ballykinler Training Unit."

Then, he tilted his head slightly.

"Well, what have you got to say after all that?"

I felt browbeaten, to say the least.

But I was not about to let him think he had put me on the spot.

If he wanted training to start on Monday, that meant I had until midday tomorrow—Friday—to give my answer.

I took a moment, weighing my words carefully before responding.

"If I could have all the intelligence information and the recent terrorist history on the areas of danger, I could start on Monday next."

The dye was cast.

At that moment, I knew next to nothing about the areas I was being sent to cover.

But one thing was clear—my brief was fused with untold dangers.

And yet, I had accepted it, without question, as one does when orders come from a Brigade Commander.

This job would demand everything I had, and if I had it in me, I would make sure the Brigadier's objective was achieved.

But at what cost?

That was the question that gnawed at me.

I turned to leave, but just as I reached the door, his voice stopped me in my tracks.

"Well done, lad."

I turned back.

His voice was no longer simply commanding—it carried conviction, depth, and something else I hadn't expected… sincerity.

"This action will save many people—both civilians and military—from being killed or maimed with life-changing injuries."

He paused, exhaling slowly before continuing.

"Too many are being injured and killed. Families are suffering. Lives are being destroyed because of these troubles. It will be worth it if we can save just one life."

His eyes met mine once again.

"I know you will be totally dedicated to your job and come through."

I gave a small nod.

"I'll try, sir."

And with that, I left.

As the door clicked shut behind me, a thought settled in my mind.

What have I got myself into now? I must be mad.

That door had closed on one chapter of my life…

…And opened another, into a dark, sinister, and unknown wilderness.

I now knew the name of that wilderness. South Armagh.

Eventually, I found the Officers' Mess and was shown to my room by the Mess orderly.

As soon as I stepped inside, I looked around in disbelief.

Was I supposed to live in this?

The room was six feet by five feet, barely big enough to move in. A single wardrobe and a bed made up the entire furnishing. The walls were marked with years of wear, and the air carried the stale scent of damp fabric and boot polish.

Thankfully, it would only be for a few nights.

Alec soon tracked me down, and as soon as he stepped through the door, I let out a half-laugh, half-grumble.

"This room is small and filthy."

He looked me up and down with a knowing smirk, arms crossed.

"Be thankful," he said. "The enlisted men have it far worse."

I raised an eyebrow, waiting for him to elaborate.

"They're sleeping in shifts, hot bedding."

For those unfamiliar with the term, hot bedding meant that as one soldier got up for duty, another took his place in the same bed.

No personal space, no privacy—just a constant rotation of bodies in the same sheets.

That put things into perspective.

The only redeeming quality of my cramped room, I thought, was that at least it was warm and safe.

Or so I believed.

The mess hall windows overlooked a courtyard, and as I stood there, something caught my eye.

The ground was strewn with rubble, a mess of twisted debris and shattered brick.

I frowned.

"What's happened out there? It's a hell of a mess."

Alec wandered over, glanced out the window, and shrugged as if it were nothing unusual.

"Oh, that?" he said, almost casually. "We had a bomb placed under one of the windows. A milk churn filled with Ampho."

I turned to him sharply.

"Ampho?"

"Homemade explosive."

There was no shift in his expression, no weight to his words.

"Lucky no one was killed."

His tone was so matter of fact, so unshaken, that it took me a second to process what he had just said.

Then it hit me like a gut punch.

Who were these faceless people I had come to fight?

And more importantly—why was I here?

Alec, sensing my silence, began to fill me in on the history of the conflict we had just stepped into.

He spoke of how religion had been turned into martyrdom, how men chose to die or rot in the Maze prison, sacrificing themselves for what they believed to be Ireland's heritage and freedom.

They were alienated from any form of authority—except the Church.

Following the Church's callous dictates, they remained short sighted, unaware of the long term destruction they inflicted upon themselves and their people.

And then there was us—the British Army.

Once again, we had been brought in to "keep the peace" by force, a third element in a war between Protestants and Catholics.

But now, both sides had turned against us.

This conflict had become so bitter, so political, that even the British soldier no longer knew who or why he was fighting.

My mind drifted to my family back home in England.

At least the Irish had their homes, their wives, their children.

What did a soldier have? Nothing. Nothing but the constant fear of a bomb, a bullet—a split second of bad luck that would make him just another victim, another statistic in this war of religion.

I struggled to understand how any so called Holy body could condone this. How could priests, bishops, and clergymen—men who preached peace and righteousness—encourage their congregations to take up arms? They claimed to fight for peace, yet they cold bloodedly justified the murder of innocent people. Who were they, these alleged believers in faith, pretending to strive for peace?

They only understood the law of the gun and the bomb. And the more they killed for their cause, the more righteous they seemed to believe they had become. I once heard a story, one that I never doubted for a second was true. An Irish bomb maker, whose device had killed twenty people, went to confession. He told his priest exactly what his bomb had done. The priest listened carefully, then asked him one question…

"Were those you killed Protestant?"

The bomber looked the priest straight in the eye.

"Yes, for sure."

And with that, the priest forgave him—for conducting God's will.

A British soldier, acting in self-defence, often as a last resort, could find himself on trial for murder, his actions scrutinised by courts, politicians, and the public.

Meanwhile, the Irish terrorists, those who had planted bombs, ambushed patrols, and massacred civilians, were eventually granted political status and freed.

Their violence was excused, their actions condoned by British politicians, forgiven by national leaders, and even blessed by Cardinals of the Church and the Pope himself.

What Pagans were these men who claimed to hold moral authority?

What right did they have to deal with death, to assign a price to human life, to manipulate the innocent into doing their dirty work, all while claiming their cause was rooted in Christian virtue?

The truth was—they had none.

A wild animal, when it hunts, will at least give a warning to its prey. The terrorists offered no such courtesy.

They struck without warning, only revealing themselves when it was too late—when the blast had already torn through flesh and steel, when the bullet had already found its mark, when the screams of the wounded and dying filled the air.

Only then would you understand the horror of their instrument of terror. Only then would you see the sickening aftermath of what they had inflicted upon the innocent.

And yet, for all the chaos and uncertainty, the soldiers caught in the middle of this religious conflict still had something the terrorists never would.

They had a country. A Monarch. A purpose in life. And, above all, they had a reason to live. That night, I lay in my small, cold bed, my mind racing.

I thought about everything Alec had told me, the truths I had just been forced to confront, and the daunting task ahead.

How was I supposed to integrate myself into a land that saw me as the enemy? How was I supposed to become part of a place where my presence was unwanted?

It felt impossible, but come morning, I would have to begin the attempt. My thoughts swirled in an unorganised mess, a tangle of uncertainty and tension that I knew I wouldn't be able to untangle in a single night.

But physical exhaustion took over where my mind failed, dragging me into a deep and dreamless sleep. I woke the next morning to a thick frost covering everything.

The cold clung to the air, creeping into bone and muscle, making every movement stiff and slow. If you ever find yourself in Ireland in winter, wrap up well.

Because the cold here doesn't just settle on the skin—it sinks deep, burrowing into the very core of you. And once it's in, it takes a hell of a long time to get warm again.

Chapter Two
Preparation - Ballykinler

After washing in freezing water, which was not by choice, I might add—the hot water system had yet to be repaired after the recent bomb attack—I made my way to breakfast, unknowingly walking straight into another brush with authority.

To set the scene, dining in Northern Ireland was a little different from what one might expect.

Due to restricted space and kitchen facilities, the dining area was split—on one side, the junior ranks and soldiers, and on the other, officers and senior ranks, separated by a screen.

Food was served buffet style, meaning both groups helped themselves and then took their seats in their designated areas.

So far, so good. Or so I thought.

Now, tradition in the British Army plays a significant role, particularly within certain regiments.

Some traditions are respected, some are endured, and some, quite frankly, seem outright ridiculous.

This morning's experience would soon prove to be one of the latter.

As I entered the dining room, I immediately noticed a man eating his breakfast—with his hat on.

I couldn't believe it.

His rank insignia made it clear—he was a Warrant Officer.

I turned to the soldier ahead of me in the queue and asked,

"What's he doing?"

The reply, delivered without a hint of amusement, was an education in regimental customs.

"He's a Colour Sergeant in the Guards. By tradition, he must wear his hat at breakfast. And he doesn't talk while eating."

The first part, I could accept. If the man wanted to wear his hat indoors, that was his business.

But the silence?

That little detail had been left out of the explanation.

Strangely, the only vacant seats in the entire dining hall were at the table where the "Hat" was sitting.

With no other choice, I took a seat and turned my attention to my plate—eggs and bacon, a breakfast I wasn't about to let go to waste.

I reached for the salt, only to realise it was just out of reach, at the top of the table.

I glanced at the Hat and, keeping things polite, said,

"Could you pass the salt down, please?"

Nothing.

He didn't even look at me.

I tried again, this time a little louder.

"Pass the salt, please."

Still no response.

And still no salt.

I frowned and turned to the chap sitting next to the Hat.

"Is he deaf?"

At that, I received a sharp scowl as if I had just committed some unspoken sin.

But at least the salt finally made its way down the table—though not from the Hat himself.

I ate the rest of my breakfast in silence, causing no further disturbance.

But as the Hat finished his meal, he shot me a distinctly disapproving look before standing up and leaving.

It was then that someone decided to finally explain the full story behind this peculiar ritual.

Long ago, an RSM (Regimental Sergeant Major) had missed a Royal command while talking at breakfast.

By the time he received the message, he had rushed off in a hurry, only to realise—too late—that he had forgotten his hat.

As a result, and by Royal dictate, the RSM of that old and proud regiment had, ever since, been required to:

1. Wear his hat at breakfast.

2. Remain completely silent, ready to receive a Royal command at any moment.

And so, the tradition had continued to this very day.

On Saturday and Sunday, I buried myself in preparing my kit. There was a lot to get done, as I was set to leave for Ballykinler on Sunday evening.

By 4:00 p.m., I left Londonderry, travelling in a unit supplied car—a rundown heap that had probably been round the clock twice over but was still expected to keep going.

Ballykinler, located south of Belfast, was home to the Black Watch Regiment, a Scottish unit that had recently begun a two-year tour of duty.

The journey itself was uneventful, apart from my driver's incessant chatter, which—if I were being generous—could be described as uninspiring at best.

When we finally arrived, the gate sentry was expecting me. After a quick check, he sent for the orderly officer, a Colour Sergeant, who eventually turned up in a beaten-up Rover.

With little ceremony, he drove us deeper into the camp. The sheer size of the place made it feel endless, its layout sprawling in every direction. In reality, Ballykinler covered seven to eight square miles, incorporating a variety of terrain within its perimeter.

After what felt like an eternity, we pulled up to a cluster of twelve huts. They were arranged like two capital 'E's, reversed and joined at their centres, forming an odd yet practical layout. As I stepped out of the vehicle at the main entrance, a Warrant Officer was already waiting.

The orderly officer made the introductions. "(WO2) Mr Hunter." He seemed jovial but firm, the type of man you could work with.

Instantly, I knew we'd get on. We entered the nearest hut together, and as we walked, he explained that he ran this replacement training centre himself, with the assistance of two sergeants.

Their job?

To prepare replacement soldiers for active duty by providing a centralised training facility.

Every unit stationed in Northern Ireland would receive reinforcements from here, and it was Hunter's responsibility to ensure these men were indoctrinated into the type of work they'd be undertaking during their tours.

His office was a plain, no-frills space. The floor was covered in worn lino, and the small window let in just enough light to be useful. A desk and two chairs made up the entire furnishing.

We both sat down, and Hunter immediately launched into an overview of the training programme. The priority, he explained, was fitness—extreme fitness.

A six-mile run in full kit would kick off every morning, designed to push everyone to their peak—and beyond. Now, soldiers are fit, but even the fittest aren't thrilled about long-distance runs before a cup of tea.

But there was no room for complaints.

The first week's mornings were dedicated to what was called "positive training". This involved working with real-world scenarios and learning the rules and procedures essential for operating in Northern Ireland.

Subjects included:

- Arrest procedures
- The Emergency Powers Act
- The role of the RUC (Royal Ulster Constabulary) and UDR (Ulster Defence Regiment)
- Opening fire procedures

- And a host of other legal and tactical essentials.

Admittedly, much of it was dry, administrative material, but knowing these regulations could be the difference between an approved action and a court martial. The afternoons, by contrast, were practical and hands-on. Field exercises and range work took priority, with the aim of getting every soldier up to a marksman's standard—regardless of the environment they would operate in.

The course itself seemed straightforward, following the usual procedures for training rotations.

But there was no doubt—by the time we were finished, every man would be ready for whatever Northern Ireland threw at him.

After finishing our chat, I remarked that I was looking forward to meeting the lads, especially if I was expected to run six miles with them in the morning.

Hunter laughed. "You need not go. It's only for the lads."

I took that as my cue to make my position clear.

Turning to Hunter, I stated in no uncertain terms—

"This course is to select an incredibly special team. If I expect them to give their all, then I will do exactly the same. No special treatment. No advantages. I will take part in everything they do."

If I was going to earn their respect, I had to work alongside them—train, eat, sleep, and push through the same struggles. Only then would they trust me as their leader. Beyond that, it would give me critical insight—I would see first-hand their capabilities, limits, and strengths.

When the time came for real decisions in the field, I needed to know who could be counted on, who could push further, and who needed support. Respect was one thing, but motivation was everything.

The future was uncertain and volatile.

At some point, we would be placed in situations where we would need every last ounce of energy, dedication, loyalty, and determination. If I couldn't instil that in them now, we wouldn't survive then.

Hunter seemed taken aback by my attitude, but he respected my reasoning. After a moment, he nodded.

"Well, I suppose you'll want to meet them all?"

"Of course," I replied. "As soon as possible."

"I'll get them all in the lecture room," he said, then left.

This moment was crucial. The first introduction.

I sat, going over in my mind what to say and how to say it. I had conducted countless introductions in the past, but this was different. Imagine the scene—thirty men, all looking for answers.

They had no idea what was coming. And truth be told, neither did I. A strange situation, indeed.

After about five minutes, Hunter returned.

I could hear movement outside—boots against the floor, men filing into the lecture room.

Hunter glanced at me.

"They should all be seated in about two minutes. If you're ready, we can go down now."

I nodded, stood up, and we walked towards the room. As we entered, the murmur of quiet chatter filled the space. Then, as soon as they saw me, silence fell over the room. I walked to the front of the room, facing them.

If you've ever stood before a group of strangers, knowing that they don't know you, don't trust you, and are waiting to judge you, then you'll understand the feeling that crept over me.

It is not a comfortable one. Not for the weak of heart. My pulse quickened. My legs felt unsteady. I could feel the colour drain from my face. I reached for the small wooden rostrum, gripping it firmly.

Then, I took a deep breath. Every man in the room was watching me, waiting. Time to break the ice.

"Gentlemen," I said, keeping my voice firm but calm.

"My name is West—Captain David West. However, for the purposes of any future contact, you can address me as 'Boss,' because that is what I am to be."

I paused, letting that sink in.

"You may smoke if you wish, and please, relax. I don't intend to keep you too long—I know you have a lot to do."

It worked. I could see the tension ease—shoulders relaxed, a few men glanced at each other, sizing up the situation.

I had them.

Now, I could carry on.

"You're all wondering why you're here."

I met their eyes, scanning the room.

"Be patient. You'll be told everything in due time."

And with that, the real work began.

I let my eyes sweep across the room, taking in the faces staring back at me. Some curious, some sceptical, others simply waiting for answers. I didn't make them wait long.

"Firstly, you all want to know who I am and why I'm standing before you."

"Let me tell you."

I kept my voice firm but measured, ensuring they understood this wasn't just another briefing.

"I have been in the regiment for fifteen years, coming up through the ranks to my present position."

That much was straightforward.

But they needed to understand why I was here.

"I have been closely linked to the training of Special Forces, military, and diplomatic close protection personnel—primarily in anti-terrorist projects."

"These have covered all areas of military and civilian responses, with a special focus on the causes these organisations fight for and believe in—to find the best ways to defeat them eventually.

I let that sink in.

No one moved.

"I classify myself as a reasonable soldier—by my own standards. And I command a high degree of dedication from everyone who works with me."

I could feel a few shifts in posture, men sitting up slightly straighter. Good. They were listening now.

"I will be working and learning alongside you. I will lecture you on occasion. But know this—I will never ask you to do anything I cannot do myself."

I could already tell who understood that sentiment and who didn't. Some nodded. Others simply stared.

Either way, they would soon find out for themselves.

"Our relationship will be unique. But let me be clear—I demand respect for my rank and authority."

"You will not question my methods."

I let the weight of that settle. "From this moment on, you have one boss—me."

"As long as we work together, no orders will come to you from anyone outside this course. The only commands you follow are those given here."

Some eyes flicked around the room, quiet exchanges of glances as if assessing whether I was serious. I was.

"I have the authority to say this from the General Officer Commanding the Northern Ireland Theatre of Operations."

That got their attention.

A few funny looks spread across the room. Expressions shifted—some doubtful, some intrigued, some suddenly more focused. Now came the crucial part.

"Regarding the future operations we are to undertake—I say this now: anything said here stays within this unit."

I paused, making sure every man in the room had time to let that sink in.

"At this point, I need twenty-one men."

"These will be selected from you."

A flicker of tension moved through the group.

"Please do not be alarmed—any more than twenty-one would make the exercise futile."

I anticipated the thought forming in some of their minds, so I addressed it immediately.

"If you are not chosen, do not feel it is because you are not good enough."

"Every single one of you has reached a standard high enough to be selected for this programme."

"You are here for a reason—because of your individual qualities."

That seemed to settle some of them. Others remained rigid, unreadable. I shifted my stance, letting my arms rest lightly on the edge of the rostrum.

"This operation is a pilot experiment. At this stage, I cannot tell you much. What I do know is that we will be operating in South Armagh."

"We will be involved in both overt and covert roles."

The words hung in the air, and I could see more than a few men absorbing the implications.

I continued.

"This will require men who can hold their nerve, men with patience, men who can remain impartial under pressure."

"And above all—men who can handle the frustrations and challenges that will come with the job. For the next three weeks, you will undergo the same training as any soldier new to Ireland. However, you will receive more than the average soldier."

I scanned their faces.

"During this time, I will be assessing each of you. In the final week, I will select the men I need."

No one spoke.

Every man was listening now.

I straightened slightly, my voice sharp but steady.

"The first priority—before anything else—is to bring you all to the absolute peak of fitness."

I let my next words hang for a moment before delivering them.

"This starts at six o'clock in the morning."

A few glances were exchanged. Some men set their jaws in preparation. Others gave off the smallest hints of reluctance. That was expected. It wouldn't last.

Then came the moment I had been leading up to.

"Now, one thing I will say—if any of you, for whatever reason, do not wish to be part of this operation, say so now. No one will carry you. But everyone will be helped. If you have any problems during training—any reason at all—you come to me."

I let my gaze move deliberately across the room.

"And I will tell you why."

I let my next words land with absolute clarity.

"I do not want a soldier who cannot give one hundred percent. To himself, to his comrades, to this job. Because if he cannot—someone could die."

I let silence take over the room, studying their reactions. There was no chatter now. No fidgeting.

Just thirty men processing what had just been laid out before them.

After a long moment, I spoke again.

"Well, gentlemen, if there are any questions—let me have them now. If not, I will stop."

And I waited. I scanned the faces in front of me, looking for any sign of what they were thinking. Some expressions spoke volumes; others gave away nothing at all.

Had I got through to them? I wouldn't know until we got started. They looked uncertain, but then again, so was I. Had I made the right impression?

Well—none of them walked out, fainted, or told me to take a running jump. That had to count for something.

"Thank you, gentlemen, and good day."

With that, I turned and left the room with Mr Hunter. As soon as the door closed behind us, the murmur of conversation erupted. I couldn't hear what was being said, but I could certainly imagine it. Hunter glanced at me.

"Fancy a drink?"

I hesitated for all of half a second. After the past few days, I needed one. Back in his office, I watched as he poured a generous measure of Irish whiskey into a tumbler. He handed it to me, then leaned back slightly.

"Well, lad, if you want my opinion—"

Here it comes, I thought. The criticism.

"You came over quite well. I thought the lads seemed to accept you for what you are. You said all the right things and kept their attention."

I took a small sip, letting his words settle.

Then I replied.

"I need more than attention, Hunter. I need their total dedication."

I paused, setting the glass down.

"I can't afford to lose even one of them. I'd never get that off my conscience."

Hunter nodded, considering my words.

"I suppose it went okay. Let's see what the next few weeks bring."

I raised my glass, looked at him, and thought—here goes. That night, I didn't sleep well. I lay awake, going over everything in my head. Would this work out? Would I be able to forge this group into what was needed? Eventually, morning came—as it would so many times over the coming weeks.

That first six mile run was brutal. Sweat poured off me, and I felt every step in my legs. But I wasn't about to slow down—not now, not ever. And neither were the men running beside me.

By the end of the first week, the change was already visible. What had started as a group of soldiers who barely knew each other was beginning to mould into a team. The comradeship was building, the trust forming. No one was bad, but some had weak areas. Nothing that couldn't be fixed over the next two weeks.

Major Skinner came down to see us. Officially, he was there to report back to the Brigadier. But it was clear he wasn't particularly interested. He struck me as the type of officer who preferred sitting behind a desk to standing in the field—a paper soldier, not a real one.

Still, the programme was progressing well. And now, we had new kit to work with. We were issued with specialised equipment, including:

- "Starlight" Night Sights – which picked up light from stars, magnified it and turned the dark into something resembling daylight.
- "SUIT" Sights – another night scope, easily attached to a rifle, providing even better night vision capabilities.
- Infrared Scanners – able to detect body heat, vehicle heat, or any object recently handled.

The infrared system was proving to be invaluable. It allowed us to see what the naked eye could not—whether it was a man with a rifle moving through a field or even his footprints tracked along a riverbank. By all accounts, terrorists used river routes frequently to avoid detection. With this kit, that advantage was beginning to disappear.

We had now been issued our vehicles—three Land Rovers and three armoured Austin 1800 saloons. The Land Rovers were standard issue, but they had been reinforced with Macaron Shields across the roof, doors, bonnet, belly, and wings. Every window was covered in mesh, and large angle irons had been welded to the front, extending two feet above the top of the vehicle.

These modifications were not for aesthetics—they were there for survival.

One man was always assigned to shotgun duty. He would stand in the back of the Land Rover, his arms and shoulders exposed through an opening in the roof. It was a miserable position, uncomfortable, and dangerous. But from up there, he could see what the driver and co-driver could not. And in this theatre, seeing first meant staying alive. We had been warned about one of the terrorists' favourite tactics.

They would stretch a wire about seven feet above the road, perfectly positioned to decapitate the unfortunate soldier standing in the back of a Land Rover.

A human cheese wire trap.

The angle iron welded to our Rovers would now ensure the wire was cut before the soldier was. What had once been a highly effective and gruesome tactic had just been rendered useless. The armoured Austins, on the other hand, were less sophisticated.

They had basic reinforcements but no bulletproof glass. A weak point, but at this stage, we took what we were given. One of the lads, a mechanic in civilian life, had appointed himself unofficially as 'keeper of the wagons.' I didn't object—he had already done a better job of maintaining them than the Army ever had. And in this line of work, a vehicle in peak condition could mean the difference between life and death.

During our first week, we covered a brief history of Ireland. By the end of this training, we would know far more than we probably wanted to. But one fact was already crystal clear—weapons would be our only real friends. That message was being drilled into us, day after day.

As a result, I spent two to three hours daily on the range, ensuring that every single man met my exacting standards. I made one thing absolutely clear—

"If you cannot hit a one-inch patch on a target by week three of this course, you might as well pack your kit and leave."

Beyond rifles, we trained on the Gas Grenade and the Rubber Bullet Launcher. Now, there were plenty of stories about the rubber bullet. Many civilians thought of it as a 'harmless deterrent'. That was far from the truth. At a range of thirty feet to fifty yards, the launcher could knock a man clean off his feet.

If aimed twenty yards before the target, allowing the round to bounce off the ground, it would increase in speed before impact. That extra momentum meant the subject would be hit harder, in a less stable condition—and in some cases, kill.

Then there was the unspoken modification.

A trick that had spread across the province—one that we were taught, but never supposed to acknowledge. By prying out the rubber round, removing its contents, and adding the powder from a second round, the projectile doubled in power.

It became a lethal weapon. I made my position absolutely clear.

I had been told that this practice was happening across Northern Ireland—but officially, the high command denied it. I found it deeply unsettling. And I would not allow it.

"None of my men are to use this modification. Ever. You fire the launcher as instructed—no exceptions." Some officers turned a blind eye.

I wouldn't.

I had no interest in playing that game.

If we were to fight, we would fight by the book—because in the end, there was only one thing worse than dying in battle. Being the one left to answer for it.

The RUC (Royal Ulster Constabulary) and RMP SIB (Royal Military Police Special Investigation Branch) gave us lectures on arrest and detention procedures. I could hardly believe what I was hearing.

According to them, if we ever arrested anyone, we needed doctors to examine the individual both before and after screening. At first, this seemed excessive—even absurd. Later, I would understand exactly why.

Every soldier was given a series of history lessons on why the conflict had started—a potted history, as they called it. But even then, I sensed something was off.

This was not an unbiased account.

It was designed to fit a particular narrative. The Army, as an institution, followed the beliefs and dictates of the politicians—who, of course, believed they were always right. But history had already shown that both sides had been wrong. Yet, within the forces, loyalist Protestant factions were subtly favoured.

The Army imposed a form of controlled thinking—not overt, not obvious, but effective nonetheless. A subtle form of brainwashing. They wanted their soldiers to believe, without question, that they were one hundred per cent right. Even now, I still believe we were at least eighty five to ninety per cent right.

But to think that we had never been wrong?

That was a dangerous and deliberate lie.

In recent years, the security forces had grown so dominant that the politicians stopped asking questions.

They were simply pleased with the results.

But they never asked—Why?

Or more importantly— How?

The Brutal Reality —Why?

Because the methods used, legal or not, had systematically dismantled terrorist factions.

By doing so, we had suppressed the volume of propaganda that could have been used against us.

We had crippled the Republican movement and prevented them from advancing their cause.

How? By methods so far outside the accepted rules of war that they could never be officially acknowledged.

Methods that we were ordered never to reveal to anyone outside the close knit family of the armed forces. I will explain some of those classic examples later.

But for now, I will say this—The soldier on the ground, the man in uniform, had little to no support. Not from his officers. Not from politicians. Not even from the Protestant forces of terrorism, whom many assumed were his natural allies. The Numbers Never Lie. In Northern Ireland, the Protestant population vastly outnumbered the Catholic population. Yet, the detention figures painted a different picture.

Who were the ones always arrested? The Catholics. Who were the ones always held as the scapegoats?

Again, the Catholics.

There were many occasions when the Protestants were caught with arms and explosives.

The forces on the ground knew about it. It was not a secret. But nothing was done.

Why?

Because allowing Protestant factions to attack Catholics made the Army's job easier. It shifted the burden. It kept the Catholic community in fear. It gave justification for further operations.

Strong words?

Perhaps.

But think long and hard about it. Because it's true. At that time, I found myself falling into the trap—hard. I had begun to believe fully that we were always right, that stopping the violence by any means necessary was justified. The Protestant cause—the Royalist cause—was the only one worth acknowledging.

The Protestant terrorist saw himself as a modern day Cromwell, enforcing his rule with the same iron grip and brutal tactics. He looked to the Monarch for his motivation and justification. Bitterness had become second nature, not just to me, but to my men as well.

Every film we were shown in training had been edited to show only one side. It was meant to instil hatred, to fuel our resolve, to justify our actions.

For most, it worked. But not for me. I have never been one to accept things at face value.

I always ask why.

I analyse, question, and seek to understand from every angle.

Most of the soldiers in Northern Ireland were there because they had no other options. Many were unemployed, from rough backgrounds, or poorly educated.

This was deliberate.

The Army tapped into these areas constantly, recruiting new blood—men who could be moulded into believing what they were told. The method was tried and tested.

It had been used for centuries. And nothing could ever break it. Would I try to change it?

No.

This was one area in which the system excelled.

If a soldier was managed well, fed properly, and treated fairly, he would give you his best. If, however, he was left to live in squalor, barely fed, treated like dirt—he would react exactly as nature intended.

He would become a survivor. And survivors see anything that threatens them as an enemy. That's how a soldier is motivated. It's instinct—to hunt, to rise above the pack, to become the best, by any means necessary.

Some of the more enlightened soldiers saw this and tried to fight against it. But their efforts were futile. They were mocked, dismissed as 'softies' or 'do-gooders'. The system crushed them.

Now, apply this psychology to Ireland.

Give these same men a series of deadly weapons. Give them a clear target. Induce hatred into them. And you end up with a dangerous and highly effective force. It became clear to me that this was exactly how my men were reacting. They were absorbing the outside messages, taking in what was being fed to them, and responding exactly as expected.

I needed to change that—fast.

In the second week, I began to alter my methods. I changed my approach to the course, aiming to neutralise their thinking. I spent long hours with them, breaking away from the official training structure. I presented them with both sides of the conflict, not just one. I wanted them to think for themselves, to see beyond what they had been told.

I hoped it would work.

At the time, I was unsure. Now, I can say with certainty—it did. The second week went well. Training had taken on a new form—a far more human approach. The men were still soldiers, still capable of switching back to hard line tactics instantly. But there was now a difference in their mind set. One thing was clear—in the Irish theatre of operations, soldiers held the power of life and death.

Not just in theory, but in brutal reality.

And that reality was beginning to shape my future role in ways I had not expected.

Taking all of this into account, I contacted Major Skinner. He had a reputation for getting things done. I couldn't afford to air my personal thoughts outright, so I had to be careful—perhaps even cunning. When he finally answered the phone, I kept things straightforward. I told him how well the course was progressing. I highlighted the areas that I knew would sound good to him—

- Weapons training
- Bomb disposal
- Lectures
- Specialist unit rotations
- History lessons on Ireland

I mentioned the writings of James Cranford (1592–1657), "The Teares of Ireland", which chronicled the deep seated Irish hatred of the English. Then, I made my request.

"Would it be possible for us to spend a couple of days attached to a working unit in Belfast?"

Skinner saw no issue with it.

He assumed it was to gain policing experience, as all units on the ground were performing that role anyway. He agreed to arrange it. And he did.

We were split into three sections of ten men. One section would be deployed to the mission in the market area of Belfast, while the other two sections would be sent to the Grand Hotel for a two-day assignment. This was my chance to prove everything I had been teaching my men—to see if they had truly absorbed the lessons I had drilled into them.

The evening before deployment, I gathered them together. I looked them over, knowing this was a pivotal moment.

"Use this time to your advantage," I told them. "Pay attention. Observe everything. Weigh the situation against what I've taught you. Use every skill you've been given—but do not express any opinion except to me when you return."

They nodded, some more serious than others, but I could see the message had landed. Tomorrow, they would get a first-hand taste of what real operations in Belfast looked like.

The following morning, we were taken by truck to our detachments in the heart of Belfast. It was a Saturday, and as I watched my men disperse to their assignments, I wished them well. The next time I would see them would be at the debrief the following Sunday evening.

Chapter Three
Belfast and Beyond

I went with my section to the mission—a building that had once served a very different purpose. Before the Army had taken it over, the mission hall had belonged to The Salvation Army. It had been a shelter for the homeless, a place where they could get a hot meal and a bed for the night.

What I saw now horrified me. The entire place had been fortified beyond recognition. Barbed razor wire surrounded the perimeter. Heavy meshing, corrugated iron sheeting, and sandbags blocked every weak point. On each corner stood a Sanger position—concrete turrets manned by armed soldiers tasked with keeping an unblinking watch on the streets outside. If there was a terrorist attack or a car bomb, these sentries were the first line of defence. They would return fire and sound the alarm.

We were let inside, and as the heavy doors closed behind us, I felt an uneasy shift in the atmosphere. This was not a military base—it was a bunker, a war zone within a city. As we walked through the narrow passage into the main hall, the first thing that hit me was the stench.

A thick, putrid mix of sweat, damp clothing, and stale air.

It was overwhelming.

The hall itself was packed with soldiers, crammed together in appalling conditions. I couldn't believe what I was seeing. Armchairs were clustered around a TV, where men sat watching football in soaking-wet uniforms—clothes that hadn't been properly washed in months. Cigarette smoke hung in the air, thick and unmoving. In one corner, there was a makeshift kitchen—a couple of gas rings with an urn of tea boiling on top. Plates and mess tins were piled haphazardly on a nearby table—I had assumed they were dirty dishes waiting to be washed. I was wrong— these were what the men were expected to eat from.

Kit was strewn across the floor, left there for what seemed like weeks. The amount of dust, grime, and general filth told me this place had not seen a proper cleaning in a long time. Strings had been hung across the walls, makeshift drying lines for socks, underwear, vests, and shirts. The men were unwashed.

The place reeked of neglect.

The walls were covered in torn-out pages of nude magazines—a crude attempt at decorating this miserable, suffocating space. Discarded wrappers from Mars bars, crisp packets, and old newspapers were littered across the floor. It felt like a prison, a place where men had been left to rot, forgotten by those higher up the chain. I pushed through the mass of bodies, searching for someone in charge.

That's when I spotted a corporal—a coloured chap, standing off to one side. I approached him, explained who I was, and he pointed me toward the back of the hall, where a screened-off area had been set up. I told my boys to stay put and made my way through the crowded space.

Behind the screen sat a lieutenant slouched in a chair. This was the Ops centre of the mission. It was as basic as it got—A couple of maps tacked to the walls. A logbook is open on the desk. A radio set crackled in the background. This was the nerve centre of our detachment.

And from what I had already seen, I could tell—Morale here was in the gutter. I introduced myself and was given a quick briefing about the area. This was the main market district of Belfast, a predominantly Catholic area with strong anti-British sentiment. Hostility towards soldiers and Protestants was open and aggressive.

Many of the streets, shops, and pubs were known to be frequented by IRA sympathisers. The lieutenant explained how they kept the population under control—a constant, unrelenting presence to ensure they knew who was in charge. "We make sure they never forget it's the British soldier who runs these streets."

His words were matter-of-fact, not gloating—just stating what he saw as a simple reality. I nodded but said nothing. He outlined our patrol strategy.

We would split into two sections of five men. Each section would be integrated into one of their existing patrols, following their orders without question.

"You do exactly as you're told," he said.

I agreed and gave him the names of my men. I was assigned to a corporal named Greaves, along with four of my men. The rest of my team was placed with a corporal named Nixon.

Everything seemed straightforward—until I asked about sleeping arrangements.

They laughed.

"Sleeping? You're joking, right?"

We would be working four hours on, two hours off—on a constant rotation. This was standard practice for the soldiers here. They had been operating like this for three months—and still had another three to go before their tour ended. I was told my "bed" was anywhere I could find a free space.

If I wanted to claim it, all I had to do was chalk my name and my section on the wall. That was it. I had come here to experience this first-hand, to see what life was really like on the ground. And now, I was getting exactly that.

I could see the unease on my men's faces. This was a different world from our training compound. But I told them to hold their opinions until after the operation. "We'll talk when we get back," I said. For now, we had to focus on the task at hand.

Still, I couldn't help but voice my immediate concern about the facilities—or lack of them. I had seen some rough conditions before, but this was something else. One single toilet for all the men. Three sinks, one shower—which doubled as a wash tub. That was it.

If you wanted to wash your face, you first had to remove the pile of socks and underwear soaking in the sinks. The state of the shower was worse. It was as black as the floor—a thick layer of dirt and grime that hadn't been scrubbed in months. It only reinforced what I already knew—You can turn men into animals very quickly.

Just treat them like animals, and they become them.

I finally tracked down Corporal Greaves and had a long conversation about the area. Naturally, I also brought up the shocking conditions in the mission. He chuckled, shaking his head.

"You think this is bad? You should see the officers' quarters."

Eventually, I did.

Under the pretence of introducing myself to the OC, I headed upstairs. A stairway marked 'Out of Bounds' led up to the officers' rooms. There were three officers stationed here—a captain and two lieutenants. The captain had his own room. The lieutenants shared one. Though the rooms were sparse, each had:

- A bed.

- A desk.
- A telephone.

They even had a separate lounge with a colour TV. One shared bathroom between the three of them. It was clean, functional, and—by comparison—luxurious.

I was welcomed politely.

They seemed curious about me, asking questions about my role. They were trying to pump me for information, but I wasn't stupid enough to give them anything useful. After a short exchange, they wished me well and hoped I would "enjoy" my stay.

I knew I wouldn't, but I kept that to myself. Corporal Greaves' section was scheduled to go out at 10 o'clock. I joined him five minutes before. He explained the patrol formation. We would move in two bricks—each consisting of up to six men. Three on each side of the road. Four men paired as opposites. The lead man on the left moved ahead alone, without an opposite number. The rear man on the right did the same, except he walked sideways and backwards, acting as tail-end security.

This was the standard patrol method throughout Northern Ireland. At road junctions, a leapfrog and cover movement was used, ensuring the team always had protection. This was everything we had been taught over the past few weeks.

And now, I was about to put it into practice.

We moved out, and I took my position—right side, opposite Corporal Greaves. He would guide me, and I would watch him closely. Up ahead, I could see the other bricks moving in formation, about thirty yards between us. I took a steady breath and stepped forward. Now, it was real.

We loaded our weapons and moved out quickly. Once outside, every movement became calculated. In the open, you never linger—you cross the ground fast, moving from cover to cover. A doorway, a wall, an alleyway—anywhere that offered protection was an opportunity to stay alive.

Being out here, in the heart of it, felt surreal. This was real now, no longer training drills or exercises. We moved at a slow but deliberate pace, constantly scanning—A curtain twitching at a window. A parked car that looked out of place. A face that didn't belong. Anything unusual could be the difference between life and death.

This was a hardened IRA area. You could see it in the people's faces, in the way they moved. On street corners, scruffy men stood watching. Greaves knew every single one of them. A silent message rippled through the streets.

Word spread instantly—The patrol is here. The British soldiers are in the area. I quickly learned that these people didn't just dislike us—they despised us. The soldier behind me muttered under his breath—"Don't worry, mate. As long as the women and kids are out, we're all right. But if the doors start shutting and the streets empty—start looking over your shoulder."

I took his advice.

But the doors remained open, people still moved about, and so I began to feel more at ease. A small, creeping confidence settled in me. That was a mistake. A big mistake. Never be overconfident in Ireland.

We had been out for about an hour when we paused at a row of terraced houses. All the homes looked the same—Two rooms up, two rooms down. One front door. One back. Many windows bricked up. Walls covered in slogans and graffiti, filled with hatred. I tried to understand it.

Why did people live in these conditions? Why stay in such squalor? Of course, I understand now—This was the only place they felt safe. This was their community. Here, amongst their own people—They were protected, they were the law, and they were in control.

In the Army, we called them "TAIGS"—a crude, derogatory term for Irish Catholics. But to them, we were the invaders. Then, I saw her. A small girl, no older than four or five. She was thin as a rail; skin stretched tight over bony limbs. She wore a filthy, ragged dress, her greasy black hair clinging to her face. Her fingernails were chewed to stubs, her bare feet were black with dirt. She scratched at her thin arms, her eyes watching us closely. Then, in a strong Belfast accent, she shouted out—

"Go home, Brits!"

She stepped forward, her eyes locked onto me. I had a daughter around her age. I smiled and said, "Hello, little lady."

She stopped about a foot away, staring at me. "What's your name?" I asked. Her small lips curled into a sneer. "Not yours to know, Brit." The words were sharp, cold, and full of venom. I hesitated, surprised.

"Why are you being so nasty?" I asked. I shouldn't have. A few other children had begun to gather around. She saw her audience—and what came next stunned me. She screamed—"Ah, bollocks, you Brit pigs—fuck off!"

The words were vile, spat from a mouth far too young to know such hate. Before I could react, she lifted her skirt—And pissed all over my boots. I was kneeling at the time. She looked at me with defiance and grinned.

"You smell sweeter now, Pig."

Laughter erupted from the others. It was a joke to them. To her. To the watching men on the corners. Corporal Greaves' voice cut through my shock.

"Move out—now."

We left quickly, but I was seething. I needed to understand. I needed to know why. Why would a child behave like that? Why would she say those things?

I had a daughter her age—She had never even heard language like that. She wouldn't dare expose herself in front of a man. What kind of hatred had been fed into this child's mind?

And by who? As we walked, I knew—I wouldn't be able to forget this.

We approached a covered shed, its entrance barely noticeable beneath a heap of discarded rubbish. Corporal Greaves signalled for us to go inside. Two of our men remained outside, taking up hidden watch positions to keep an eye on the street beyond.

I stood there, silent, still trying to process what had happened with the little girl. I kept turning it over in my mind, searching for some kind of reason—but I couldn't find one. Greaves noticed my distraction.

"Don't dwell on it," he said. "That happens every day. Treat them as they treat you, but always keep the upper hand."

Then he added, almost casually—"You should've given her a kick in the arse—that would've shut her up." I looked at him, disbelieving.

"Surely we should try making these kids our friends, not enemies?"

He laughed, shaking his head.

"If we befriend that scum, they'll lull you into a false sense of security—get you to trust them, then lead you into a come-on."

I frowned. "A come-on?"

"A setup."

His tone darkened, his expression turning serious.

"Next thing you know; you've got a bullet in your head. Don't ever try talking sense into these kids."

"Your human concerns are the best weapon the IRA have against us. They know we won't fire near children, so they use them as human shields."

He continued, his voice filled with barely contained frustration.

"A gunman will hide in a crowd of kids. The second a patrol comes near, he'll open fire. The kids get caught between us and him—he knows we won't shoot back."

Then, in a low, muttered voice—"Sometimes I wish I could shoot all the little bastards, but we can't."

I let his words sink in, but my mind was still grappling with the bigger question.

"Who puts this hatred in their heads?" I asked. "Who teaches them, from birth, that Brits are the enemy?" Greaves didn't hesitate.

"It's drilled into them. Their parents, their teachers, their priests—it doesn't matter. They're raised to hate us. They grow up believing that killing Brits is the only way to free Ireland." I thought about our own training, our own doctrine.

The Army had its own methods, its own black-and-white version of history. Both sides believed they were right. Both sides had been successful, in their own ways, in furthering their cause. It made everything more complicated. And for the first time, I felt an uneasy doubt creeping in. We left the shed, but my mind wasn't on the job.

I was still turning over Greaves' words, trying to make sense of it all. Then Greaves called me over as we walked. "Right, sir—let's have a bit of fun to break the monotony." I glanced at him, wary.

"Fun?"

He smirked.

"It'll upset the locals, but let's do a few checks—to bring you up to speed. I'll do the first one, and then you can have a go. Watch me."

I was still lost in my own thoughts, too distracted to think too much about what he meant. So, without much consideration, I agreed. We continued walking. Ahead, I saw a young lad, about nineteen, approaching on the opposite side of the road. Tall, wearing jeans and high boots, with a green combat jacket—the type favoured by IRA members. His head was down, avoiding eye contact.

Greaves gave me a quick nod.

"Okay," he murmured. I nodded back. As the lad came closer, Greaves stepped directly in front of him, blocking his path.

His voice was sharp, aggressive—"Where are you going, Sullivan?"

I immediately realised—Greaves knew this lad. Greaves called me over. The rest of the patrol immediately took defensive positions, positioning themselves to cover us. They were trained for this moment, their eyes scanning every possible threat. The lad hesitated.

"Nowhere," he muttered. I could see the fear in his face. He was from a poor home; that much was clear. A kid caught in the middle of a war he didn't start. Greaves' voice hardened. "Assume the position."

The lad obeyed instantly—hands up over his head, his body leaning against the wall of one of the houses. Greaves positioned himself behind him, then kicked the boy's feet apart, widening his stance. The frisking began. The lad started protesting, shifting uncomfortably as Greaves' hands searched him from head to toe. Greaves wasn't gentle. He was thorough, checking every pocket, waistband, and seam.

The lad's face burned with embarrassment. Greaves leaned in, his voice mocking.

"Shut your face. If I want you to talk, I'll tell you to."

Then, with a sharp smirk—"Not carrying anything for Daddy today, then, Sean?"

The boy stiffened. He answered carefully—"Don't know what you mean."

Greaves glanced at me, grinning slightly. "This one runs a few jobs for his dad. His old man's a villain—likes to make up little presents for his friends."

I knew exactly what he meant. This boy was a courier. Moving weapons, explosives, or information.

Another small cog in the IRA's machine. As I watched, I realised—this wasn't just about patrolling a hostile area.

This was psychological warfare, and I was right in the middle of it. Greaves leaned in close to the lad, his tone mocking. "Presents, Sean. You know, little gifts—nail bombs, incendiary devices." He smirked. "But Sean here knows nothing about that... do you, Sean?"

Without warning, Greaves kicked the boy in the back of the knees. Sean crumpled onto the pavement, landing hard on his knees, a sharp gasp escaping his lips. The pain was clear on his face, but he bit down, saying nothing at first. Then—"It's all lies! My dad's away; I don't know where he is!"

Greaves snorted. "Crap." He crouched down, his voice low and deliberate. "Listen, sunshine. You're lucky I'm in a good mood today. Otherwise, we'd be taking you in for a nice long chat."

He tilted his head, watching Sean closely. Then, after a moment—"Go on. Piss off." Sean got slowly to his feet, his eyes flicking between Greaves and me. I could see it in his face—he was memorising me. The new face. The stranger in his streets. Then, as if nothing had happened, he turned and walked away.

One of the soldiers called out, laughing—"Should've gobbed him, Corp!" Greaves grinned. "Next time—don't want to give a bad impression, do we?"

They were enjoying this. I saw it now—clear as day. And it sickened me. The stories I'd heard before coming to Ireland—The ones I thought were exaggerated, soldier's tales, twisted truths—They were real.

I couldn't change any of this, not now, not yet. But when I had my own command, my own men, I would run things differently. At least, I hoped I would. After about half an hour, I started to feel it. My feet burned in my boots, a strange fatigue creeping in. I wasn't physically tired—I was tense. Every muscle coiled, ready to react to the slightest movement, the slightest threat. This was the strain of real situations.

Your mind sharpens, and your body prepares—watching, waiting, anticipating the unknown.

What's around the next corner? Who's waiting in that alley? Is that just a shadow—or a man with a gun? Fear fuels you. And over time, they told me, you get used to it. Then, it becomes second nature.

And the first? Survival.

The streets of Belfast were all the same—Row after row of crumbling terrace houses, poverty in every doorway. To an outsider, they blurred into one another. But to an Army patrol, each one was as familiar as your own home. Every house, every resident, every routine—memorised. Any change—noticed immediately. Every face—recognised. Every stranger—scrutinised.

If someone was missing, they were found.

They had to explain themselves.

Where they'd been…

Why they'd gone…

Who they'd met…

If a visitor came to stay, they were recorded and vetted.

Who were they?

Where had they come from?

What were they doing here?

Why had they come?

Even the smallest details mattered. An extra pint of milk on a doorstep? Who's it for? Is someone expected? Every detail was logged, kept in notebooks—A small sign that someone might be helping the IRA. A tiny shift that could signal an attack was coming. Everyone was treated as hostile. Not because of orders, not because of doctrine—But because of fear, instinct, and survival.

As we moved forward, the street narrowed, the walls closing in around us. Ahead, we approached what looked like a bricked-up building, its windows sealed, its presence oddly foreboding. On the corner, a man in his mid-twenties leaned against a doorframe, arms folded, his stance casual but defiant.

A hard-looking bastard—the type who wouldn't take any nonsense from anyone. As we drew closer, he backheeled the door behind him—a subtle signal. Greaves didn't break stride. He turned to me, "Do you want to do the honours, sir?"

He nodded toward the man. "He's a lookout. Behind that door? A Republican club. We're going in."

I nodded.

"OK."

Greaves gave the rest of the patrol a silent signal. Instantly, they moved into covering positions Crouching low, rifles raised. Eyes sweeping windows, alleys, rooftops. Every shadow is a potential threat. We were deep in hostile territory, and now, it felt real. I walked up to the lookout, stopping just inches from him.

"Hello."

He didn't reply. I spoke again, this time sharper. "I'm talking to you, mate—not the bloody wall." That got through. His gaze shifted to me, eyes cold, assessing. Then, in a low, unbothered voice—

"You won't find anything here, Brit."

I glanced at Greaves, who gave me a slight nod—then flicked his eyes toward the wall. I got the message. I stepped in closer. "All right, chum. Against the wall—hands high, feet apart." To my surprise, he complied without a word. I frisked him quickly, my hands brushing over the sweat-drenched fabric.

The smell hit me—stale sweat, smoke, and something sour. It turned my stomach. He didn't flinch—didn't even twitch. Just stood there, passive, waiting for it to be over. Greaves finally spoke.

"OK, leave him. I know there's no problem. Let's go in."

Greaves pushed open the door. I followed, two of our lads slipping in behind us, taking positions by the entrance. The stench hit me instantly—a mix of stale beer, sweat, and damp wood. I was getting used to it now, the filth, the unwashed bodies, the feeling of unease.

As we moved through the room, I kept my rifle close, careful not to bump into anyone. The drinkers barely acknowledged us, as if we didn't exist. Only when we passed a group deep in conversation did I notice the shift. The tone of voices changed, the subjects altered mid-sentence.

Their eyes flicked toward us, then away again. Identifying the Players. We reached an empty corner, backs against the wall, facing the room. Greaves started pointing people out, murmuring their histories like a roll call of violence. "That one—lifted for possession of a weapon."

I followed his gaze. A thin man, eyes sharp, fingers tapping idly on his pint glass. "That one—his brother's in the Maze. Twelve years for murder." A stocky bloke, arms tattooed, knuckles bruised and scarred.

"That one—was involved with his brother-in-law. A known explosives man." I glanced over. A man in his forties, calm, calculated—the kind who knew how to stay just out of reach. "We can't pin anything on him—yet." It went on and on. Every face, every name, every crime. And through it all, I felt it. The hatred in the room. Not just the hatred of today, but the hatred of generations.

A hatred that ran deeper than war, deeper than politics. A hatred of the British. We shouldn't have been there. But we were. Walking into a room full of known killers armed with nothing but authority and arrogance. We were playing a game. A game of chance. A game of one-upmanship. But thinking back—They were playing a far deadlier game. A game that felt more like Russian Roulette.

We moved through the room once more, weaving between tables and stepping over discarded chairs, but this time, the hostility was more pronounced. The women, in particular, had no hesitation in making their feelings known. Unlike the men, who exuded silent contempt, these women did not hold their tongues. Their abuse was relentless, their words laced with venom, and their voices shrill with fury.

What poured out of their mouths was not just insult but something far worse—disgusting, vile threats, spoken in such a violent flurry that it was almost difficult to comprehend. They described, in grotesque detail, what they would do to us if they had the chance, reducing us to objects of degradation, using language so filthy that even the hardest of soldiers would have flinched. I had never heard anything like it, nor could I ever repeat it. It was more than hatred; it was raw, unfiltered loathing deeply embedded within them.

Greaves nudged me and muttered, "Time to get out. The women are bad news." I didn't argue. Their words clung to me like filth, something I couldn't shake off, something that made me feel that, in their eyes, I was not just the enemy but something less than human. As we turned to leave, their shouting only grew louder, the men in the room laughing as if they were watching a well-rehearsed show.

I could feel my back burning under their gaze, and when we finally stepped out into the street, I let out a breath I hadn't realised I was holding.

Back at the mission, I found myself feeling oddly relieved, even though I had previously thought the place was a hole. But now, in comparison to the hostility outside, it seemed almost welcoming. At least here, there were no shrieking voices, no spit-flecked insults hurled in our faces. It was still cramped, still filthy, but it was, at the very least, a place where I didn't feel exposed.

Our meal, however, did little to lift the spirits. The food was awful—fat-drenched, overcooked eggs floating in grease, limp chips that had the texture of cork. But it was warm, and after the stress of being out in the streets, we needed it. I forced it down, more out of necessity than appetite.

After eating, I turned my attention to the scrapbook—a crude collection of newspaper clippings, photographs, and handwritten notes compiled by the unit. Every mission had one, a visual record of their time in the area.

I flipped through the pages, seeing the same faces appear over and over again—men who had been arrested, gunmen who had been killed, weapons that had been recovered. There were pictures of sacks of explosives, some weighing over a hundredweight, alongside descriptions of snatch squad raids and intelligence reports.

But it was the sections about the women and children that truly unsettled me. I read article after article detailing how they played an integral role in the IRA's operations—how they acted as decoys, luring soldiers into the sights of waiting gunmen; how they smuggled weapons, hiding them under their skirts or in prams, knowing full well that soldiers would hesitate before searching them; how they provided safe houses and protection for men who had taken lives in the name of their cause.

The IRA did not have to force these people into submission; they were willing participants, deeply embedded in the structure of the organisation.

There was one story that particularly stuck with me. It told of how women used their own bodies to distract soldiers, deliberately stripping down to slow them during searches, using nudity as a weapon of war. One cutting showed a woman standing before a patrol, progressively undressing while her comrades smuggled a wounded IRA man to safety.

The soldiers, all young men who had not seen their wives or girlfriends for months, were momentarily stunned, distracted just long enough for the fugitive to escape. And when the woman later confessed her actions to a priest, she was granted absolution. In the eyes of the church, she had not sinned—she had simply done her duty, protecting a man who was serving a "just cause" in the battle against the British.

The more I read, the more I realised how deeply ingrained this conflict was, not just in the men who fought but in the very fabric of society. It was not just the IRA and the Protestant factions who were at war; it was an entire way of life, a belief system passed down from generation to generation.

Over those two days, I learned more than I had ever thought possible about the motivations behind both the Catholic and Protestant causes and about the army's precarious position between the two. I even found myself in an unexpected discussion with a

Catholic priest after an incident in which he had been stopped and questioned.

He was calm, articulate, and polite, but when I pressed him on the issue of forgiveness—on how the church could absolve those who had taken lives—his response sent a shiver down my spine.

"The church does not condone evil," he told me. "But a Catholic is permitted to kill on three occasions. One, when the Christian cause is just. Two, when one engages in a holy war. And three, when execution is called for by Christian duty."

I stared at him, letting the words sink in.

"So, you're telling me that a terrorist—someone who guns down a soldier in cold blood—can still be forgiven?"

The priest met my gaze without flinching.

"If his cause is just if he is fighting in a war, and if he is executing the will of his leaders—then yes, the church will forgive him."

It was in that moment that I understood the true horror of what we were facing. We were not fighting, just a group of men with guns. We were fighting an ideology, one that had been given religious legitimacy, one that had been woven into the very fabric of their existence.

And worst of all, I realised that to them, we were no different. We were the enemy, faceless and foreign, oppressors and invaders.

It didn't matter what we believed.

To them, we were already condemned.

The church protected them, encouraged them, and gave them justification for their actions. It was not just the gunmen or bomb-makers that were driven by this cause but the women and children, too. They were taught from birth that revenge was their duty and that the years of oppression, bloodshed, and betrayal had to be avenged.

Meanwhile, the British soldier was bound by law, restricted by the Emergency Powers Act and military regulations that left no room for retaliation. He was expected to operate within a legal framework that often felt deliberately designed to leave him vulnerable.

Yet, in the field, that framework was flexible. Loopholes were found, grey areas exploited, and orders interpreted in ways that allowed necessary actions to be taken while still appearing lawful. It was a balancing act, one that every soldier understood, though the line between right and wrong blurred more often than not. It was an impossible position, a war fought in the shadows where the enemy had no such moral constraints, no bureaucracy to hold them back.

By the end of my two-day experience in Belfast, the relentless routine had drained me. The constant patrols, the endless cycle of being in and out of the mission, the ever-present hostility—it was exhausting in every possible way. I could see now how the soldiers stationed here were ground down, how their patience was tested beyond limits, how their tolerance had been eroded to the point of hatred.

The bitterness was understandable. They were stuck in an unwinnable war, despised by the people they were supposedly there to protect, and governed by politicians in Westminster who had never walked these streets.

And that, I realised, was the core of the problem. The men making the decisions had no real knowledge of what was happening on the ground. Their policies, rigid and outdated, were relics from another era, based on political strategies that had been carved in stone centuries ago.

England's sovereignty, the so-called integrity of its empire, was built on this refusal to bend. Any deviation, any compromise, would mean admitting failure. And so, nothing changed. The conflict dragged on, men died, hatred deepened, and the cycle continued.

Back at Ballykinler, I called the full course together in the lecture room. The cold air lingered, but there was no sense of formal instruction this time. I did not stand at the front and deliver orders. Instead, I sat with them, face to face, and we talked. I wanted to know what they thought of the weekend, what they had learned, and how they felt about what they had seen.

What struck me most was how many of them shared my views. They, too, had been shocked by the reality of Belfast, by the hostility, by the conditions, by the unrelenting tension. But there were others—men who had enjoyed the control, who had felt a sense of power in their encounters with the locals.

They saw the methods used by the more seasoned soldiers and believed them to be justified. Maybe, in some cases, they were. But I could not allow that kind of thinking to take root in my unit. If a man thought himself judge and jury on the streets, if he believed he had the right to make those decisions on a whim, then he had no place in my team.

The next morning, I made the decision to suspend training. Instead, I spent the day speaking to each man individually. By now, we had developed into a well-moulded group, a team that had built trust, discipline, and camaraderie. But now was the time to understand them on a more personal level. I wanted to know their thoughts—not just about the training, but about me, about the role they were about to step into, about the Irish, about how their families felt about them being here.

One by one, they came in. I listened to their concerns, their motivations, and their doubts. Some were here because they believed in the mission. Others were here because they had no real alternative. A few harboured the kind of aggression I could not afford to let fester.

In the end, four men did not meet the standard. It was not that they were bad soldiers—far from it. But they were not right for this unit.

That left me with twenty-six men. I needed twenty-one to form my bricks, but I was reluctant to let any more go. With leave, training courses, and the ever-present risk of sickness or injury, I had a strong case for keeping the full number. The next step was to put my argument forward to the Brigadier.

I went straight to Major Skinner, the man who could make things happen. Now, it was time to see if he would listen.

The pace was accelerating now, and the time for final preparations was upon us. Wednesday morning arrived, bringing the answer I had been waiting for. The approval came through—I could keep all twenty-six men I had requested. I could have jumped for joy. It was a small victory but a crucial one. Major Skinner also informed me that I was to report to Brigadier Woodford on Friday at 10:00 a.m. for my final briefing. The real work was about to begin.

That evening, I gathered my men. The atmosphere in the lecture room was heavy, the weight of expectation hanging in the air. They knew what was coming. The uncertainty of selection had left them all on edge. I could see it in their eyes, the silent questions, the anxious energy.

I got straight to the point. "Well, gents, as you know, not all of you will be staying with me." The room was deathly quiet. I read the four names aloud. As expected, their faces dropped, but there was no outburst, no argument—just quiet resignation. I reassured them.

"May I say this does not reflect upon your capabilities whatsoever. However, I feel you would be better suited to work with one of the other detachments in the province. Of course, you will all have a course report to accompany you, which I hope will help you in the future. May I say it has been a pleasure to know you, and I wish you all well. Mr Hunter, who is in his office, will give you the details you need. Thank you."

The four men stood up, exchanged brief nods with the others, and made their way out. They were disappointed, naturally, but they accepted it without protest. I had made the right choice.

I turned back to the remaining men. "Well, now for you lot," I said, allowing a small smile. "You may recall that initially, I needed twenty-one for my crew. Well, I put it to the Brigadier that I do not want tired, exhausted men whose alertness, keenness, and interests soon become affected.

I, therefore, have asked for an extra five men because we all need a day off. Also, to cover sickness and leave, etc. He has agreed, so I have pleasure in telling you that you are now the twenty-six that are with me for good."

A loud cheer erupted in the room, fists clenched in triumph. The tension that had been there moments before had transformed into something else—pride, excitement, relief. The morale was exactly where I needed it to be. Now, the challenge was keeping it there.

I continued. "I would just like to say I will have my final briefing on Friday with the Brigadier. I hope we will be able to assume our new role next week, but before we get into full swing, I feel we should see both our new accommodations, which I gather will be

Gough Barracks in Armagh—a newly built barracks. Also, our new town, Newry, is on the border with the South."

They listened intently as I laid out what was ahead. I explained how we would work to gain the confidence of the people in Newry, to earn their support if possible, and how I hoped we could operate. I could feel the mood shift. The lads were keen now that they knew what was expected of them. Enthusiasm bubbled beneath the surface, but I knew better than to let it get ahead of us.

"To keep things in perspective," I added, bringing the mood back to reality, "we still have two days more training, and I will not let up. Where we are going, fitness is our key to the future success of this operation."

Those final two days exceeded all my expectations. The men pushed themselves to their limits and beyond, refining their techniques, honing their instincts, and improving at a level that left me with no doubts. They were ready.

Friday came. When I arrived at the Brigadier's office, he was waiting for me. There was no ceremony, no wasted time—just straight to business. As I had been told, our unit was to be posted to Armagh, using it as our home base. From there, we would operate out of the security headquarters in Newry, as well as the police station. By day, we would coordinate from these locations, gathering intelligence and carrying out operations as needed.

Night-time activity would be dictated by the situation on the ground, with infantry, air corps, and covert operatives taking the lead. If I required them, they would be at my disposal.

This was it. The pieces were falling into place. The mission was about to begin.

Satisfied with how things were progressing, I found myself in fifty percent agreement with the Brigadier's arrangements. While I wanted my men to stay fresh and unwind at night—unlike in Belfast—there was always the option to rotate personnel if required. He instructed me to report to Major John Smythe in Armagh, my new OC, who would be responsible for administering all our needs. Armagh would be our base of operations, and once in Newry, we were to report to Major Stam at the security headquarters. He commanded the backup troops in the area and could provide assistance within minutes if necessary.

Our integration into the region was moving swiftly. The Royal Ulster Constabulary (RUC) expected us on Sunday for a briefing on their role, and later that evening, the local intelligence cell would update us on everything they knew.

Everything seemed to be falling into place. I was to submit a weekly report to the Brigadier through my new OC, but if I ever felt the need to speak to him directly, I had only to ask. His parting words stuck with me: "I hope you will succeed; there's a lot counting on it."

On the way back to Ballykinler, I allowed myself a brief moment of relief. The first stage was complete. What I did not know then was that we were about to write ourselves into the troubled history of this country. I thought of my lads—Benny, Colin, Carey, Andy, Tom, Wing Nut, Vic, Paddy. Each name held weight now, each man had proven himself in ways I had come to respect. From the outset, I had made it clear that on the ground, we would be equals.

We would address each other by first names, except for me. No one was to use my Christian name or my rank. Instead, I became simply "The Boss" or just "Boss." I never had to repeat that instruction. It was a mark of respect among us, and none of them ever allowed anyone outside our unit to call me Boss. It was their choice, and I respected it.

Arriving back at Ballykinler, I found Hunter had the lads on the range. I grabbed my rifle and headed down for one reason—I had previously told them that if they could not land thirty rounds into a one-inch square at two hundred yards, they were out.

I knew Hunter was pushing them hard, ensuring every single man was up to standard. As I reached the range, the last shots were being fired. Only one rifle was still cracking—Wing Nut's.

Wing Nut had earned his nickname due to his large ears, which stuck out like the wingnuts on an old bolt. Small in stature, he was as nimble as a mole, able to squeeze into places a larger man could not. He climbed like a monkey and had nerves of ice—qualities that would prove invaluable in the field.

I walked up behind him and called to the control tower, "How many?"

A voice replied, "Twenty-six, four within two inches of the marker."

Wing Nut looked up at me, waiting for my reaction. I gave him a nod. "Come on, lad, you get up. Let's see what I can do."

I took my position, shouldered my rifle, and fired off thirty rounds. I had no illusions about showing off, but as I examined the target, I saw that I had placed one round just outside the four corners of the marker. Close, but not perfect.

Wing Nut grinned. "Not bad, Boss."

I smirked. "Aye, but you still owe me four shots inside the square."

The lads laughed. The test was over, but the real challenge was yet to come.

The move to Newry the following morning was quiet, yet the journey itself held a deep sense of interest. As we passed through the notorious Glen Shane Pass, I knew that our approach would not go unnoticed. The so-called jungle drums had already begun to beat, spreading the word of our arrival through unseen networks, ensuring that the right people—on both sides—were well aware of our presence.

As we neared the town's boundaries, the weight of the situation settled more heavily on my shoulders. It was clear that we were not just entering another location; we were stepping into a place where tensions simmered just beneath the surface. The security forces headquarters in Newry was an old Territorial Army centre fortified to the hilt. Razor wire coiled around its perimeter, meshing stretched across every possible opening, and iron sheeting covered the walls for added protection.

The entrance was guarded heavily, with gates that swung open only to allow our convoy through before slamming shut behind us with a finality that was unmistakable. Soldiers dashed out, weapons at the ready, assuming covering positions as we drove between two Saracen armoured cars that remained stationed outside at all times—just in case.

Inside, I wasted no time finding Major Stam, who had been fully briefed by the Brigadier on our arrival. He was direct, experienced, and knew his area well. He suggested that for the first few days, it would be wise to take along a couple of his men who had a solid understanding of the town's layout, routines, and key players. I agreed immediately. My men had studied maps; they knew street names, but nothing could substitute for real-time, on-the-ground familiarity.

He informed me that a helicopter reconnaissance had been arranged for us at 11:00 a.m. We were to be picked up from Bessbrook Mill, the company headquarters. This old cotton mill had been taken over by the army back in 1969 when British forces had first been deployed in the area.

Now, it served as a critical hub for operations in South Armagh, housing a screening centre, a helipad, and an intelligence post. It was here that much of our information would be processed, and any actionable intelligence would be directed.

At 4:00 p.m., we were scheduled to meet with the RUC to inspect various designated rest areas in town. Everything was moving swiftly, and I could feel the momentum building.

Before heading to Bessbrook, Major Stam gave us a full tour of the Newry base. The conditions were, to put it bluntly, dreadful. Men were packed into overcrowded rooms, fifteen to twenty per room, with barely any facilities to speak of. It reminded me of the mission hall in Belfast, though these soldiers at least knew they had slightly more freedom when it came to personal time and space.

They had adapted to their conditions, but it was clear that morale was stretched thin. Still, they welcomed us as best they could, knowing that our arrival might bring some degree of change.

At the rear of the base stood a small recreation hall and what they called a chogie shop. The term "chogie" was one commonly used by soldiers to refer to Asian traders who catered to military personnel. Since soldiers were not permitted to shop in civilian stores, these traders set up within the base, supplying everything from burgers and coffee to basic clothing and toiletries—twenty-four hours a day.

It was a lifeline of sorts, a small comfort amidst otherwise bleak surroundings.

Also located at the rear of the base was a pipe range, a narrow concrete drainage tunnel fitted with a target at one end, designed to allow soldiers to keep their marksmanship sharp without the risk of stray rounds causing damage beyond the perimeter.

We were given access to a small office, a briefing room, and a rest area. The officers' facilities, unsurprisingly, were significantly better—separate quarters inside the main building, adjacent to the operations control centre.

At 11:00 a.m., we were lifted off in Wessex helicopters, leaving Bessbrook Mill far below. As we gained altitude, one of the intelligence sergeants accompanying us pointed out key landmarks, drawing our attention to the distinct divisions between Catholic and Protestant communities. From above, the contrasts were startling.

The Protestant areas appeared better maintained, though their curb stones were painted in bold red, white, and blue—the colours of the Union flag. Their patriotism was on full display. The Catholic areas, in contrast, were marked in green, white, and orange, the tricolour of the Irish Republic dominating every visible space.

Murals were splashed across building walls, depicting masked gunmen clutching rifles, their figures towering over passersby like shadowy sentinels. Some portrayed past victories, others served as recruitment propaganda, while some issued stark warnings—You Are Entering a No-Go Area.

It was one thing to hear about these divisions in lectures and intelligence briefings. It was another entirely to see them from the air, to witness just how deeply entrenched they were in the fabric of daily life. This was a battleground unlike any I had encountered before, and the weight of what lay ahead was becoming ever more tangible.

The town of Newry was relatively small, yet its geography and layout told a story that echoed the broader history of Ireland. A tangled network of adjoining roads, narrow alleyways, and a patchwork of derelict and modern buildings defined its landscape.

At the town's heart stood a towering Catholic church, meticulously maintained, a stark contrast to the surrounding structures. The marketplace nearby catered to goods arriving from the South, less than a mile away. What was really sold there, I wondered? I knew I would eventually find out.

A river split the town in two, flanked by small docks and coal yards scattered along its banks. Surrounding the town were housing estates Protestant and Catholic communities perched on the hills, looking down onto the town below. Some were newly built, while others bore the scars of time.

Only one main road led into Newry and another out, though numerous small roads snaked through the estates and into the countryside—ideal escape routes for those who wished to come and go unnoticed.

Beyond the town limits, the hills rolled into vast stretches of green scrub, punctuated by poorly maintained fields and crumbling farmhouses. Many of these farms had been abandoned, their owners having given up in the face of constant conflict. Some of these derelict properties dated back to the potato famine, their walls bearing silent testimony to a history of suffering.

The very existence of these ruined crofts was a legacy of past oppression. Centuries ago, Irish peasants had been driven from their lands by English landlords, their homes set ablaze, their livestock seized, and their families left destitute. The cruelty of those times had planted the seeds of a hatred that endured to this day. Now, these abandoned crofts served a different purpose—hidden sanctuaries for terrorists, caches for weapons, and safe houses for those evading pursuit.

Our tour took us along the border with the South, an invisible yet powerful divide. The boundary was poorly marked, easy to stray across—both for the army and for those we were hunting. Warren Point and Ross Trevor fell within our operational area.

Ross Trevor, once a bustling deep-water port, now lay mostly dormant, its waters opening out into Carlingford Lough and the Clanrye River, also known as the Newry Canal. Hills rising from the South provided an advantageous overlook of the port, making it a vulnerable spot.

The road between Warren Point and Newry was another dangerous stretch—open, exposed, and utterly unforgiving. On one side, the river formed the natural border with Southern Ireland, while on the other, fields stretched toward the towering Mourne Mountains.

The first sign of Newry that greeted incoming travellers was its cemetery—a place strictly off-limits to soldiers, for it was considered hallowed ground by the locals. Yet, for those of us entering the town in uniform, it felt more like a silent warning.

Further afield, Crossmaglen and Fork Hill stood as bastions of Republicanism, deeply entrenched in their loyalty to the IRA. These were not places to take lightly; they were strongholds where even the most experienced soldiers trod carefully.

The people there were hardened, unyielding in their beliefs, and fiercely protective of their way of life. The presence of British troops in these areas was met with open hostility, a constant tension simmering beneath every interaction.

Had I known then what I know now, I might have turned back before stepping foot in Crossmaglen. No one would ever tame that town. It was not merely a Republican stronghold; it was the living heart of the IRA, the very pulse of their movement.

The defiance that fuelled the conflict across Ireland was cultivated and nurtured here. This was where the fight for Irish identity had been waged for generations, and no foreign force, no amount of military strategy, would ever break the will of these people.

Newry, Bessbrook, Crossmaglen, Fork Hill—these were the names that defined the conflict, the battlefields where history was being written in blood and ideology.

We arrived back at Bessbrook around 1:00 p.m., weary yet more informed. A quick lunch was followed by an exhaustive briefing on the various stations and units we would need to liaise with during our time here.

It was an education like no other, a stark realisation of the scale and complexity of the task ahead. What lay before us was not just another military deployment. This was something else entirely.

The sheer volume of intelligence compiled and logged at the base was staggering. It seemed as though every family's history, every name, and every suspected link to the ongoing conflict had been meticulously recorded. The screening area, in particular, piqued my interest. It was a stark, no-nonsense facility—nothing more than a tall brick enclosure with a gravel-covered yard.

The sound of footsteps carried sharply in the enclosed space, ensuring that no movement went unnoticed. The perimeter was topped with razor wire, a constant reminder of the nature of the work carried out here.

Inside the compound, three large porta cabins formed the operational centre. Two of them were divided into five subsections, each furnished with little more than a table, two chairs, and harsh overhead lighting. These were the interview rooms, where detainees were questioned under the scrutiny of powerful lamps that left no place to hide. The third cabin was split into three functional areas.

The first phase was the reception, where all individuals brought in were recorded, their details taken, and their photographs snapped for identification. From there, they moved to the medical examination room, where a cursory health check was conducted before the final stage—the initial interrogation chamber. This room was adjoined by a small toilet and wash area, offering basic facilities, but it was the heavy door leading out to the walled yard that caught my attention.

Many men had passed through that door, and I had no doubt that many more would. Some of their stories, I knew, would stay with me long after my time in Ireland.

Our next stop was the police station. The moment we stepped inside, it was clear we were not welcome. The reception from the RUC officers was far from warm—cool, guarded, and tinged with an undercurrent of resentment. It was evident that they viewed us as intruders, stepping into their domain and undermining their authority. Their hostility was unmistakable.

We were introduced to the senior officers and given a brief tour of what could only be described as a fortress. High walls, reinforced security, and an air of paranoia surrounded the place, but it was not the physical structure that concerned me—it was the attitude of the men within it.

I sensed fear amongst them. They wore their uniforms and went through the motions of law enforcement, but there was a distinct lack of conviction. They were, by and large, Protestant and their allegiance to the British state was clear, yet they did not exude confidence in their role.

They carried out their duties because they had to, not because they believed in the cause they were upholding. It was a chilling realisation—how could we hope to succeed in an operation when even those entrusted with law and order seemed unwilling to stand firm?

We left the police station within the hour, but the encounter left a sour taste in my mouth. It was evident that I would face significant obstacles in this area, not only from the IRA but also from those who were supposed to be on our side. The RUC's reluctance to work with us would be a problem, one I would have to navigate carefully.

Our final stops were the hospital and the fire station. Here, too, the reception was less than friendly. Both institutions were said to be heavily anti-army, their staff leaning towards Catholic nationalist sympathies.

It was made clear that while they would not outright refuse assistance, they would not go out of their way to cooperate with us either. It was yet another example of the deeply entrenched divisions that ran through this town.

As I stood there, absorbing everything I had seen that day, I realised the scale of the challenge ahead. Winning over the people of Newry would not be easy. Even securing basic cooperation from those in positions of authority would be an uphill battle. The distrust ran deep, fuelled by years of resentment, fear, and bloodshed.

The old ghosts of the past were still very much alive in this town. The RUC, for all its modern branding, still carried the echoes of its predecessor—the infamous "B Specials." Once little more than a state-sponsored militia, they had been notorious for their brutality against Catholics. Though officially disbanded, their legacy lingered, and the scars they left behind had not yet healed.

I knew then, beyond any doubt, that my time in Newry would test me in ways I had never imagined. This was not just another military posting. This was stepping into the heart of a conflict that had been raging for centuries. And whether I liked it or not, I was now a part of it.

CHAPTER FOUR
THE DEEP END

On the 6th of February 1976, we arrived in Newry at 07:15 on a bitterly cold morning, our breath misting in the air as we left our vehicles. There was a quiet tension among us, an unspoken awareness that from this moment on, everything would change. None of us knew exactly what to expect, only that the coming days would test us in ways we could not yet comprehend.

I quickly organised the section into three bricks, each supplemented with an additional NCO from Major Stam's company. Our task was to patrol the estates, each brick covering a different sector while maintaining radio contact. The weapons were loaded, final checks completed. Then, with a brief nod, I signalled to the lads—we moved out.

The Brigadier's operation, once just an idea in the planning rooms, was now a reality. Whether it would serve the good of Ireland, I could not say. Whether our efforts would be counted, our actions acknowledged, or our sacrifices appreciated—I would never know.

We left the Newry base under a sky streaked with frost, the early morning silence punctuated by the steady crunch of our boots against the frozen ground. Our approach was firm but measured; we needed to establish our presence without immediately stirring up hostility.

Newry's centre, now a pedestrian precinct, was under restricted vehicle access—standard in most large towns across Northern

Ireland. An RUC post guarded the main entry point, its officers watching the streets with practised wariness. The patrol, by now, had drilled their movements to instinct. Junctions were crossed swiftly, every angle covered. Buildings were scanned with a precision that had become second nature.

As we stepped onto the High Street, all eyes were on us. Women pausing whilst shopping, glancing over their shoulders, the tension barely concealed. It was clear we were something new, a different set of faces. I knew word would spread fast. The jungle drums would start beating, and soon enough, the local IRA battalion would know we were here.

One shop caught my attention. Outside, a table was laid out with books and records, all undeniably Republican in nature. I stopped, running my fingers over the covers—not out of curiosity, but to be seen. I wanted to provoke a reaction. The woman inside clocked me immediately. Yet, instead of approaching, she remained frozen, staring as if she could not believe what she was witnessing. This was a break from the norm, a deviation from what she expected of a British patrol. And that, at least, meant we were already making an impression.

Our first area of focus was a predominantly Protestant estate, and it proved to be an education in itself. The small terraced houses, though simple, were well-kept, clean, and in noticeably better condition than their Catholic counterparts.

Our first pass through was about learning—mapping out the shortcuts and identifying key vantage points. From the upper streets, we could see right down into the town centre, an ideal lookout for tracking movements below. Yet something about the place was unnerving. It was too quiet.

Beyond this Protestant enclave lay another small estate, this one Catholic. We knew it would be vital to understand the layout, the streets, the exits. Now was as good a time as any. Moving carefully, we eased through the narrow roads, pushing deeper into what was considered a no-go area—for both Protestants and the Army.

Ten minutes later, we reached the heart of the estate.

And then, everything changed.

Hatred.

It was not subtle, not something you had to look for. It hit you immediately. The moment the locals saw us, doors slammed shut. Women vanished inside. The only things left out on the streets were the stray dogs.

We spread out instinctively, adjusting our formation. This was a lesson we had already learned—never bunch up in hostile territory.

This was a different world altogether. And we had just walked into its core.

If you ever find yourself in a situation like this, surrounded by stray dogs, you must abandon any sentimental feelings you have for animals. Whether you're in the forces or simply on the wrong side of the divide, these creatures can sense it. Believe me, they do.

Their hackles rise the moment they see you. First, one bark, then another, until suddenly, the whole street erupts in a chorus of snarls and snapping teeth. Not just a handful—but twenty, maybe thirty, moving as a pack, their mangy coats hanging off their skeletal frames. They take great delight in humping on your legs or arms if you give them the chance. There is only one way to deal with them—either kick them away or kill them.

I remember one particular animal, meaner and more savage than the rest. It became such a menace that we eventually planned its demise. A large piece of steak, sliced deep and filled with the contents of three emptied 7.62 cartridges of cordite, sealed its fate.

We knew its owners kept it starving, ensuring its aggression remained unchecked. After it was gone, life became easier. I often wonder if they ever figured out what had happened to it.

Over the next week or two, we learned the town inside out—its estates, its pubs and clubs, the workplaces, church halls, youth centres, and the local haunts where people gathered. Once we had a solid grasp of the layout, we were finally able to operate without escorts. Now, we could focus on the real objective—the people.

Up to that point, life had become somewhat uneventful. We had pulled in a few individuals for screening but not with any real intention of making arrests. It was more about sending a message—letting them return home with a story to tell. A warning that we were not a soft touch, that we could be hard when necessary.

Still, I knew we had to start showing results. The Brigadier had been pressing Major Stam for updates every few days, checking whether we were settling in.

I spent hours reviewing weapon seizures, hoping to identify a pattern, but with little success.

One place in the Protestant area, however, had proven unexpectedly welcoming. We even dropped in for tea on occasion.

It was there that an elderly woman, speaking in her usual matter-of-fact way, mentioned something curious. Her brother had recently seen unfamiliar figures in the upper part of the estate—strangers lurking near the derelict houses.

She assumed they were Catholic youths, loitering where they had no business being.

"You should get those places bricked up," she said.

I dismissed it at first, but Andy wasn't so quick to brush it aside.

"Why do Catholic youths—not kids, but young men—hang around near a Protestant estate in a derelict building, bearing in mind the deep division between the two factions?" he asked.

He had a point. Something about it felt off. I decided we needed to take a closer look.

The next day, we adjusted our route to take in the derelict house.

I left a few lads outside on watch, then approached the building cautiously. From the outside, nothing seemed out of the ordinary—just another forgotten structure left to decay.

Benny stepped forward, reaching for the front door, but I stopped him with a sharp shake of my head. "Don't," I warned.

We had learned that doors in places like this were sometimes wired to explosive devices. One wrong move and the whole thing could go up—along with the poor bastard who touched it.

Instead, we searched for another way in. A side window caught my attention. The undergrowth beneath it was trampled, the dirt recently disturbed. Someone had been through here.

Peering inside, I saw the usual signs of squatters—a mess of discarded rubbish, signs of someone having slept rough. The roof was riddled with holes, as were sections of the upstairs floorboards. But aside from the decay, everything else seemed intact.

I pulled myself through the window. Benny, following close behind, cautioned me, "Mind the floorboards under the window." I grinned. "You think I don't know that by now?"

It was one of the oldest tricks in the book—booby-trapping loose floorboards with explosives. Step on the wrong one, and you were done for. I had learned quickly that in places like this, trust nothing.

Moving carefully, I scanned the room. The air was damp, the stench of mould clinging to the walls. Despite the decay, nothing looked immediately suspect.

Benny and Andy followed, each of us taking a different room to check over.

We weren't even sure what we were looking for—if anything at all. Then Benny called out.

"Boss! Front room upstairs—you better come up here a moment." His tone was sharp enough to put me on edge.

I climbed the stairs, stepping into the room where Benny stood just inside the doorway.

"Look up there," he said, pointing at the wall above the fireplace.

I scanned the room. The walls were covered in peeling wallpaper, an old wooden crucifix hanging just above the fireplace. The floor was strewn with rubbish, the air thick with dust. At first glance, nothing seemed out of place. "What's up?" I asked. "Have a look at that cross," Benny insisted.

I stepped closer. It was a plain, old wooden crucifix—two bits of wood mitred together.

"What's wrong with that?" I asked, frowning. "Have a close look," he replied.

I sighed. "Come on, Benny, stop playing games. You're getting too jumpy." "Look at the nail on the top," he said, his voice deadly serious.

I hesitated, then leaned in. That was when I saw it—a single, brand-new nail holding the crucifix in place.

Everything else in the house was old, rotting with time. So why was this the only thing that had been recently disturbed? A prickle of unease crawled down my spine.

I turned to the wallpaper, running a hand along the seam. It was loose. Too loose.

"Penknife," I called to Benny.

He threw it over, and I carefully peeled back about an inch of the wallpaper. Beneath it, the plaster looked normal. No sign of fresh repairs.

I reached up and lifted the crucifix off the wall. Nothing. Benny stepped forward. "Anything?"

I shook my head. "No, nothing. Plaster looks fine."

Benny wasn't convinced. He ran a hand over the exposed section of the wall, then frowned. "No, it's not," he said.

I glanced at him.

"When this house was built, they used lime plaster," he explained. "Not grey."

I looked again. He was right. Something wasn't adding up. "Outside. Now."

We moved faster than we had come in.

We all assumed covering positions around the building, weapons at the ready.

I got on the radio, informing control of the situation and requesting a search team. Within minutes, a Pig armoured car rumbled up the road, flanked by a couple of Rovers.

They didn't waste time.

Major Stam arrived in the first Rover, stepping out as the vehicles screeched to a halt.

"What is it, lad?" he asked. I quickly explained what we had found.

The search team moved in, working through the house methodically, leaving the suspect nail untouched until they finally reached the upstairs room.

One of the men took a large spike and drove it into the wall. It went through effortlessly, like a hot knife through butter.

The sergeant in charge turned to us. "There's definitely something behind here."

He carefully chipped away at the plaster, pulling back enough to slide a light tube into the hole. A cavity was revealed—reasonably sized but, at first glance, empty.

Nothing immediately seemed out of place.

The hole grew to about eight inches wide. The sergeant pushed the nozzle of a Sniffer—our device for detecting explosive substances—into the gap. Nothing.

"OK, let's get it down," he ordered.

Within minutes, the section of the wall was torn away, revealing six large packets wrapped tightly in polythene.

The team checked for traps, then carefully pulled them out, unwrapping each one with deliberate caution.

Inside, packed in grease and in full working order, were three American M1 carbine rifles per package.

Major Stam was ecstatic. I was over the moon. Our first real find—and a good one.

The discovery didn't go unnoticed.

By now, word had spread. Both the upper Catholic estate and the lower Protestant one knew we had uncovered a weapons cache.

At the very least, these rifles wouldn't be used to kill anyone. After the investigation, they would all be destroyed. Still, something about it didn't sit right.

Why were these weapons so well hidden, almost as if they were meant to remain untouched? Why had they been preserved so carefully? And why had they been stored in a lone house between two rival areas?

This was no ordinary stash. This was part of something bigger.

We talked it over among ourselves, and the conclusion seemed unavoidable. These rifles were part of a larger quartermaster's store.

The only question was—whose? Which side had hidden them?

One thing was certain: a quartermaster was active in the area.

I suggested we keep the group of houses under twenty-four-hour surveillance to see if anyone came looking.

A covert observation post was set up about half a mile away, hidden on the roof of another derelict building. With powerful night sights, we could monitor the area without being detected.

For three days, we watched. Nothing. There was no movement. There were no curious onlookers. No one was trying to reclaim what we had taken. Eventually, the post was stood down.

I reached my own conclusion—the cache had been Catholic. My reasoning? The only people who asked about the derelict house were from the Protestant estates.

The following days saw more house searches and more screenings.

Some people were openly furious at our actions. Others kept their anger hidden behind tight-lipped silence.

But every lead took me nowhere.

I had hoped—no, I had been certain—that if I could find the quartermaster, I could trace the supply routes feeding the north.

For now, though, the trail had gone cold.

By this point, I had unknowingly become a well-known figure in Newry—and not in a good way. Suspicion surrounded me from every corner, but it didn't deter me.

We had been relentless in our searches, pushing past long-standing taboos and disregarding the so-called "No-Go areas." The Derry Beg estate was one such place—a large Catholic stronghold where British soldiers had learned to tread carefully, if at all.

For years, it had built a reputation as a place to be feared. Any patrol that dared set foot inside risked walking straight into an ambush, a volley of gunfire waiting to greet them.

We ignored the threats.

We pushed on, searching houses, questioning people, and moving barricades that had once been seen as untouchable. Information was our goal, and we would get it—one way or another.

It was a dangerous game, and one particular incident made me realise just how cautiously we had to play it.

In our time around Newry, we had encountered all sorts of people. Some were open to conversation, others were hostile. A few, with the right approach, could be persuaded to talk.

And then there were those who had no intention of speaking—except to set a trap.

We had been patrolling Derry Beg for about an hour when a woman called us over.

"Would you lads like a cup of tea?"

It seemed innocent enough. Maybe, just maybe, it was a chance to make some kind of inroad. I accepted.

Before long, twelve steaming cups appeared—one for each of us. Then the door shut.

We knew better than to let our guard down. Something felt off.

This kind of warmth—this kind of hospitality—was completely out of character for the area. I told the lads to hold off on drinking. Instead, I dipped two fingers into my own cup.

You might think it strange to scald my fingers like that, but in Newry, caution was worth far more than comfort. I felt the bottom of the cup.

There it was—an unwelcome addition.

I tipped the tea out onto the ground. Sure enough, shards of crushed glass glinted at the bottom, the remains of what had once been a light bulb ground down into a lethal powder.

If we had drunk it quickly, as she had no doubt hoped, the glass would have torn through our insides—causing serious, if not fatal, damage.

Silently, we gathered the cups, making sure not a single man had taken a sip.

Then I walked next door, rapped sharply on the door, and waited. A woman answered, hostility written all over her face. I handed her the cups.

"Be sure to thank your neighbour for the lovely tea she gave us." She slammed the door in my face. We moved out without another word.

Later that day, I passed by the same house again. The woman who had offered us the tea was sitting on her doorstep. Her face was bruised, her head bloodied. Every window in her house had been smashed in. The ground was littered with shattered china.

Her neighbours had given their verdict. Justice, in its own brutal way, had been served.

She glared at us, hatred burning in her eyes. "British bastards!" she spat.

That little incident sealed my reputation in Newry. If I had been hated before, now it was set in stone.

The next day and the one after that, we continued our patrols, but frustration mounted.

We were getting nowhere.

Determined, we shifted focus, turning to the docks and the local workplaces. Maybe there, we could find someone willing to talk.

It was a complete waste of time. No one would say a word. So, I changed tactics.

We began picking people up off the streets—mostly those who stood out, those who looked just a little too wary of us.

That, at least, started to produce results.

Our main targets were the young lads. We pulled them in for as little as failing to say hello.

At Bessbrook, the treatment was harsh. It had become standard practice to leave detainees out in the pouring rain, stripped of their clothing, a pillowcase over their heads.

I wasn't keen on the method. But it worked.

Our first real break came from a seventeen-year-old. He didn't last long.

After an hour standing naked in the freezing rain, his hands tied, the pillowcase clinging to his face, he broke.

Tears streamed down his cheeks. Benny shoved him to his knees. The gravel beneath him was sharp, cutting into his skin.

Benny pressed his boot into the lad's leg, grinding the stones deeper. The boy let out a scream of pain.

Then the questions started.

His family. His friends. The people he mixed with. The IRA. Who did he know? Who were the members?

It worked.

The words spilled out. He had joined the IRA recently. He had taken the oath. He was ready to fight. The interrogation had given us what we needed.

The lad had cracked, spilling names—members, high-ranking officers, all active in the Newry Battalion of the IRA.

And the location? A room above an old antique shop in town. It was a jackpot.

Once the youth had been taken away to the RUC and charged with IRA membership, we moved quickly.

Straight to the town centre. Straight to the street he had given us.

I knew the man who ran the antique shop. Hard as nails. A long-time player in the game.

But now, we had the excuse we needed to go through his place like a dose of salts.

And that's exactly what we did.

We stormed in, pinning him against the wall as we moved through the shop. He was cuffed within seconds and secured to a heavy piece of antique furniture.

Then we headed upstairs. Nothing. Absolutely nothing.

If we didn't find anything soon, we had just wasted our best lead.

The shopkeeper was dragged up, interrogated on the spot. He gave us nothing. Not a word.

Meanwhile, Wingnut had been ferreting around when he found something—a doorway hidden behind a large wardrobe.

This was it.

The door led into an adjoining house, one that had been bricked up years ago. From the outside, it looked like any other derelict building. No sign of life. No indication of what lay within. We went in.

IRA flags hung on the walls. Anti-British posters were plastered everywhere. Maps.

Routes marked—ones commonly taken by security forces. Photographs of security bases. But most importantly—a folder. Inside, addresses of IRA members.

This was a goldmine. A find of massive intelligence value. And yet, as I stood there, I realised something else. My presence here was now a problem. We had to be careful.

I warned everyone—this place had to remain quiet. Of course, it didn't.

Later, I was summoned to Bessbrook.

The Senior Intelligence Officer didn't waste time. In no uncertain terms, he told me a complaint had been lodged against us.

Not only that, but our actions had sent every IRA terrorist in the area underground.

I was furious.

Annoyed at myself, yes. But even more at the fact that my actions—effective as they were—were now being questioned. The frustration boiled over.

"How the hell can a British soldier be expected to do his job when he's bound by red tape?" I demanded.

We were told to produce results. And yet, when we produced them—when we got intelligence, when we took action—we were hauled in and reprimanded.

If we played by the terrorist's rules, we'd be court-martialled. Imprisoned.

If we hesitated, followed procedure, or gave them time—our targets would either get away or kill us first.

And when we did get valuable information and acted on it? A report for cruelty was lodged.

It didn't matter that the lad we had picked up was IRA. That he had taken an oath to fight.

No—he was the victim now. He was later even awarded compensation for his "troubles."

How could a soldier work under these conditions?

The rules were a joke.

We weren't even sure who the real enemy was anymore. The Protestants? The Catholics? Or the politicians who sent us here?

All we knew was that it was the soldier who was blown up. The soldier who took the hit.

And we had no say in it.

None of us had chosen to come to Ireland. We weren't asked. We were sent. Told what to do. Given no option.

The gun in our hands was meant for defence, not attack.

At least, that was how I saw it. That was how most soldiers saw it.

But the terrorists? They weren't here to defend. They picked up guns and planted bombs to kill.

They weren't interested in talking through the old grievances, in working towards a solution. They wanted death. They wanted destruction.

And we? We were told not to fire on a known terrorist. Not to take action to stop them.

To let them go. To let them kill. Only then—when they had struck first—were we allowed to act. It was madness.

We were stoned, abused, restricted from troubled areas, then told to "get on with it."

And we did. Because we had no choice. We became the fall guys in a war where both sides hated us. We were expected to protect known terrorists, yet couldn't even arrest them.

Meanwhile, politicians, councillors, and church leaders told their people to rid the nation of its "undesirables."

Then they demanded payment. Not just from one side, but from both.

In their churches, no coin was ever heard in the collection plates—only the rustle of notes. People sent money by post, week after week, and were openly thanked during services.

Their contributions, they were told, would be put to "good use." To support the martyrs.

But we knew what that really meant. This wasn't about faith. This wasn't about righteousness. This was about buying weapons. Buying ammunition.

Fuel for the cause. And the men of God—the ones who preached about morality—were just as guilty as the terrorists. Hypocrites. Worse than the men with the guns.

Because they weren't just killing with bullets. They were funding the war.

My views were scorned. I was reprimanded—treated as if I had become one of them.

But no matter what the officers thought, the soldiers knew where I stood. Many of them agreed with me, though none would openly say so.

Their attitude was simple:

"We've only got a few months of this—let the problems take their course. We'll play piggy in the middle, let the politicians think we're doing a great job, when all we're really doing is surviving. Dealing hardship to any faction."

It was a mindset born out of frustration. Out of exhaustion. Out of a complete lack of faith in the system that had put us here.

Yet that feeling only fuelled me.

And whether it was my approach or something else, my men followed me. They supported me. We became something of an outlawed society within the Army. A unit apart.

They called us "The Hades People." Hades—the mythical land of exile, where the dead wandered among sinners. I knew, deep down, that every man wished he could be part of my team.

The only thing that stopped me from being moved was the Brigadier. Not because he agreed with me. Not because he approved. But because we were producing results. And results mattered more than politics.

Still, I knew he fought tooth and nail to justify my continued presence, desperate not to lose face among his peers.

Word spread fast.

Before long, people in the streets were talking to us. Not just shouting abuse—actually talking. I had spent months trying to get into their minds, trying to break through the wall of hostility. At first, it had felt impossible. But now? Now, they were listening. That's not to say all of them.

There were good people on both sides—Catholics and Protestants—who wanted nothing to do with the violence. People who wished for peace, who wanted to be free from the oppression and corruption of their so-called "leaders." And little by little, some of them began to trust us.

My big break came when I met a woman who knew I had been speaking to an acquaintance of hers. I had spent months trying to talk to both of them.

Eventually, I managed to build a connection with her friend, Martha. Then, through her, I met Moira. Moira was Catholic. And yet, strangely, she agreed with much of what I said about the troubles.

She had no love for the British Army, but she saw the truth for what it was. Her sons were all in the Provisional IRA—though, of course, they never admitted it.

She was sorry for what had happened to Martha's son. The boy had made a fatal mistake—he had spoken too openly. He had told his IRA superiors that he had met Protestants, that he had found their views weren't so different from their own. That both sides wanted the soldiers gone. For that, he was punished. They shot him in both kneecaps. Left him a cripple for life. When Moira told me this, she broke down in tears.

"Why did they do it?" she asked me.

But we both knew the answer.

The people at the top didn't care about peace. They didn't care about the cause. All they wanted was power—wielded at the barrel of a gun.

Moira would go on to play a significant role in the future of our operations in Newry. I told her the only way to end the war was to put the terrorists away. To stop the flow of weapons and explosives from the South. To expose the leaders for what they were. To educate the young—the next generation—that the gun was not the path to peace. In time, she agreed.

She said she would try to help. She was an unseen friend of Martha. She owned a shoe shop in Newry. And despite everything—despite the violence, despite the war—she quietly did more to help bring peace to Ireland than anyone ever realised. Few would ever know what she had done.

Moira's family was steeped in the conflict. Her son was in the Maze prison, part of the blanket protest, convicted of murdering a soldier. Her husband had been killed in a Protestant sectarian attack. Her two other sons were training in Southern Ireland, preparing to follow in their father's and brothers' footsteps. Terrorism was a family trade. And yet, despite everything, she spoke to me.

It had taken months to gain her trust.

At first, it was just a brief hello here and there. Then, one day, I walked into her shop. I knew I was standing on IRA-hallowed ground. We talked—or rather, she swore at me. Called me every name under the sun. But I was still standing by the time she finished. And that, in itself, was a victory.

She had attacked soldiers before. Beaten them. Driven them out of her shop. The only reason I was still in one piece was because, somehow, she had decided I was different. And maybe, in some twisted way, I had earned a sliver of respect. She blamed the British Army for what had happened to her friend's son. I defended my views.

We argued—bitterly. She would never openly admit I was right. But she didn't walk away, either. We nearly came to blows over the blanket protest in the Maze prison. I asked how a murderer could demand special privileges. How could someone claim political status for taking a human life? For planning, executing, and carrying out a cold-blooded killing?

She had no answer. And yet, I knew—this was only the beginning. Moira would go on to become one of the most important figures in my time in Newry. Whether she knew it or not, she had already started to turn. And once someone starts to question the cause, there's no going back.

Even in prison, the training continued. Bomb-making. Sabotage. The skills needed to kill even more people. The men inside called themselves political prisoners. Protested their innocence. Yet they sat in their cells like petulant children, smearing excrement over the walls when they didn't get their way. Outside, the ones who had sent them there carried on with their daily lives, never thinking of the suffering of their so-called martyrs.

They let others tell tales of glory. The young men—idealistic, angry—went out, did their deeds, and ended up in one of three places. Prison. A grave. Or, if they were lucky, on the run—hunted for the rest of their lives, only to return to terrorism and die the same way.

But the cause had to continue.

Why? Because those at the top needed it to. Moira and I talked often. She warned me to stay away. I didn't.

Even now, I can't explain why I kept going back. Persistence, maybe. Or something deeper. Whatever it was, it paid off. Little by little, my views were accepted. Not by the Army. For us, things were harder than ever. We had become outcasts, getting no support from above. But something had shifted on the ground.

Unbeknown to me, my team had become recognised—and accepted—by the people. Mostly by the women of Newry. Wives and friends of the Provisional and Official IRA. Of Protestant paramilitary groups like:

The Ulster Volunteer Force (UVF)

The Ulster Freedom Fighters (UFF)

The Irish National Liberation Army (INLA)

It unsettled me. They saw me as fair. Impartial. But I questioned their motives constantly. What was their true intention? Were they agreeing with me or simply watching?

By this time, my men were moving into places no British soldier had dared to go before. Forkhill. Crossmaglen. The outlying villages. It was dangerous ground.

Then, two off-duty Ulster Defence Regiment (UDR) soldiers were shot in their homes. One of their wives was murdered alongside them. It triggered a storm. Catholic estates were raided. House searches. Screenings. Doors kicked in. Damage everywhere. Resentment boiled over. Then, a soldier was sniped at. It was an open war. Armoured cars tore through garden fences. Chaos took over.

We were back on high alert. And yet, I knew—if we showed no fear, we might get something out of this mess. That was when I made a decision. I ordered my men to take off their flak jackets. The reaction was immediate. Shock. Horror. Resistance.

Flak jackets were our only real protection against bomb fragments. But they were also heavy, slowing us down when we needed to move fast.

The real reason? I wanted to show the people we weren't afraid. Moira and I later discussed the killings. I told her I wanted to meet someone high up in the organisation. Someone who could explain the real motives behind these attacks. I expected her to explode at the suggestion. She didn't. Instead, she said she'd see what she could do.

A week later, I got my answer. Moira had arranged a meeting. But it had to be far from Newry. Somewhere secure. Somewhere neutral. I suggested Newcastle. A quiet lane near the foothills of the Mourne Mountains. It was far enough away to be considered safe. Remote enough for us to control. And most importantly—we could be watched from a distance. The location was accepted.

We met the following Saturday at 8:00 a.m. Of course, my men were already in position—hidden, armed, covering every angle. We were all in civilian clothes. It wasn't unusual for a few people to meet for a chat at the base of the Mournes. His name was Michael Hogan. About 43 years old. Moira was with him. I felt the tension in my gut. Be careful. And yet, another part of me thought, to hell with it. We sat for two hours, going over past and present troubles. Hogan was an old campaigner.

His time had been in the days of the B Specials. A front-line fighter for the IRA. Now, he was part of the Official IRA's political wing. Not the active side—the Provisional IRA had broken away, as he put it, "a power-crazy lot." He disagreed with their methods. But he had no power to stop them. Or to stop the splinter groups that were springing up, refusing to take orders from anyone. Hogan had been pushed to the background. But he was far from useless. We both knew the risk of talking like this. But the humanitarian side had to be put forward. An agreement had to be reached. He had information. I needed a way to get it. That was the problem.

He refused to meet anywhere visible. Anywhere he could be seen. And yet, the intelligence he had would need to be acted on quickly. We couldn't afford to arrange meetings that took days to set up. That was when Moira stepped in. She offered to be the go-between. There was just one condition—I couldn't be seen talking to her. She would pass messages through trusted friends. Possibly through Martha. It wasn't a perfect system. It wasn't safe. It put all of us—Moira, Martha, Hogan, and myself—in an incredibly dangerous position. But at that moment, I had no choice.

I had to trust them. And trust, in a place like this, was deadly. The whole thing could have been a glorified setup. I knew that. But the choice had already been made for me. I trusted Moira. I trusted my own judgment. Maybe the information would flow. If I didn't put my full faith in this agreement, I could easily become a target myself. This was my only trump card now. As a show of faith, I agreed to the arrangement—but with one condition. If I didn't receive anything within a week, it was over. Moira and Hogan understood what I meant.

If I wanted to, I could have had them both lifted and locked away for a very long time. As a seal of our new alliance, we shook hands and went our separate ways. I stayed behind for a while, thinking over everything that had been said. Something about it didn't sit right. Andy must have sensed it. He came over, reading my expression. "What's up, boss?" he asked. I exhaled. "I don't know, Andy. Everything seems to be going in the opposite direction." He listened as I laid it out.

"Michael Hogan has agreed to finger a few baddies and to give us anything he can find, but strings are attached. We have put ourselves in their hands and have to do what they say. If we do, the whole section's lives may be put on the line for the whim of an Informer. We must now be even more cautious in how we manage all situations. If we are seen to be siding with the Protestants, our own lives could well be over."

"On the other hand, if the Protestants see us to be soft on the Catholics, we lose what little face and confidence we have with them." Andy saw the problem straight away. But in his usual calm way, he reassured me. "The lads are behind you, boss. Whatever you decide, we'll stand with you." That was all I needed to hear. I made my next decision then and there. Any information we received would not be passed to the other Army units until the last possible moment. I didn't want the jungle drums beating before we even had a chance to act.

The drive back to Newry felt endless. I made another decision on the way. I wouldn't mention the meeting to any of the officers at my base. Telling them would mean betraying my agreement. And worse—it would sign my lads' death warrants. If the IRA found out we had knowledge that could harm them, they wouldn't just come after us. Moira and Hogan would be executed in the foulest way imaginable. When we arrived at Newry, I gathered all my lads in the briefing room. I swore them to secrecy and told them everything. Their reaction was exactly as I expected. They agreed with me completely. Each man walked out, knowing that from this moment on, secrecy was paramount.

Afterwards, I found myself wandering the base. Soldiers were scattered everywhere—some trying to sleep after 50 or 60 hours on duty, too exhausted to even take off their boots or flak jackets. Rifles were strewn across the floor. Some of the men had even taken theirs into their sleeping bags with them.

If their families could see the conditions they lived in, they would have been outraged. But they never would. And the saddest part of all? None of it mattered.

Their efforts, their exhaustion, their suffering—it was all a waste. They weren't doing any real good. They were just marking time. Going through the motions. Making sure the politicians could say they were doing their job. The truth was, they weren't helping the situation. They were fuelling it. MPs sometimes visited. Not one soldier ever complained. They knew that if they did, their careers would be over in an instant. These visitors never saw the real Ulster. Never heard the soldiers' side of it. And they never would.

How lucky I was to have my lads. I would never let them live in a hovel or work the kind of hours the rest of the regiment did. If I could do that for my men, why the hell couldn't it be done for all of them? It was a question that would never be answered. I felt then that my group had been used in a very clever way. They kept us relatively happy—just enough to ensure we produced results. High morale meant effectiveness. Effectiveness meant success. And success meant the Army could pat itself on the back.

Eventually, I ended up in the OPS room. Major Stam was hunched over a map, deep in thought. I asked him what was on his mind. "Everything I try turns sour," he admitted. "But you've made headlong progress since you turned up." He pointed to a SAS observation post overlooking a farm. They suspected the occupants were about to receive a supply of something. What, exactly, they didn't know? I wanted to tell him about my meeting with Hogan. I stopped myself. I also wanted to drag him down to where the soldiers were living and rub his nose in it. But I knew it would be futile. He wouldn't understand. We lived in two different worlds. Unlike me, he was an officer and a gentleman. I had come through the ranks. I knew what it meant to live like a soldier. The men had no choice. They did what they were told. They lived where they were put. And that was that.

In the days that followed, something changed. More people in the community began to accept our presence. They spoke to us and engaged with us. But much of the conversation revolved around the Army's role. I listened to their hatred of soldiers. To their Dickensian attitudes towards the opposing faction. When I put my side across, the majority admitted that our small group was different.

We didn't cause wanton destruction. We treated them as human beings, not animals. They had a point.

The Army's tactics were brutal. It was standard practice to ram a Saracen armoured car or a Pig personnel carrier straight into houses. To drive over cars. To flatten obstacles—even people—if necessary. These weren't random acts of destruction. They were tactics. And in the right situations, they worked. If a gunman needed stopping, they stopped him. If the only protection a soldier had was his vehicle, he would use it. It wasn't about malice. It was about survival.

By late November 1976, Ireland was still on fire. The whole province was on high alert. A literal war was being fought between Catholic and Protestant terrorist factions. Bombs were going off across Northern Ireland. Sectarian killings were a daily occurrence. And we were right in the middle of it.

Chapter Five
Results

After receiving a call to go to Londonderry for a meeting with the Brigadier, I knew exactly what he wanted—results. I reviewed everything we had achieved since February when I had first been tasked with forming this unit and gradually earning the confidence of the people of Newry and South Armagh. The goal had been clear from the start: gather intelligence to disrupt the movement of explosives and ammunition coming up from the south. A tall order, to say the least.

Looking over our records, I assessed what we had managed to recover: eighty rifles, submachine guns, and pistols. Over 1,300 kilos of explosives. Thirty detonators. Six hundred rounds of ammunition. All of this is within nine months of operations. Not bad, considering the pressure we had been under. Yet, I knew we had only scratched the surface. I could only gauge the Brigadier's thoughts on the matter once I was in front of him.

We had gained acceptance, of sorts, from both sides—mainly among the women and older men, many of whom had once been hardliners in the IRA and Protestant movements. These were the ones who, little by little, passed on snippets of information. Some leads were good, some were worthless, and some were deliberate traps. Each one had to be assessed—was it genuine, or was it an attempt to set us up? I never trusted any of them completely.

Moira had helped establish a secure method for passing information. We used "drop boxes" hidden in the walls of old buildings or beneath loose stones—mostly in cemeteries, once considered untouchable by security forces. The terrorists had long used these graveyards as safe havens for storing weapons, confident that we wouldn't dare enter. But we had ignored that old taboo, and they now knew we conducted searches there.

Moira had also arranged for local children to deliver written messages to these drop boxes. To signal a drop, they would alter one of their "hopscotch numbers" in the play areas—using blue chalk instead of white. A simple but effective system. Each time we passed by, we would check for any marked numbers. If we saw blue, we knew a message was waiting. We would then move to the drop box, ensure the area was clear, and retrieve it. It was a method that worked well.

As I had previously warned Michael Hogan, if I didn't hear anything within a week, the deal was off. True to his word, he sent word through Moira—he would meet me at the same place as before that evening at 5:30 p.m.

At that meeting, he provided valuable intelligence. A large shipment of Ampho—a homemade explosive made from agricultural fertiliser—was on its way. It was being transported in sheep carcasses, sealed in polythene bags, wrapped in muslin cloth, and then frozen solid. There were about seventy bags, totalling around 800 pounds of explosives, along with detonators and Cordex wire. He gave me the expected time and location of its movement north, along with a description of the vehicle—a green refrigerated truck. No registration number, though.

His final warning was clear: "The driver's a bit of a cowboy." Armed, as was his co-driver. If we stopped the truck, we needed to be extremely cautious.

I had less than twelve hours to get the operation in place.

I immediately contacted Major Stam, briefing him on the situation. The shipment needed to be intercepted—but not too close to Newry. I had to protect my source. I requested helicopter surveillance with infrared cameras to shadow the truck's movements. The ambush had to be set between 3:15 a.m. and 4:40 a.m. —the window in which the vehicle was expected to cross from the South. I provided the grid reference of the roadway and the crossing point my informant believed would be used. Now, I could only hope he was right.

"I'll have my men in concealed positions at the crossover point," I told Stam. "I'll be there to confirm whether or not the vehicle is on its way."

I suggested that he pass the details to 2 Para Regiment and arrange a spot "Vehicle Checkpoint." However, it had to look routine—not a targeted stop. The RUC needed to be present as well. I requested at least two platoons to cover the area beyond the checkpoint in case things turned ugly. I was certain there would be an escort vehicle trailing the truck.

Some of my men would remain at the crossing point, keeping watch for any other suspect vehicles passing through. If anything seemed off, they would alert Stam.

Now, it was a waiting game.

Major Stam later informed me that the "Vehicle Checkpoint" would be established, and the requested helicopter would be ready to lift off upon my instruction. His reasoning was sound—setting up the checkpoint too early might attract attention. If the driver had a radio, he could be warned, especially if this cargo was as valuable as we had been led to believe. I agreed.

The night was dark, cold, wet, and miserable. Rain lashed down as we remained in cover, waiting.

At 5:20 a.m., we spotted a truck approaching. The only indication that this might be our target was the fact that it was refrigerated. I relayed the message over the radio, instructing the checkpoint to begin proceedings. They were also to ensure that any vehicles following the truck were searched—one of them could be an armed escort.

Five minutes passed. A few more vehicles followed behind the suspect truck, but in the dim light, I couldn't tell if any of them were escort vehicles. Slowly, we continued trailing.

About twenty minutes later, a cluster of headlights illuminated the road ahead—the checkpoint. I pulled over before reaching it, ensuring I wouldn't be seen as part of the stop. At this point, I was satisfied. The operation had gone smoothly so far. Now, I would wait for the results at Bessbrook.

I radioed Major Stam. "I'm returning to Newry. Call me when the op is complete."

Back in Newry, I sat down to enjoy a well-earned bacon sandwich and a cup of tea. I barely had time to take a bite before a duty corporal approached.

"Sir, Major Stam's on the phone. Wants to speak to you."

I went straight to the OPS centre, picked up the receiver, and heard the excitement in his voice.

"We've got a massive haul," he said. "Operation went without a hitch—though the driver and co-driver took a few bumps, as you might expect."

He went on to explain that they had intercepted an escort vehicle three cars behind the truck and had recovered weapons from it as well. All suspects were now in custody at Bessbrook, along with the entire shipment. Then, in a rather curt voice, he added:

"Now, what do you expect me to do with seventy frozen sheep carcasses?"

Without missing a beat, I replied, "How about lamb for Sunday roast? I'll search for the mint sauce."

That got a laugh out of him.

Gathering a few of my lads, we headed over to Bessbrook Mill to check the haul and screen the new suspects.

The haul was bigger than expected—highly lethal material, all of it. Spirits were high. The entire find was later handed over to the RUC for disposal. I never did find out what happened to the lamb.

RUC intelligence and army intelligence interrogated the detainees, trying to uncover who had produced the explosive and how it had been made. It was of remarkably high quality. I had shared everything with them—every lead, every piece of intelligence—yet, as always, I doubted they would share anything substantial in return. Without my unit's efforts, they wouldn't have had the leads they were working with now in South Armagh. But when it came to getting information back from them, it was like dragging blood from a stone.

This lack of cooperation was becoming infuriating. The army, the RUC, the intelligence cells—they were all quick to act on my intelligence. They reaped the benefits: seizing explosives, recovering weapons, and taking more terrorists off the streets. They were quick to take the credit. Yet, when it came to reciprocating—providing me with crucial intelligence gained from interrogations—they clammed up.

I needed to know who these people were. Where they came from. Who their contacts were. Where they were based. This information was critical for gathering further intelligence, identifying upcoming arms shipments, and preventing more attacks.

It became clear that certain senior officers—intelligence officers, RUC officials—were more interested in the prestige of a successful operation than the actual mission itself. Their concern wasn't about lives saved or operations succeeding—it was about who got the recognition. That realisation did not sit well with me.

I decided then and there that I would take this matter up with the Brigadier at my upcoming meeting.

No more games. No more withheld intelligence.

The RUC and the company commanders wouldn't like being told what to do, but I couldn't allow my men's lives—or my own—to be jeopardised by a lack of accurate, up-to-date intelligence.

I wouldn't stand for it.

Back in Armagh Barracks, I ironed my suit, making sure I looked the part for my meeting with the Brigadier later that day. I had briefly considered travelling to Londonderry in uniform, but the Brigadier's Staff Officer, Major Skinner, had advised against it. "Come in civilian clothes," he had said. And so, I prepared accordingly.

I had gathered all the relevant documentation and telexed an initial programme for discussion to Skinner's office. Then came the surprise—my OC informed me that I would be driven to Brigade HQ by my crew, with an armed response vehicle as backup.

"Why?" I asked, though I already suspected the answer.

"Orders from Brigade," he said. "You're now classed as a high-risk target. The RUC will escort you."

That caught my attention. What had changed? What intelligence had come through to warrant such precautions? No one would tell me. Just that "the information received required these measures."

The drive to Londonderry was uneventful, though my mind kept circling back to that question. What had happened?

To break the tension, I chatted with the lads about the future—how things were shaping up and what could be improved. Then, inevitably, the topic turned to leave.

"When's Christmas leave happening?" one of them asked.

They all wanted a break—to see their families their girlfriends. And truthfully, they deserved one. Every man in this unit had put everything into the operation's success. How could I refuse them this?

"I'll speak to the Brigadier," I said.

At 11:00 a.m., we arrived at Brigade HQ. I told the lads to head to the reception waiting area—set up for visitors with refreshments and reading material—while I continued towards the Brigadier's office. My escort had been unnecessary in the end, but the fact that it had been ordered still weighed on my mind.

I knocked on the door and stepped into the anteroom. Major Skinner was seated at his desk.

Jovially, he said, "Hello, right on time. How was the trip?"

"Fine," I replied. "No problems at all. It's a nice day, and I'm looking forward to my meeting with the Brigadier."

He nodded. "We'll go over some admin details first, then meet the Brigadier. He's suggested a preamble discussion before lunch, then we'll head to the mess for a bite to eat. After that, we'll get into the details of future plans."

That all sounded reasonable. I nodded in agreement.

With a hint of sarcasm, I added, "I trust my newly acquired security escort and the lads in reception will be fed and looked after?"

Skinner smirked and instructed his chief clerk to see to it.

For the next half-hour, we discussed shortages, replacements, and the usual administrative necessities. It was dull but essential. Fortunately, he approved everything I needed, ensuring replacements would arrive without issue. My only concern was that they wouldn't be "snaffled away" at Armagh before I could get my hands on them. I made sure to warn against that.

Once everything was finalised and the paperwork sealed in folders, we made our way to the Brigadier's office.

Inside, Skinner introduced me as if I were a stranger. I stood to attention.

"Good morning, Sir."

The Brigadier beamed. "David, David, my good fellow, come in! I've been looking forward to this meeting. How the hell are you?"

He got up, stumbled around his desk, and extended his hand.

"Very well, thank you, Sir," I replied, shaking it firmly.

His greeting surprised me. There was a warmth to it—almost an old friend's welcome.

We sat down around a coffee table by the window, overlooking a neatly lawned area. The atmosphere was unexpectedly relaxed. I had been dreading this meeting, convinced that our results had not met his expectations. But now, sitting across from him, my tension began to ease.

He quizzed me on several fronts—how I was getting on with the people in the South, what methods I had used to gather intelligence, how I was working with the RUC, and my relationship with the standing security forces in Newry and Bessbrook. He also wanted an assessment of IRA strength in the area and Protestant activity in the outlying regions.

I trod carefully. He needed to know the basics, but I was acutely aware of the security risks in sharing too much. The last thing I wanted was to compromise an informant or leak sensitive details outside my group. It was a fine line to walk.

At last, Skinner glanced at his watch and announced, "How about lunch? It's time!"

Clearly, lunch was a high priority for the Brigadier.

We headed to the Officers' Mess, where I was seated at his prized table. I wasn't asked what I wanted—I was simply served. And what a meal it was.

The best Lemon Sole I had ever tasted, followed by Lemon Cheesecake and coffee.

How the other half live?

As I ate, I couldn't help but feel a twinge of disgust. The officers dined in luxury, completely disconnected from what the soldiers endured in the field.

After coffee, we returned to the Brigadier's office. Now, the real meeting would begin.

He had already been briefed on our achievements—what we had found, what we had seized, and how we had operated over the past nine months.

"I had great hopes for this plan," he said. "I have to say, I didn't expect you to upset so many people in the process."

That caught my attention.

Someone had been complaining.

I suspected that certain officers weren't happy with my methods, and now those whispers had made their way up the chain. If that was the case, then I would need to stand my ground.

I looked the Brigadier in the eye. "Sir, my approach has never been political or biased—it's been fair. And fairness has delivered results."

I outlined my approach—how I had worked across every perspective: the IRA, the Protestants, the Army officers, the RUC, the intelligence personnel, the soldiers on the ground, and even those who outright opposed my methods. I had made difficult decisions, took risks, and faced resistance at every turn.

But I knew one thing for certain—I was succeeding.

And so far, I believe I have achieved not only my own aims but his as well.

That said, I was not willing to change my attitude or methods to appease a minority of senior officers and civilians—especially not to accommodate their prejudiced opinions and narrow views.

I took a bold step.

"Sir, you initially posted me here," I said firmly. "If you recall, you gave me carte blanche to achieve the objectives of this operation. You brought me in for my experience, my understanding of the terrorist mindset, and my ability to demoralise it. I have done this and continue to do so with increased vigour and determination.

I feel that I have them on the run, and with your continued support, I will succeed."

"If you are hearing dissatisfaction from uninformed officers and civilian parties, I believe they do not understand—or perhaps are unaware of—the reasons behind the continued secrecy of this operation or even its very purpose. These officers seem to dislike being requested—or should I say ordered—through your authority to assist in stopping the perpetrators of these vile acts."

"They fail to grasp the extent of our efforts and the gains we have made. Consider the lives we have saved, the property we have protected from destruction, and the terrorists we have removed from the streets—who now reside in the Maze prison. These individuals are no longer part of the equation; they cannot kill again. Their terrorist organisations are now weakened, with fewer front-line personnel to carry out their agendas."

"The fact is, gunmen and bombers in Northern Ireland are now being starved of arms, ammunition, and explosives to kill and maim innocent people. In my mind, that alone is proof of the operation's success. This is what my unit has achieved in a short time."

"If you are not happy with my methods and my results, then here and now, I am willing to resign my commission, Sir."

Silence.

Major Skinner's mouth fell open. He was visibly shocked—not just by my words but by the tone in which I had delivered them. I doubted he had ever heard anyone stand up to the Brigadier like that before.

I braced myself, expecting the Brigadier to call for me to be removed.

But that call never came.

Instead, the Brigadier remained silent. He got up, walked over to the window, and stared out for a long moment. The room hung in thick silence. Two minutes passed. Then, he turned back, walked slowly to his desk, and sat down.

Finally, he spoke.

"Finished?"

"Yes," I replied.

"Right, young man," he said, his voice measured but firm. "I will tell you a few things now.

"I agree with everything you have just said, and I have heard everything from these alleged uninformed officers. When I first heard about your methods, trials, and tribulations, yes, I had doubts about appointing you for this task."

"But since that time, I have kept a very keen eye on you and your progress. This progress, in my eyes—and in the eyes of the General Staff at the MOD—has been more than satisfactory. It has allayed my previous fears that the operation might fail. It is now my opinion that it will not fail if it continues in the same vein as it has been."

He paused briefly, then continued.

"I have been considering extending the operation province-wide. However, after speaking with you and hearing your assessment, that may be a mistake. It would only make the entire province wary of saying anything to anybody. Terrorist organisations would go deeper underground and become even more secretive than they are now."

"I agree with everything you have said, and I will give you my utmost support."

"On a more personal note, I will contact all of these senior officers who have approached me and my office. I will put them in the picture—make it clear that they are to support you and your group in any action you deem necessary."

"They will also provide you with the required assistance—whatever, whenever, and wherever you need it."

Then, his voice took on a harder edge.

"As for your threat of resigning your commission—I do not take kindly to threats, and I will refuse any resignation you may now or in the future submit."

"In fact, you have never said these words." He locked eyes with me. "So, I do not have to take this into consideration when I make any recommendations in your annual confidential report regarding your future career."

"Do I make myself clear?"

"Yes," I replied boldly.

The afternoon continued without a hitch.

I felt that the Brigadier had turned a corner—he now seemed to respect me in a way he hadn't before. Instead of dictating tactics, he discussed them. He even backed down on certain views when I presented solid reasons against them, drawn from my experience on the ground and the local knowledge I had gathered.

We achieved a forward-looking plan, and I was satisfied with how he had received my reports so far.

Finally, I broached the subject of leave.

"Sir, is there any possibility of standing down over Christmas? Just for a few days," I asked. "The lads need a break."

He considered it for a moment. "Would your absence cause any lasting problems?"

"I don't think so," I replied. "But if you have concerns, I'm willing to stay behind with a few lads."

He nodded. "I don't see why not, but I don't want you away for more than a week."

That was good enough for me. I thanked him. Our meeting was over.

Then, just as I was preparing to leave, he brought up a distinctly unpleasant subject.

"The intelligence sector has informed me that you are not a liked person amongst some terrorist active cells," he said. "Which isn't surprising, given your current involvement with them."

He paused, watching for my reaction.

"By all accounts, they want you out of the way. It seems you're a thorn in their side."

I remained silent, waiting for what was coming next.

"As a cautionary measure, I have ordered that you be escorted when not on duty in Newry."

I clenched my jaw. I knew I wouldn't like what was coming.

"I know you won't like it, and neither will the plain-clothed RUC officers who will be performing these escort duties," he continued. "But I cannot have you stopped at work. Until this threat is gone, your movements will be very restricted. That is a fact you must live with."

His tone left no room for argument.

"You must be one hundred percent on your guard from now on until this threat is no more."

He didn't ask for my thoughts. Instead, he walked me out through Major Skinner's office, wished me well, and told me to keep him informed.

I had never really considered that I might become a target. If anything, I had assumed that any hostility directed at me would come from my own senior officers, given the way I had taken on my role.

But this?

This was different.

This put a whole new perspective on the operation. I would have to be even more cautious, more alert—watching every word I spoke, every person I confided in because I had no idea who might pass something on to a gunman.

Life had just become a lot more valuable.

Outside, the lads were waiting for me, along with my new, unwanted RUC escort.

They had been told my meeting was over and to collect me. I could already see how this arrangement would interfere with my day-to-day activities.

I would have to put a stop to it.

The drive back to Armagh was long and uneventful, though the lads kept the conversation light. They wanted to know more about my history and what had landed me in this role.

Kenny, sitting beside me in the back seat, smirked.

"You must have really pissed off some high-ranking officer to get stuck with us in South Armagh."

That brought a laugh from everyone. At least it helped ease the tension of our new unwanted tail.

By the time we arrived back in Armagh, darkness had settled. There was little to do but change and relax for the evening.

I had paperwork to get through—something I didn't relish, but it had to be done.

Looking at the roster and upcoming Christmas dates, I worked out who could go on leave. I had told the Brigadier I was willing to stay, and he hadn't objected to my suggestion, so I decided—I was going home.

It had been nearly a year since I had seen my wife and family. I would admit, even now, that the strain on my relationship was growing. I needed to get home.

I left it to the lads to decide amongst themselves who would stay. Six volunteered to remain over Christmas, while the rest put their names forward for leave.

I never questioned their decision.

I submitted all the names to Major Smythe, along with leave applications, requesting two-way flights and transport to and from the airport.

There was no issue. Transport was arranged.

Then, at last, the day arrived.

We all went home for Christmas.

CHAPTER SIX:
FEAR

Christmas came and went. I must admit, when the lads regrouped, I felt a sense of relief. They seemed more relaxed, even happier—a welcome sight, given that we needed to get back to work. The momentum couldn't slip.

According to the intelligence briefings I attended, the province had remained relatively quiet over Christmas. Terrorist activity had been minimal, explosions were down, and Belfast was seeing the lowest levels of bombings in recent memory. That should have been good news, but something about it unsettled me. Over the same period, sectarian killings had risen. I couldn't help but wonder why.

The lull between Christmas and New Year gave us a brief respite, but it didn't last. By early January, we were back in the thick of it.

By February 1977, I had been in the province for over a year, and the strain was beginning to show. It felt like a weight pressing down on my shoulders, the kind that never truly lifts. But despite the exhaustion, I knew the operation was yielding results.

In April, the Brigadier made an unannounced visit to Armagh to meet with Major Smythe and me. His mood was noticeably upbeat. The statistics told the story: explosives recovered, arms seized, arrests made—all reflected in the reduced number of bombings. The terrorists were on the back foot, struggling, their movements increasingly restricted. It was clear from the Brigadier's demeanour that he had already reported this to the Ministry of Defence, and his superiors were pleased.

With the military gaining the upper hand, he believed it was time for politicians to capitalise on the momentum. Pressure could now be applied to the political factions that had emerged within the terrorist ranks. The hope was to force them to the negotiating table and push for a peaceful resolution. But despite the optimism, the continued car bombings and rising sectarian violence remained deeply concerning. Yet, there was progress—real progress. In fact, these early discussions would eventually lay the groundwork for what would become the Good Friday Agreement.

Once our meeting with the Brigadier concluded, I gathered the lads, and we returned to Newry. No sooner had we arrived than I received contact through the drop boxes—messages from my regular informants.

Michael Hogan had been busy. There were several messages from him, each marked urgent. He wanted to meet immediately. I wasted no time arranging it.

What he had to say stunned me.

He was risking his life by sharing this intelligence. According to him, the IRA in the South was struggling—desperately short of experienced manpower and, more importantly, running out of funds. Their American pipeline of cash was drying up. In response, they had launched an aggressive fundraising push among Irish immigrants in the United States, and it had paid off. They had amassed enough money to acquire a significant weapons shipment.

The result?

A shipping container packed with military-grade Semtex explosives, Armalite rifles, pistols, machine guns, ammunition, and even uniforms. A stockpile large enough to fuel their campaign for years.

But it wasn't coming north by land. That route was too risky. Border patrols and vehicle checkpoints had increased, making overland smuggling of such a large load nearly impossible. The IRA leadership wasn't willing to take that chance.

Instead, they had devised an alternative route—by sea.

The plan was simple yet bold. A fishing trawler would transport the weapons from a small port in the south, Mizen Head, across the Irish Sea to the Isle of Man. From there, under cover of darkness, it would cross to Strangford Lough in the North, slipping past intentionally unmanned customs observation posts. A Newry-registered fishing trawler would rendezvous at the lough—nothing that would raise suspicion. The cargo would then be transferred onto smaller vessels before making landfall near Newtownards.

Once ashore, the weapons would be loaded onto concealed vehicles waiting on the Portaferry Road. From there, they would be driven into Belfast.

A flawlessly executed smuggling operation—if they pulled it off.

All I knew was that it was happening soon. Days, maybe less.

I needed help. And fast.

Safe houses had been designated in case of security force activity, but the IRA hierarchy believed this route was their best chance. It bypassed all vehicle checkpoints and British patrols, reducing the risk of interception. The operation involved hardened, dedicated IRA men—individuals who had been given a clear directive: ensure this shipment got through at all costs.

The entire movement would take place over three nights, using well-known fishing vessels that wouldn't attract suspicion. It was bold and meticulously planned, and if successful, it would flood Belfast with enough weapons and explosives to sustain the IRA's campaign for years.

I needed to stop it. But how?

I was landlocked in Newry, unable to intervene directly. I racked my brain for solutions. An interception at Newtownards? Too risky. The cargo could be offloaded at any point during the journey across the lough, making any attempt at a land-based capture unpredictable.

The only viable option was the Royal Marine Commandos at Warrenpoint. Their RIB crafts had the speed and manoeuvrability to track, board, and seize the vessel once it entered Northern Irish waters. But for that to happen, I needed precise intelligence—vessel identification, movement patterns, and confirmation of the cargo. I also needed coordination with the Isle of Man police and a surveillance operation covering the southern and eastern approaches to Belfast.

It was a massive undertaking, all hinging on the word of an IRA informer.

I had no exact date, no confirmed vessel, no hard evidence—only the knowledge that it was imminent.

I returned to Newry Security Base and immediately phoned Major Skinner. I kept my language veiled, giving away as little as possible, but made it clear that I needed to speak to the Brigadier in person. This was beyond my remit. I needed his authority to bring the necessary forces into play.

Skinner told me to wait at Newry while he reached out to the Brigadier. I paced the room, the minutes stretching into what felt like hours. Finally, the call came.

The Brigadier's voice was clipped. He didn't fully grasp the message I had sent but understood its urgency.

"Can you get to Londonderry immediately?"

"If I can get a helicopter, I'll be there within the hour," I replied.

"If it's that important, I'll wait."

That was all I needed.

I went straight to Major Stam. "I need a helicopter to Londonderry immediately," I told him.

His eyes narrowed. "Is it that urgent?"

"Yes. No delay."

He nodded. "Get to Bessbrook. I'll have one ready."

I had already told Benny to stand by in case I needed him. We drove straight to Bessbrook, and sure enough, a helicopter was waiting on the pad.

As we lifted off, I radioed ahead to inform Major Skinner that I was airborne.

When we arrived in Londonderry, a vehicle was waiting to take me to brigade headquarters. I wasted no time getting to the Brigadier's office, closing the door behind me as I entered.

I laid everything out—what I knew, what I suspected, what I needed. I detailed the scale of the operation and the significance of the potential seizure. This was beyond a standard arms haul—this was a strategic shift in the IRA's operations. The Brigadier was the only man with the authority to allocate the necessary resources. Military, naval, and intelligence assets would all have to be engaged.

He listened intently, then called in Major Skinner. Without hesitation, he ordered an immediate meeting that evening at 8 o'clock. The attendees:

- The commanding officers of 2 Para, the Argyll and Sutherland Highlanders, and the Green Jackets
- The Officer Commanding the Marine Commandos
- The Army Air Corps detachment commander
- The Chief Constable of the RUC
- The Intelligence Officer in charge of operations

Top priority. No excuses. This was a military matter under the Emergency Powers Act of Northern Ireland.

For once, I was speechless.

The Brigadier turned to me. "I intend to put the Colonel of 2 Para in charge of this operation, but I want you as his assistant. You know the background. He knows the deployment of troops. You will guide him on the key arrests—we need to get as many as possible."

He nodded approvingly. "Well done, lad. Now get back to Newry and find out exactly when this movement is starting."

"Thank you, sir," I replied.

"Liaise with Skinner. I'll need to be in direct contact when we get the green light."

I flew back to Newry, my mind racing.

The next few days were tense. Everyone knew something was coming, though they didn't know what. I kept my mouth shut, but the uncertainty gnawed at me. I needed confirmation.

Three days passed. Nothing.

Major Skinner called—there was concern at higher levels. The longer we remained on standby, the more other operations across the province suffered. The Brigadier was beginning to feel the pressure.

I was beginning to feel the embarrassment.

By Friday afternoon, I had resigned myself to the fact that it might be a false lead. I was looking forward to a quiet weekend when the message finally arrived.

The operation was on.

The shipment would depart Mizen Head that night at eight o'clock. The vessel: a large fishing trawler, Newry-registered EA51. The name: JESSIB. Red and white in colour. The cargo would be buried under a layer of herring and mackerel.

That was all I needed.

I grabbed the phone and relayed the information to the Brigadier. He wasted no time. Within minutes, the operation was in motion.

Nothing would move until JESSIB entered Strangford Lough. As soon as it did, standby companies would silently move into capture positions, awaiting the go-ahead.

That order would come from the Marine Commandos, who would shadow the vessel using night vision and infrared equipment.

I took three of my lads with me, standing the rest down for the night.

The following morning, we reported to the ops centre of 2 Para.

Lieutenant Colonel Lindsay Davies was waiting for us.

After some brief formalities, he got straight to the point. "What's the strength of your intelligence? How reliable is it?"

I told him exactly what I knew.

He nodded, processing the information. "Where do you suggest we position our men for the capture? Or do we follow it into Belfast and take down everyone involved?"

I thought carefully before responding.

"The last thing we want is to blow the whole operation wide open. Firing should only occur in self-defence, and every man involved must be briefed on that. As for when we strike—I suggest we wait until the entire cargo is landed. The moment it touches the road; we risk losing it. If we hit them as it's offloaded, we can seize the lot—vessels, cargo, and suspects."

He considered this.

"And positioning?"

"It needs to be done today. All troops concealed along the Portaferry Road in staggered positions. We don't know the exact landing site, so rapid response is crucial. Each unit must be ready to move the moment we confirm the drop point. Some will form backstops to cut off any potential escapees."

He nodded approvingly, but I had one more point to make.

" Sir, one sticky point I would like to make is this. The members of the RUC, those who have been informed of this op and who will play an active role in the operation, will be kept away from the frontline until it is known that the cargo has been landed and the suspects are apprehended. It will then be up to the RUC to be seen to be in an assisting role rather than a pre-emptive role."

Davies studied me. "Do I take it from the last comment that you do not wholly trust our friends in the RUC?"

I met his gaze.

"Sir, much as I respect that the RUC do a decent job, in assisting us. I have learnt during my time in Newry that they are predominantly a Protestant force. I also know information gained that could be of advantage to the Protestant Terrorist organisations seems to somehow make its way through to them very, very quickly. These organisations get to know the salient, helpful points of any operation. I do not want this to happen with this operation. I want this haul destroyed rather than fall into the wrong hands, if you get my drift."

Davies held my stare for a moment, then gave a decisive nod.

"Understood. The RUC will be kept back, focusing on keeping civilians away from the operational area. That's their role, anyway. Would that be a satisfactory solution to your fears; if so, let it be."

That was the answer I needed.

I added one final point: the seized haul would be transferred to security forces, fully catalogued, and systematically marked for destruction in Belfast.

That was the plan.

Now, we just had to pull it off.

CHAPTER SEVEN: TAKEDOWN

I knew the Colonel, and I would get on well. We took over a disused factory warehouse to the south, well outside the precinct of Newtownards. To secure our position, 2 Para personnel monitored all approach roads, ensuring no unauthorised access—not even from the RUC.

Inside, we got to work. Maps were pinned to the walls, and communications were established with various security forces, including the Marines. We planned for a full briefing once it was clear the target vessel was turning for Strangford Lough. Intelligence on its movements would come from the Isle of Man police and Marine surveillance craft.

Saturday passed in relative silence. Company commanders were briefed on the utmost secrecy required. One misstep, one sighting of security forces, and the operation could be blown. Worse still, it could erupt into an open gun battle—these men were desperate to get their haul through.

By late Sunday afternoon, Isle of Man customs, who had been shadowing the vessel, confirmed it had departed. Darkness had already fallen by 4:00 p.m., offering cover. Now, we had to wait for the naval contingent to give the go-ahead once it reached the mouth of Strangford Lough.

At 7:45 p.m., the radio crackled to life. Call sign "Hotel," the Air Corps helicopter tasked with high-altitude surveillance, came through urgently:

"Get those damned Marine RIBs out of the mouth of the lough, get them beached and static; we can see them on infrared! If we can see them, the target will also be able to see us on its radar. If they are seen, the op is over!"

The Colonel erupted. "What the hell do those idiot Marines think they are up to?" He grabbed the radio and barked into it.

"You have been compromised in open water, identified by friendly forces, using infrared. The subject of this exercise can also see you on radar. You are instructed to secure your vessels and keep them out of radar vision immediately; is that understood?"

The reply came instantly.

"The transmission from 'Hotel' was monitored, and we are moving without delay to a concealed beach position, ETA one minute, over."

Had the target seen them? The only way to know was if the helicopter detected a course change or slowdown. All we could do was wait.

The next hour was agonising. Nothing came through. Though the temperature outside was below freezing, I was sweating. Then, suddenly, "Hotel" was back.

"The principal target is now entering the Op location."

We immediately instructed the Marines to continue monitoring at a safe distance. If the vessel attempted to turn back, they were to board and arrest the crew. Nearing 9:00 p.m., all units were informed the operation was now in full green mode. Orders were active.

"Hotel" updated us again. The target had entered the lough, heading towards its destination. Marine Commando vessels took their positions carefully, avoiding radar detection. The infrared surveillance proved invaluable—without it, we would have been blind. We waited.

Then, another transmission.

"We now see four smaller vessels approaching from the north towards the principal target, awaiting your instructions."

The Colonel responded immediately. "Wait and observe, over."

The company commanders, all listening in, understood the stakes. They were on high alert, ready for the next move. No action could be taken until "Hotel" signalled the time was right.

Forty-five minutes of silence followed. Then, "Hotel" came back on.

"The four smaller target vessels are now alongside the principal target. It appears that items are being transferred to these vessels. I will keep you informed as to what we understand is happening."

The next message was one none of us wanted to hear.

"Hotel" reported, "Low on fuel, will have to abort this operation. However, 'Hotel 2' is on its way to take over my commitment. He will be on-site within the next ten minutes. I cannot wait any longer to observe the target vessels; I must withdraw."

"Damn, damn, damn!" The Colonel slammed a fist against the table. "Not now, at this crucial point. Why did they not have enough fuel for the whole period of this op? We are blind without them; the whole op can turn into a bucket of worms!" He turned to me.

"What do we do?"

I rubbed my forehead, feeling the sweat on my palm.

"This situation is no one's fault. 'Hotel' has been in the air for hours, moving from Ireland to the Isle of Man and back, hovering at high altitude to remain undetected—that takes up a lot of fuel. We have little choice, sir. We must wait for 'Hotel 2' and warn all outposts to be on high alert for any unexpected developments. If any vessel is seen about to beach, they must take initiative and act accordingly. That is all we can do."

That was it. Nothing more could be done. We relayed instructions to the outlying units and waited.

Those ten minutes felt like an eternity.

Finally, "Hotel 2" crackled onto the airwaves.

"Requesting call sign acceptance to join the operation."

We confirmed immediately and then requested a status update. The response was precise and reassuring.

"I see one large principal target and four smaller targets, all in a group together. I will monitor and report anything further."

A collective exhale swept through the control room. I watched as the Colonel seemed to age ten years in as many minutes. My own nerves were shot.

I turned my attention to the maps on the wall, studying our ground forces' positions. The Highlanders were stationed along the west of the lough, ready to intercept any escapees heading in that direction. The Green Jackets controlled the northern routes along Portaferry Road. On the east side, 2 Para had concealed themselves at multiple locations. Altogether, three hundred men were in position.

Every soldier had been given strict orders: capture was the priority. Weapons were only to be used as a last resort, if absolutely necessary, to prevent an escape.

The next hour and a half passed in tense silence. Then, the radio broke through.

"Hotel 2" reported, "Four minor targets moving toward the east of the location, the principal target heading toward the mouth of the lough, over."

The Paras, already monitoring, were immediately alerted.

Another message followed. The Green Jackets confirmed two trucks moving south on Portaferry Road.

"Are we to stop them?" they asked.

We responded. "No, let them come."

These were the pickup vehicles. Now, we needed "Hotel 2" to relay any sign of unloading.

The waiting game continued.

The radio blared out again; it was "Hotel 2." They reported that the targets were heading for an outcrop of land north of Anna's Point, near Mount Stuart House. They provided the grid reference, stating that the location appeared to be a canoe quay with an isolated parking area and a hut or café concealing an area behind it.

We confirmed that 2 Para had received the transmission and awaited further updates. Before long, the Green Jackets reported that the two trucks had pulled into the quayside on Portaferry Road near Mount Stuart House. Simultaneously, "Hotel 2" confirmed that all four vessels were now stationary at the quayside. We instructed all parties to hold their positions until we were certain the cargo was being transferred.

After forty minutes, the radio crackled to life again.

"2 Para here. The four vessels have been unloaded. Both trucks are now fully loaded and about to move."

Colonel Davis gave me a thumbs-up before picking up the radio handset.

"All parties, move, move, move now. Stop and arrest all suspects, and stop all vehicles. Treat this move with extreme caution. Minimum force is authorised. Permission to open fire is granted only if fired upon. Report progress back when the op is clear."

He then turned his attention to the Marine call signs.

"Stop the four minor target vessels and the principal target vessel. Arrest all occupants. The use of weapons is to be contained as far as practical. Any firing is to be reported when the operation is complete."

The Green Jackets were ordered to advance toward the contact point to assist 2 Para as needed. The Highlanders were instructed to detain anyone observing the operation from the western side of the Lough and reposition north and west to provide additional support if required.

All parties responded with a crisp, "Wilco, out."

Then, we waited.

Minutes later, gunfire erupted—the last thing we wanted. The risk of exposure had just increased tenfold. We immediately directed the Green Jackets to seal off the area and ordered the Highlanders to establish a secure perimeter. We contacted the RUC, informing them of the situation. They provided additional support, monitoring and preventing anyone from approaching the site. Now, we had to wait for further details.

Then came the message we had been waiting for.

"2 Para here. Location secure. Twenty suspects were detained. Six injured following gunfire are receiving treatment; we require medical transport. Three friendlies have also been injured and are being treated. All cargo from the trucks is secure. The vessels have been impounded by the Marines, awaiting further instruction."

That was it. The culmination of eighteen months of effort had resulted in perhaps the most significant haul in Northern Ireland's history. For all intents and purposes, a bloodless coup.

The Colonel turned to me.

"Well then, I think we have achieved something that will go down in the history of this country as a great victory. Shall we go and see what we have caught?"

Around us, soldiers exchanged congratulatory pats on the back. I couldn't quite understand the enthusiasm. To me, it was just another operation. I turned to my men.

"This is your victory; you earned it."

The Colonel ordered medics and ambulances to be brought in and the entire area to remain sealed. We still had no update from the Marines regarding the principal target, but we were confident it would come soon.

Before heading to the contact site, I called Major Skinner.

"Operation successful. Please relay my compliments to the Brigadier. I will brief him once I've assessed the situation."

I added that six suspects had sustained gunshot wounds after opening fire on security forces. We had three casualties with similar wounds.

Now, all that remained was to secure the site and assess the full extent of our success.

We drove down the Lough-side road to the contact point at Mount Stewart Quay. On arrival, the area was a hive of activity. The Paras efficiently lined up all suspects, securing them with Plasti-cuffs and taking their details before screening. The process was methodical, ensuring every individual was accounted for before being loaded into vehicles. They were to be transported to various screening centres—Lisburn, Aldergrove, or possibly back to Newry or Bessbrook.

I wanted to be involved in the screening process, knowing this "well" of intelligence could prove invaluable. We waited for about an hour while final preparations were made. Then, the convoy moved out. The two trucks, laden to the gunwales with crates of arms, ammunition, explosives, and assorted paraphernalia, would soon be sorted, catalogued, and secured. The final tally of the haul would be interesting to see.

The RUC joined the Para vehicles in escorting the convoy, a necessary precaution against potential civil unrest. Now, in full daylight, we followed the column, some twenty armed vehicles strong, bristling with soldiers alert to any possible threat. Colonel Davis had chosen Aldergrove as the best destination for securing the haul. I was somewhat surprised by the RUC's response when the Colonel practically ordered them to secure all pinch points along the route and ensure the convoy was not stopped. Nonetheless, they did an excellent job, with patrols stationed at each junction to hold traffic as we passed.

Upon arrival at Aldergrove, I ensured the two trucks were under secure military custody before formally standing down this phase of the operation. The suspects were taken to various undisclosed locations across the province, isolated from their co-conspirators until the initial interrogation phase was complete. Even then, I doubted they would be able to communicate with one another. The intelligence extracted from these interrogations would be crucial.

Before returning to Armagh, I contacted Major Skinner, requesting that the operation be stood down. The Intelligence

Corps, alongside the RUC, assumed responsibility for interrogations and further arrests. I also made it clear that I expected to receive all intelligence gathered. Major Skinner later relayed that the Brigadier had informed the commanders of 2 Para, the Highlanders, and the Green Jackets to stand down. My request for access to all intelligence obtained from the suspects has also been approved. Furthermore, the Brigadier instructed that once I had compiled a detailed count of the seized haul and any additional intelligence, I was to submit a full report for immediate review.

I was utterly drained. There was only one place I wanted to be: bed.

In the days that followed, between my regular duties in Newry, I focused on compiling the intelligence gathered and maintaining close contact with the intelligence services handling the interrogations. I provisionally briefed the Brigadier, as did the Colonel of the Paras. The task of consolidating all findings into a comprehensive report proved to be a challenge in itself. Below are the key points of the recovered arms and explosives:

Arms & Explosives Recovered:

- USA Semtex C4 Plastic Explosive: 1400 Kilograms
- USA High Explosive Quarry TNT: 1600 Kilograms
- USA Detonators: 600
- USA Radio-Controlled Detonators: 100
- USA Radio Signal Detonating Devices: 20
- USA Anti-Personnel Claymore Mines: 200
- USA Cordex Rolls (300 metres each): 25
- USA RPG7 Rocket-Propelled Launchers: 120

- USA RPG7 Rocket HE Shells: 300
- USA M27 LAWS Anti-Tank Weapons: 40
- USA M16A1 Carbine Colt Rifles: 200
- Israel-Made UZI 9mm Machine Pistols: 150
- Soviet Military Kalashnikov Rifles: 100

Ammunition Seized:

- Rifle cartridges (7.62 calibre): 18,000
- Rifle cartridges (5.56 calibre): 15,000
- Pistol cartridges (9mm calibre): 7,000

It became evident just how significant this operation had been. The sheer quantity of arms and explosives recovered represented a major blow to terrorist operations. The next steps would involve careful analysis of all intelligence extracted from the detainees and determining what further action needed to be taken.

Over the next few days, I remained busy compiling detailed reports for the Brigadier. Locked away in my room, I focused entirely on finalising the report, leaving my crews to continue operations in Newry. Gathering the necessary information was arduous, as little could be discussed over the telephone. I had to verify certain points with the Colonel of the Para regiment the Intelligence Companies, and seek input from the Green Jackets, the Argyle and Sutherland Highlanders, and the RUC regarding the names and locations of the twenty-two arrested terrorist suspects.

After finalising my notes, I had them typed up and prepared for the Brigadier. It took four solid days and most evenings to complete. Throughout, I was under constant pressure from Major Skinner, eager to know when the report would be ready. On the fifth day, I phoned him to confirm its completion but insisted that I preferred to deliver it in person rather than telexing it. He consulted the Brigadier, then arranged a meeting for the following Tuesday at eleven in the morning. The Brigadier would review the report beforehand and then discuss necessary follow-up actions with me. That was fine by me; all I wanted at that moment was to set the report aside and get some much-needed rest. I had not been monitoring Newry closely, though I was confident everything was under control. I had left Benny in charge, and I knew he would reach out if any significant developments arose, though I doubted he would require my guidance.

That evening, Major Smythe knocked on my door, entering with two glasses and a bottle of "Bushmills" Irish whisky.

"I hear congratulations are in order. You're the talk of the town," he said.

I looked at him, puzzled.

"How the hell do you know what's happened? I've only just finished the report for Brigade, and my lads have been sworn to secrecy about the operation," I replied.

He smirked. "You can't keep a haul like this quiet; it's all over the officers' mess. The Colonel of the Paras says he wants you to transfer to his regiment."

I shook my head. "That's the last thing I need. I think I'll find a hole and hide."

We shared a few drinks, laughing at the absurdity of it all. The next twenty-four hours passed in a blur. I only remembered being woken on Monday morning by an orderly announcing that Benny was waiting outside.

I quickly dressed and stepped out to meet him, expecting a problem. There was none.

"Are you coming to work, boss, or do I have to keep doing the dirty work?" he asked with a grin.

I gave him a wry smile. "Give me ten minutes, and I'll come down with you."

After a quick wash and a week's worth of beard shaved away, I skipped breakfast and headed out, greeted by sniggers from the lads. I was grumpy, exhausted, and overworked. More than anything, I needed to get back up to speed with ongoing operations rather than dwell on the mission we had just completed.

Benny briefed me on recent developments. It appeared that Protestant communities were becoming more active. There were whispers that some sectarian killings originated from within the Protestant community in Newry. These claims needed to be substantiated, investigated, and, if necessary, acted upon. I had to admit that our recent efforts had largely focused on the Catholic community and the IRA terrorist organisation. It was clear that our attention had to be split, stretching our resources to their limit, but it was a necessary step if we were to uncover the truth.

I headed to Major Stam's office and asked if he had ten minutes for a chat. He readily agreed. I inquired about any intelligence his soldiers had gathered regarding Protestant activity in the area. He confirmed that the Protestant communities seemed more aggressive and confident than usual, while the Catholic communities remained notably quiet. He suspected this quietness could be a prelude to an escalation in activity. Though he could not be certain, he was concerned about the significant losses the IRA had suffered following our operation—news that had spread like wildfire among their ranks. He had never encountered this exact situation before during his tour of duty and had instructed all his troops to remain on high alert.

I asked about his intended course of action. He admitted that he had planned to discuss the situation with me before taking any steps, though I had pre-empted the conversation. I assured him that now I was aware, I would take measures to substantiate the rumours, investigate where necessary, and check with my local informants for any relevant intelligence. I promised to keep him informed of any significant findings.

Despite my calm exterior, I couldn't shake a growing unease. The terrorist organisation would undoubtedly be reeling from our success, and their reaction would not be far behind.

CHAPTER EIGHT
REPRISAL

The following morning, I picked up my usual escorts; by now, they had become a fixture. We travelled up to Londonderry for my appointment with the Brigadier. The journey passed without incident. With my report clutched under my arm, I entered Major Skinner's office. He sat me down, informing me that the Brigadier would not be long, and then left, taking the report with him. For the next twenty-five minutes, I sat idly, growing increasingly impatient. However, this was clearly the Brigadier's way of doing things.

Eventually, the office door opened, and I was summoned inside. I walked in, saluted, and was gestured to sit. As I did, I noticed a third person in the room, dressed in civilian clothes, though no introduction had been made.

The Brigadier looked up from his desk, his expression grim, which perplexed me.

"Lad, this report is a very, very precise, complex, and amazing record of what has recently happened in this most successful operation. I congratulate you and your team on a job really well done. I have spoken to the commanders of the other companies involved in this op; all say that your initial briefings on the situation and the knowledge and quick thinking during the op were nothing but brilliant. I hope you realise that this haul of ammunition, explosives, and arms may be the biggest haul ever recorded in Northern Ireland. The arrests made have been of immense benefit to the intelligence services, and this operation has resulted in the removal of top operatives in the IRA frontline offensive strategy. I can now tell you that we are winning this war because the operation has put the opposition's forces in a position of extreme weakness. This will allow us to look forward to bringing these troubles to an end."

He gestured towards the man in the corner.

"Now, may I introduce the party sitting in the corner, who is over from London and the Northern Ireland desk of military intelligence? He is collating and investigating all the information gained from the arrested terrorists and will add these findings to the findings of the overall picture. This, in turn, will form the content of the subsequent briefing to both MOD and the relevant politicians as to future actions in the province. That being said, some information that has become known is very disturbing, and you must know. I doubt if you will like it, but I will leave it to our friend to tell you. We will discuss it in full detail later today."

I felt a deep sense of pride in what we had accomplished. Nothing the Brigadier had said was new to me, but hearing that the British Army's mission in Northern Ireland seemed achievable lifted my spirits.

The man in the corner stood up, glanced at the Brigadier, and then addressed me.

"Thank you, sir. May I concur with everything that you have said, and may I add? The captain has produced a remarkable result based on his and his team's actions since the team was first established following your recommendations to MOD.

That brings me to a more delicate subject. Captain, do you realise that you and your team have, by your actions, achieved what has not been achieved in Ireland since the start of the troubles in 1969? In all, you have, by your previous actions and the current operation, crippled the IRA's hierarchy to the point that they have very few trained operatives left, not only in manpower on the ground but in the knowledge of bomb-making and tactics. This can be put directly at your feet. As you can imagine, the hierarchy that is left is not happy. This is what intelligence sources have brought to my attention, and I do not doubt its source. That source is deeply embedded with in-house Special Forces operatives.

This is not an acceptable turn of events; meetings have taken place within their hierarchy as to what they can do to stop this constant drain on their resources. These resources have now been reduced to a trickle. This is evident by the reduced bombings and, subsequently, the reduced destruction of property throughout the province. The recent starvation of arms, evidenced by the use of shotguns rather than military rifles and hardware, has affected their frontline operations. There have been meetings taking place not only in the North but also in the South of Ireland. It is also known that fundraising in the States has been severely affected, and any future aid will be vastly reduced.

The initial information from these meetings has resulted in a proposal that I do not like. It is that you and your team be removed from the province! I do not know how they intend to do this. However, I do feel that it will not be a soft action. It will be a hard strike designed to bring about a high degree of publicity in order to renew morale in the IRA frontline organisations and to bring them back into prominence afterwards.

It is, therefore, my recommendation to the Brigadier to bring this special operation to an end and return all personnel to their units. This, obviously, will include you, captain. It could, perhaps, save not only your own but your team's life as well. Not to mention any civilians who may innocently be involved in any attempt to remove you from the province. The decision is up to the Brigadier and you; I gathered from a previous discussion with him that you two will discuss it after I leave."

He turned to the Brigadier.

Once again, I thank you on behalf of the military intelligence for your actions and for what you have achieved in maybe bringing this theatre of operations nearer to a peaceful conclusion."

With that, he shook hands with the Brigadier, then approached me.

"It has been a great pleasure to meet you. I would have liked to meet your team, but unfortunately, time constraints do not allow it. Please convey my gratitude to them."

With one final nod to the Brigadier, he departed the office, accompanied by Major Skinner.

The Brigadier looked at me and said, "Perhaps this is a suitable time for light refreshments and a cup of tea. I have arranged to have a little snack brought in; then we can chat."

Shortly after, Major Skinner entered with an orderly carrying a tray of sandwiches, tea, and coffee.

The Brigadier started, "Look here, lad, the last thing I want is to have this operation stopped. I agree with most of what our MI friend has said. First, I want us to chat about things in general. You must feel as if you have just been hit in the stomach with a bat, so I do not intend to go on and aggravate the situation.

"What I suggest is that we go over the salient points and consider our options. In turn, I would like your views. That being said, I will ask what you feel the future holds and how you think I will get over this problem. Then, I suggest you take on board what has been discussed today and return to Armagh to put it to your team.

"I would like to hear their feelings about the matter and therefore suggest we all meet, maybe at Ballykinler, to finalise the outcome of these latest revelations. The outcome can only be decided by you and your team, but do bear in mind that they will withstand the worst of this new threat. I have no intention whatsoever of recommending cancellation of this operation if anything can be salvaged."

The Brigadier was right—I did feel as if I had been hit in the stomach. My head was reeling, and I felt physically sick as I turned over everything that had been said.

After all the work we had put into this operation, all the contacts we had made since we arrived, and all the lives we had saved, it was impossible to quantify it all. The children could now play without fear of the soldiers; they were no longer being educated to hate them. The young men were looking for career paths rather than being encouraged to pick up a gun and fight for the cause. That alone was a massive step forward.

The locals, particularly the mothers, respected what we were doing. Now, instead of mourning deaths and injuries from bombings, they felt relieved that the threat to their lives was diminishing.

But what would happen if we were to disappear? How could we simply up and leave, abandoning our newly found informers and friends to the mercy of the terrorist organisations? I had no doubt that retribution would be swift. What would the result be?

For the next two hours, I spoke candidly with the Brigadier and Major Skinner. I talked about how we had worked with civilians, gaining their trust and identifying those willing to provide vital intelligence. If only he could truly grasp what we had achieved—

what we had taken away from the terrorists. The arms, the ammunition, the morale.

We had systematically diminished every attempt of theirs to be a dominant force in their so-called fight against the British yoke. We had formed allies not only within the Catholic and Protestant communities but also within the RUC.

It was clear that soldiers on the ground in Newry, Bessbrook, Fork Hill, Crossmaglen, and Warren Point were beginning to see things our way. Their officers had told me openly what a welcome change had taken place within the population since our arrival. It was evident in the lack of soldiers firing upon suspects—there was no longer a need. Even in direct contact situations, capture had become the objective rather than lethal force.

Surely, this was enough to present a case to the MOD for continuing the operation rather than shutting it down. Stopping now would be a step backwards, a victory for the terrorist organisations. It would set the progress of the British Army in Northern Ireland back by at least five years, further prolonging the conflict. This was not a decision to be taken lightly.

Surprisingly, Major Skinner did not disagree with any of it. In fact, he supported most of what I said, though he challenged certain points with the Brigadier. I understood that it was he who would have to justify our existence to the Generals and the MOD, especially given the direct threat we now faced.

That threat was not just to our unit—it was designed to stifle our entire operation.

I could see the Brigadier's position completely. Still, I pushed back, perhaps overstepping the mark. I told him that the MOD had to consider our views and our feelings.

We were the ones on the ground, not them. We knew the risks, the people, the ways to navigate the dangers. The MOD had no knowledge of what we knew; they did not understand the lay of the land or the nuances of the communities.

With all due respect, they could play at being soldiers as much as they liked, but they were not here. And if they decided to disband the unit, it could be the worst decision they ever made.

I said I would take everything we had discussed back to my team and let them decide. Their opinions would guide my next move. That was the best I could offer.

The Brigadier nodded, looking uncharacteristically downcast. He said he would arrange a meeting at 11:00 a.m. at Ballykinler in two days. I agreed and left his office feeling far more despondent than when I had arrived.

The drive back to Armagh was consumed by turmoil.

How the hell was I going to break this to my team?

After all their hard work, would it all amount to nothing? That was how I felt—a sinking, gut-wrenching waste.

I had no idea how they would take the news. But one thing I did know—I was not the type to give up in the face of adversity.

I would fight for this unit. I would fight for this operation. We had worked too hard to make it a success. I believed we had achieved something significant.

I was certain the lads would agree with me, but if they didn't—if they were hesitant about their future in light of the threats against us—then I would accept their decision. And I would stand with the Brigadier.

CHAPTER NINE
DECISIONS

It was just after five in the evening when I arrived back in Armagh. There was no point in delaying the news any further—any hesitation would only give rise to rumours, and that was the last thing I needed.

I got on the radio to the patrols, who were already on their way back, and told them I needed to speak to them as soon as they returned. I instructed them to meet me in the briefing room and made sure that the other lads still in Armagh would also be there.

On my way, I stopped in to see Major Smythe, giving him a brief rundown of my meeting with the Brigadier. Maybe I was looking for guidance, or maybe I just needed to voice my frustration—I wasn't sure. He was astounded, to say the least, but assured me he would support me in any way he could.

By the time I reached the briefing room, the lads had already gathered. I asked them to sit and lock the doors—I didn't want any interruptions.

I stepped up to the rostrum, scanning the faces before me. These men had stood by me through some of the worst situations imaginable. Now, they were looking at me with the same questioning expressions I had seen when I first addressed them during selection training.

My legs felt like jelly. My stomach churned.

I took a breath and began.

"You must be wondering why I have called you here. Well, all I can say is that I did not want this meeting to happen, but it is vital.

During my meeting with the Brigadier today, He asked that I pass on his congratulations, and the congratulations of the General staff and the MOD, as to your recent success in the joint operation a week ago.

Following this, he went on. He said he had received some unpleasant news from a third party visiting the province from the Military Intelligence Northern Ireland desk, working with the MOD London.

The long and short of this is that we have, and this includes me, been put on the top of a terrorist hit list. This information has been received from a reliable, embedded source.

Unfortunately, these successes have resulted in the IRA deciding to take us out of the picture. According to this source, we have practically crippled the organisation and its ability to mount any sustained attack or bombing campaign in Northern Ireland.

They now feel the only way to get back to prominence and not lose face with their supporters is to come up with a shock strategy to remedy the situation. This strategy is to take out our unit very publicly, making sure it is done in such a way that it attracts as much publicity as possible.

This has resulted in the MOD not wanting the IRA to get this publicity, thus avoiding what could be seen as a high-profile IRA victory over the Army.

They have decided, in their wisdom, "for this unit to be disbanded."

A stunned silence fell over the room, followed by an audible gasp.

I continued, my voice steady.

"However, following the formal meeting, where the report on the recent op was discussed. The Brigadier told me he would put up a case to continue or go along with the MOD after receiving the deciding factor."

That factor is what you have to say, your thoughts on this decision, and the subsequent connotations that would result from our absence from South Armagh.

This decision was only made after I had vehemently challenged his views and the actions proposed by the MOD. I said that I felt the decision to disband would put back the progress of the British Army to peacefully end the troubles by five years at least and, possibly extend it.

The forces would have to remain in Northern Ireland for maybe a further five years, and nobody wants to see these troubles continue for perhaps another ten years.

It would be political suicide for the government to warrant that expenditure.

All the work we have put in and our successes can be counted in the recovery of arms and ammunition. What could not be counted as the goodwill that we now enjoy from what was, for all intent and purpose, the enemy?

We have succeeded in making them friends, where before they were not.

He took on board everything I said and stated to me that he would delay any decision until he had spoken to each one of you, following a meeting he has set up in two days at Ballykinler.

Therefore, Gentlemen, we will all be going to our old training ground on Friday morning to speak with the Brigadier.

Before then, I want you all to discuss what I have said, what you feel, and the pros and cons of this unit being disbanded.

Most importantly, do remember your decision will be the resulting outcome for the local communities in South Armagh.

I am not going to go on and on only to say that tomorrow, we have patrols as normal.

Thursday will be a free day for you to prepare for the meeting on Friday.

Should you wish to put anything in writing, please do so through me; otherwise, there will be an open forum after the meeting with the Brigadier.

After this evening's meeting, I will openly discuss any points with you.

"Thank you."

Discussions lasted over two hours after I had spoken. Most of the points raised reflected what I had already said to the Brigadier. All I could do now was encourage the men to bring their thoughts directly to him at the meeting in Ballykinler. The decision rested with him.

I could do no more.

That night, I tried to put my mind at rest, but it was impossible. The men felt just as I did—helpless, frustrated, and completely demoralised. I think all twenty-six of us left that briefing room feeling as though a black cloud had settled over us.

The next day in Newry, morale was at an all-time low. The men were miserable, inattentive, and distracted by the uncertainty of what lay ahead. Their lack of focus was obvious, and it put all of us at risk.

By midday, I had had enough.

I ordered everyone off the streets and back to the security base in Newry.

Once inside the briefing room, I let them have it.

I practically screamed.

"What the hell do you think you are doing out there? Your sulking is only making you and me bigger targets than we already are."

"I want you all to face up to the situation. Get a grip and function as the competent soldiers you are trained and supposed to be.

"Work for today is finished—we are going back to Armagh. I am unwilling to put you or anyone else at any further risk."

"It appears to me that is all we have been doing all day. You are fortunate the opposition does not know how poorly you have reacted to their latest threat."

"I am extremely disappointed with you."

"Let us hope tomorrow you put on a better face for the Brigadier. Because if you don't, we can all say goodbye to Newry, this unit, and this operation."

"Do I make myself clear?"

Silence.

"Shall I repeat myself?" I bellowed. "Do I make myself clear?"

This time, they responded—albeit sheepishly.

"Yes."

The drive back to Armagh was silent.

I could almost hear them cursing me under their breath, angry that I hadn't given them space to wallow in their own misery. But I didn't care.

All that mattered was keeping them alive.

Their lack of focus today had put us all in danger.

I refused to let their despondency weaken my resolve. This situation was beyond our control, but that didn't mean we would allow it to define us.

When we finally arrived back in Armagh, I ordered them to wash down the vehicles and ensure everything was in top condition for the trip to Ballykinler.

I knew that keeping them busy would stop them from dwelling on what they could not change.

They could curse me all they wanted, but I knew from experience—that the only way to get men back into the right frame of mind was to get them working.

Friday morning came, and we all climbed into two minibuses that Major Smythe had arranged for the trip. We arrived at Ballykinler in exceptionally good time, with about 45 minutes to wait for the Brigadier.

I spent most of the time chatting with Mr Hunter. He already had an idea that something was wrong, as the Brigadier's Staff Officer, Major Skinner, had been in touch with him. He had asked for the briefing room to be set up in an informal manner for this meeting.

I briefly went over recent events with him, as he was particularly interested in how the lads had developed. I told him how well things had been going—how we had gained the trust of both the Catholic and Protestant communities in Newry, as well as securing a good footing in the surrounding villages and towns of South Armagh.

Of course, I also told him that we had made a few enemies and that the Brigadier had called this meeting because the MOD wanted to determine the future of the operation.

He wasn't surprised. In fact, he said Major Skinner had hinted that there was an issue at the higher levels that needed addressing.

The Brigadier arrived at about 10:45 a.m. I met him as he got out of his car, accompanied by Major Skinner. They both seemed rather buoyant—quite the contrast to the mood of the men sitting in the briefing room, who looked thoroughly miserable.

Mr Hunter saluted the Brigadier and said the briefing room was ready for him and that he would not be disturbed. The Brigadier thanked him, and we walked inside.

When we entered, the lads stood up to attention. The Brigadier waved his hand and beckoned them to sit down.

Unbeknown to me, Mr Hunter had arranged the seating in a semi-circular, tiered fashion. At the front, there was no desk or rostrum—just three armchairs. I assumed they were for the Brigadier, Major Skinner, and myself.

The Brigadier asked us to sit down, and so we did.

He then began, his approach to the men particularly measured.

"I have asked you all here to discuss the latest news regarding your present operation. I do not intend to make a speech; I do not want you to feel that you cannot openly say what you think."

"We are here today following the meeting you have recently had with your OIC. He has made it clear to you what the lay of the land is in respect of recent developments, following your considerable successes with our fight against the local terrorist organisations."

"Information has come from the MOD that I am not happy with. What they have recommended is that this unit be disbanded. They feel the new threats from the IRA are such that if they come to fruition, it would put the army in a bad light."

"The recent operation, where you have recovered vast quantities of arms and explosives, has put the IRA on its back foot. Now, the IRA wishes to take this unit out in a highly public manner."

"I want to hear what you all feel about this decision and what you think the unit's future role should be. You chaps are on the front line of this conflict. I am here to take on board all your comments and reasoning. Whichever way it goes; I will fight your corner with the MOD."

"Well, gentlemen, the work that you have done in the brief time you have been in existence has been of immense value to the overall planning and strategy of the Army in the province."

"Now, I will ask my two fellow officers to leave the room, as I do not want you to feel restricted in your response or criticism of any previous or future operations you may have undertaken."

"Thank you, gents."

Major Skinner and I exchanged glances. He gave a small nod towards the door, and we both stood up, asked to be excused by the Brigadier, and then left the room.

Mr Hunter, looking slightly puzzled by our sudden reappearance, met us in the corridor.

"Problems?" he asked.

"I do not think so, Mr Hunter. The Brigadier asked us to leave, as he wanted to chat with the men without us being there to restrict their comments," I replied.

"Well, may I suggest my office, and I will get some coffee organised."

Both Major Skinner and I took the offer with open arms.

I never knew what was said in that briefing room and never asked. If anyone wanted me to know, they would tell me. As far as I was concerned, it was between the Brigadier and my men—no one else.

After about ten minutes, the coffee arrived. I didn't quite know how I felt—both Major Skinner and I were a little dumbfounded. Mr Hunter did his best to put our minds at ease and went on to say

"What's happening in that briefing room? We don't know; the meeting might go on for a maximum of half an hour."

However, as the minutes stretched past thirty, I glanced at Major Skinner.

"Something interesting must be going on in there."

"It is very strange," he said. "Usually, the Brigadier gets meetings over very quickly. I cannot imagine what is taking all this time."

Mr Hunter chimed in. "Gentlemen, what will be, will be. I'm sure the Brigadier is just ensuring he has all the facts. My only comment would be, is that it is a good sign that this meeting, informal as it is, is taking such a long time. The Brigadier is gathering all the information from the men in there, ensuring that everyone is of the same opinion. If not, he is asking why not! I doubt very much that the Brigadier will leave without turning over every stone before he makes any decision."

We both looked at Mr. Hunter and nodded, agreeing with his assessment.

After some two hours, the sound of chairs shuffling reached us, and the Brigadier appeared in the doorway of the briefing room. Both Major Skinner and I went out to greet him.

In my view, he looked a little browbeaten. I asked how the meeting had gone.

"You have a remarkable bunch of men in there, Captain. You should be proud of them; they are most supportive of you, and they have given an excellent account of the situation, both in the past and what could be in the future. However, I get the impression that they would gladly desert if my decision does not gel with their thinking. We will see."

"They can be a bit forward sometimes, sir, but I hope you got what you came for."

"I did, thank you. I will speak to you in a few days."

He left without further comment and returned to Londonderry.

I stepped into the briefing room, now filled with animated discussion, as everyone expressed varying points of view. Raising my voice, I called out, "Right, playtime is over. I do not know what you have said to the Brigadier; he has left and now has me wondering if I have a bunch of would-be deserters on my hands. I do not want to know what was said, although we should hopefully have an answer to the future of this unit in a few days. Let us all get back to base and get some work done."

On the drive back to Armagh, I noticed that, strangely, everyone seemed rather happy, as if they had won some sort of victory. This was not the impression I had gathered from the Brigadier's comments as he left Ballykinler. I said nothing. I let them feel what they felt. My only concern was that they returned to the ground in a better frame of mind than when we had left—it would make them more efficient and focused on the job at hand.

When we arrived back at Armagh, I was informed that Major Stam had been asking for me to call him as soon as I returned. Clearly, it was important, so I went straight to the phone.

As soon as he answered, I could tell by his voice that something was very wrong.

"I have some unwelcome news: two Catholic men travelling in a painter's van have been shot and killed in an ambush in Newry. The gunmen escaped the scene into the Protestant estate in north Newry. The RUC have found no trace of them. I expect that there will be repercussions due to this action. Can you help?"

There was no point in heading to Newry that late in the afternoon—it wouldn't help anyone.

"I doubt there will be any repercussions this soon after the event, perhaps tomorrow or in a few days. I will investigate through my contacts to establish the facts and see if they know anything. I will discuss it with you in the morning."

That was all I could do for now.

Still, the turn of events made me uneasy. The Protestant sector of Newry was growing bolder, and this ambush had taken their actions to an entirely new level. It would have to be addressed.

The following morning, I briefed the lads before leaving Armagh, outlining the situation with the shootings in Newry and how we needed to handle it. I decided that we would tour the Catholic estates, listening to the locals and gauging the overall mood. We needed to determine what kind of retaliation, if any, was being considered and what action we could take to prevent further trouble.

After about an hour, I realised that calming tensions was a lost cause. The anger in the Catholic estates was palpable, and there was no question in my mind—reprisals were inevitable. We, the army, had no choice but to be in the middle of it.

The security level had to be raised immediately.

Upon returning to the Newry base, I went straight to see Major Stam. I relayed what we had gathered from the Catholic communities and made my recommendation. Every military personnel and base in South Armagh needed to be placed on security level Red for the next forty-eight hours—at the very least until the threat level had reduced significantly.

It wasn't a move I wanted to make, but it was necessary.

I just hoped it wouldn't lead to even more bloodshed.

My fears soon became a reality. Neither side was happy with the increased level of security forces' activity.

Two weeks after these measures were introduced, the first incident occurred. A bus was hijacked in the Protestant area, fitted with petrol storage and an incendiary device, and then driven into the Catholic area of Newry. It was parked alongside a community centre and ignited.

This, I felt, was an act of defiance—one that would not only draw the security forces into the Catholic area but also provoke a reaction from the terrorist activists. The intention was clear: to incite conflict between the security forces and the IRA.

We had no choice but to respond.

By the time we arrived outside the community centre, the bus was almost completely burned out. The fire brigade was finishing up, eager to get out of the area as quickly as possible. A fair-sized crowd was gathering in the opposite car park, a few of them already shouting profanities at both the Protestants and the army.

This was not good.

I knew that this car park had previously been used as a local marketplace, as well as a meeting area for those who wanted to air grievances—whether genuine or incited. It was a known hotspot for stirring up unrest. More than once, demonstrations here had escalated into full-blown riots.

As I scanned the growing crowd, I recognised several well-known troublemakers. They were already waving their arms, shouting, drawing others into their orbit.

This was about to escalate.

I signalled my men to move back to the far end of the car park. Our presence alone could be enough to tip things into violence, and I wanted to give the situation as little fuel as possible.

At the same time, I radioed back to control, informing them of the situation and requesting immediate reinforcements. If this turned into a riot, we would need the numbers to contain it.

The response came quickly. Two support platoons were en route and would be with us in approximately ten minutes.

Ten minutes was too long.

The crowd had swelled to over a hundred, maybe two hundred people and their agitation was growing. Without vehicles, we had no cover if things got out of hand. If the crowd surged, we would be vulnerable.

I ordered two lads with rubber bullet launchers to get ready.

Then, suddenly—from within the crowd—a shot rang out.

My response was immediate. I ordered my section to take up a defensive firing position, safeties off, ready to engage if necessary.

The crowd surged forward by twenty or thirty metres, clearly trying to provide cover for the gunman. But when they saw us crouch down, weapons at the ready, they hesitated.

The shot had been heard by our reinforcements, still en route.

Moments later, two Saracen armoured cars came screaming into the car park. Soldiers poured out of the back, taking defensive positions, rifles raised and ready to fire.

It was then that I realised the full extent of the Protestant plan. They had set the fire to bait us in. Now, we were in the exact situation they had wanted—armed British soldiers in a standoff with an angry Catholic crowd.

A powder keg, waiting for a spark.

Something had to happen.

Then, over the noise and shouting, I heard them—two helicopters approaching fast.

They came in low, hovering just twenty feet above us before moving forward, pushing directly towards the crowd.

It was like watching a broom sweep across the car park.

Men, women, and children ran in every direction, scattering under the downwash of the rotor blades. Within a minute, the car park was clear.

The helicopters rose, hovering at about one hundred feet, watching.

The Sergeant in charge of the reinforcements came up to me.

"Are we still needed, sir?"

I shook my head. "No, you can stand down. Return to Bessbrook."

Back at the Newry security base, I met with Major Stam to debrief. I laid it all out—how the Protestants had baited us, how they had designed the situation to drive a wedge between the Catholic community and the security forces.

By making us respond aggressively in the Catholic area, they hoped to shift the balance—making themselves appear the lesser threat in the eyes of the army while increasing the Catholic hostility towards us.

If we weren't careful, we would be playing right into their hands.

Major Stam agreed with my conclusions about the bus attack. He also agreed that things were escalating fast and that we needed to be prepared for further sectarian violence.

I knew the Catholic community well enough by now. They would not let this pass without retaliation.

We had to be on high alert.

I told Major Stam I would push my informers for any intelligence on possible uprisings or retaliatory attacks. If there was action brewing, we needed to know about it before it happened.

Before leaving, I asked that my thanks be passed on to the helicopter pilots. Without their intervention, the situation could have turned into something far worse.

Their manoeuvre should be considered a standard tactic in the event of future riots.

Major Stam nodded. "I had actually sent them to your location to observe and assist if required. Their actions were most beneficial in calming the situation. I'll pass on your comments and thanks to the Air Corps."

We both knew, however, that this wasn't over.

The next few weeks were hectic, to say the least. Both factions in Newry were playing a dangerous game of cat and mouse. A few shootings had taken place, and we had been involved in some of them—none of which were pleasant. The loss of life on either side of a conflict is something one wishes not to talk about.

With all these incidents, along with the constant reports I had to forward to brigade headquarters, life felt increasingly stressful. However, without our informers on both sides, the number of casualties would have been far worse. The actions we took based on the intelligence received had prevented many killings, and for that, everyone was grateful.

Still, I had yet to hear anything from the Brigadier about what our future would be—whether we would continue the operation or be disbanded. The uncertainty was not conducive to good soldiering.

It was taking a toll on my men.

Frustration, short tempers, inattentiveness—these things were creeping in, and I feared it would lead to problems I could not resolve. I needed word from the Brigadier soon.

It was now nearing the end of May 1977. With the constant unrest in Newry, weeks were blurring into months, making it even harder on the men. I decided that when I returned to Armagh, I would contact Major Skinner and ask for an update on the Brigadier's negotiations with the MOD regarding the future of our operation.

The day was over, and it was time to pack up and head back to Armagh. Everyone was exhausted, the strain of the last few weeks etched into their faces. I wished I were taking back a happier bunch.

As if someone had read my mind, a message was waiting for me when I arrived in Armagh. I was required to be at the Brigadier's office at eleven o'clock the following morning.

I knew immediately what this meant.

The only reason I would be summoned was to be informed of the outcome of the Brigadier's discussions with the MOD.

I felt a little sick.

I had been waiting for this moment for what felt like an eternity. Now that it had arrived, I almost didn't want to face it. But I had no choice. I had to hear the verdict.

Major Smythe was with me as I read the message. He took one look at my face and instantly realised I was troubled.

"Is it bad news?" he asked.

"It's the message from the Brigadier I've been waiting for," I admitted. "But now that I have it, the future seems uncertain. If the news were good, I feel he would have told me straight away by phone. The fact that I've been summoned to his office makes me think he wants to break the news to me gently. We'll see what tomorrow brings."

Major Smythe was understanding. "Come on, let's go to the mess for a drink."

I accepted his offer. That evening, I drank too much and paid for it the following morning with a splitting headache.

A cold shower and a few cups of strong black coffee sorted me out.

I went out to check on the lads but didn't tell them about my meeting. They were only informed that I wouldn't be with them that day, that I had a prior engagement, and wouldn't be back until late in the afternoon.

"Should any problems occur, contact Major Stam. He will advise and keep me informed by radio if necessary."

Benny gave me a strange look.

"Is there anything wrong, boss?"

"No, Benny, I have things to do. I need to do them alone. You make sure everything in Newry runs smoothly today. Be careful—it's getting dangerous out there."

"OK, boss, you be careful too and don't worry. We will be all right."

We went our separate ways.

I could sense the tension among my men. They knew I had something weighing on my mind, but I couldn't confide in them.

They were right.

I pushed the thought aside and arranged with Major Smythe for transport to Londonderry.

The entire journey, my mind raced.

What would I say to the Brigadier when he told me it was all over?

How would I take it?

More importantly, how would I break the news to my chaps?

When we finally arrived at brigade headquarters, I went straight to the Brigadier's office, where Major Skinner met me.

His greeting was cool.

I understood why—I had been pestering him for answers for weeks.

"The Brigadier is expecting you," he said. "He will be free in a few minutes."

Sure enough, within five minutes, the Brigadier's door opened, and I was beckoned inside.

He was sitting behind his desk, looking through some papers. Without a word, he gestured for me to take a seat. I did.

For a few moments, he continued reading. Then, finally, he looked up.

"I am sorry you have been called here at such short notice. I gather you have been terribly busy with increased activity in Newry. I am sure you want to finish this meeting as soon as possible so you can return to your duties."

I met his gaze but said nothing.

If he was about to say what I thought he was, would I even have duties to return to?

He placed the papers he had been reading into a folder and leaned back slightly.

"Well, finally, I got a response from the MOD regarding the operation in Newry. I have to apologise for the length of time it has taken."

"However, I have had to fly over to London twice to the MOD and put forward my case to the powers. I also have had to produce reports and evidence to support what I had requested."

"At one point, I felt like giving up—at least once. But then I thought back to my meeting with your men at Ballykinler. Their loyalty, their commitment to the success of this operation, and what it meant to them."

"At that meeting, they put forward many strong arguments for continuing the operation. They made a case that the future of many sectarian disputes within the province could be changed by carrying on with this work."

"At one stage, while at the MOD, I was tempted to request your presence to corroborate what had been said to the generals, politicians, and Military Intelligence personnel."

"Finally, I received a telex yesterday."

"It stated that, after considerable discussion and deliberation, and against much opposition, it has been decided that the operation will continue."

"It was felt that to disband your unit may, as you have said in the past, give the terrorist organisations within Northern Ireland a significant boost to their morale."

"Retaining the unit, as has already been proven, will eventually destroy both their morale and their ability to mount any sustained actions in the future."

"So, Captain, it is with my blessing that you return to Newry and tell your men to get their chins off the ground."

"Yes, I, too, have my spies. I know how down in the mouth they have been during a very disconcerting period of events in South Armagh."

"Let's hope it can be sorted quickly and these killings be stopped."

He paused before continuing.

"I am not going to invite you to lunch today, as I am sure you are in a hurry to get back".

"Thank you for the excellent job you and your men have been doing up to date. I ask that you continue this work in the excellent way you have executed your duties to this point."

"I will not forget your contribution to these troubles and implore you and your men to be extremely cautious of the continuing high terrorist threat to remove both you and your unit from the province."

I was literally speechless.

Composing myself, I finally managed to thank him for his efforts and assured him I would keep the operation going at the pace it had been. I was of the same mind as he was about its eventual success.

I thanked him again and left.

When I stepped out of the office, I felt like punching the air in satisfaction with the outcome—but I controlled my emotions.

I quickly found my driver, and we headed back to Armagh.

On arrival, I went straight to Major Smythe's office. The door was open, so I knocked and stepped inside. He was sitting behind his desk and looked up as I entered.

"Come in, what news?"

"Well, John, unfortunately, you have me under your skin for the foreseeable future. The Brigadier has been able to secure the continuation of operations in Newry."

He got up from his desk, came around, and slapped me on the back.

"Well done. I knew you would be able to swing it. However, I did have my doubts as to whether the Brigadier could pull it off in London. Well done to both of you. Now, perhaps we can get a smile back on your face and get some real work done; great news."

We exchanged a few more comments before I left his office, feeling considerably happier.

I got on the radio to the lads on the ground.

"When you return to Armagh, meet me in the briefing room. I have news for you."

I had a couple of hours before the crews would be back, so I headed to the mess and asked the orderly if he could rustle up a sandwich and some coffee. I hadn't eaten all day, and anything would be appreciated.

He soon returned with a mug of black coffee and a plate of ham sandwiches.

Taking them to the briefing room, I sat down and waited.

At about half past six, the men arrived. They looked exhausted, their uniforms a little dishevelled. I waited until the last stragglers appeared, then told them to sit down and lock the door.

I stood in front of them, keeping my tone calm.

"Well, we have all been waiting for the Brigadier's answer regarding the future of our operations in Newry."

"Today, I had a meeting with the Brigadier, who has just received a final telex from the MOD regarding the continuation or disbandment of this operation."

The Brigadier did say his decision to continue with his arguments with the MOD was coloured by the meeting he had with you all at Ballykinler. He went on to say how impressed he was with the arguments you put up to him in support of the continuation of our duties in Newry.

So, gentlemen, as a result of your efforts and your reasoning regarding our future presence in South Armagh. After many meetings and much discussion and opposition at the MOD, the views were taken not only of military intelligence but also of the RUC and the General in command of operations within the province.

Due to the successes of this operation, they have decided to continue it until otherwise stated.

The mood in the room shifted instantly.

I saw the relief wash over their faces, the tension they had been carrying for months finally lifting.

I knew exactly how they felt—I had been living with the same uncertainty.

Now that the air was cleared, it was time to get back to work.

"This isn't the end of our challenges," I told them. "We need to uncover the underlying cause of these sectarian disputes within South Armagh."

"These tensions are spreading across the province, and we cannot allow them to escalate further."

"Starting tomorrow morning, we will double our efforts within both the Protestant and Catholic communities in Newry and the surrounding villages."

"Our objective is clear: gather intelligence, identify motivations, and find a way to prevent this from spiralling out of control."

I paused, looking around at the men who had fought alongside me through everything.

"Finally, you should all be proud of the way you handled yourselves with the Brigadier. You gave the right answers, you made a strong case, and we got the result we needed."

"I'll see you all in the morning, bright and early. Let's get back to work."

CHAPTER TEN
THREAT

South Armagh was known as "Bandit Country," two hundred square miles of the most dangerous and hostile terrain in Northern Ireland. Open, desolate, and unforgiving, it served as the perfect training ground for IRA gunmen. Since 1969, this land has claimed the lives of one hundred and fifteen soldiers.

To the Republicans, it was "God's Country"—the only region in the six counties where they believed they had successfully resisted the British Army. Both geographically and politically vital, South Armagh was a powder keg, always on the verge of explosion.

We travelled the road between Armagh and Newry daily, and more often than not, shots were fired at our vehicles.

The morning arrived, and the lads were in good spirits. With the uncertainty over our future behind us, there was a renewed sense of focus.

We moved out of the barracks in Armagh and headed down the now all-too-familiar road towards Newry. The A28 was narrow, winding through Ballydogherty, its verges lined with high banks and thick hedgerows. There were long stretches of desolate road, the kind that made perfect ambush sites. We had learned to take them at speed.

This morning was no different.

We were pushing sixty-five miles per hour when, without warning, the lead vehicle veered off the road, skidding onto the verge before coming to an abrupt stop.

The convoy reacted instinctively. The following vehicles swerved to avoid a collision before coming to a halt. Within seconds, we were out, taking up defensive positions.

A loud volley of gunfire cracked through the air, bullets ripping over our heads from somewhere further up the road.

"Contact! Contact!" I shouted, my voice carrying over the noise.

The order was clear—return fire immediately if a gunman was spotted.

Sporadic shots continued from a ridge above us, but the thick hedge line made it impossible to get a clear visual. A couple of the lads scrambled up the embankment, breaking through the undergrowth. I heard the warning called out—a gunman had been sighted.

Another volley of gunfire rang out, the rounds striking our vehicles.

Then, from the far side of the hedge came the distinctive crack of an SLR rifle. One of our lads had taken the shot.

Silence followed. No return fire.

We advanced cautiously towards the ridge, and there, lying motionless in the undergrowth, was the gunman. A Thompson submachine gun lay beside him.

I knew immediately that the situation had just escalated.

I radioed Newry HQ, reporting the engagement and requesting immediate support. The RUC needed to be on-site, and I wanted a platoon dispatched to seal off the area in case there was further movement.

They responded quickly, but the rest of the day was spent making statements, dealing with the RUC, and reporting the incident to the necessary authorities.

Two of my men had sustained minor injuries—one with facial cuts from a shattered windscreen, the other with a graze to the left arm from a gunshot.

Apart from a few bullet holes in the vehicles, we had been lucky.

This was just the beginning.

A few days after the shooting at Ballydogherty, intelligence came through from a reliable source.

A tip-off suggested we should pay a visit to the local Catholic church hall. Something was amiss—someone had recently fitted a new Chubb security lock to the doors, and it wasn't clear why.

Coincidentally, we were already planning to move into that particular estate that morning. I decided to take a look.

We moved cautiously through the estate, eyes scanning for anything unusual. The church hall was a single-storey stone building with a slate roof. It looked as unremarkable as any other, except for the new security lock.

Leaving a few of the lads in covering positions, I did a lap around the hall. The doors were locked, just as expected. The windows revealed nothing unusual.

I wandered over to the church, hoping to find someone with access to the hall. Before I could even knock, the vestry door swung open.

A local priest stood before me, his stance defiant.

Before I could say a word, he snapped, "And what do you want, coming here? There's nothing here for you."

"I need to have a look in the church hall. You being the keyholder, you can let me in."

He folded his arms. "And what will you do about it if I don't want you to go into my church hall? Arrest me?"

"If I have to, I will," I replied. "I'm doing my job, and I need access to this hall. Now, do I get the key or not?"

The priest hesitated, then fumbled in his pockets and pulled out a ring of keys. He pushed past me with obvious irritation.

"All right, I will let you in, but be quick about it. I have other things to do that are more important than your silly inspection of my church hall."

I gestured for two of my men to stay outside while the rest followed me in.

The priest turned to me. "So that is it—my church hall. All that happens here are meetings of the women's institute, the youth club, and the girl's netball club. So you have seen it. Can I now lock up?"

My eyes drifted to the far end of the hall, where a door was secured with a padlock.

"Where does that door lead to?" I asked.

"Oh, it goes to the toilets. There's nothing in there," he said quickly.

I frowned. Why would a toilet need a new padlock on the outside?

Andy, one of my lads, sidled up to me and muttered, "Something's not right here. Look at the ceiling—it's been fitted low, not open to the eaves like most church halls. And for a building this old, the plasterwork is pristine. No loft hatch, either. Seems odd."

I nodded. Something wasn't adding up.

Turning to the priest, I ordered, "Open that door."

"Why?"

"If you don't open it, I will have it opened for you."

"Now look here, there's nothing in there, there's no reason for you to go in there, and that's final."

I gave a nod to Colin—built like a bus—who stepped forward and positioned himself in the doorway, blocking any escape. Then I signalled Benny and Andy.

"Get that door open."

A few well-placed kicks and a firm shoulder charge sent the door flying open.

The priest was livid, his face turning crimson as he began shouting about police complaints and compensation for damages.

I ignored him and stepped inside.

It was just a small toilet—nothing more. No window, no other exit.

I sighed, feeling a flash of disappointment.

Had we been misled?

Then Wingnut, who had followed me in, pointed upwards.

"There's your loft hatch, boss."

I looked up.

Tucked away in the corner of the ceiling was a small access panel.

"Benny, lift Wingnut up," I ordered.

Once through, Wingnut shone his torch into the space above.

Seconds later, his voice came down.

"Boss, we're going to need some help up here. There are hundreds of weapons stacked to the eaves."

I turned to the priest, whose complexion had drained to a ghostly white.

"Nothing here, eh?" I said. "You are under arrest."

He said nothing.

I radioed Newry HQ and reported the find, requesting immediate reinforcements and engineers to dismantle the ceiling for proper access.

Moments later, Colin called out from the entrance.

"Boss, you better come here. We've got trouble."

A crowd had gathered—angry locals, around eighteen of them, a mix of men and women. Their faces were hard, their stances aggressive.

I quickly ordered my men into defensive positions and radioed for more troops.

The tension in the air was thick, the kind that precedes a riot.

For the next ten minutes, the standoff held. Then, a low thudding sound filled the sky.

A Wessex helicopter roared overhead, hovering just above the graveyard.

Moments later, fourteen paratroopers fast-roped to the ground, securing defensive positions. A second helicopter followed, bringing another platoon.

The mood in the crowd shifted.

Then, the RUC arrived in force.

The numbers were no longer in their favour.

One by one, the locals began to disperse.

For now, at least, the storm had passed.

For the next seven days, the church hall remained under strict guard. A cordon was placed around the building, manned day and night as engineers worked to dismantle the ceiling and uncover what lay hidden within.

The scale of the find was staggering.

More than two thousand weapons and thousands of rounds of ammunition were removed from the loft space—an arsenal both modern and deadly, the kind that could inflict devastating harm in the wrong hands.

Among the haul were wartime rifles and pistols, some relics that belonged in museums rather than a hidden weapons cache. Every last item was seized, taken away, and destroyed.

The soldiers remained in the area throughout the week, combing both the church hall and the church itself for any additional caches. It was an exhaustive search that stopped just short of exhuming recent graves—though, at one point, even that was suggested.

Unsurprisingly, this operation did little to help our standing with the Catholic community.

To them, we were the ones responsible for the disruption, the ones who had uncovered the truth they wished had remained buried. Their resentment was palpable, but we had no choice—we had a job to do, and we would see it through.

The fallout came swiftly.

Within days, protests erupted, growing into small, coordinated riots. Tensions ran high, and the unrest became relentless, stretching across two to three weeks of near-constant clashes.

It escalated so severely that I had no choice but to call in reinforcements—the Paras and the RUC—just to hold the line.

For the soldiers on the ground, it was a daunting task.

They were deployed to maintain law and order, yet they now faced a violent, unrelenting crowd. Outnumbered and increasingly outgunned, they had to rely on their training and discipline to prevent the situation from spiralling into open warfare.

The rioters were well-prepared.

They wielded concealed weapons, hurled stones, and used any makeshift device they could find to inflict harm. At times, the situation teetered on the edge of all-out battle.

For us, every moment was tense and unpredictable.

We had to remain alert, anticipating every possible threat, and be ready to respond instantly. The attacks were constant, and while we held our ground, we felt the weight of the pressure.

Beyond the physical danger, there was the emotional toll.

Facing a hostile crowd day after day, enduring the taunts and verbal abuse—it wore on even the hardest of men. Yet we had to stay composed, to keep our emotions in check, never allowing ourselves to be baited.

For some, the conflict cut even deeper.

Many of the soldiers were Irish themselves. They faced a brutal internal struggle—loyalty to their country versus duty as a soldier. They were forced to make impossible choices, deciding when and how to use force against people who, in another life, could have been their neighbours.

And still, the violence worsened. The rioters grew in number, now in the hundreds. Firebombs rained down. Gunfire crackled from the crowd. We were reaching breaking point.

This was no longer just a protest—it was a battlefield.

The riot was fuelled by years of pent-up frustration, grievances that had simmered beneath the surface for too long. Economic disparity, social inequality, and a deep-seated belief that the British government had failed them—these tensions had built to an inevitable explosion.

The discovery of the arms cache had simply been the final spark.

To the IRA and their supporters, our operation had been an act of British supremacy, a blatant attack on their cause.

To the Catholic community, it was a humiliation, a loss, a moment of reckoning that was too much to bear.

With media attention amplifying the unrest, the situation spiralled further. Inflammatory messaging and misinformation spread like wildfire, feeding the flames of anger and outrage.

The streets were becoming ungovernable.

A decision had to be made.

The retreat was not taken lightly.

It was a calculated move based on careful assessment. We considered every factor—the sheer size and intensity of the crowd, the presence of armed individuals within their ranks, and the likelihood of further escalation.

Staying meant inviting disaster.

The Brigadier had been monitoring the situation closely, in constant communication with the MOD in London. His guidance was invaluable. He knew, as we did that this was not a battle we could afford to fight on these terms.

So, we withdrew.

The retreat was strategic, not an act of defeat.

We executed it with discipline, establishing defensive formations to ensure a controlled withdrawal.

Soldiers carried riot shields, helmets secured, and every movement calculated.

Communication was vital.

Through radio updates and hand signals, we maintained order, ensuring that no man was left behind and that our lines remained intact.

We fell back to the security base in Newry, regrouping behind reinforced defences.

But retreating did not mean hiding.

As soon as we returned, we took swift action to fortify our position.

Barricades were reinforced. Obstacles were strategically placed, making it near-impossible for any would-be attackers to breach our perimeter.

Security measures were heightened—access control was tightened, surveillance was increased, and monitoring systems were enhanced.

We made it clear: if they wanted a fight, they would have to come to us on our terms.

Resource management became critical.

We deployed personnel where they were needed most, ensuring that every point of weakness was covered. Equipment was allocated efficiently—every bullet, every ration accounted for.

The retreat had not been an act of surrender.

It had been a move to secure our position, to reassess, to plan for the next phase.

Ultimately, it was the right decision.

But it came at a cost.

There were injuries. There were casualties. The impact on morale was undeniable.

No soldier walks away from a riot like that unchanged.

The psychological strain of facing down a relentless, hate-filled crowd—knowing that, in another life, some of them might have been friends or family—was something that weighed on all of us.

But war does not allow for hesitation.

We had done what was necessary.

Now, we had to prepare for what would come next.

Reflecting on the retreat, it is essential to analyse both its strengths and weaknesses. Understanding what worked well and where improvements can be made will help us refine our strategy for any future riot situations.

Among the key strengths was our ability to think quickly under pressure. The decision to withdraw to the Newry base was not only tactical but crucial in preventing further escalation. Once there, the reinforcement of base defences and the immediate implementation of additional security protocols ensured the safety of both personnel and resources. These actions collectively contributed to the overall success of the operation.

Following the retreat, I compiled a full report and passed my findings on to the Brigadier for his review.

Several recommendations were forwarded, including:

- Conducting regular training exercises to simulate riot scenarios.
- Establishing and maintaining clear communication channels.
- Continuously updating security protocols to adapt to evolving threats.

By implementing these measures, we would be better equipped to handle similar situations in the future.

The retreat also underscored the importance of ongoing training and preparation. Complacency was not an option—our ability to respond swiftly and effectively in moments of crisis depended on maintaining a high level of readiness at all times.

One of the most crucial factors in the success of the retreat was communication.

In times of crisis, clear and concise communication is paramount. By ensuring that vital information was relayed efficiently, we were able to coordinate our actions effectively, make informed decisions, and execute the retreat without unnecessary confusion or delay. This level of communication was equally vital in strengthening our defensive position once we reached the base, allowing us to organise and secure our perimeter without disruption.

In conclusion, the retreat from the riot was a critical decision made in the best interest of safety and operational stability. While it presented challenges, it reinforced the necessity of prioritising personnel protection in volatile situations.

Lessons were learned—not just in how to manage a withdrawal but also in how to fortify our defences and reassess our approach to riot control. Moving forward, the implementation of enhanced riot management strategies will be crucial in ensuring the safety of soldiers while mitigating potential risks.

Through continuous improvement, training, and preparedness, future riot situations can be better managed—keeping both our soldiers and the wider community as safe as possible.

Chapter Eleven
Building Bridges

The retreat had drained the energy from the riot, and eventually, the crowds dissipated, retreating into their homes. With the tension slowly easing, the reinforcements—some four hundred men—returned to the barracks at Bessbrook, leaving me and my small band of men behind to pick up the pieces.

Rebuilding trust would be no easy task.

For weeks, we had to tread carefully. The riots had left scars on the community, deepening the divides we had fought so hard to bridge. It was, perhaps, the most difficult period of my entire tour in South Armagh.

I gradually re-established my contacts, but the flow of information had all but dried up. Getting anyone to talk felt like pulling hen's teeth. No one wanted to be seen with us. Whenever we approached a group—whether Catholic or Protestant—a veil of silence would immediately descend. Conversations, if they happened at all, were brief and cautious.

We had a long road ahead if we hoped to regain the trust we had once built.

By early August 1977, the oppressive heat of summer settled over the region. Days were long and stifling, but little by little, things were improving. The streets were quieter. The fear in people's eyes had lessened. Youth clubs had reopened, and children played outside once more.

I allowed myself to think, just for a moment, that we were on the right path.

Then came the day that changed everything.

That fateful morning in Newry, I—a British officer whose duty was to serve and protect the community—became the target of an IRA gunman.

It happened just as I was leaving the Security base at the start of a routine patrol.

A shot rang out.

I felt the sharp sting of a bullet grazing my shoulder. The pain was instant, but the shock hit harder.

Had the gunman aimed just a fraction lower, I wouldn't have walked away from that moment.

The attack sent a shockwave through Newry, sparking both fear and outrage. It reinforced what I had already suspected—the recent threats against my life were not idle words. The IRA had marked me as a target, and they were determined to see me gone.

Everything we had worked for—the fragile trust, the uneasy peace—was now crumbling.

The attack underscored the relentless danger my team faced daily. My injury was minor—a graze to the shoulder and a dented ego—but the implications ran far deeper.

The shooting sent a clear message: the IRA was still very much in the fight.

It had a devastating impact on the local communities. Fear crept back into the streets, undoing months of effort. Families kept their children indoors once more, frightened by the increasing violence.

The fragile truce we had worked so hard to build now seemed all but shattered.

It was yet another tactic in the IRA's playbook—using terror to deepen divisions, to sow anger, fear, and resentment between the factions. And for their supporters, it was a statement of strength, proof that they could strike at the heart of the security forces whenever they pleased.

In response, security measures in Newry tightened overnight. More boots on the ground. More patrols. More tension.

It seemed as though everything we had tried to do to bridge the gap between the communities had been in vain.

But I refused to accept that.

My team had a job to do, and we would continue doing it.

Orders from brigade headquarters came thick and fast, outlining new security measures for all military personnel.

One directive, in particular, enraged me.

Due to a recent wave of bomb hoaxes designed to lure security forces into ambushes, bomb disposal operatives were now being deliberately targeted. The IRA had adapted their strategy—placing bombs then shooting the men sent to defuse them.

As a result, trained bomb disposal personnel were in short supply, and training new operatives took time.

The consequence? A chilling new order.

From now on, before a bomb disposal unit was called, soldiers on the ground had to confirm that a reported device was indeed real.

In other words, a private soldier would now be expected to risk his life to check for a live explosive.

To me, it was nothing short of madness.

What the order effectively meant was that a private soldier's life was deemed expendable, while a bomb disposal expert's life held more value.

It was a sickening mindset—one that reminded me of outdated military thinking, as though we were still fighting in the days of the Crimean War, where soldiers were treated as cannon fodder.

When I relayed this order to my team, the outrage was immediate. They were just as furious as I was. But orders were orders, and whether we liked it or not, we had to follow them.

Still, I refused to let it stand without challenge.

I raised my concerns, and eventually, the order was amended. Now, only a senior officer or NCO could conduct the assessment—not a low-ranking soldier.

It was a small victory, but one that could save lives.

Since the riots and the shooting, the Brigadier had urged me to take a step back from frontline operations. He wanted me to be less visible to let my senior NCOs take the lead.

For a while, I obliged.

But it wasn't in my nature to sit back. I joined my team on the ground as often as I could despite the warnings.

My shoulder was still healing, and the medic charged with overseeing my recovery became increasingly frustrated with me. He had orders to ensure I took it easy, but I wasn't interested in taking it easy.

Even in my absence, the patrols continued to gather useful intelligence. The arms and explosives were still coming in from the south, and we continued our efforts to intercept them.

Despite everything, the operation was succeeding.

But I knew the Brigadier was facing mounting pressure from the MOD.

The riots. The shootings. The continued instability.

It was only a matter of time before London overruled him, bringing our mission to an end.

If that day came, I knew he would fight tooth and nail to keep us in place for as long as possible.

The morning of the 13th of September 1977 started as any other.

The sun was shining. The drive to Newry was uneventful.

After settling at the Security base, I had a short briefing with Major Stam before leading a two-hour patrol through the Protestant estates. Nothing was out of the ordinary.

We exchanged pleasantries with a few locals, but none of our usual informants were around.

At 10:30 a.m., we returned to the base.

Major Stam had mentioned earlier that he was short on manpower. He had sent three platoons to Bessbrook to assist the Paras in an operation further north. With his resources stretched thin, he appreciated any assistance we could offer.

We sat down for our first coffee of the day when a private soldier entered the briefing room.

"Captain, Major Stam needs you in the Ops Room. ASAP."

I set down my cup and headed straight there.

The Major wasted no time.

"David, I am sorry, but I have had a report of a suspect device in a large handbag on the counter at the Hermitage Bar, behind the Town Hall, next to the canal. I do not have anyone to check it out. Could I ask you and your patrol to take the necessary action, seal it off, and see if we need to act on this report for bomb disposal?"

"No problem," I replied.

I returned to my team and briefed Benny on the situation.

By now, the RUC had already evacuated the surrounding buildings, but they had not approached the bar itself. I contacted the local fire station, instructing them to attend at a safe distance in case they were needed.

With everything in place, we moved out.

As we arrived, I spotted the RUC and the fire brigade pump tender stationed at a safe distance.

My men dismounted, taking up defensive positions with clear lines of sight to the entrance. There was nothing left to do but go forward and assess the scene. I signalled my lads, then advanced. Kenny followed close behind, covering me. I crouched low as I reached the entrance, my eyes scanning the corridor ahead. There, on the bar counter, twenty feet inside, was the device.

Not a handbag.

A ten-gallon oil drum wrapped in cortex explosive wire.

And on top of it, a block of plastic explosive—with a shiny antenna protruding from its surface.

Radio-controlled.

A trap.

I had seconds to react. As I turned to withdraw, I heard it—A sharp crack of detonation. The bomb had been triggered.

I had barely taken my first steps away when the world exploded.

The force of the blast lifted me clean off my feet and hurled me out of the bar entrance, flinging me nearly thirty metres through the air. I was weightless for a moment, tumbling towards the canal below. As I twisted in mid-air, I realised—most of my clothes had been blasted off my body.

Then I saw it.

A monstrous fireball erupted from the bar entrance, roaring towards me like a living thing.

Instinct screamed at me—don't breathe.

If I did, I was dead.

The fireball swallowed me whole, engulfing everything in its path. The heat was unbearable, searing my skin, and then—impossibly—I was yanked backwards, sucked into the inferno as if the flames themselves had claimed me.

That was when the real explosion hit.

A deafening, skull-rattling detonation tore through the air, the loudest sound I had ever heard.

My ears rang. My vision blurred. A searing pain tore through every inch of my body.

Everything went black.

Then blue.

The primal urge to survive took over.

I must not breathe.

I was trapped in a raging firestorm. My body burned—face, arms, hands, legs—everywhere, the flames licked and devoured. My skin peeled, raw and screaming in agony.

I wanted to scream with it.

But I couldn't.

My voice had vanished, lost in the blaze.

I couldn't move.

I could only watch as my body disappeared into the flames, an unbearable heat consuming everything in its path. Somewhere, deep in my mind, I thought—this is it. This is how I die. Then, something pushed me. A force I couldn't explain.

Maybe it was my men dragging me clear. Maybe it was my family, willing me to live.

All I knew was that I was moving—out, away.

Later, I would learn that it was Kenny who had saved me. Despite suffering burns to his hands, he had fought his way into the inferno, found me, and hauled me out. By then, the roof and ceiling of the bar had collapsed, flames devouring everything. But somehow, Kenny got to me.

And outside—I was still burning.

The fire had consumed my clothing. My skin had become fuel. I was on fire.

Forensics would later confirm the oil drum had been filled with petroleum jelly. That explained why, as the lads tried desperately to put me out, the flames kept reigniting.

Again and again, my body flared up, embers embedded in my flesh glowing like molten coal as the wind breathed life into them.

Each time they doused me, the fire returned.

They tried everything.

It was futile.

I watched as my own flesh burned.

Finally, a fireman turned a hose on me, drenching me with water.

The flames died. But the pain—oh, the pain—remained.

By some miracle, Benny and the lads managed to bundle me into the back of a Rover and raced me to the local hospital—less than half a mile away.

That was where the real battle began.

The moment we arrived, the doctor took one look at me and shook his head. I would later learn what happened next. Benny—covered in my blood, his hands still shaking—pleaded with the doctor to help me.

The doctor refused.

"This hospital is for the Catholic community, not British Protestants," he said coldly. "I won't risk my life treating him. Get him out."

That was when Benny snapped. He pulled his pistol, pressed it against the doctor's temple, and growled, "Then give him something for the pain."

Under duress, the doctor administered an ampule of morphine.

That was the last thing I remembered before everything turned hazy. Somewhere in the background, Andy had been relaying the situation to control, calling for urgent medical assistance.

Then—

A Wessex helicopter roared into view, touching down in the Town Hall car park. I was lifted onto a stretcher and carried towards the waiting aircraft.

The last thing I remember was the heat.

Wessex helicopters have front-mounted engines. Their exhaust vents sit right where I was being carried. As I passed beneath them, a blast of heat rolled over me.

Then—darkness.

I lost consciousness.

I woke briefly in the military wing of the Royal Victoria Hospital in Belfast. I didn't know how much time had passed.

The world was a fog of pain and morphine.

A nurse leaned over me. "How are you feeling?" she asked gently.

My mind drifted to my wife. Tears burned my eyes as I tried to speak. I had to tell them her phone number. I had to reach her. The nurse held the phone to my ear, and suddenly—she was there.

I could barely form words, my voice a garbled mess of agony, but she understood.

I wanted to see her.

I needed to see her.

Major Smythe appeared at my bedside. His voice was distant, but I caught his words.

"Do you want her to come?"

I tried to respond, but my body betrayed me.

I don't remember what happened after that.

The next time I surfaced, she was there. She had flown in via a private jet—one usually reserved for political passengers. At the time, I didn't realise why she had come so urgently. The truth was, they didn't expect me to survive.

My injuries were severe—too severe.

I was kept in a medically induced coma, pumped full of drugs and morphine. Life became a hazy swirl of pain, numbed only by the floating sensation of sedation. Within days, I was casevaced to the burns unit at the Royal Military Hospital in Woolwich, London. A Hercules aircraft carried me there. I remember only flashes.

My wife is by my side.

The flight.

The police escort from RAF Northolt to Woolwich, sirens blaring.

Then—nothing.

Darkness swallowed me once more.

CHAPTER TWELVE
RECOVERY

I remember coming around in the hospital at Woolwich, though I had no idea at the time that I had already been there for five days. The doctors had placed me in an induced coma, assessing the extent of my injuries before daring to wake me. When I finally surfaced, I found myself lying on an air bed—a strange, unsettling sensation, as if I were floating on a fragile cushion of air. The bed prevented my body from touching any solid surface, a necessity for burns patients, where even the slightest friction could tear away healing skin.

The room was bathed in daylight, though everything appeared hazy, as if I were peering through a veil of mist. My hands and arms were wrapped in plastic, sheathed as if they belonged to someone else. Beneath the plastic, my skin was coated in a thick, white cream—aqueous cream, as I later learned. It was smeared over every inch of my body, a feeble barrier against the relentless assault of pain that awaited me.

This was only the beginning of a long and torturous journey.

Two men entered my room, both clad in white coats. One was a Colonel, the other a Major—both surgeons. The Colonel spoke first, his voice clipped and clinical, devoid of emotion.

"Well, young man, you are in a bit of a mess. You have some forty percent full-depth burns; your arm is nearly severed, and the skin on your right leg is nearly all either burned or blown away. Your hands are very severely burnt, and your face is half covered with your melted beret. The rest of your body has suffered superficial burning.

We do not know if you have any internal injuries. Over the past couple of days, we have conducted an extensive assessment of your condition; we need to do much preparatory work before we can start the rebuilding process. This is going to be a long and painful process, which will cause you a great deal of suffering. That being said, the hard painkillers you have been on since the explosion are going to stop! As I do not want you to become addicted to morphine, so from this moment, no more. Do you understand?"

I nodded weakly. He continued.

"You have much muscle and skin loss; veins and muscles have been melted and destroyed. The only way to recover, unfortunately, is to suffer for a long time. Firstly, flesh has to be grown, and then skin has to be grafted. Tomorrow, we will take you down to the theatre and de-slough all of your burns. This process involves the removal of necrotic or non-viable tissue from the wound bed. De-sloughing plays a vital role in preparing the wound for a skin graft, as it promotes optimal healing of the wounds, reduces the risk of infection, and improves the adherence of a graft. Following this procedure, the wounds will be dressed and re-dressed every few days to promote the growth of flesh in order to eventually have a base to carry out grafting."

With that, they left.

That was my introduction to hell.

The dressing changes began every two or three days, a cycle of torment that defied imagination. Each time, the nurses would expose my raw wounds, pouring peroxide solution over them before wrapping the burns in sterile towels, squeezing them tight, and then ripping them away. Iodine followed, searing my flesh with white-hot agony. Finally, paraffin gauze mesh was strapped around my arms and legs, and a pressure bandage was applied to force the flesh to grow through the mesh—only for it to be torn away again at the next change, repeating the process. Again and again, new flesh was ripped away, only to grow back through the gauze, locking me in an endless cycle of pain.

I wanted to die. If I had been able to move, I might have tried. I would have given up my family, as much as I loved them, if it meant an end to the agony.

Sleep was a cruel joke. Every time I closed my eyes, I was back in Ireland, burning, screaming, trapped in the nightmare that had become my reality. The memories came in waves—heat, fire, the acrid stench of seared flesh. And then, the worst trial of all—I had to try to stand.

The first attempt broke me. I collapsed after a single step, my legs buckling under the weight of pain and atrophied muscle. I lay on the floor, helpless, a wreck of a man. My wife had been at my side, whispering encouragement, but as I looked at her, the shame overwhelmed me, and I burst into tears. The scabs on my legs split open, revealing the ash beneath.

For weeks, it continued—day after day, dressing change after dressing change. When, at last, the new flesh had grown, it was hypersensitive, every nerve exposed. The pain was unbearable, racking my body until I screamed aloud. And then, at last, the grafting began.

I had spent two weeks dreading the possibility of rejection, knowing many patients lost their grafts. The surgeons had exhausted all available donor sites on my body. Instead, they used meshed pig skin on my right arm and leg. In all, I underwent thirty-five skin grafting operations under full anaesthetic over five months. One of these surgeries involved peeling away the melted remains of my beret from my face. When I first awoke and saw my reflection, my skin raw and angry, I broke down again. But later, the surgeons told me that the delay in removing the charred remnants had, in some miraculous way, allowed my facial structure to recover. Time had healed it beyond anything I could have expected.

When the last of the dressings were removed, small patches remained where the grafts had failed to take. These areas had to heal naturally, aided by salt baths. I was winched into a bath filled with intensely strong salt water, where I had to remain for forty minutes as the salt worked its way into the raw wounds, cauterising them to allow scabs to form. The pain was excruciating, and I finally understood why the ward had been soundproofed—to muffle the screams of patients enduring the same ordeal. After a few days, those scabs were forcibly removed so that new skin could grow in their place.

I won't go on about the hospital treatment any further except to say that, looking back, I am eternally grateful for the dedication, expertise, and care of the surgeons, nurses, and staff who guided me through that hell. I will never forget what they did for me.

Six months later, I had come to terms with my injuries—at least, as much as one can. But I had become a nuisance to the staff, desperate to regain my independence. I wanted to use my rebuilt hands to feed myself rather than being fed. I wanted to use the bathroom alone rather than rely on a nurse to hold a bottle or bedpan for me. I still couldn't walk and had limited use of my right arm.

Then, they dangled the carrot before me.

I was told that if I worked with the physiotherapists for two weeks—if I could stand, walk, and use my arms unaided—I would be allowed to go home for the weekend. The thought of it filled me with determination.

I could barely shuffle three or four centimetres. Blood pooled beneath my new skin grafts, seeping through the pores. But I had a new wheelchair, controlled with a single finger on the joystick. I was far from the most popular patient on the ward—reckless in my attempts, weaving through the corridors like a would-be Damon Hill, Formula One champion. But I didn't care. I had a goal. And nothing would stop me.

I was soon restricted in my movements by the nurses. One of the male nurses, whom I had struck up a particularly good friendship with, had been my lifeline throughout the healing process. He had encouraged me, helped me, and pushed me forward when I felt like giving up. But now, he looked at me with doubt in his eyes.

He shook his head. "I don't think you'll be able to achieve the level of movement required to go home for a weekend break in two weeks."

My response was immediate. "By hook or by crook, I will get home for the weekend, come hell or high water."

He laughed, a knowing glint in his eye. "Well, Sir, let's see what we can do."

The following morning, they wheeled me out of the burns unit. It was the first time in seven months that I had seen the world beyond those hospital walls. The air hit me like a shockwave—fresh, crisp, unfamiliar. It was overwhelming. Frightening, even.

We reached the gym, its large swing doors opening to reveal a vast space filled with equipment and determination. Waiting inside was a physical training instructor, Warrant Officer 2. He was a giant of a man, his muscles carved like stone, his presence commanding. He greeted me with a broad smile.

"Good morning, Sir. I have been expecting you. I know we are going to get on, and in this first session, I need to assess you and judge your abilities in order to see what programme of rehabilitation will suit you. Now, let us see you stand."

With effort and a bit of help, I pushed myself upright. My legs trembled beneath me, but I stood.

"Great," my physio said. "Now your nurse can go, and I will ring the ward when he can return."

Then, with an air of casual cruelty, he pushed my wheelchair away. "I have a few details to take from you; take your time, don't rush; just come over to my office, where I can fill out a few forms!"

Before I could protest, both my nurse and the physio were gone. My trusty wheelchair—my one source of stability—had vanished with them. And I was left there, standing alone, staring at the long, agonising journey ahead of me.

That, I think, was the hardest walk of my life.

I would have preferred a forced march over the Brecon Beacons to that gym floor. Each shuffle forward was agony, each centimetre gained a battle. Blood seeped from my skin grafts, leaving a trail in my wake. The journey took me one hour and thirteen excruciating minutes. I cursed the physio with every step, every movement sending lightning bolts of pain through my body.

Finally, I reached his office. I leaned against the doorway, my body drenched in sweat, my breath ragged, my legs trembling in a pool of my own blood. I glared at him.

"You bastard."

He looked up, entirely unfazed. "Sir, well done! By getting across that gym, you have proved to me that you have the guts and determination to get through the programme I have in mind for you.

If you had not done that or had given up, then I could do nothing for you. Now, I will ensure that you will be able to walk and get back to a level of fitness that will be acceptable for the medics to discharge you, OK?"

He went on, his voice resolute. "Your nurse is on the way to take you back; I will see you every morning at 10 o'clock and every afternoon at 3:00 p.m.; we have much work to do."

I would be thankful for that physio for the rest of my days. Over the next two weeks, he dragged me through pain barriers I had never imagined possible. I swore at him, and he swore back. He built up my body, my resilience, and my mind. He prepared me for the uncertain future ahead.

After two weeks of relentless training, he looked at me after a particularly gruelling session of gym circuit training and nodded. "I'm recommending that you are fit and able to go home for the weekend."

If I could have, I would have jumped for joy.

Back at the ward, the Colonel came to see me. "Well, young man, you have exceeded all our expectations and have earned, through your hard work with the physio, a much-needed break away from us for the coming weekend. All that is needed is for us to arrange transport for you. Have a good weekend."

The following Friday, dressed in a loose-fitting tracksuit and armed with my medical supplies, I was told that a staff car was waiting to take me home to the Midlands. The entire ward—nurses, surgeons, staff—gathered to see me off, helping me into the car.

I should have been elated. Instead, fear crept over me. After so long in the security of the hospital, the outside world felt alien. I wanted to hide. Anyone who has spent months in isolation will understand that feeling. At the time, PTSD was called "cowardice." I knew otherwise.

That weekend was painful in every sense. My wife and children walked on eggshells around me, unsure of how to act. I could not hold them, could not embrace them. That, more than anything, broke me.

By the time I arrived at my flat, I already wanted to return to the hospital. Monday morning could not come fast enough.

When I finally stepped back into the Burns ward, it was like stepping into sanctuary.

The next two months passed in a blur of healing, rehabilitation, and specialist visits in London, where I was fitted with pressure garments for my arms and legs. These had to be worn day and night for two years to prevent scar tissue from hardening and restricting movement.

Recovering from severe burns is a battle of endurance—physical, emotional, and psychological. After nine months, countless surgeries, and more pain than I could have imagined, the day finally arrived. I was going home.

The transition was daunting. Leaving behind the security of the hospital meant facing a world I no longer felt part of. The prospect of caring for my wounds, managing my pain, and navigating my new reality filled me with anxiety. Could I do it alone? Could I cope with the fear that clawed at me?

Conversations about my discharge intensified. Healthcare professionals assessed me and made plans for home care, follow-up treatments, and rehabilitation. Then, at last, the decision was made.

I could now walk—slowly but unaided. Standing no longer sent fire through my body.

The Colonel had warned me that the muscle loss in my right leg meant I would need a walking stick, at least for a while. I was being posted to the south of England, close to an Army hospital and the central London specialists who would continue my care.

The day finally arrived when I was to leave this place that had been both my sanctuary and my prison for the past nine months. I had entered as a broken man, shattered in both body and spirit, and now, though rebuilt, I was leaving a shadow of my former self. A part of me clung to the comfort of the hospital—the routine, the security, the people who had fought so tirelessly to put me back together. But it was time. Time to step back into the world beyond these walls, no matter how uncertain my footing felt.

As I made my way to the main entrance, every nurse, every surgeon, and every member of staff who had been part of my journey followed behind. I walked proudly, albeit with the aid of my sticks, savouring this moment of triumph. At the threshold, I paused. Turning to my physiotherapist, the man who had dragged me through hell and back, I held out my walking sticks.

"I won't need these anymore; perhaps you can find a home for them. I thank you for everything."

There were no grand speeches, no dramatic goodbyes—just gratitude, deep and unspoken, between those who had fought this battle with me. I bid farewell to the nurses and surgeons, stepped into the waiting staff car, and as we pulled away, I waved to them one last time.

But even as the hospital receded into the distance, the real battle was only just beginning.

Returning home after nine months meant confronting a new reality. My living environment had to be adapted—handrails installed, the bathroom modified, and spaces reconfigured to accommodate my new physical limitations. But the practical adjustments were nothing compared to the emotional ones.

Rebuilding my relationships with my wife and children proved to be the hardest challenge of all. I had survived, but I had not returned the same man. My injuries, both seen and unseen, formed an invisible barrier between us. My wife, despite her best efforts, struggled to accept what had happened to me. The scars on my body were nothing compared to the ones forming in my marriage. These fractures, small at first, would only grow deeper with time.

Life was no longer what it had been. What should have been heartwarming—being back with my family—was instead fraught with tension. Simple tasks that I once performed without thought now required immense effort or assistance. Every moment was a reminder of what had been taken from me. Frustration mounted as I fought to reclaim my independence, pushing myself daily to regain what little strength I could. It was exhausting, both physically and emotionally.

I had six weeks before I was due to report for my new posting in Hampshire. Whatever my next role entailed, I was determined to be ready for it. But those six weeks tested not just my resilience but my family's as well.

The reality of my new life soon set in. I needed help with everything—dressing, applying creams, soaking my grafts with lanolin, washing myself. Even the smallest tasks felt monumental. Then came the question of transport. Could I still drive? My beloved MGB convertible, once my pride and joy, was now an impractical relic of my past. It was clear I needed something more suited to my new limitations.

My father stepped in, calling on an old friend who owned a garage in the Midlands. A solution was found—a large, fully automatic car that I could handle. It meant saying goodbye to my treasured MGB, a painful but necessary sacrifice. In exchange, I received a Wolseley 1800 saloon automatic. Not the sleek sports car I had once loved, but something I could drive. Something that gave me back a measure of control.

And with that, I was on my way.

Chapter Thirteen
A Step Forward

I became painfully aware of how much I had to rely on my wife. Simple tasks I had once taken for granted were now insurmountable obstacles, leaving me feeling helpless and dependent. My flat in the Midlands, once a symbol of stability, had become an encumbrance rather than a benefit. I needed my wife and children with me—I had to hold my family together. I could feel our life teetering on the edge of a precipice, and the thought of losing it all filled me with dread.

We decided to rent out the flat and move into married quarters in Hampshire. A month's leave passed in a blur, and then I moved south alone, arranging to stay in the Mess until I secured a house. The military housing department was efficient, and soon, they found me a semi-detached house in one of the military estates. Meanwhile, my wife handled the rental arrangements for our flat and, once everything was settled, moved down with the children to join me.

We tried to settle in.

The children hated their new school. My wife hated our married quarters.

I had hoped this move would provide a fresh start, but instead, it felt like a slow descent into something far worse. The entire process was stressful, frustrating, and ultimately deeply disappointing. This wasn't the life I had imagined for us. Instead of a sense of purpose, I felt a crushing inadequacy creeping in—an overwhelming fear of everything happening around me.

The local medical officer saw it. He saw the hollowed-out version of me sitting in his office, the exhaustion in my eyes, the way my shoulders slumped with the weight of everything I had endured.

His solution was drugs.

Antidepressants. Painkillers. A cocktail of medications, all prescribed to dull the edge of what had become my existence.

In the following weeks, I had several visits from officers within my regiment, briefing me on my rehabilitation programme and outlining my new role. Then, the day finally came—I was to report to district headquarters. This was meant to be the start of something new, a fresh career path, an opportunity to rebuild.

I put on my uniform, got into my car, and drove to my 11 o'clock appointment with the Southern District General Commanding Officer.

Major General Jeremy Cullen greeted me warmly, his manner surprisingly unmilitary.

"Come in, sit down," he said, waving me towards a chair.

I sat, feeling uncertain, waiting for whatever was coming next.

"I have looked at your record of service and am very impressed with what I see," he began. "I have also spoken to Brigadier Woodford, who may I say is most disappointed to lose you from his command but stressed how much of an asset you have been to recent operations in Northern Ireland."

"I realise you have a long way to go in your recovery following the unfortunate bomb incident that you were injured in. I have given a great deal of thought as to how I can help in this lengthy process. Obviously, you cannot return to active duties with the regiment, and your presence in Ireland is now untenable, which means you are restricted to UK duties."

"So, I have decided to put you into a staff position within headquarters; your new post will be as staff assistant to the Brigadier here at Southern District headquarters. It will give you as much time off as you need for your various requirements. It is a rather sedentary position compared with your last posting; however, it will also involve us taking advantage of your unique insight into the various terrorist organisations that you have studied and been involved in their demise over many years."

"To this end, I have arranged for you to be a member of the tutors at the staff college in Sandhurst. To lecture on the history of the various terrorist organisations and how to overcome the threat from them. It will also allow you the necessary time for your various stages of physio with the medics, as and when you need it."

"Obviously, I would require you to give a concise overview of the subject to a group of senior officers prior to the permanent position. However, I doubt that will be a problem for you. How does that all sound?"

I was taken aback.

Could I do this? Was I capable?

Would my nerves hold up?

"Thank you, sir," I managed to say. "I did not think that I would be given such a responsible position, bearing in mind my recent injuries; however, I will try to fulfil my duties to the best of my ability."

The General nodded.

"As you may know, Staff College is for Majors selected for higher field rank to pass through in order to process their career. So, I do not wish to embarrass either you or your prospective pupils with your rank as captain. I therefore intend that you will be promoted with immediate effect to Major."

"I will ask my staff officer to introduce you to the Brigadier and to instruct you in the necessary formalities regarding your promotion. I wish you well in your new position. Should you need anything in the future, please do not hesitate to ask me."

I left the General's office with my mind spinning.

There was so much to prepare—so much research to be done. I would have to put together an entire syllabus, compile lesson plans, and structure detailed overviews. This wasn't just a job; this was about shaping the minds of the officers who would lead future operations. If I got this wrong, people could die.

That weight settled deep into my chest.

Major Richard Dower, the General's aide-de-camp, escorted me to meet my new boss, Brigadier Mike Mathews.

On the way, Richard turned to me.

"I've recently been through Staff College myself," he said. "I still have all my notes on the lectures. If you need to know the course content, I'll gladly let you have them."

I accepted his offer without hesitation.

Richard would become an invaluable friend in the months ahead—a wealth of knowledge and an unspoken source of support.

Brigadier Mathews was nothing like I had expected.

Short, stocky, with a rosy face and a gung-ho attitude, he greeted me like an old friend.

We sat for an hour and a half, talking about Ireland, our pasts, mutual acquaintances, and—eventually—my new role.

It seemed simple enough.

I was to manage his diary, oversee the office administration, book his visits, and keep the paperwork under control. I wouldn't be deskbound, he assured me, but I'd be on call most days.

It seemed like an easy job.

It wasn't.

His staff of twenty civilians ensured that everything within Southern Command flowed through his office. Every morning, mountains of paperwork landed on my desk, needing distribution, action, or review. It was monotonous, but thankfully, I had two incredibly efficient clerks who made my life easier. They handled most of the tedious work, leaving me to approve and oversee rather than drown in endless documentation.

It was a system that worked.

That evening, I arrived home exhausted.

I sat down heavily, recounting everything to my wife.

"You are now the wife of a Major," I told her.

She did not look impressed.

She sighed, folding her arms. "So that means I have to play the part of a Major's wife?"

By nature, she wasn't sociable, and she had never cared for the officers' wives' fraternity. I knew this would be a problem down the line.

However, she was pleased with the substantial pay increase.

The children were overjoyed to see me, their chatter about school a welcome distraction.

Later that night, I went through my routine—creaming and redressing the wounds that still marked my healing body.

Physically, I was improving.

Mentally?

I was drowning.

The nightmares came every night. The same scene, over and over—the Hermitage Bar, the fireball, the unrelenting heat. I would wake drenched in sweat, gasping for air, my heart pounding like I was still there.

I wasn't myself anymore. I avoided everything. The drive, the fire, the unravelling of my marriage—it all consumed me.

And one day, I snapped.

I got in my car and drove deep into the woods.

Tears streamed down my face. I didn't know where I was going.

I only knew I couldn't live like this.

Then, something inside me shifted.

I wiped my eyes.

Got back in the car.

Drove home.

If life was going to throw everything at me, then I would throw it right back.

I wasn't done yet

It was now November 1978. In one month, I would face a meeting with the General Commanding Officer of Headquarters Southern Command, alongside generals from the Ministry of Defence, brigadiers from various commands, the Officer

Commanding Sandhurst Military Academy, the Officer Commanding the Staff College Sandhurst, and other dignitaries. Among them were high-ranking civilians and various majors from companies within the command. In all, some twenty-five senior figures would be present to hear my presentation.

My boss, Mike Mathews, had briefed me beforehand. The General, after reviewing my history and the increasing tensions in various theatres of operation, believed it essential to examine this phenomenon closely. The goal was to assess the growing threats and devise strategies to counteract them, making this presentation a pivotal moment. According to Mike, the government was already on the back foot regarding these emerging threats.

Over the next few weeks, I worked relentlessly—day and night—researching and refining my paper. When I finally finished, I approached my boss for feedback, but to my surprise, he refused.

He simply said, "I'm not qualified to comment on the content. I'll wait for the presentation. The attendees will be asked to fill in a critique regarding the content, its importance, and any relevant comments they wish to make. It wouldn't be in your interest to have my comments beforehand."

I was stunned. It felt like a weight had been dropped onto my shoulders. I left his office thinking, what next?

As I stood before the audience, I could feel their inquisitive eyes scanning me from their seats in the small auditorium at the Staff College Sandhurst. Rows of high-ranking officers, each with gleaming brass badges on their epaulettes, waited for me to begin. This was a room filled with immense power and influence.

Mike had given me a few words of encouragement during the drive. "Just give it to them as you see it."

Easier said than done. Standing behind the small rostrum, I felt exposed. The moment reminded me of Ballykinler when I first addressed my selected soldiers before our deployment to South Armagh. I took a deep breath, cleared the lump in my throat, and decided to present it with measured confidence—slow, expressive, clear. This wasn't just about relaying facts; it was about ensuring they understood the depth of what we were facing.

I began.

"Good morning, gentlemen. I hope this morning I can partake with you some interesting, factual, informative history on a subject that I have studied and been involved in for quite a few years, that subject is "Terrorism and the Terrorist." In the brief period, I am with you this morning, I can but scratch the surface of this very in-depth subject; if you wanted, we could continue for the next week without a break and without repeating anything previously said. So, I hope I am not going to bore you with a very brief overview of the subject. I would ask that if you have any questions regarding anything on the subject, please ask them at the end of this presentation."

A pause. Silence. Their eyes locked onto me.

"What is a terrorist, and what is terrorism? This subject is going to become increasingly important in today's activity within the British Army's role, bearing in mind its role within a civil unrest scenario. You may ask what it has to do with civil unrest. It has a lot to do with it. One could say it is the main cause of action by dissatisfied civilians against our political leaders or governments."

I could see a few nods from the audience.

"The history of the terrorists involves many historical figures and entities. These incidents are associated with what we now call terrorism. Governments and rulers agree that terrorism is a disputed term, and very few of those who are labelled terrorists actually believe they are. It is now common for governments whose opponents are in violent internal conflicts or even international disputes to describe the opposing side as zealots, troublemakers, or rebels. They are practising terrorism.

The act of Terrorism is not a modern-day occurrence; it stems back to Roman times, the first century AD. Sicarii Zealots assassinated collaborators during the Roman occupation of Judea; although called rebels, their actions and methods were, in fact, terrorism.

The French Revolution's Reign of Terror. Brought the word to prominence, as the Jacobin rulers of this revolution used violent methods as well as executions in vast numbers to ensure obedience to their rule. By these actions, the population was cowed to submission by instilled fear.

The terms Anarchism, nationalism, and anti-monarchism are the forewords in understanding the topic. This association was only linked with non-governmental groups. Toward the end of the 19th century, anarchist groups, as well as individuals, when the Russian Tsar and a U.S. president were both assassinated.

Terrorism can also be labelled as an intentional political tactic. "Robespierre", a French Lawyer and anarchist, used this tactic as a part of the agitation of sympathisers, whose resulting actions brought about the fall of the French Royal Families on the 10th of August 1792.

The terms "Terrorism and Terrorists" were also now being used to describe the intimidation and violence by Governments or Rulers. We only need to look at the "Terrorism by police" in recent Russian history and the population's fear of the KGB within its boundaries as well as outside. This has to be described as Oppressive

Military and Civilian Terrorism, a well-used tactic condoned by the governments of those countries.

Terrorism is the use of violence against a sovereign state; this was established in the early 1870s. The Governor of St Petersburg in 1878 was shot dead by Vera Zasulich, whose claim to fame is that she was generally recognised as the first female terrorist; she was a twenty-six-year-old social revolutionary who protested against the Russian state's policies. Her intention was for a social revolution in Russia. The Russian Revolution, until now, had only used non-violent methods to be heard. However, Zasulich's shooting of the Governor opened a new way to communicate political messages: violence.

This action produced worldwide publicity amongst political activists and showed these groups a new way to protest, a totally incredible tool, Terror, or "propaganda by deed." Future assassinations were carried out of European politicians by terrorist groups. By the early 1900s, this tactic, known as "The Russian method", had spread worldwide. This new practice of extreme violence was soon an institution with all the new emerging terrorist groups.

A new group known as "Navodaya Volya" (The People's Will) was a known terrorist organisation. In 1881, assassinated "Tsar Alexander II", with the use of a "dynamite bomb. It is said that "Mark Twain" commented about this attack, "Well, if that is the only way to overthrow the Russian Government, then thank God for dynamite!"

These Russian terrorists,' although struggling against the Russian state, found their tactics were now the accepted way to attack the government."

I glanced at the audience. Many were taking notes. Some sat back in thought, absorbing the weight of what I was saying.

"Following the 1881 assassination of "Tsar Alexander II" it was becoming a great concern that the availability of modern weapons of war and new communication devices were assisting terrorists. These emerging terrorist groups, the founders of today's terrorists, were making it possible to create far more attention to their cause through the use of modern weaponry, such as the newly manufactured rifles, handguns, explosives, and two-way radios; these were easily obtainable through underground arms contacts.

The use of these commercial technologies quickly spread a very worrying political message internationally through media channels that seemed to thrive on newsworthy horror stories. These terror campaigns were transmitted and glorified by mass media companies, giving front-page publicity to these terrorist groups, which, in fact, increased membership amongst sympathisers.

Also, these first examples of this type of violence and the use of terror tactics gave birth to the Modern-day term known now as "Terrorists", and their actions were known as "Terrorism." "

I let the final word linger in the air before pausing.

Then, I looked up at my audience and continued.

"When the terrorists moved with their modern-day tactics against governments and the civilian population of Western Europe and the United States of America, Initially, the governments tried to play down these acts of Terror, describing them as an outrage or assassination. This is despite the fact that these groups used the same terrorist tactics and methods as Russian terrorists. The new terminology was apparently only used to describe anti-colonial actions being experienced in greater numbers throughout the British colonies. Following World War 2, this form of terror emerged and was mainly used against Western governments; now, these acts were labelled as terrorism. This is the genuine starting point for the more widely recognised form of violent political expression that we know today and is described as terrorism.

I will now move on to some of the known modern-era terror groups that have become synonymous with the outrages committed by terrorists, who are now etched into the history of terrorism through their callous, murderous methods, to which all burgeoning terrorist, anarchist, or idealists base their protestations and actions upon.

In 1968, The Red Army Faction (RAF) was a West German left-wing radical group named after its leaders, Andreas Baader and Ulrike Meinhof. It later became known as the Baader-Meinhof group. Born out of the radical student university movement, the Red Army Faction comprised mainly of educated youngsters who saw themselves as soldiers fighting the West German capitalist establishment. They apparently believed that the present government was little more than a reincarnation of the Third Reich. I was at this time serving in Berlin; I participated in the investigations of these student demonstrations together with the German Police. This group's actions first sparked my interest, and thus, my study of the terrorist was subsequently born.

It was in 1967 that the killing by police of a young activist during a demonstration in Berlin against a visit by the Shah of Iran apparently persuaded Andreas Baader that the post-war government was little better than the Nazis they had replaced. The group increased their campaign, and Baader, following the bombing of a Frankfurt store, vowed to mount a violent, bloody campaign against the German government. In 1968, he detonated homemade bombs in two Frankfurt department stores. He was, following a nationwide investigation, arrested and imprisoned. In 1970, during a prison library visit, he escaped with the help of his left-wing campaigning journalist, Ulrike Meinhof.

The Baader-Meinhof group was firmly established within Western Germany by now. In 1970, several members of the group headed off to Jordan, where they were taught how to use the Kalashnikov rifle by the Palestinian Liberation Organisation, who had established a camp solely for the purpose of raising funds for their terrorist actions and to pass on their methods to other terrorist groups. The Bader-Meinhof group then spent the next two years robbing banks, raising money to start their intended bombing campaign.

Around a quarter of young West Germans expressed some sympathy for the group at its height of popularity. Many others condemned their tactics; however, they expressed their disgust with the newly established government due to the fact that they saw former known Nazis enjoying prominent roles. Critics meanwhile denounced them as murderous political thugs - desperate for a cause, however, with no real political goal. It could be argued that the allied powers, who encouraged these ex-high-ranking Nazis, although experienced engineers and industrialists, started the rebuilding of the German government and economy; maybe they were responsible for the subsequent formation of these anti-Nazi groups and the birth of the German terrorist.

This group, as previously mentioned, had its origins among the radical elements of the German university protest movement of the 1960s, which decried the United States as an imperialist power, characterising the West German government as a fascist continuation of the Nazi era. From its early days, they supported themselves through bank robberies and engaging in terrorist bombings and arson, especially of West German corporations and businesses; these attacks also included U.S. military installations in

West Germany. That being said, Baader decided they needed a more immediate strategy to get the authorities to act. Thus, he decided on a more personal approach to his planned atrocities, kidnapping and torture. They decided that kidnapping, torture, and assassination of prominent political and business figures were the mainstay of the future. The goal of this terrorist campaign was to trigger an aggressive response from the government, which they believed would ultimately be the spark for a broader revolutionary movement to emerge. As West German government response tactics became more violent, much of the support it had enjoyed among the political left was lost.

The Baader-Meinhof Terrorist group was firmly established in the public mind. Horst Mahler, a socialist lawyer who is by now a key figure within the German neo-Nazi movement, was at this stage also heavily involved with this fledgling organisation. Baader was captured together with his accomplices Jan-Carl Raspe and Holger Meins in a Frankfurt shooting on 1st June 1972. Baader's girlfriend, Gudrun Ensslin, was arrested a week later, and Ulrike Meinhof was caught, arrested, and imprisoned.

By the mid-1970s, the group had expanded its scope outside West Germany and allied itself with militant Palestinian groups, a move that I fear may have untold future consequences.

In 1976, Ulrike Meinhof hanged herself in her prison cell. Shortly after this, two Baader-Meinhof terrorists, intent on showing the world that Baader-Meinhof was still very much an active force, took part in the Palestinian hijacking of an Air France passenger jet, which ultimately ended after the successful Entebbe raid in Uganda by Israeli commandos.

As a result of Baader-Meinhof allying themselves with the Palestine rebels, this modern terrorist group, the PLO declared, themselves freedom fighters against the oppression of Israel, their intention to use all the Baader-Meinhof terrorist tactics to ensure their successful goals. That is a separate subject on its own for later discussion.

Three months later, the chief executive of the Dresdner Bank, Juergen Ponto, was killed by Baader-Meinhof terrorists at his home in Frankfurt. It was the abduction of Schleyer, head of the German Association of Employers and a former member of the Nazi party, which started a series of events known as the German Autumn. In Cologne, a woman with a pushchair stepped out in front of a car. The driver, who was chauffeuring one of West Germany's most powerful industrialists, "Hans Martin Schleyer," the vehicle was forced to a stop. The woman pulled out two machine guns and opened fire; Schleyer's bodyguards were killed at the scene, and her accomplices, following behind, dragged Hans Martin Schleyer out of the car. Schleyer's captors offered his release in exchange for Baader, Ensslin, and nine others. One month later, after many failed attempts for his release and after various body parts of his, which had been sent to the West German Authorities, his body was found in the boot of a car. Schleyer is but one name on a list of more than thirty industrialists and politicians killed by the Baader-Meinhof during this period.

But even as these negotiations were being conducted, Arab sympathisers of the group were finalising a plan to hijack a plane full of German tourists bound for Frankfurt from Majorca to increase the pressure on the authorities. The aircraft, seized on 13th October, went first to Italy, then Cyprus, Bahrain, and Dubai, before finally landing in Mogadishu. The captain was shot dead by the hijackers, and shortly afterwards, German elite commandos stormed the plane, killed three of the hijackers, and freed the hostages. This successful assault provided a ray of hope for a country where many felt under siege. But it was the final blow for the group's leaders in prison.

News broke on the 18th of October 1977 that Baader, Ensslin, and Raspe had committed suicide. There is still some controversy about how they obtained the weapons they used.

These are a few of the recent actions conducted by the now notorious Baader-Meinhof Terrorist Group:

7 April 1977: Chief public prosecutor killed.

30 July 1977: Head of Dresdner Bank, killed by a motorcycle assassin.

5 Sept 1977: Hans Martin Schleyer abducted.

13 October 1977: Lufthansa Plane hijacked.

Whether there was any tremendous ideological design behind the killings of the 1970s is unclear. Some analysts believe the Baader-Meinhof group had hoped to whip up anger within the left, possibly to spark some form of civil war. Comparisons have been drawn with the crackdown on some civil liberties.

Laws were quickly introduced to limit suspects' rights in order to bolster police powers. While it initially enjoyed some sympathy from the left, the Baader-Meinhof group found itself increasingly isolated as the years went by. However, it did find assistance from communist East Germany, where a number of its members were given refuge. Given all the measures taken by the German authorities, the Baader-Meinhof group continued to grow and spread its influence and terror tactics throughout the world at an alarming rate. It is now accepted that Baader and Meinhof forged the modern-day terrorists and the ideals of terrorism. Their commitment to the cause has echoed throughout terrorist circles and is now ingrained in the philosophy of these various groups. Every action conducted by this terror group has been copied. It has been carried out with remarkable success by other terrorist groups, resulting in their actions becoming a blueprint for many resurgent groups bent on getting their causes heard at any cost.

Let us see where the Baader-Meinhof group went, trained, and encouraged civil unrest within these communities by the use of exceptionally severe action and what we now know of those locations, with a view to any terrorist action the group encouraged in these countries.

Mogadishu, Somalia: Al-Shabaab is the most prominent rebel faction/terrorists; it now rules within Mogadishu, and despite the growing challenges, al-Shabaab still controls large swathes of territory in southern Somalia. It is the most influential in many rural areas and now prioritises guerrilla and terror attacks. It funds itself by mainly kidnapping western hostages and pirate activities on major shipping lanes around the Indian Ocean.

Saudi Arabia: Saudi Arabian Terrorism has been mainly attributed to Islamic extremists. Their targets included foreign civilians, Westerners affiliated with its oil-based economy, as well as Saudi Arabian civilians and security forces. The known terrorist organisations are Al-Ashtar Brigade and Al-Mukhtar Brigade. The United States Department of State reports that terrorist incidents in Saudi Arabia include external attacks by Iranian and Houthi Terrorist groups. The Saudi Arabian rulers refute these claims and state that no terrorist cells operate within Saudi Arabia. It is felt that this belief is used to allay fears about the growing tourist trade emerging within Saudi Arabia.

Iran: leaders of Iran regard the "Shia Muslims" as heretics; they have attacked their mosques and gatherings with terrorist-type tactics. It considers Shia civilians to be legitimate targets. Iran has been designated a terrorist safe haven and has been classed as hostile by many other countries. The government of the Islamic Republic of Iran has been accused of training, financing, and providing weapons and safe havens for non-state militant terrorist factions, such as Hezbollah in Lebanon, Hamas in Gaza, and other Palestinian groups, such as the Palestinian Islamic Jihad (PIJ) and the Popular Front for the Liberation of Palestine. These groups are designated terrorist groups by a number of countries and international bodies; however, Iran considers such groups to be "national liberation movements" with a right to self-defence against oppressive governments.

Greece: Formed in 1975, the 17th of November group is a far-left paramilitary terrorist faction known for its attacks on Greek government buildings. It is a Greek far-left Marxist–Leninist urban guerrilla organisation led by Alexandros Giotopoulos. Both the Greek government and the media widely describe it as a terrorist organisation.

Jordan: The Salafist-jihadist movement is, according to its history, related to terrorists who have visited the Gaza Strip, where they were trained in making explosives. Who later returned to Jordan and recruited other sympathisers to plot attacks "with bombs against buses and trains, they introduced the now infamous explosive vests, for use in populated patrolled areas." Tel Aviv and Amman have been embroiled in political tension as Israel revealed its plans to annex the occupied West Bank and the Jordan Valley, which has instigated extremist activity against Israeli targets. Jordan is known to be sympathetic and accommodating to Iran-backed Houthi rebels, the Palestine Liberation Organisation, and the Hezbollah group. Jordanian authorities have a state security court, better known as a military tribunal, that typically deals with terrorism-related cases. To date, no Salafist-jihadist has been charged with any offence.

Syria: The Muslim Brotherhood, known as a front for the Arab Socialist Baath party, has had a "long campaign of terror." The government blamed it for the terror activities. However, the insurgents used names such as Kataib Muhammad (The Hand of Muhammad) to refer to their organisation, which began in Hama in 1965 but has now moved to more extreme modern terrorist activities.

Gaza: The terrorist group Hamas is at the epicentre of this conflict. It is the dominant force in Gaza, notorious for its extensive rocket arsenal and lethal assaults. Labelled a terrorist organisation by Israel, the U.S., and several European countries, it is supported by the Palestinian Islamic Jihad and the Popular Front for the Liberation of Palestine.

Lebanon: Terrorist organisations operating in Lebanon include the radical Shiite militia Hezbollah, several Palestinian groups, Hamas, Palestinian Islamic Jihad, the Popular Front for the Liberation of Palestine, and the Popular Front for the Liberation of Palestine "General Command" as well as the Abu Nidal Organisation, al-Jihad, Asbat al-Ansar, the Japanese Red Army, and some local radical Sunni Muslim organisations.

Ireland: Throughout Northern Ireland's present troubles, a number of loyalist Protestant paramilitary groups have been born and are active, being responsible for hundreds of murders. Loyalist paramilitary groups in Northern Ireland have 12,500 members. These groups are, in fact, terrorists and commit extreme acts of terrorism. Many of the paramilitaries are now involved in criminality and drug dealing, with tensions between and within groups resulting in serious disorder at times, as well as shootings, bombings, and sectarian attacks. The largest loyalist terrorist groups throughout the present troubles are the Ulster Defence Association and the Ulster Volunteer Force; they remain the most prominent active group. The Ulster Volunteer Force has murdered more than two hundred people in the province to date. It was formed in 1966. It has adopted the names and symbols of the original UVF; the movement was founded in 1912 by Sir Edward Carson to fight against Irish home rule. The UVF shot dead, the first police officer to be murdered during the present-day troubles. The organisation has since been involved in various atrocities, including the bombing of McGurk's Bar in Belfast in 1971 and the sectarian killings of the Shankill Butchers (a group of known assassins), who are still active today. The Red Hand Commando is affiliated with the UVF and is considered the most secretive of the loyalist paramilitary organisations. It emerged in the early 1970s and, according to recent records, has killed thirteen people, including twelve civilians, although the number could be much higher.

The IRA (Irish Republican Army) is a Catholic paramilitary organisation whose structure, tactics, training, subculture, and function are similar to those of a professional military force. They are a fully-fledged terrorist organisation operating in Northern Ireland, whose sole objective is to create a united Ireland and to rid Northern Ireland of British rule within the province by any means. They also want to rid Ireland of all protestants by any means. This, as you know, is being achieved by the use of force, i.e. terrorist activities and creating civil unrest. Paramilitary units perform duties that a country's military or police forces are unable or unwilling to do. That being said, the IRA has no remit from the Republic of Ireland to conduct any actions in the North whatsoever, according to the Irish government. However, sympathy for the cause is well supported in the South.

Lastly Black September:

The group's name is derived from the Black September conflict, which began on 16 September 1970, when King Hussein of Jordan declared military rule in response to “Fedayeen” attempting to seize his kingdom – resulting in the deaths and expulsion of thousands of

Palestinian fighters from Jordan. The BSO began as a small cell of Fatah men determined to take revenge upon King Hussein and the Jordanian Armed Forces. Recruits from the PFLP, As-Sa'iqa, and other groups also joined.

The group was responsible for the 1972 Munich massacre in which eleven Israeli Olympic athletes were murdered, nine of whom were first taken hostage, and the killing of a German police officer. Following this attack, the Israeli government, headed by Prime Minister Golda Meir, launched an assassination campaign, ordering Mossad to assassinate those known to have been involved in the massacre. To date, at least one Mossad unit has assassinated eight Black September and PLO members, including Ali Hassan Salameh, nicknamed the "Red Prince", a wealthy, flamboyant son of an upper-class family, and commander of Force 17, Yasser Arafat's personal security squad. Salameh was also behind the 1972 hijacking of Sabena Flight 572 from Vienna to Lod. He was recently killed by a car bomb in Beirut. During a raid in Lebanon in April 1973, Israeli commandos killed three senior members of Black September in Beirut. In July 1973, in what became known as the Lillehammer affair, Ahmed Bouchiki, an innocent Moroccan waiter who was mistaken for Ali Hassan Salameh, was killed in Norway. Six Israeli operatives were arrested for the murder.

There are far too many countries to list; it goes on and on, for instance, Yemen, South America, The African states, and North America. Many of these countries, and I have not mentioned all of them, have come to follow the diktats of the Baader-Meinhof's group policies. I can see you will be asking, "What can we do"? It is not up to me to say all I can do is express my views based on the experiences and studies that I have been involved in, i.e., those that have to do with terrorism. I feel terrorism should be looked at by governments and by the military high command with a completely new and different approach. If we do not, we will not be prepared for what is to evolve from these "Terrorist Pioneering Groups." In the UK alone, some recent terrorist events of note are The Guildford Pub Bombings in October 1974, where 5 were killed. Birmingham, November 1974. 21 Killed, and 182 injured. Woolwich pub bomb 1974. 2 killed, 35 injured. Nearer to home, The Officers Mess of 16 Para Brigade in February 1972, at Aldershot.

Be very aware that more groups will come to the fore in the future, and their tactics will be similar to their predecessors. However, I feel the methods will be far more visual and the personal atrocities far more pictorial. There will be "High jackings, kidnappings, and assassinations. Beheadings will be the usual way to exact their demands. We must look at our role in a scenario of civil disobedience. What are our capabilities to protect the country and government against these burgeoning threats, including the rise of various infiltrating religious faith followings? We must look at permitted marches and demonstrations, which are also increasingly turning violent. This is mainly caused by agitators and known sympathisers of illegal organisations; this is just a start. We must look at strikes and the agitators. We must look at civil liberties and restrictions placed against them. Would any new laws encourage dissent among the civil population, and would these restrictions turn the government and our security personnel toward a police state? This all has to be looked at, studied, formulated into plans, and acted upon. Perhaps I am going too far; it is up to the specialists within the fields of security and government to decide what to do.

That said, I do feel that many in this audience should take heed of what they have heard and look towards the present national and international state of government. Also, the protests could lead to civil unrest, anarchy, and internal conflict, which will ultimately involve the use of military force. Perhaps International military conflict will quell these factions. All that has been highlighted in this presentation is purely for your information and hopefully will pre-arm you for what I feel is to come from the now hard-line burgeoning terrorist organisations and new radical movements emerging throughout the Arabian states. If terrorist history is anything by which to measure the future, in that case, I fear atrocities involving unthinkable numbers of deaths, executions, high jackings, and casualties, as well as incredible property destruction. It is only a forethought of things to come.

Thank you for your attention, gentlemen."

As I scanned the room, I saw the weight of my words settle upon my audience. Concerned expressions replaced the initial air of curiosity. Over the next two hours, in the mess hall, I fielded numerous questions. Many attendees were deeply troubled by the implications of my lecture. I sensed that for some, difficult decisions about counterterrorism strategies would soon have to be made.

CHAPTER FOURTEEN
CONTINUANCE

It had been three weeks since I had given my lecture at the staff college, yet there had been no feedback—no word, no response, just silence. I had kept myself busy with mundane tasks, but pushing paper could only keep me occupied for so long. Then, one morning, one of my assistants stepped into my office and said, "The Brigadier would like to see you in an hour if that was convenient."

I nodded, keeping my expression neutral. "That's not a problem. Inform the Brigadier's staff assistant that I will be with him shortly."

I walked to Richard's office, my footsteps steady despite the unease settling in my gut. I knocked firmly on the door, determined to appear calm and collected. This meeting, I knew, was about my lecture and its aftermath. I was apprehensive, to say the least.

Richard's clerk opened the door and gestured for me to go straight in. "He's expecting you."

Inside, we exchanged pleasantries before heading into the Brigadier's adjoining office.

Mike Mathews was one of the finest officers I had ever served under—a man both respected and, at times, feared. His knowledge of military strategy, both in combat and within civilian scenarios, was second to none. He beckoned me to sit—not in front of his desk like a reprimanded schoolboy, but in one of the large armchairs by the bay window, which overlooked the manicured lawns outside.

He began with a measured tone. “I’m pleased with the way you’ve taken on your new role and the efficiency at which it’s running now.”

Then, he got to the point, “I have asked you here, as I have had a long discussion with the General, about the content of your lecture recently given to officers at the Staff College. Both he and I, although impressed with how it came over, are most concerned about the content and the future implications regarding civil unrest. The implication of further, more intense, terrorist activities throughout the world, and what the repercussions for UK governments could be.”

I sat still, listening intently.

“To this end, after studying the attending officer's comments, which may I say are glowing, we ask that you continue your research into this subject whilst also taking up the position at the staff college as our permanent Instructor on “Civil Unrest within the community.” At the same time, we would ask that you compile a dossier, which will be forwarded to the MOD for onward transmission to various political Ministers within the government. “

He paused briefly before continuing, his tone firm. “We realise this is a big ask of you, but your lecture has highlighted areas of extreme importance that have not been given the credence that they deserve. They should be acted upon, and future plans must be made in the event of civil unrest coming to the fore. We find that both we, the Army, and the government are put into a position where we are found to be sorely unprepared.

Well, what do you say after that?”

I knew what was coming next.

In the military, phrases like "we would ask that" or "we were thinking perhaps" were never requests. They were orders wrapped in the illusion of choice. Declining wasn't an option—unless, of course, you wanted your career to come to a grinding halt.

So, I answered exactly as expected. "Yes, Sir."

With that, my future was set in stone.

The next six months were relentless. Between lectures at the Staff College, hospital visits, operations to release scarring, physiotherapy sessions, and the increasing strain of home life, I barely had time to think. Physically, I could match most other soldiers—though my skin remained fragile. I was assured that, with time, it would toughen.

The mental side, however, was a different story. The flashbacks still came. The nightmares persisted. But I forced myself to carry on, refusing to let them interfere with my duties.

Finally, I completed the dossier—a weighty document spanning fifty internal folios. Every avenue of research had been explored, and every piece of information was meticulously sourced. It was, without doubt, the most comprehensive analysis I had ever compiled.

I handed it to the Brigadier, marking it Highly Confidential. He flipped through it briefly, then looked at me.

"This looks like a very comprehensive document and will take some time to digest. You must have worked endlessly on it; I will definitely give it the attention it deserves. Thank you in advance for your efforts."

I nodded. "Thank you, Sir."

I left his office and returned to mine, relieved it was finally out of my hands.

Months passed with little consequence—mundane, even boring. Then, in early May 1979, everything changed.

I had recently undergone my annual medical examination, a routine requirement for all soldiers. The medical officer delivered the verdict bluntly: he never believed I would regain my full operational medical grade due to my injuries and the condition of my skin.

It was disappointing—but not surprising. Deep down, I had never truly expected a different outcome.

Shortly after, I was summoned to the Brigadier's office. Something about his tone unsettled me. It had been some time since he last called me in, and I assumed it was to discuss parts of the dossier. I had included recent events—such as the assassination of Conservative Minister Airey Neave in a car bombing at Westminster in March 1979. Perhaps he thought it too raw to be included.

But as soon as I walked into his office, I knew this meeting wasn't about the dossier.

The Brigadier looked uneasy, which immediately put me on edge. He hesitated before speaking.

"David, I have been discussing your history with both the general and the medical officers conducting your recovery programme. They are quite pleased with the way it has been going."

He paused. I could sense the weight of what was coming next.

"However," he continued, "the medics have categorically said they feel certain you will not attain acceptable medical grading, which is a requirement for you to continue service with the army."

I stiffened.

"The reason, they say, is that the next war or military campaign the army will be involved in most certainly will involve the use of chemical warfare products. They feel that in that scenario, your injuries and skin grafts would not hold up to these chemicals, and you would be unable to fulfil your duties as an Officer."

His words hung in the air, heavy and final.

"The General and I have to agree with this assessment and feel that you should look to your future life outside of the military. To this end, bearing in mind the outstanding service you have given over many years and the circumstances that have brought about this turn of events, we must assist you in every way we possibly can. Firstly, the medics are confident they can present a case to the medical board for a medical disablement discharge, which would grant you a disablement pension and open the pathway to other tax-free war disability payments. Secondly, you are still technically on a twenty-two-year contract with the army, as you were commissioned from the ranks. This will hold you in good stead to secure a mortgage, which I suggest you arrange without delay. Finally, we will ensure you receive the best follow-up treatment within the military medical sector for as long as you require, as well as future assistance with employment opportunities. We have agreed that you would be offered a civilian position at the Staff College on a casual contract, allowing you to continue lecturing on terrorist matters within a civil environment.

The alternative is that you remain in the army, retaining your present rank with no further promotion. You would be restricted to UK postings, unable to serve abroad, or participate in active service or wartime operations. You would, of course, complete your current contract and receive a pension at the end, though it would be taxable. You have less than a year to decide which path to take; however, I will need your decision within the week. Perhaps you should discuss this with your family and come back to me shortly."

I cannot say I was surprised by this conversation—it had only been a matter of time before I would have to make this decision. I went home to discuss it with my wife, who was unsurprised. She had wanted me to leave the army years ago, never truly enjoying the military lifestyle. I viewed the decision from both a practical and financial perspective. I was still relatively young—one could say in the prime of my life—and yes, I could start over. It was not worth discussing with my children; they were too young to grasp the full implications. Instead, I ran some financial calculations, weighing what I would need to establish myself in civilian life against the assets I had to support this transition.

Three days had passed since receiving the news from the medics, and it was time to give the Brigadier my decision. I rang his staff assistant to request a meeting. Within ten minutes, my phone rang—the Brigadier asked me to come up and see him.

As I entered his office, he gestured for me to sit. A coffee pot and two cups sat on the table. He poured me a cup before speaking.

"How did the discussion with your wife go?"

I replied, "It was not so much a discussion but an acceptance of the inevitable cessation of my time in the forces, bearing in mind what had happened. It was not really a surprise to her; we both agreed that we must accept what had happened and move on."

He nodded thoughtfully. "That is a most admirable way of approaching the situation."

He then assured me that he would begin the process of arranging my medical board and oversee the necessary documentation with the chief clerk, whom he suggested I liaise with regarding the general arrangements.

"You can take as much time off as needed, duties permitting," he added. "I imagine you will need it, considering house hunting as well as job hunting."

I left his office and went home to reflect on what had just happened. I had just said goodbye to my career.

CHAPTER FIFTEEN
STANDING ALONE

I had never truly grasped what life in the army entailed—what it provided and, just as importantly, what it took away—until I found myself preparing to leave it. In many ways, being a soldier meant living under an all-encompassing shield. Every aspect of daily life was taken care of: food, clothing, accommodation, even transport. There was never a need to worry about financial security or the logistical burdens of everyday living. The army fostered a sense of certainty, of belonging, of knowing exactly where you stood.

Then, suddenly, that security was gone. The moment you stepped out, you became entirely responsible for yourself and your family, with no institutional safety net. The mental strain of that realisation was immense. When the choice to leave isn't yours—when fate, rather than personal ambition, dictates your transition—it is an even greater burden. There was no choice but to face it head-on.

I quickly found a house and moved out of married quarters, settling into my new home. Though sparsely furnished at first, we soon made it liveable. Securing a mortgage posed no issue, and thankfully, my daughters remained in the same school, avoiding further disruption. My medical board had gone as expected, my attending officer assuring me there would be no complications with the Ministry of Defence's final approval. It was now just a matter of time.

To prepare for civilian life, I took a three-week resettlement course on corporate management strategies—an area where my leadership skills could be put to good use. I spent my days drafting letters, refining my CV, and reaching out to companies that might benefit from my experience. Then, out of the blue, the Brigadier summoned me to his office.

That meeting would stay with me forever. It was unlike any military discussion I had ever had. The usual formality was absent, replaced by an almost casual atmosphere as if we had just come off the golf course discussing the day's game. It put me slightly off balance.

He asked how my job search was going, mentioning that the chief clerk had informed him of my imminent departure. My official discharge was set for the 1st of February 1980, but with accumulated leave and medical recovery time, I was effectively free from duty by the 1st of October 1979. He inquired about my new home and whether I had secured employment yet.

I joked about learning to mow the lawn—one of many small adjustments to civilian life. As for work, I admitted the search had been slow so far.

Then came the offer.

"I have been discussing you and your history with an old friend of mine; he is an ex-Danish resistance leader from the last war who is the present consultant with a German engineering firm. They are, in fact, looking to expand into the UK. They want to set up a showroom, operating from prestigious offices in the centre of Mayfair in London. He is looking for a British Gent of standing, preferably an ex-military person, to take on and administer the operation and establish an import exports depot and warehouse in London Heathrow to oversee a UK distributorship."

He continued, “The intended export market will be all the old British Commonwealth countries, including places like Hong Kong, Singapore, and the Philippines; they feel that the British approach will produce far better results than the German one, if you understand. You would have carte blanche with a budget of some three million pounds; it would also involve a lot of national and international travel."

Then he asked the question that would change everything.

"Is this something you might be interested in?"

There was only one answer.

"Of course I am," I replied.

The Brigadier nodded, satisfied. "I'll contact Joren and tell him you'll call to arrange a meeting if that's agreeable to you."

We chatted for a while longer. He assured me that he wished to stay in touch and that I would always be welcome at regimental dinners and functions. I thanked him for the introduction, deeply appreciative of the opportunity. Leaving his office, my mind was racing—was I truly ready for this? Would I live up to expectations? Only time will tell.

Joren Egeberg was the kind of man who put you at ease instantly, the kind of person you could discuss anything with. Over the phone, we spoke about my background and the German engineering firm he represented. He invited me to lunch at a top London hotel, where we could go into more detail.

That meeting stretched into four hours. Joren explained how difficult it had been to find the right person for the role—most candidates lacked either the experience or the ability to speak German. That, at least, worked in my favour. My first year of married life had been spent living with a German family, and I had become fluent in the language.

He outlined the company's vast scope—electronic components for the mining industry, aircraft-engineered parts, switchgear, and electro-turbines. Many projects involved bespoke development, meaning an architectural design department would be necessary.

Then, we toured the company's newly acquired offices in Hay Hill, just off Berkeley Square—a five-story building with a large basement. Joren envisioned an elite workspace: a staff restaurant, an overnight apartment for management, a sales office in the basement, and a state-of-the-art showroom and hospitality suite on the ground floor. The first floor would house executive offices, including those for himself, the Managing Director, and me. The remaining floors would accommodate sales teams, conference rooms, and boardrooms.

It was, quite literally, a blank canvas.

"We will mould this into a thriving headquarters," Joren said. "It must exude luxury—no expense spared. This company must be seen as first-class in every way."

Back at his hotel, he laid out the terms. The salary package was substantial, complete with a fully funded pension, an expense account, and a prestigious company car—essential for entertaining clients.

"This is not a job for the faint-hearted," he said. "But if you're happy with what you've seen and heard, the position is yours."

I accepted.

With a month of leave remaining, we spent that time finalising my contract, selecting a car, and handling logistics. And just like that,

I became the UK Development Administration Manager for a major German engineering firm.

The next stage of my life had begun.

I won't bore you with the finer details of my time in London, but suffice it to say, the experience was invaluable. I successfully established the showroom, recruited and trained staff, and secured an outstanding female manager to oversee daily operations. It was one of my better decisions—she was both elegant and ruthlessly efficient, which freed me to focus on setting up the warehouse and distribution network.

It was hard work—long hours, relentless challenges—but I thrived on it. The role sharpened my corporate management skills and honed abilities that no classroom could ever teach. More than anything, it reinforced a crucial lesson: psychology is one of the most powerful tools in business, and when used correctly, it can open doors that would otherwise remain locked.

Over the next two years, the company became fully established in the UK, earning a solid reputation as a respected exporter to far-off markets. My newfound interpersonal skills proved invaluable as I travelled extensively with sales managers, entertaining prospective distributors and securing new business opportunities. However, this constant travel took an additional toll on my marriage. It became painfully clear that the only thing holding us together was the money I was bringing in. My wife was certainly enjoying the high life, and, unfortunately, I was the one funding it.

On numerous occasions, I tried to reason with her, stressing the need to save rather than spend. But my words fell on deaf ears. Each time I broached the subject, her reaction made it clear she had no intention of changing her ways. Eventually, I realised my best move was a tactical retreat—maintaining the status quo rather than igniting further conflict.

Despite the growing tensions at home, I found certain aspects of my job in Mayfair thoroughly enjoyable, particularly the more refined side of business—entertaining high-level clients. My role required me to escort prospective distributors and important figures, usually at the director level, to some of London's most prestigious venues. I soon became well acquainted with the city's finest establishments: Ronnie Scott's Jazz Club, The Ritz Restaurant & Casino, and Claridge's, to name but a few. Many of my clients, being foreign executives, struggled with the language, and I often found myself accompanying them on their insatiable quest to experience the best that London had to offer.

It was during one of these visits while dining at the Ritz Hotel—arguably the most prestigious eatery in Mayfair—that I was approached by the Maître d'. With an air of quiet sophistication, he arrived at the table carrying a silver platter, upon which lay a folded note.

"Sir," he said, excusing his interruption, "this is from a gentleman who was dining here but had to leave unexpectedly."

I took the note and unfolded it.

"Hello, David. I thought it was you; how are you? Long-time no see. Call me. Nick Page."

A London telephone number was written below.

I thanked the Maître-d' and slipped the note into my pocket, returning to my lunch with my Japanese clients. Later that afternoon, after seeing them off at Heathrow for their return flight, I headed back to my office for a well-earned break.

As I sat at my desk, my secretary brought in a fresh coffee and a few messages, none of any real significance. Reaching into my jacket pocket, I retrieved the note from Nick.

We had first met years ago during a close protection course, where we had quickly struck up a strong friendship. Over the years, we had stayed in contact throughout our military careers, but after I left Germany, we lost touch.

I picked up the phone and dialled the number.

After a few rings, a pleasant voice answered.

"Bordergreen International, Mandy speaking. How may I help you?"

I introduced myself and explained the note I had received.

She responded warmly. "Nick mentioned you might call. He asked me to take your number so he could get back to you—he'd love to meet up."

I left my details and waited for his call. When we finally spoke, our conversation was easy, as if no time had passed. We arranged to meet for lunch the following afternoon at the Officers' In & Out Club in Piccadilly.

The next day, I strolled along Piccadilly, enjoying the rare warmth of the afternoon sun. Green Park was alive with office workers escaping their desks, basking in the brief respite of their lunch break.

Arriving at the In & Out, I was ushered to the reception desk, where I signed in. Luckily, I had kept my membership—it was the perfect place to meet like-minded individuals who appreciated a certain level of refinement. The club exuded an air of timeless tradition, its oak-panelled walls adorned with military history, the lounges and bars filled with deep leather chairs and polished mahogany. It was the epitome of an ex-officer's gentleman's club, offering fine dining, accommodation, and an unspoken camaraderie among its members.

As I entered the lounge, I spotted Nick seated in a corner booth. He waved me over, and within moments, we were deep in conversation, catching up on everything that had transpired since we had last seen each other.

For three hours, we spoke about our lives—my time in Ireland, the explosion, my recovery, and how my career had unfolded since leaving the army. He had heard about my injuries and how I had made a name for myself at the Staff College with my knowledge of terrorism.

We decided to continue our reunion over dinner. I had no objections—after all, I had the use of the apartment at my office.

Nick laughed. "I live in Devon, but I stay at the office during the week and only head home at weekends."

Before dinner, he needed to drop off some paperwork at his office in Chiswick and invited me along. I agreed, and we spent the rest of the evening enjoying good food, good conversation, and the easy companionship that only old comrades share.

It's strange how the years melt away when you reconnect with someone who truly understands you.

Over the next couple of months, Nick and I met regularly, rekindling our friendship over fine meals and long conversations.

Meanwhile, at work, I had growing concerns.

The head office in Germany was overjoyed with the UK operation—far exceeding their initial expectations. However, this success seemed to bring unintended consequences. They began sending over German specialists—engineers and designers—to assist with critical projects. While this was initially understandable, it became troubling when they started replacing key staff members I had personally hired. These were individuals who had played a vital role in developing the company's strong reputation in the UK.

I expressed my concerns to Joren Egeberg, who had just returned from a visit to Germany. His response left me stunned.

"They've offered me a golden handshake to resign," he admitted. "A very generous one. I'm being replaced by a German national."

I couldn't believe it.

Joren sighed. "I suspect most of the staff will eventually be replaced by Germans. They've already assigned a German understudy to assist you with the more complex engineering aspects of your job."

The writing was on the wall.

CHAPTER SIXTEEN
WIND OF CHANGE

A few weeks later, Nick phoned my office. His tone was calm and measured, but I sensed an underlying urgency. He wanted to meet that evening, saying he needed to discuss something he couldn't talk about over the phone. That alone piqued my interest. Conversations with Nick were never trivial, and if he was insisting on a face-to-face meeting, I knew it had to be something important.

He was staying at the Dorchester Hotel on Park Lane, a place of polished luxury and quiet discretion. He was on a job with a client for a few weeks and had to remain close to his principal. I glanced at the clock and considered my schedule. There was no question of declining. I phoned home, telling my wife I might have to stay overnight due to the meeting. She was surprisingly unbothered, even pleased, saying she'd take the opportunity for an early night. With that sorted, I put the phone down, informed my secretary I was leaving early, and made my way out.

The walk down Piccadilly was brisk, the familiar hum of London life surrounding me. The traffic rolled past, headlights cutting through the early evening haze. Park Lane, with its grand hotels and sweeping views of Hyde Park, had an air of wealth and exclusivity. I stepped into the Dorchester hotel, greeted by the soft glow of chandeliers and the quiet efficiency of staff who had long mastered the art of making guests feel important.

At reception, I asked them to inform Nick of my arrival. The "Maître-d'" gave me a courteous nod and gestured towards the reception lounge. "Please take a seat, sir. Mr. Nick will be down shortly."

I settled into one of the plush armchairs, the scent of expensive polish and fresh flowers lingering in the air. On the coffee table in front of me, a bowl of sugar-coated almonds sat invitingly. It was a small detail but one I'd come to associate with the Dorchester—an odd little indulgence in a world where luxury was expected, not questioned.

Ten minutes later, Nick appeared, striding towards me with the relaxed confidence he always carried. We exchanged greetings before making our way upstairs to his suite.

Once inside, we settled into a comfortable rhythm, chatting about various subjects—nothing significant at first, just the usual back-and-forth of two men who had known each other long enough to skip the formalities. Then, after a while, he steered the conversation towards work.

"How's it going?" he asked casually, but there was something in his tone that suggested he already knew the answer.

I exhaled, leaning back slightly. "It's OK, Nick," I said, though even as I spoke the words, I knew they weren't entirely true. "I don't like working for this German company. They're bringing more of their own people into the UK, which is leaving a bad taste, especially after all the work I've put in."

Nick nodded as if he'd expected that answer. "That's actually quite fortunate," he said. "I've been discussing you with my co-directors."

I raised an eyebrow, waiting for him to continue.

"They're all ex-military or from diplomatic protection," he explained. "And they think you could be an asset to the company."

I watched him carefully, processing his words.

He leaned forward, his expression serious. "Look, considering your security background, your knowledge of terrorism, and your experience, you're more than just another guy with corporate management skills. You've got leadership ability, confidence in public speaking, and, most importantly, the capability to run a crew on the ground if needed. The thing is, we're overstretched. We need someone who can handle corporate sales, manage high-level negotiations, and build strong client relationships."

He let that sink in for a moment before adding, "I want you to attend an informal meeting before the next board meeting. You'll meet everyone, get a feel for things, and we can discuss the ins and outs of the proposal."

Then he paused, his gaze steady. "Would you be interested?"

I hesitated. Not because I wasn't tempted—because I was. But this was a significant shift, and I wasn't the type to leap without looking.

I took a moment, weighing my options. "I'd like some time to think it over," I said finally.

Nick nodded, unfazed. "Of course. Take your time."

The following morning, fate seemed to have made its decision for me.

Joren Egeberg called me into his office, his expression unreadable. "We've both been called to Germany for an important meeting," he informed me.

By the next morning, we were en route to Munich. The flight was uneventful, but there was an unspoken tension in the air. We landed around ten o'clock, met by a company chauffeur who drove us straight to headquarters. Joren, ever the composed professional, led the way with an ease that suggested familiarity.

As we stepped into the chairman's office, the atmosphere shifted.

Herr Kris Hertzman sat behind an imposing desk, his gold-rimmed spectacles perched on the bridge of his nose. I had never met him in person, though I'd spoken to him over the phone several times. He greeted us with the kind of forced politeness that barely concealed his true feelings.

Joren leaned slightly towards me and muttered under his breath, "It's all show. We now enter the tiger's lair."

I could see it clearly—the words "nice to see you" stuck in Hertzman's throat. He didn't like Joren. He didn't like me. He was a relic of old Germany, a man who resented the shadow of defeat that lingered over his nation.

Without much preamble, he got straight to business.

He praised the UK division's profitability and expressed his satisfaction with the investment. But then came the real purpose of the meeting. The company was expanding, and the next phase required expertise in engineering and design—areas in which neither Joren nor I were qualified.

And so, it had been decided. We were both being let go.

Just like that.

There were no theatrics, no drawn-out justifications. It was cold clinical. He thanked us for our contributions and then addressed Joren directly. "I presume the settlement package we discussed is agreed?"

Joren gave a curt nod.

Hertzman then turned to me. "You will receive three months' gross salary, an end-of-service bonus, and as a gesture of goodwill, you may keep your company car. Replacement personnel will be arriving in London next week. You may leave at your convenience."

I gritted my teeth, every instinct telling me to leap over that desk and throttle the man. But before I could act on impulse, I felt Joren's hand on my sleeve, a subtle but firm warning.

Hertzman, oblivious to my seething anger, continued. "I assume you will want to return to London as soon as possible. My car will take you to the airport."

There was nothing left to say.

We left the office, escorted out as though we had never belonged there in the first place.

The flight to London was tense, the air between Joren and me thick with frustration. Neither of us spoke much at first, both lost in our own thoughts, but there was no mistaking the mutual disgust we felt at how we had been discarded. The sheer arrogance of it all—being summoned like schoolboys to Germany only to be dismissed in a matter of minutes. A business decision, they had called it as if the years we had dedicated to building the UK branch from the ground up had been nothing more than a footnote in their grand expansion plans.

But as the hours passed, our anger settled into something else—something closer to grim acceptance.

We might have been unceremoniously cast aside, but at least we could leave with our heads held high. No one could say we had not put in the effort. The results spoke for themselves. We had taken that company and made it a success in the UK, and though we were leaving under circumstances beyond our control, it was a chapter we could still look back on with pride.

A week later, after tying up loose ends, I walked out of the UK company offices for the last time. I didn't look back. Instead, I climbed into my car—my so-called "gesture of goodwill"—and drove home, a vow forming in my mind as I pulled away from the building.

I would never work for a German company again.

Joren returned to Denmark, and before long, we lost touch. That was the way of things. In this line of work, people came and went, paths crossing for a time before diverging once more.

And perhaps, just perhaps, Nick's proposal had come at exactly the right time.

At home, my wife was unsurprised when I told her everything—the way things had unfolded, my final departure, and the fact that Nick had offered me a job. I had already spoken to her about my feelings, my dissatisfaction with my career in London, and my growing concerns about my future.

Now, with my resignation official, I told her I planned to take a few weeks off. Some time to clear my head. Some time to just be with her and the kids.

But in the back of my mind, I knew my next move was already in motion.

It came as no surprise to Nick when I rang him, asking if we could meet for lunch to go over his proposal in more detail. We arranged to meet at Browns Hotel in Dover Street. The setting was understated but elegant, the kind of place where serious discussions took place over quiet, civilised meals.

After lunch, Nick wasted no time outlining exactly what my role would entail.

He was eager for me to meet the other two directors, as well as a few key members of the staff. He wanted me to get a feel for the company, for the men I would be working alongside, and for the scale of the operation.

That same afternoon, I was introduced to the core team.

Chic Downing, an ex-military close protection specialist, ran the daily operations on the ground. He was the kind of man you wanted watching your back—experienced, sharp, and unflappable.

Tony Francis, a former staff officer from the 22 SAS regiment, handled administration and payments. The kind of man who ensured everything ran smoothly, from logistics to finance.

Alan Pardoe, an ex-MI6 intelligence officer, brought a different kind of expertise to the table. He was the man with the connections, the one who knew how to navigate the murky world of international intelligence and security.

Then, there was Brian Fellows. I had known Brian from my early days with the regiment, and it was good to see a familiar face. He was in charge of the "Celebrity" section—high-profile clients, some of whom were household names.

Looking through the list of personnel, I felt a strange sense of familiarity. It was like stepping into a home away from home.

These were my kind of people. Men with a shared background and a shared understanding of what it meant to operate in high-stakes environments. And they were just as eager to have me on board, seeing me as someone who could help push the company towards a more corporate, structured future.

The only thing left to discuss was my salary package and start date.

Strangely, I accepted a lesser package than what I had been earning at my previous job. But with a bonus structure tied to client turnover and revenue, as well as a solid pension plan, it was a fair deal. More than that, I knew I could increase the company's turnover. And unlike my last job, I was stepping into an environment where I belonged, surrounded by people I could trust with my life.

I had only one request—that I be allowed to continue giving occasional lectures at the staff college, as I had done every four to six months since leaving the Army. Nick saw no issue with that, provided it didn't interfere with my company responsibilities.

And so, in August 1982, I joined Bordergreen.

I have never looked back. Not once.

The first few weeks in my new role were spent settling into my office, familiarising myself with ongoing operations, and visiting the London hotels where our teams were stationed. I made a point of meeting the men on the ground, listening to their feedback, and assessing how things ran on a practical level.

Our primary clients were members of various Arab royal families. These were powerful, wealthy individuals who required the highest level of discretion and professionalism. I had to tread carefully, ensuring I was always respectful and aware of cultural sensitivities.

Part of my role involved gauging client satisfaction—understanding how they felt about the security provided and whether any improvements could be made.

What I hadn't anticipated was how interested they would be in my background.

They were keen to hear about my history, my experience in counterterrorism, and my analysis of emerging threats. These discussions, casual at first, became a crucial part of my role. Unbeknown to me, these visits were cementing my reputation.

Before long, my name became well-known among Arab circles. I was seen as someone who could be trusted to protect their interests and ensure they had the best security coverage possible during their time in the West.

It was Alan Pardoe who took me to Scotland Yard, introducing me to the diplomatic protection group and key figures in charge. These connections proved invaluable.

Since the clients we provided security for were neither British Royalty nor Government Ministers, they were outside the jurisdiction of state-provided security. However, many were high-profile industrialists—Americans, Japanese, and South Americans—whose insurance policies required them to travel with close protection specialists trained in anti-kidnap procedures.

Word spread quickly among high-level insurance companies. Before long, many of them began recommending our services to their clients.

By February 1983, it was clear my efforts were making an impact.

Nick came into my office one afternoon with a broad grin. "I think I owe you a slap-up meal," he said. "You're heading for a big end-of-year bonus. Tony's been going through the accounts, and since you joined, our turnover and client list have risen by eighty per cent. That's incredible. We can safely say that's down to you. I don't know how you've done it, but keep it up."

I was pleased, of course, not just for myself but for the team. We had built something solid, something that was growing stronger by the day. That night, the entire staff joined in the celebratory meal.

We were riding the crest of a wave.

Time passed quickly. Months turned into years, and the work never slowed. My time was no longer my own—I spent more hours in the air than on the ground.

I visited nearly every Arab country, but the trips were rarely about the logistics of their visits to the UK.

They wanted to discuss something else.

Terrorism.

Not threats from the outside but from within their own borders. Internal rebels. Insurgents.

I was careful. I kept my distance. I didn't want to become embroiled in the political entanglements of these nations.

But the more I tried to keep my distance, the more they pulled me in.

By 1985, after three years with Bordergreen, I was exhausted.

Something had to change.

And so, I made a decision. It was time to sit down with Nick and have a serious conversation about my future.

I remember it well. It was late on a Thursday afternoon when I arrived at the office. Most of the staff had already gone home, leaving the building unusually quiet, the usual hum of activity replaced by a stillness that felt almost foreign. The air carried the faint scent of polished wood and lingering cologne from earlier meetings.

Nick, however, was still in his office, enjoying a well-earned drink. I knocked on his door and stepped inside. He barely looked up before gesturing towards the chair opposite him, already reaching for a second glass. Without a word, he poured me a rather generous measure of whiskey, the amber liquid catching the light as he set it down in front of me.

He had been waiting for me. I could tell. He knew this conversation was coming.

I took a deep breath, steadying my thoughts before diving in. I explained everything—how I was feeling, the exhaustion, the constant travel, and the weight of the conversations I had been having with Arab leaders. The work itself wasn't the problem; it was the shifting nature of it, the way the discussions were becoming increasingly political. I told him outright that it was not my place to take sides, nor did I want to be seen as doing so. More than that, it was dangerous for the company. If we were perceived as favouring one group over another, we risked stepping into treacherous territory.

Nick saw it immediately. His expression darkened as he absorbed my words, rubbing a hand across his chin. He knew better than anyone how delicate these matters were.

"You're right," he admitted, exhaling. "We can't afford to be put in a political position—it doesn't matter what the government's stance is on any of these countries. We keep neutral. Full stop."

He leaned back, staring at the ceiling for a moment before scratching his head in thought. Then, finally, he looked at me and said, "Let me sleep on it. We'll talk again in the morning. You go home, and don't worry."

The following morning, I arrived at the office a little later than usual, just in time for the first round of coffee. The place was livelier now, the usual rhythm of the workday already in motion.

Nick called me into his office as soon as he spotted me.

We chatted for a few minutes, keeping it light at first before he finally got to the point. He had given my situation a great deal of thought overnight and had come up with a solution that, in his words, might just work.

The company, he explained, was severely overstretched. They were trying to do too much with too few hands. That had to change.

To that end, he suggested pulling me off my marketing role with new clients—at least temporarily. Instead, I would take charge of a couple of the crews on the ground, running the operations directly.

He had already spoken to Mandy, his secretary, and she had agreed to filter incoming enquiries, forwarding only the most critical ones to me. This way, I would be free from political discussions while still maintaining my value to the company.

Nick studied me for a reaction. "What do you think? You happy with that?"

I considered it for a moment. It was, in many ways, the perfect solution. I wouldn't have to navigate the dangerous waters of political entanglements, and yet I wouldn't be entirely removed from the business either. It allowed me to step away from the part of the job that was wearing me down while keeping me firmly in the thick of things where I thrived.

"Yes," I said finally. "That works."

And just like that, overnight, my role in the company changed.

Looking back, Nick had been rather crafty in his approach. By solving my problem, he had also solved one of his own—gaining an extra manager on the ground, someone who could handle operations directly.

But I wasn't complaining. In fact, I welcomed the shift.

I was back at the sharp end, back on the ground where things mattered. No more endless meetings, no more corporate handshakes. Now, I was actively involved—directing operations, making decisions in real time.

Of course, the nature of the work was different from my earlier military days. It wasn't combat, but in many ways, it required just as much awareness, strategy, and discipline.

The job now revolved around close protection for Arab royals and their families. To the outside world, it may have seemed like a simple task—high-profile figures enjoying their time in the West, shopping in luxury boutiques, dining in five-star restaurants. But beneath the surface, it was a different story.

Some might joke that it was little more than "holding their hands while they walked around the chocolate factory." In reality, it was far more sinister than that.

The truth was that these high-profile figures were prime targets.

The threat wasn't just from organised terrorist groups; it came from a variety of sources—opportunists, fraudsters, con artists, and even internal rivalries. My job wasn't just to keep them physically safe but to ensure they weren't taken advantage of.

That was one part of the job I disliked—the financial side of things.

It was standard practice for the close protection team to handle large sums of money on behalf of the clients. We would withdraw cash from Arab banks in London or in the cities we were stationed in, sometimes holding more than a hundred thousand pounds at a time.

Then, we would follow our clients from store to store, working alongside floor managers who kept track of their purchases. At the end of the day, we would settle the total in cash—an unsatisfactory system, to say the least, but one that the clients insisted upon. It was their way, and there was no changing it.

From the outside, it may have seemed like a dream job. We dined in the finest restaurants, stayed in the most luxurious hotels, and travelled in high-end, bulletproof vehicles. Money was never an issue.

But the reality was something else entirely.

The exhaustion was relentless.

We were constantly on high alert, always watching, always assessing potential threats. It wasn't just the usual security concerns, either. We had to be mindful of cultural sensitivities, ensuring that everyone around our clients behaved appropriately.

Arab royalty operated by a strict set of customs, very different from Western norms.

A person from the lower station was not permitted near them unless authorised. Women could not be in the presence of any male who had not been approved by a husband, guardian, or, in our case, the reigning prince or sheikh.

A single misstep—a wrongly addressed greeting, an accidental breach of etiquette—could cause serious offence.

And so, every interaction had to be carefully managed, every movement calculated.

At the end of a long day, when the public façade was dropped and the security protocols were momentarily eased, I often found myself reflecting on the nature of the work.

It wasn't war, but it was its own kind of battlefield.

The threats were different, and the stakes were just as high.

And every night, as I collapsed into bed, drained from the constant vigilance, I knew one thing for certain.

The job may have changed, but the pressure never did.

At the end of the day, our work was far from over. While the clients retired to their suites or continued their evening engagements, we remained hard at it. The security aspect of our role may have eased slightly once the public eye was no longer upon them, but the logistical side was only just beginning.

Every single purchase made throughout the day had to be collated, itemised and logged into an inventory. This was not a mere formality—it was an essential part of the operation. The sheer volume of luxury goods acquired during these trips was staggering, and each item had to be accounted for. Watches, jewellery, designer clothing, bespoke suits, fine art—nothing could be overlooked.

Once the inventory was finalised, the next step was organising the transportation of these goods. Everything had to be packed meticulously, ensuring the items were ready to be transferred to the airport and loaded onto the clients' private jets.

This alone was an operation in itself, often dragging on into the early hours of the morning. Despite the official end of our working day being four o'clock in the afternoon, the reality was that we were often still on duty long past midnight. Sleep became a luxury in its own right.

But it wasn't just about logistics.

Every single invoice had to be collected, checked, and verified. Why? Because the tax paid on these high-value goods could be reclaimed upon departure from the country. This was not something our clients were willing to overlook. If there was money to be retrieved, they would ensure it was done.

One thing was certain—Arabs were never slow when it came to handling taxes. They paid them when necessary, but if there was an opportunity to reclaim, they pursued it with absolute precision. It was an accepted practice, entirely legal, but it added yet another layer of complexity to our responsibilities.

For airport customs personnel, this was a recurring nightmare.

The moment our Arab clients arrived at the airport, they would present an overwhelming number of invoices, seeking reimbursement for every eligible purchase. The sheer quantity of claims, combined with the high value of the goods, caused endless delays.

For us, it was just another part of the job. A relentless, exhausting, but necessary task that had to be completed before we could finally rest—if only for a short while before the whole cycle began again the next day.

CHAPTER SEVENTEEN
DÉJÀ VU

For a few months, I worked alongside Brian Fellows, who was becoming increasingly involved with a well-known member of the famed "Rat Pack." Brian had always handled the celebrity clientele—those who required our discreet assistance in maintaining their privacy—and during my time with him, I gained a new appreciation for that line of work.

It was a world unlike any other, a whirlwind of film stars, household names, and high-powered industrialists who relied on us to ensure their safety as they moved through the UK and abroad. The work was different from the high-risk operations I had previously been involved in, but it had its own intensity. For the famous, privacy was a commodity just as valuable as wealth, and the measures required to maintain it were often intricate and demanding.

I enjoyed this time immensely. There was a certain novelty in escorting people whose faces were known worldwide, ensuring they could move freely without the intrusion of the press, overzealous fans, or anyone looking to take advantage of their status. Unlike the structured discipline of military service or even the rigid expectations of diplomatic security, this role required a different kind of strategy—reading people, anticipating threats before they arose, and navigating the unpredictable nature of the entertainment industry.

Eventually, Brian left the company to work full-time as a personal protection officer for his Rat Pack client. Nick wasn't thrilled about losing him—there was always a risk when men of our expertise were lured away by wealthy benefactors—but he let Brian go with his blessing. It wasn't long before Brian moved his family to America, where he built a new life, eventually becoming a US citizen.

With Brian gone, I briefly took over his responsibilities before shifting back to the international sector, returning to the side of the business that dealt primarily with Arab clients.

My first assignment in this transition was a significant one—establishing a security detail for the Omani royal family at the Sultan's private UK residence in the south of England. It was a prestigious commitment, but I took it in my stride. After years of navigating high-stakes operations, it was simply another mission, another objective to be carried out with precision.

Three weeks into the job, however, I received an unexpected call.

I was instructed to go to Heathrow Airport's Alcock and Brown suite to meet the Sultan of Oman, who was arriving on an unofficial visit. His plan was to spend time with his mother and the princesses staying at the estate I was securing.

I had heard much about Sultan Qaboos bin Said Al Said, but this would be my first direct interaction with him. By all accounts, he was a man of vision, a ruler dedicated to modernising his country while remaining deeply committed to the well-being of his people. His rise to power in 1970 had been swift and decisive—a bloodless coup, orchestrated with the assistance of British forces, had removed his father, Said bin Taimur, from power. The elder Sultan had been a despised ruler, infamous for keeping Oman in a state of near-poverty despite its vast oil wealth.

When the plane touched down, I was there to greet him. I introduced myself formally, briefed him on the security situation, and laid out the measures I needed him to follow while outside his estate. I was firm but respectful—this was not a request but a necessity for his safety.

He took it all in with a measured nod, offering no argument.

That was my first insight into the kind of leader he was—a man who understood the necessity of protection and who did not allow ego or personal pride to cloud his judgment when it came to security.

Over the following weeks, I found myself in conversation with him on several occasions. The meetings were always in the evenings, informal yet thought-provoking. It became clear early on that the Sultan had done his research on me. He knew about my background, my time studying terrorism, my understanding of insurgent movements. He was deeply interested in the transformation of rebels into organised terrorist cells and even more so in the way outside governments funded and fuelled these groups for their own ends.

Our discussions were not mere small talk. They were in-depth, strategic, and, at times, unsettling. Here was a man who ruled a country under constant threat from internal factions, who had first-hand experience dealing with the very dangers I had spent years analysing.

We spoke about the British involvement in his ascension to power—the coup that had removed his father and placed him on the throne. He acknowledged the role the UK had played, but there was a weight to his words when he admitted, "Perhaps the price I paid was too high."

He explained how he felt beholden to the British government—not just for their military assistance, but for freeing him from imprisonment under his father's rule. It was a rare moment of vulnerability from a man who, to the outside world, carried himself with absolute control.

It struck me then that I wasn't just speaking to a head of state. I was speaking to someone who had lived through extraordinary circumstances whose path had been shaped by forces beyond his control. In those moments, I felt less like an employee and more like a confidant.

When his visit came to an end, he thanked me personally, telling me he had valued our conversations and would take time to reflect on everything we had discussed.

As the Omani royal family departed, I found myself considering the experience in a way I hadn't with previous assignments. It had been one of the most enjoyable commitments I had undertaken—not just for the professionalism of the job but for the rare insight it had given me into a leader's mind.

Shortly after the Sultan's departure, I went on annual leave, taking my family on a much-needed holiday. I tried, in earnest, to make up for lost time.

The truth, however, was that time was not something that could be reclaimed.

Looking back over the past year, I realised I had only spent three months in England—two of which had still been consumed by work. My absences had become the norm, and while I had been focused on establishing myself in this new career, life at home had continued without me.

It was a sobering realisation.

Since leaving the military, I have thrown everything into my work, carving out a reputation for navigating the complexities of the private security world. But in doing so, I had side lined the people who mattered most.

My wife had adapted. She had taken charge in my absence, becoming more independent and more self-sufficient. What I hadn't realised—what I hadn't seen happening—was how far we had drifted apart.

The most telling moment came when I discovered she had opened separate bank accounts in her name, using the money I had sent home.

She had built her own world while I had been busy elsewhere.

It hit me then—I was on the verge of losing my family.

When I returned to work after the holiday, I sat down with Nick and laid everything out. I told him about my concerns, about how my marriage was slipping through my fingers.

He listened without interruption, then gave a simple nod.

"I understand," he said. And I knew he did.

We agreed that I would scale back my hours, spend more time at home, and delegate more of the night-time operations to the senior operatives on the ground.

For the first time in a long while, I felt as though I was taking control of something other than my work.

But deep down, I couldn't ignore the feeling that it might already be too late.

For the next year, everything seemed to run smoothly. I settled into my adjusted work schedule, balancing my commitments while trying to salvage what remained of my marriage. But I was not naive. Though I continued to make an effort, deep down, I knew things were beyond repair. The distance between us was not just physical—it had become something far more profound.

Then, in June 1986, everything changed.

I was working at the Four Seasons Hotel on Park Lane, overseeing the security of a high-profile member of the Qatari royal family. It was mid-morning, around ten o'clock when my principal called me into his suite. The tone of his voice told me this was not a request—it was an order.

"I have been informed that you are required at the Dorchester," he said flatly. "The ruler of Oman has requested you personally."

I blinked, momentarily taken aback. This was unexpected.

"Sir, I understand," I replied, keeping my voice measured. "However, I cannot leave you without protection."

My client met my gaze, his expression unwavering. "You have left me with plenty of protection. And I am in no position to refuse the wishes of the ruler of a sister Arab country. You may go."

There was nothing more to be said.

Still, I had to clear it with my office. I stepped out into the hallway and phoned Nick, briefing him on the situation. After a short pause, he simply said, "Might be more work. Go meet the Sultan."

And so, I left the Four Seasons and made my way up Park Lane towards the Dorchester.

As I walked, a strange thought settled in my mind. The Dorchester was not just another hotel—it was where the Sultan's father had been placed in exile by the British government after his overthrow in 1970. The irony of him choosing to stay there now did not escape me.

But it was not my place to question his reasoning.

Upon arrival, I informed the reception of my presence, and they swiftly made the call upstairs. Moments later, the concierge approached me.

"The Sultan's suite is on the fifth floor," he said, gesturing towards the lift.

As soon as the doors slid open on the fifth floor, I was met by two large Arab men in Western suits. Their attempt at frisking me for concealed weapons was poor—more symbolic than effective—but I let them do their job. Without a word, they motioned for me to follow them down the hallway.

When I stepped into the suite, I was greeted in a way I had not expected.

The Sultan of Oman welcomed me like an old friend, his warmth taking me slightly by surprise.

"Come," he said. "I have ordered a light lunch for us. We can talk while we eat."

I nodded, though I couldn't shake the lingering curiosity.

Why had he called me here?

There was no small talk about how I had been or what I had been doing. No polite inquiries or pleasantries. That in itself made me cautious.

We began by reminiscing about our previous meeting during his last visit to the UK. He spoke about how much he had enjoyed our conversations and how he valued my company. He told me about the new golf course he was building in Oman, as well as other projects he had in the pipeline.

Eventually, I asked about his mother.

"She is well," he replied simply.

And then, at last, we arrived at the real reason for my presence.

The Sultan leaned back slightly, his expression thoughtful. Then he spoke.

"David, I have given much thought to our previous discussions when you looked after my mother."

I listened carefully, noting the shift in his tone.

He continued, "Following our talks regarding the internal conflicts in my country, I have come to a decision. Although I have strong deterrent forces on the ground, I lack something essential—close protection for myself and my family. The threat is real, and it stems from the fanatical supporters of my father's regime. As you know, he was deposed, and I took his place with the help of British forces. These rebels want my head. They want to destroy my family and restore another despot to power—one who would bring back the slave trade and turn my country into a haven for terrorists."

His words carried weight.

"It is only a matter of time before these current rumblings escalate," he went on. "I am confident that my security forces will eventually capture these rebels and dismantle their cause. But in the meantime, my family is at risk. And that, David, is why I am making you a proposition."

I remained silent, waiting.

"I ask that you, with a small team, come to Oman to train and establish a royal close protection unit under my personal supervision. This would be a fixed-fee contract for no more than six months. Accommodation, health benefits, and a completion bonus will be included. You will have full control over the inventory and resources required."

He met my gaze, his expression serious.

"I understand this will cause considerable upheaval for you—both in your current position and your family circumstances. If necessary, I will personally speak with your company directors regarding your temporary leave, and I am sure we can reach a satisfactory compromise. I will be in London for the next week, and I ask that you give this serious consideration. Ideally, I would like the project to commence within the month."

He paused.

"With the correct resources, this can be achieved."

I had listened intently, absorbing every word.

I knew I should respond, but for a moment, I was unable to speak. This was an honour—not just to be considered, but to be personally offered such a role. It was not the kind of opportunity that came along twice.

My reply was, if I recall, as disjointed as my thoughts.

"I… I will certainly consider your proposal," I said at last. "I will need to speak with my boss and, of course, discuss it with my wife. I should have an answer for you within the next 24 hours."

The Sultan nodded. "My agents in London will arrange payments and the necessary paperwork for anything you require. However, if you accept, it would be helpful to provide them with a rough estimate of costs and an initial inventory."

And with that, our meeting ended.

I left the suite and made my way back down to the lobby. I remember walking down Park Lane in a daze, my thoughts colliding in my head.

How I didn't walk straight into a wall, I will never know.

By the time I arrived back at the Four Seasons, Alan had already taken my place. He greeted me with a knowing look.

"Nick's waiting for you at the office," he said.

That meant one thing—I was in for a grilling.

Without delay, I made my way to Chiswick.

When I arrived, I told Nick everything—the details of the meeting, the Sultan's offer, and the exact wording of our conversation. I left nothing out.

Nick listened without interruption, his expression unreadable. Then, after a long pause, he gave me a quizzical look and said, "Go for it, boy. And best of luck. If there's anything I can do to help, you only need to ask. As for your job here, it will still be waiting for you when you get back—if you still want it."

His confidence in me was reassuring.

"You'll need some time off," he added. "You've got a hell of a lot to do if you want this up and running within a month. Take whatever time you need. Don't worry about your commitments here—we'll manage."

I thanked him for his support. Then, after a moment of hesitation, I admitted, "The sticky part will be telling my wife."

Nick smirked knowingly but said nothing.

I already had an idea of the men I wanted for this mission. The problem was that they were part of our part-time manpower force.

"If I approach them with this proposition, it could deplete our available personnel," I pointed out.

Nick shrugged. "We'll cross that bridge when we come to it. They're free to work wherever they like."

And with that, my next challenge was clear.

I had to break the news at home.

That evening, I went home and sat my wife down to discuss the proposition I had received from the Sultan. I expected some resistance—concern, perhaps even frustration—at the idea of me disappearing for six months on another assignment.

But to my surprise, she was unbothered.

"As long as you keep the bank topped up and stay in touch, six months will go by quickly," she said matter-of-factly.

I studied her for a moment, trying to gauge her reaction. There was no anger, no disappointment—just calm acceptance. She went on to tell me how, over the past few years, she had made many friends and enjoyed spending time with them. The children were growing older now, she added, and she could converse with them "woman to woman."

Something about the way she said it unsettled me.

It wasn't just the words but the meaning behind them. It was as though she was subtly reminding me that life had moved on without me—that she had built something separate from what we once had. And I realised, perhaps more clearly than ever before, that she had.

She had her own life.

I had mine.

And unfortunately, the twain would not meet.

The decision had been made for me. I was going to Oman.

I rose from my seat without another word and made my way to the study. Sitting at my desk, I picked up the telephone and dialled the Dorchester Hotel. Within moments, I was put through to the Sultan's secretary.

"I'd like to request an interview with His Majesty tomorrow at his earliest convenience," I said.

I explained that we needed to finalise the necessary requirements following our earlier discussion and that I would appreciate confirmation of the meeting time, preferably that evening or, at the latest, early the next morning.

The secretary assured me I would be informed as soon as possible.

I placed the receiver back in its cradle, poured myself a large whiskey, and settled into my chair, the glass cool against my palm.

Now, all that was left was to wait.

The following morning, I arrived at the Dorchester at precisely 11:00 o'clock—the time I had been asked to attend.

As I pulled up to the entrance, a uniformed parking attendant stepped forward. I handed over my keys, watching as he drove my car towards the private parking area before making my way inside.

The lobby, as always, exuded an air of quiet luxury, the polished marble floors gleaming under the grand chandeliers. A doorman directed me to the lift, and soon, I was ascending to the Sultan's suite.

This time, there was no preamble.

The moment I stepped inside, the Sultan gestured for me to take a seat, and we got straight down to business.

"I have spoken with my managing director," I began, "and later discussed the proposal with my wife. The outcome was positive on both counts. Therefore, I accept your offer—subject, of course, to a satisfactory agreement on the contract price."

The Sultan gave a small nod, waiting for me to continue.

"I have calculated a project fee of £125,000," I said, "plus an open-ended incidental expenditure account. For my four trainers, I am proposing £25,000 each, plus incidental costs. Additionally, I require twenty-five per cent of these fees to be paid prior to departure, with the remaining balance settled in two monthly payments."

I paused, watching his reaction.

He did not contest a single figure.

"Agreed," he said simply.

With the financial terms settled, we moved on to the logistical aspects of the operation.

My primary concern was the vehicles.

"I will require four powerful Mercedes S-Class 500 limousines—two stretched, two standards. Naturally, they must be fully bomb- and bulletproof. However, these are not vehicles one can simply purchase off the shelf. They require specialised manufacturing and armouring, a process that will take at least six months."

The Sultan listened intently as I outlined the issue. Then, I presented my solution.

"Given the time constraints, I suggest we transport the four existing limousines from your UK residence to Oman. Once there, they can serve as immediate replacements while new vehicles are ordered to take their place in England."

For a moment, he considered my words. Then, with a satisfied nod, he said, "A first-class solution."

We spent the next two hours going over the finer details of the project.

The Sultan was eager to see it move forward as quickly as possible, and his enthusiasm was clear. His desire for absolute perfection in execution was evident—he would accept nothing less than the best, and I fully intended to deliver just that.

As our discussion drew to a close, he handed me a slip of paper.

"This is the address and telephone number of my agent in London," he said. "They will draft the formal contract and arrange the initial payment, including the transport of the vehicles to Oman."

He leaned forward slightly, his tone firm but courteous.

"My agent has full legal authority to sign any necessary documents on my behalf. However, if you encounter any difficulties with purchases or arrangements, do not hesitate to contact me directly in Oman."

I nodded in understanding.

He then instructed his secretary to relay everything we had discussed to his agents and strongly encouraged me to meet with them as soon as practically possible.

With the meeting concluded, I rose from my seat and shook his hand.

There was no turning back now.

The next stage of my journey was about to begin.

CHAPTER EIGHTEEN
OMAN

The next few weeks were not only hectic but utterly exhausting. The first task was assembling the right team to accompany me. I needed men with close protection training, solid field experience, and instructional expertise. More than that, they had to be reliable, physically fit, available, and, above all, attuned to my way of working.

Nick provided me with a list of part-time operatives he frequently used for his assignments and permitted me to approach any of them as I saw fit. I quickly selected four, three of whom I had previously worked with and knew to be competent. The fourth came highly recommended as a seasoned professional in the field.

John Brackwood was an ex-Metropolitan Police diplomatic protection officer, experienced in safeguarding high-profile figures. Philip Keys had a similar background, having also served in diplomatic protection. Fred Isles had spent fourteen years with 2 Parachute Regiment before transferring to the Royal Military Police and specialising in close protection. Finally, there was Gary Upton, a former training sergeant with 22 SAS Regiment. Each possessed a wealth of knowledge and the hardened composure required for the task at hand.

I made it clear from the outset that they would be required to sign a contract, including a strict non-disclosure agreement. Upon signing, they would receive twenty-five per cent of the agreed fee and would be bound to my directives from that moment onwards.

There was no hesitation from any of them, and each signed without question.

The next step involved liaising with the Sultan's agents in London. I had previously spoken to Cyril Fuller from Hamilton's in Bond Street, who instructed me where to go for our meeting. Bond Street, known for its exclusivity, is home to some of the world's most prestigious fashion houses and high-end consultants. Hamilton's, however, was discreet.

The entrance was marked only by a polished brass plate embossed with the name. Above it, a camera watched silently. I pressed the intercom, announcing my name and the purpose of my visit. The door unlocked with a muted click, and I stepped into a long, well-lit corridor leading to an opulent reception area. A charming receptionist greeted me, informing me that Mr Fuller was expecting me. She led me to the lift, taking me to the fourth floor, where I was ushered into his office.

The room exuded old-world sophistication. Floor-to-ceiling oak panelling, oil paintings depicting desert landscapes—presumably of Oman—alongside grandiose portrayals of other foreign scenes. Fuller himself sat behind an immaculate rosewood desk, devoid of clutter save for a delicate china teacup.

The man immediately struck me as educated, possibly Etonian, with the air of someone who never needed to raise his voice to command attention. He wore a flawlessly tailored three-piece Savile Row suit, complemented by a gold pocket watch chain draped across his waistcoat. A large red bow tie completed the look. When he spoke, his articulation was sharp and precise, and each sentence was delivered with effortless efficiency. There was no need to repeat oneself with this man. Every word registered instantly.

"Mr West, good morning. A pleasure to meet you at last. The Sultan speaks highly of you. Please, sit down," he said, gesturing towards a deep, brown leather Chesterfield sofa in front of his desk. He joined me there, his manner relaxed but entirely in control of the situation.

Turning to the receptionist, he instructed, "Susan, be so kind as to bring another cup of tea for Mr West. I am certain he would appreciate it."

He then settled into business. "From my understanding, you are assembling a team of specialists, acquiring substantial equipment, and securing vehicles for transport to Oman. The purpose of this mission is to train a hand-picked unit in close protection for a six-month period, beginning in less than a month. You and the Sultan have agreed on a fixed-term contract with an immediate advance payment of twenty-five per cent. Furthermore, this office has been authorised to facilitate all purchases you deem necessary. Is that correct?"

I nodded. "That is correct."

"Excellent. Let us now discuss the finer details. Do you foresee any immediate complications?"

I outlined the primary logistical challenge: obtaining armoured and bulletproof vehicles suitable for the operation. The ideal choice was the Mercedes S-Class 500 series limousines, yet these had a six-month waiting list. I proposed an alternative solution—using four of the Sultan's UK-based vehicles and transporting them to Oman while placing an order for replacements to be delivered to the UK. The Sultan had already agreed to this, but I required Fuller's assistance in arranging air transport for the vehicles, given that each weighed over one and a half tons.

I also raised the issue of securing weapons and ammunition, both live and blank, which would be critical to the training programme.

He listened attentively, never interrupting, and responded without hesitation. "The transport of vehicles by military aircraft can be arranged. As for the weapons and ammunition, I believe it would be best to liaise directly with the military attaché at the Omani Embassy. He will handle that matter without issue. Additionally, I would advise you to deal with Mercedes directly regarding the replacements, referring them to me for payment."

With the core concerns addressed, we moved on to secondary matters—security clearances, passport verifications, visas, health insurance, and required inoculations. Fuller seemed unperturbed by any of it, treating each point as a mere formality.

Finally, he leaned back slightly and said, "I will have the funds arranged today. Regarding payments, my calculations place the twenty-five per cent advance for your team at £25,000, equating to £6,250 each, along with £31,250 for your own fee. Additionally, an expense account of £20,000 has been included, bringing the total to £76,250. Do my figures match yours?"

I confirmed they did.

"Good. That will be ready shortly. Susan will also provide you with the attaché's details. I will brief him in advance."

He reached into his desk drawer, extracting two bound folders. "Now, the final matter—your contract. I have drawn this up on behalf of the Sultan. I would ask that you review and sign it today, formalising your commitment to the project."

I skimmed the documents. They were concise, to the point, and contained no clauses that raised concern. I signed both copies, as did Fuller. He then pressed the Royal Seal of Oman onto them and handed one to me for my records.

With everything concluded, he stood and extended his hand. "I believe that is all for now, Mr West. I trust you will make the necessary arrangements without delay.

I look forward to hearing of your success."

I shook his hand firmly. "You will."

With that, I departed, fully aware that the real work was only just beginning.

Once outside, I hailed a cab and gave the driver one word: "Chiswick." As we move through the streets of London, I let out a slow breath, feeling the weight of the morning's meeting settle over me. The city blurred past, a stream of polished shopfronts and hurried pedestrians, but my mind was elsewhere, replaying every detail of my conversation with Cyril Fuller.

Arriving at Nick's office, I walked straight in without knocking. He glanced up from his desk, and before he could say a word, I dropped into the chair opposite him.

"I feel like a double whiskey," I muttered, rubbing my temples. "But a coffee will do. You would not believe the morning I have had with the Sultan's agent. And, I have got a rather large favour to ask of you."

I reached down, lifted my briefcase onto my lap, and snapped it open just enough for him to see the thick bundles of cash inside.

"Can I put this in your safe? There is a small matter of £76,000 in here, and I'd rather not be wandering around London carrying it."

Nick took one look, then burst out laughing. "Oh, so you've met Cyril. He does take a bit of getting used to." He leaned back, shaking his head. "I know that man keeps a ridiculous amount of cash in his office. Many a time, I have found myself in the exact situation you are in now, rushing to get it secured somewhere sensible. Of course, you can put it in my safe. Now, how do you take your coffee?"

The next month flew by in a blur of embassy meetings and logistical planning. Most of my time was spent liaising with the Military Attaché to finalise additional training vehicles and personnel for kidnapping scenarios. Every detail had to be accounted for—weaponry, accommodation, scheduling, and transport logistics.

A trip to Germany saw me at the Mercedes headquarters, where I personally specified the exact modifications required for the new fleet of vehicles, ensuring they met the rigorous demands of both security and desert conditions. Meanwhile, the team was fully outfitted with gear suited to Oman's harsh climate. Every item was scrutinised—footwear, tactical clothing, equipment—nothing was left to chance.

Upon returning to London, a message from the Omani Military Attaché awaited me. The departure date had been set. We were to collect the vehicles, gather our necessary kit, and drive to RAF Lakenheath in Suffolk. We had precisely three days to be there, arriving by 1200 hours. Our transport? An American C-17 Globemaster, bound for USAF Thumrait Airbase in Oman. This would serve as our base of operations, with dedicated sections of the airfield and surrounding ranges secured exclusively for our training programme.

Before departure, I placed a call to Cyril Fuller, thanking him for his assistance over the past month. Without his swift actions and meticulous attention to detail, the project would never have been ready in time. He wished us well and assured me that should I ever need his help in the future, I only had to ask.

On 17th July 1986, I booked the team into the Eagle Hotel in Guildford for the night. After a final briefing over dinner, we turned in, knowing the next morning would mark the beginning of something entirely new.

Spirits were high, the anticipation unmistakable. This was more than just another assignment—it was an adventure. Light-hearted banter filled the car, laughter cutting through the hum of the engine. We were ready for Oman, eager to begin.

Fully loaded with our equipment, my car sagged under the strain, barely making the journey with its suspension intact. Upon arrival, we transferred our kit into the four waiting Mercedes limousines, each fuelled to capacity with ten extra gallons stored in reserve. Fortunately, my team were seasoned professionals already accustomed to the weight and handling of these powerful vehicles. Unlike standard road cars, the limousines required a skilled hand, their sheer bulk demanding precision and control.

A final check ensured we had everything. A quick radio test, and we were on our way.

The journey to the base was uneventful, and we arrived precisely on schedule. The gatehouse sentry, already expecting us, waved us through after a brief verification. We proceeded to the assembly point, where the logistics manifest officer took charge of our vehicles, overseeing their secure loading onto the Globemaster.

I had arranged for my personal car to be garaged at the base for the duration of our time in Oman, knowing we would need it for the return journey. With that sorted, all that remained was the flight itself.

No matter how many times I had seen them, I never ceased to marvel at the sheer enormity of these transport aircraft. Their lumbering frames seemed to defy the laws of physics, yet they would lift effortlessly into the sky, carrying unimaginable weight.

The flight to Oman took between eight and ten hours, depending on jet stream conditions. We settled in for the long haul, the steady drone of the engines a constant companion. I must have dozed off at some point because the next thing I knew; we were descending into Thumrait.

At precisely 9:30 p.m., we landed. Within moments, the vehicles were unloaded and secured. From there, we were directed to the officer's mess, where we were informed that in the morning, we would be taken to our permanent accommodation. I do not recall much else from that night other than the feel of the bed beneath me and the instant pull of sleep.

Dawn brought with it the arrival of Major Tareq Al-Hinai, a high-ranking officer in the Omani Desert Regiment. He introduced himself as our official liaison for the duration of our stay. Anything we required, whether for work or personal needs, would be arranged through him.

He wasted no time in getting us settled. Our new residence, some ten miles outside Salalah, had been prepared to the highest standard. He handed us special identity cards, explaining their significance. These allowed unrestricted access to any of the Sultan's estates across Oman. More importantly, they carried an implicit authority—anyone, military or civilian, who saw them would provide immediate assistance if required.

We were driven to our accommodation, and to say it exceeded expectations would be an understatement. It was, quite literally, a home away from home. Each day, the premises would be cleaned, the fridges restocked, and fresh provisions provided. Two 4x4 Range Rovers were assigned for our exclusive use.

Major Tareq suggested we take the remainder of the day to acclimatise, adjusting to the intense desert heat. The following morning, he would collect us for a full tour of the training facilities and surrounding areas.

As he departed, I shook his hand and thanked him. It was clear we were in good hands. This was the beginning of something significant, and we were more than ready for it.

Tareq navigated the mountain roads with the skill of someone who had driven them countless times. His hands were steady on the wheel, his movements precise, even as the narrow roads twisted through sheer rock faces and deep ravines. He barely seemed to notice the sheer drops beyond the edge of the track. I, on the other hand, couldn't help but cast a wary glance at the terrain, particularly concerned about the second Range Rover trailing behind us. My team was competent, but these roads were unforgiving. Yet, as I checked the rear-view mirror, I saw they were handling it with the same professionalism. My concerns were, thankfully, unfounded.

Tareq had arrived at our quarters at six in the morning to find a very sleepy crew. With his usual efficiency, he announced that we would be heading towards the mountains bordering Yemen, a route often used by rebel insurgents to infiltrate Oman. It was vital, he explained, that we familiarise ourselves with the territory. If we ever had to travel through this region again, we should be both armed and extremely cautious.

As we climbed higher, the landscape became more desolate, the mountains stark and imposing. They seemed endless, stretching into the horizon like jagged scars on the earth. It was immediately clear why this terrain had been favoured by insurgents for generations. A whole regiment could vanish into the craggy expanse, never to be found. The thought was sobering.

Tareq pointed out two abandoned villages nestled against the rock. Years ago, when rebel invasions were frequent, their inhabitants had fled and never returned. The emptiness of the place was eerie—stone houses left to the mercy of the elements, doorways gaping like silent witnesses to a past too dangerous to revisit.

"This could be useful," I murmured, already assessing how the ruins could serve our training programme. The structures provided excellent cover, opportunities for counter-ambush drills, and urban warfare simulations. Tareq nodded as if reading my mind.

We returned to the airfield, where I was eager to inspect the spare vehicles allocated for training. From experience, I knew that evasive driving exercises could be punishing on cars, often reducing them to little more than twisted wrecks by the end of a session.

Eight vehicles stood in the compound, a mix of powerful saloons and a couple of sturdy pickup trucks. The pickups, in particular, would be invaluable. Such vehicles were the transport of choice for insurgents and terrorists alike, their versatility making them ideal for both reconnaissance and rapid getaways. If our trainees were to defend against them, they needed to understand their handling and weaknesses inside out.

After a much-needed lunch, Tareq informed us that we would now meet the personnel selected for close protection training. All of them spoke English fluently, eliminating any language barriers. He went on to explain that the twenty individuals chosen were all serving members of the Desert Regiment. They understood the risks and had sworn absolute dedication to the protection of the Sultan and his family.

The training facilities comprised ten buildings, all in excellent condition. Tareq led us through each one, detailing their intended use. If we required additional resources, all we had to do was ask.

We concluded the tour in the lecture room, where our trainees were already assembled, sitting in disciplined silence, waiting.

Tareq turned to me expectantly. It was clear he expected me to address them.

I took a moment before stepping forward.

"I will not waste your time with unnecessary introductions," I began. "You are here because you have been entrusted with the security of the Sultan and his family. My job is to ensure that you are capable of fulfilling that duty to the highest possible standard."

I paused, allowing the weight of my words to settle. Their expressions remained impassive, but I could sense the intensity behind their gazes.

"I will be teaching you everything there is to know about close protection. You will learn how to safeguard your principal, which is the professional term for a VIP. You will master advanced evasive driving techniques, techniques that can mean the difference between life and death. But let me be clear—these methods are not to be used outside of your role. They are dangerous, and they must be treated with absolute responsibility."

Their postures straightened slightly. I had their attention.

"The programme will cover the positioning of bodyguards, vehicle formations, responses to suspicious activity, and every other detail that might seem mundane but is, in reality, crucial. These are the foundations of professional protection.

You will also be trained in live firing exercises—both in static positions and while moving at speed in a vehicle. Many of you may believe you are already proficient with weapons. I have no doubt that you are. But what I will teach you will elevate your weapon-handling skills to a level you have never experienced before."

I let the statement hang in the air, watching as a few of them shifted, intrigued.

"Before we begin, there is one final requirement," I continued. "I will assess your fitness to ensure you are capable of completing this course. And at the end, you will be required to sign an agreement."

A flicker of uncertainty crossed a few faces.

"This document will bind you to secrecy. If any of the techniques, strategies, or information shared in this course is disclosed to anyone outside of this unit, the consequences will be severe. You will be subject to prosecution and, potentially, imprisonment."

At this, a murmur rippled through the room. Tareq shot me a questioning look but remained silent.

Once the briefing concluded and the trainees were dismissed, he pulled me aside.

"Do you think that is really necessary?" he asked, his tone cautious.

I met his gaze steadily. "If an attack were to take place, and the enemy had inside knowledge of how this unit operates, they could devise a counter-strategy. If that happens, the Sultan's security is compromised, and people will die. I will not take that risk."

Tareq hesitated, then nodded. "I understand. I will have the necessary documents prepared."

Satisfied, I returned to my team.

The trainees would report at 0800 hours the following morning, dressed in lightweight Western clothing. Their first day would not be about drills or technical instruction. Instead, it would be a showcase—an opportunity for them to see what they would be capable of by the end of the programme. Only then would they begin to understand the true scope of what lay ahead.

I glanced back at the lecture room one last time before leaving. By the end of this course, these men would be transformed. They would not just be soldiers. They would be the last line of defence between the Sultan and those who wished him harm.

That evening, with the luxury of an empty airfield runway at our disposal, I seized the opportunity to put our vehicles through their paces. Though the exercises were the very ones we would soon be teaching the trainees, I could not deny the exhilaration that came with pushing the limits of these machines.

We started with high-speed manoeuvres, pushing the vehicles to 120 mph before executing the precision technique known as the handbrake turn. This method allowed for an immediate reversal of direction, an essential escape tactic in the event of a frontal ambush. It was not a manoeuvre for the faint-hearted.

Next, we set up ramps at strategic points on the road, designed to tip the vehicle onto two wheels and keep it balanced long enough to weave through narrow gaps between oncoming vehicles. It was a technique that required absolute confidence, as any hesitation could result in catastrophic failure. Only a driver completely in tune with their machine could pull it off without disaster.

Finally, we drilled convoy formations, driving three vehicles in close succession, with no more than six inches between each. The purpose was to create an impenetrable shield around the principal's car, preventing any hostile vehicle from wedging between the convoy. This was a method employed only in extreme circumstances, where the protection of the principal took absolute precedence over everything else. It demanded unwavering trust between the drivers—any miscalculation, and the entire formation could collapse in an instant.

As the days turned into weeks, the course progressed at an impressive pace. The trainees absorbed the theoretical aspects of close protection with discipline, allowing us to transition smoothly into the practical phase. What I had not anticipated, however, was their inexperience with high-speed driving. Most of them had never exceeded 60 mph in their lives. Taking them beyond 120 mph for the first time resulted in white knuckles, pale faces, and more than a few sick bags being put to good use.

Yet, despite the initial shock, their improvement was undeniable. They were becoming competent drivers, adept at maintaining convoy integrity and executing evasive manoeuvres with growing confidence.

One lesson, however, needed to be driven home with absolute clarity—the importance of remaining alert at all times.

One morning, as they practised convoy procedures, I laid a trap. One of my crew disguised himself in traditional Arab clothing and walked along the road as the convoy approached. He raised a hand in greeting, an innocent gesture easily ignored. The drivers and passengers paid him no mind as they passed. The moment the last vehicle moved beyond him, he produced a machine pistol and fired into the rear tyres of the principal's car, sending it skidding off the road.

The reaction from the trainees was immediate—panic, confusion, and a delayed response that would have cost the principal's life in a real scenario.

They learned that lesson the hard way. Complacency was a killer.

Following that demonstration, we moved on to one of the most complex and crucial aspects of the course—firing a weapon accurately while in a moving vehicle under attack.

To an untrained observer, it might seem straightforward—point the weapon and shoot. But the reality was far from simple.

At high speeds, a vehicle does not move in a straight line; it bounces, sways, and shifts with every turn and adjustment of the driver. If a shooter aimed directly at a target mid-bounce, the shot would go wide. The key was understanding how to use the vehicle's motion to one's advantage.

I taught them to aim at the lowest point of their target, allowing the natural movement of the vehicle and the recoil of the weapon to compensate. Instead of firing single shots, they engaged the automatic setting, letting gravity and momentum carry the line of fire upwards. This method took time to master, but once they grasped it, their accuracy improved dramatically.

As the weeks rolled on, they assimilated every lesson. The raw recruits who had first walked into the lecture hall had transformed into a competent, disciplined, close protection team. They had earned their place.

Christmas came and went, though the occasion passed without celebration. Omanis, followers of the Ibadi Islamic faith, did not observe the holiday in the same way as the West. While the season's spirit was acknowledged, there were no festive gatherings, no decorations, no familiar comforts of home. A few brief calls to our families were all we had to mark the day. It was a lonely Christmas, but we accepted it as part of the job. There was work to be done, and soon enough, the routine carried us forward.

The final test arrived.

I asked Tareq to assume the role of the principal for a full-scale security detail through Muscat. The trainees would escort him throughout the city, handling every aspect of his protection—from vehicle transport to foot patrols in public areas. They would execute mount and dismount drills, maintain close-quarter formations, and manage every potential threat.

Halfway through the exercise, I would rotate the teams at designated barracks, ensuring every trainee had the opportunity to perform in a different role. My crew and I would shadow them in unmarked vehicles, observing every movement and scrutinising every decision.

The operation commenced the following morning. The convoy moved through the capital, the trainees operating with a newfound sharpness. Every motion was assessed, and every procedure was evaluated.

By the time the exercise concluded, there were only minor errors—nothing critical, nothing that jeopardised the principal's safety. It was a performance I could be proud of.

That evening, I met with Tareq for a debrief. We discussed the success of the course, the progress of each trainee, and the final step—selecting the most capable individuals to lead the team going forward. I provided him with my recommendations, men I trusted to uphold the high standards we had instilled.

With that settled, it was time to report back to the Sultan. The mission was complete.

Tareq nodded in agreement. "I will arrange the meeting. You have done well."

I leaned back, letting out a slow breath. It had been months of relentless training, of pushing these men to their limits. Now, it was their turn to prove themselves. The foundation had been laid, and the Sultan's protection was in capable hands.

My meeting with the Sultan went better than expected. Unbeknownst to me, Tareq had been providing him with weekly reports on our progress. It did not come as a surprise—his discretion was characteristic—but I had not realised the extent of his updates.

We spent several hours discussing how the Sultan should best utilise his newly trained security team. I advised him to place absolute trust in them, for their sole purpose was his safety. They were trained to react decisively in high-pressure situations, and under no circumstances should he second-guess their actions. I knew this would not be easy for a man accustomed to complete autonomy, but it needed to be said. To my surprise, he accepted my guidance without hesitation.

I was especially pleased when he revealed his decision to appoint Tareq as the head of the team. It was an excellent choice. Though he had observed rather than directly participated in the training, he had immersed himself in every aspect of it. He understood the procedures, the strategies, and the necessity of discipline. More importantly, he had earned the respect of the men, and they would follow him without question.

I informed the Sultan that I would be leaving my course notes and lesson plans with Tareq, should they ever be needed. However, I assured him that should the need for further training arise, arrangements could be made through military channels now that the unit had been officially integrated into the armed forces. He agreed, acknowledging that a structured approach would ensure continued development.

Over five months had passed since our arrival in Oman. To mark the occasion, the Sultan extended a generous offer—a month-long stay at one of his beachside residences. Though the invitation was deeply appreciated, I knew I had to decline. The relentless heat had taken its toll on my still-healing body, the sun's intensity aggravating the grafted skin. Since that time, I have never been able to endure prolonged exposure to the sun. I excused myself by explaining that both my crew and I were eager to return to our families.

The Sultan understood. He assured me that his staff would arrange our flight back to RAF Lakenheath and expressed his desire to see us one last time before our departure. True to his word, he honoured the full six-month contract, including the promised £5,000 bonus for each member of my team.

Two days later, Tareq arrived with our travel arrangements. Our flight was scheduled for the following day at midday. The Sultan had requested our presence at his residence at 10:00 a.m., and Tareq would collect us at 8:30 a.m. to personally drive us there. I thanked him for the kindness he had shown us throughout our time in Oman and extended an open invitation should he ever visit the UK. It was only fitting to return the hospitality.

The next morning, we arrived at the Sultan's residence in Muscat. The grandeur of the palace was as striking as ever, yet the warmth of our welcome made it feel less like a formality and more like a genuine farewell. We were led to the reception hall, where we waited briefly before the Sultan entered, accompanied by an assistant carrying a tray.

His greeting was warm, his gratitude sincere. He thanked us for our service, for the dedication we had shown in training his men, and for the expertise we had brought to his security detail. Then, with a gracious smile, he gestured towards the tray. One by one, each member of my team was handed an envelope and a small green box.

Inside the envelope was £5,000 in crisp fifty-pound notes. The green box contained something even more remarkable—a gold Rolex watch.

When my turn came, I was presented with a similar green box but also a maroon necktie embroidered in gold thread with the Omani Royal Crest. I understood the significance immediately. These ties were not given lightly; they were reserved for members of the royal family or individuals deemed trusted acquaintances of the palace. It was an honour I had not expected, and to this day, I still have both.

Then came the final surprise.

A smaller package was placed in my hands. I opened it to find an additional £25,000 in fifty-pound notes—my bonus. The gesture was humbling, a token of appreciation that extended far beyond mere compensation.

We exchanged our final farewells and left for the airport.

Upon arrival, we proceeded through the usual embarkation procedures before walking out onto the tarmac. It was only then that I realised the full extent of the Sultan's generosity.

Waiting for us was not a standard military transport. Instead, standing before us in all its polished grandeur was the Sultan's private Boeing 747.

Our return journey would be in absolute comfort, a stark contrast to the rugged, mission-focused flight that had brought us here. As we settled into the opulent interior, the weight of the past six months began to sink in. It had been a relentless, demanding experience—physically, mentally, and emotionally. But now, as the engines roared to life and the wheels left the ground, I allowed myself to relax.

The mission was complete.

Home was waiting.

Chapter Nineteen

Turning Points and New Horizons

I drove from Lakenheath to London, the road stretching endlessly before me, my mind a whirlwind of thoughts. It was nearly midnight on the 1st of February 1987 when I finally pulled into Waterloo railway station. True to form, no trains were running. I looked at my crew, and despite our exhaustion, we all burst into laughter. Typical. There was nothing left to do but find somewhere to rest.

We drove to Hyde Park Corner and booked into the Four Seasons, grateful for the promise of a hot bath and a bed. The night melted into morning, and over breakfast, we said our goodbyes. There were no elaborate speeches, no need for them. We all knew the bond forged over the past six months would not fade. If any of us ever needed help in the future, it would take nothing more than a telephone call.

The forty-mile drive home felt longer than it should have. As the countryside rolled by, I found myself lost in thought. The work I had been doing—it was a young man's game. I was now in my mid-thirties, and though I still had the fire, I could feel the wear creeping into my body. The time had come to face some serious decisions about my future.

Stepping through my front door, I was greeted with the warm embrace of my wife and daughters, their joy evident in their eyes. It felt good to be home, but something inside me felt displaced. To make up for lost time, I had brought them gifts from Oman—a gold-inlaid jewellery box, delicate pearl necklaces for the girls, and a gold bracelet for my wife. We dined in lovely restaurants, took long walks through the woods, and I revelled in the laughter of my children. Yet, despite my efforts, I felt like an outsider in my own home, a visitor rather than a father or husband. The life I had built had carried on without me, and I was unsure how to reclaim my place in it. The restless energy within me refused to settle. I needed to work.

On impulse, I decided to head to London to drop in on Nick, my old boss, unannounced. Perhaps he had something for me. The idea of seeing a familiar face lifted my spirits. Striding into the office as if I had never left, I called out, "Can anyone get a free cup of coffee here?"

What I found instead sent a chill through me. Alan was hunched in the corner, surrounded by cardboard boxes, while Tony sat at Mandy's desk, his expression bleak. The air in the room was heavy with something unspoken. A knot formed in my stomach.

Alan and Tony stood, shaking my hand, their greetings subdued. Alan poured me a coffee, and they listened intently as I spoke about Oman. They seemed eager for distraction, but when I finished, I looked between them, sensing a weight I couldn't ignore.

"Right," I said, setting my cup down. "You can now tell me what's wrong. You both look as if you've gone ten rounds with a prize fighter."

Tony glanced at Alan, who nodded. Taking a deep breath, Tony finally spoke. "We have some bad news. Nick passed away two months ago from a massive heart attack, and Chick… he's been diagnosed with cancer. Mandy's left to have a baby. Nick's wife, as

a director of the company, wants to dissolve it, and we've agreed to her wishes. That's what we're doing now."

The words hit me like a blow to the chest. Nick—gone. I struggled to breathe for a moment, staring at them in disbelief. The loss of my old friend and mentor felt unreal. I forced myself to ask what they planned to do next. Tony told me he was taking early retirement, and Alan had secured a job as a civil liaison officer with the Metropolitan Police.

I grasped at something—anything—to hold onto. "Why don't we continue the company ourselves?" I asked.

Their response told me everything. They had lost heart. The company wasn't just bricks and contracts; it had been built on friendships and on trust. Without Nick, without Chick, it wasn't the same. They didn't have the will to rebuild. I left the office feeling hollow, the weight of loss pressing on my shoulders.

When I returned home, I told my wife everything and admitted the brutal truth—I was now unemployed. The following months were difficult. Every call, every letter, every desperate attempt to find work met with rejection. My age and my lack of long-term corporate management experience—both worked against me. For the first time in my life, I felt truly lost.

Then, an idea struck me. Why not start my own company? I toyed with the idea of a close protection firm, but the physical demands were too great, and finding the right men in sufficient numbers would be a challenge. Instead, I turned my attention to the engineering field, recalling my time working with the German company in Mayfair. Servicing and supplying replacements for specialised equipment was a niche market, one that the company had never fully tapped into. If I could build the right team, I could fill that gap.

I spent hours combing through old diaries and address books, tracking down former colleagues, and sifting through my contacts. Slowly, a plan took shape. I found a solid nucleus of engineers, and through them, I was introduced to younger professionals eager for an opportunity. This could be their chance to get in on the ground floor of something significant.

After numerous conversations, I had a shortlist of six candidates. I would take on four. Any more, and the financial burden would be too heavy in the beginning. I sat down and calculated every penny. With the savings I had from Border Green, the earnings from Oman, and the generous bonus from the Sultan, I could cover my mortgage and pay a reasonable salary for myself, my employees, and a receptionist for about eighteen months. I had enough to secure an office, buy vehicles, and maintain a small working capital.

And so, in May 1987, Advanced Relay Service Co. was born.

It was a leap into the unknown, but for the first time in months, I felt a flicker of something I had nearly forgotten—hope.

If anyone ever tells you that setting up your own company is easy, they are either incredibly lucky or deeply misguided. It is gruelling, relentless work, demanding a level of determination, confidence, and sheer stubbornness that most people cannot sustain. I had previously set up a large German engineering distribution company in Mayfair, but that was an entirely different story. That venture had an almost limitless budget, and crucially, it wasn't my money on the line. When the risk is your own, when every decision could mean the difference between success and financial ruin, the game changes entirely.

The first step was securing premises. I found a modest but functional space—far from the grandeur of my previous Mayfair offices but enough to get started. The premises included lock-up storage areas, a yard big enough to park three vehicles overnight, a small reception area, three first-floor offices, a washroom, and a tiny kitchen. It was bare-bones, but it was mine, and I was determined to make it work. Now, all I needed was a team and, most importantly, customers.

I began reaching out to my old contacts, distributors I had appointed when I worked for the German engineering company. To my relief, they remembered me well and were pleased that someone was finally offering specialised service for German-engineered switchgear. Three of them assured me they would be in touch whenever their customers had issues. It was a small victory, but one that gave me hope.

The next two months were a whirlwind of activity. I needed engineers, but not just any engineers—I needed professionals who were competent, adaptable, and reliable. Simultaneously, I had to find a receptionist who could handle invoices, type up reports, and manage the day-to-day flow of the office. After extensive interviews, I hired Alysha, an efficient and sharp-witted young woman who proved invaluable from day one. Anything I asked was done instantly, and before long, she became my right hand. When the company expanded, she was the natural choice for my PA.

Beyond staffing, countless other details demanded my attention. Work order sheets had to be designed to ensure a seamless process from job completion to invoicing. An accounting system needed to be established, tax registrations completed, and a multitude of administrative tasks handled. There were no shortcuts—every piece had to fall into place before the company could truly begin operations.

I leased four vans and secured lines of credit with suppliers for replacement parts. Stocking the warehouse was a gamble; without steady clients, I couldn't predict which parts would be in high demand. Every decision carried financial risk. To mitigate this, I offered my prospective engineers a solid proposition: instead of struggling with irregular, self-employed work, they could join me on a fixed contract with paid holidays, a pension scheme, and an insured, fuelled company van. It was an enticing offer, and all four engineers signed on, relieved to finally have stability.

With the foundation in place, I turned my attention to making the office a proper working environment. The old, broken furniture that came with the lease had to go. I invested in new desks, chairs, filing cabinets—everything needed to create an efficient, professional space. A new telephone system was installed, as well as a computer to bring our order and invoice process into the modern age. Costs ballooned rapidly, and I could only hope that the investment would pay off.

The first month of trading was painfully slow. While we managed to keep the engineers busy, the revenue was non-existent. I had set a thirty-day payment term, meaning we wouldn't see any actual income until the third month. It was a nerve-wracking time, but I stayed the course, focusing on marketing and building relationships in the industry.

By the six-month mark, momentum had shifted. Word spread and new contracts started coming in. Slowly but surely, we were establishing a name for ourselves. Our stock levels grew as we identified the parts most frequently needed, but I had to keep a sharp eye on inventory—too much stock meant too much capital tied up.

One year after opening our doors, on the 2nd of April 1988, I submitted our financial records to my accountants. When the final figures were compiled, I was called in for a review. The company, on paper, had turned a profit. However, with the ongoing lease payments, vehicle costs, and the substantial amount of my own money that had gone into the business, we still had a long road ahead before we were truly financially secure.

I had already mentally written off the money I had invested, but hearing it confirmed by the accountants made it feel all the more real. As managing director, with my wife as company secretary, we accepted that this investment was now an asset within the company, something that held value and would, in time, yield returns.

Starting Advanced Relay Service Co. had been a leap of faith, a test of resilience, and a gamble with everything I had built. But as I sat there in the accountant's office, reviewing the figures, I knew one thing for certain—I had no intention of failing.

The company continued to flourish over the next three years, expanding steadily as our reputation solidified in the industry. Financially, things had never been better, and yet, within my own home, I felt like a ghost wandering through the corridors of a life that no longer felt like mine. My wife and daughters revelled in the comfort and luxuries that success had provided, but I could feel a growing distance between us, an unspoken chasm that widened with each passing day. My wife, in particular, seemed to be indulging in the wealth with a reckless abandon, spending as if money flowed endlessly from some inexhaustible well. I had been working nonstop for years, and the price of that dedication was becoming clear: I was losing my family.

Determined to bridge that gap before it became irreparable, I decided we needed to get away, to reconnect before the bonds between us withered entirely. The opportunity arose when my uncle invited me to accompany him and his wife on a visit to his sister, my Aunt Vera, in St. Louis, Missouri. It seemed like the perfect solution—not only would I get the chance to meet long-lost family members, but I could also turn it into a long-overdue holiday. Leaving the company in the capable hands of my newly appointed service manager and my ever-reliable PA, I packed up my family for a six-week trip to America, hoping it would rekindle the warmth I feared had been lost.

The moment we cleared immigration at St. Louis airport, we met a chaotic sea of people, all holding up signs, waving furiously in the hope of reuniting with their loved ones. Among them stood a man about my age, fair-haired, with a broad, welcoming smile. The card in his hands bore our name. This was "Chips," my cousin, surrounded by a group of men and women who were, as I soon learned, the family I had never met. What followed was an outpouring of affection—hugs, handshakes, laughter, and an overwhelming sense of belonging that I hadn't anticipated.

Bundled into three waiting cars, we left the city behind and drove deep into the Missouri countryside, eventually arriving at a large residential estate. Chips' house was impressive—newly built, spacious, and set on an enviable plot of land. That evening, we gathered in his lounge, swapping stories and piecing together the threads of our shared history. As the night deepened, Chips recounted the harrowing story of his mother, my Aunt Vera, a GI bride who had crossed the ocean for love, only to find herself trapped in a nightmare. Her husband, an abusive alcoholic, had made her life a misery, hospitalising her on more than one occasion. The cycle of violence only ended when he was arrested, imprisoned, and eventually died—though Chips did not elaborate on how.

Determined to escape that darkness, Chips had left St. Louis as a teenager, forging his own path in the world. He had started with nothing, taking up a job as a truck driver. But through sheer grit and determination, he now owned a national trucking company and two successful car dealerships. He had built himself up from the ashes of his childhood, and I found myself admiring him more with every passing minute.

Eager to make our visit unforgettable, Chips had planned a stay at his lodge on the Ozarks Lake, promising days of fishing, boating, and relaxation. It was the escape I hadn't realised I needed. My uncle, Chips, and I spent countless hours on his boat, reeling in fish that we later barbecued by the lakeside. I felt an unfamiliar sensation creeping in—something I had not experienced in years. Peace. For the first time in as long as I could remember, I was at ease. The girls spent their days swimming, while my wife quickly formed a group of friends and spent most of her time with them. Our family had slipped into separate orbits, only coming together at mealtimes, but I told myself that was enough.

Evenings were filled with laughter, good food, and the intoxicating burn of Kentucky Rye. We frequented lakeside clubs, mingling with the locals, and absorbing the relaxed, carefree energy of the place. The days slipped through our fingers like sand, the first month vanishing before we even had the chance to acknowledge it.

One evening, as we sat around the fire, chips casually mentioned that he needed to travel to Utah to deliver his son-in-law's boat. Rather than simply making it a routine trip, he proposed something far more enticing: a road trip across America. He described it as a chance to see the country as it was meant to be seen, to follow the path of the pioneers who had once journeyed west in search of a new life. The idea ignited something in me—a longing for adventure, for movement, for the thrill of the unknown. Without a second thought, I accepted.

It was only later that I realised my mistake. I had not consulted my wife or daughters. They were enjoying the Ozarks, relishing the life they had settled into, and they had no interest in leaving. My enthusiasm was met with resistance, and for a fleeting moment, I wondered if this decision had been selfish. My uncle and his wife, too, declined, citing their age and the daunting nature of such a long journey. They chose instead to remain in St. Louis under the watchful care of Chips' sister, Brenda, who assured us she would take good care of them.

With my conscience eased and my heart set on the open road, we boarded Chips' Winnebago, ready to chase a piece of history across America. What I didn't realise at the time was that I wasn't just chasing adventure—I was also running from something. And perhaps I was leaving something behind that I would never quite get back.

That journey remains etched in my mind, an adventure so vivid that I believe I will carry it with me to the day I die. We travelled through Missouri and Kansas, breaking the journey to drop down into Texas, where we spent a couple of glorious days' water skiing on Lake Powell. The locals welcomed us with open arms, and we basked in their warm hospitality, sharing stories over hearty meals and experiencing the relaxed charm of the American South.

From there, our journey took us onward to Colorado, where we had the chance to pan for gold. Of course, we found nothing of value, but that hardly mattered. The experience alone was enough. As a memento, we purchased a trio of gold nuggets and had them crafted into necklaces and earrings—keepsakes that I gifted to my wife, who received them with obvious delight. We continued our trek through to Utah, where we were introduced to Cho, a Native American who had married Chip's daughter, Linda. Now a warden of an Indian reservation, Cho was a man of quiet strength and wisdom. He and Linda welcomed us as though we were family, sharing their traditions, stories, and most of all, their incredible food. The time we spent with them was both humbling and enriching.

As a group, we then made our way down to Arizona, where we stood in awe before one of the most breathtaking sights on earth—the Grand Canyon. No photograph or description could ever do it justice. The sheer scale and depth of it was almost incomprehensible, a natural wonder that seemed to defy time itself. If you ever have the chance to witness it firsthand, you must.

Time had slipped away faster than I had realised. Chip approached me, looking concerned. "We need to get back to St. Louis now," he said. "I miscalculated how long the trip would take, and your flight back to the UK leaves tomorrow." The news hit like a thunderbolt. A quick calculation revealed the reality of our situation—we had to drive solid for twenty-four hours, nonstop, across the breadth of America. The prospect was daunting.

Sensing the difficulty ahead, Cho immediately offered to come with us to share the driving. He knew that such an arduous journey with only two drivers was a near-impossible task, and his presence would make all the difference. Without hesitation, we accepted his offer, and within an hour, we were on the road, pushing eastward with a desperate urgency.

That final leg of the journey was one I would rather forget. The stress of the non-stop drive, combined with the fatigue of weeks of travel, weighed heavily on all of us. We endured relentless lightning storms that cracked the sky open in eerie, electric fury. Torrential rain hammered against the windshield, reducing visibility to mere feet, while in stark contrast, the searing heat and dust of the open plains pushed the limits of our already struggling air conditioning. Every mile was a battle against exhaustion and the elements, but the only option was to push forward.

By the time we finally rolled into St. Louis, dawn was breaking. At the airport, my uncle and his wife were waiting for us, their expressions a mixture of relief and concern. With barely an hour before our flight's departure, there was no time for long goodbyes. I hastily changed out of my travel-worn shorts and T-shirt into something more suitable for the long flight home.

As I sank into my first-class seat, the sheer exhaustion of the past twenty-four hours caught up with me. The hum of the aircraft engines was a lullaby. As the plane ascended into the sky, I drifted into the deepest sleep I had known in months, leaving behind the vast landscapes and unforgettable experiences of America.

CHAPTER TWENTY
FAMILY FAREWELL

December 1991 arrived with the usual excitement of the festive season. The company had just held its annual Christmas drinks party, and the office was abuzz with the anticipation of the upcoming holidays. The presents for the girls were wrapped and sitting beneath the twinkling tree, the cupboards were stocked with festive food, and everything was in place for a perfect family Christmas.

Two days before Christmas Eve, as the office was winding down for the holiday break, I found myself alone in my office, finishing up last-minute tasks. The phone rang, and I answered, surprised to hear my wife's voice on the other end. Her tone was eerily calm and measured.

"Are you alone?" she asked.

"Yes," I replied, sensing something was off.

Then came the sledgehammer blow.

"Since our holiday in America, where you tried so hard to make up for lost time, and the nightmare we endured after the explosion in Northern Ireland, you have done everything you could to hold this marriage together," she said. "But it's not you—it's me. The man I married wasn't the man who came home from Ireland. That man, I no longer know or love. I'm leaving. I won't be home when you get there. There's a letter from my solicitor in your study, setting out the terms for our divorce. Goodbye."

The line went dead.

For a moment, I sat frozen, the phone still in my hand, my mind refusing to process what had just happened. Then, almost instinctively, I dialled home. The unanswered ringing on the other end was deafening.

Shaking myself into action, I told Alysha, my PA, to leave early and enjoy her Christmas. I locked up the office, got into my car, and drove home, my thoughts a chaotic swirl of disbelief and dread.

When I stepped through the front door, the devastation was immediate. Something was wrong—terribly wrong. I walked into the living room, my heart hammering. The Christmas presents under the tree were gone.

I needed a drink, something to steady myself. I went to the drinks cabinet, only to find it completely emptied. My wife had taken the lot. I felt a rising panic and moved towards the kitchen, hoping to at least make myself a sandwich and gather my thoughts. Opening the fridge, I was met with stark emptiness. The turkey, the vegetables, the festive treats—everything was gone.

I stood in the silence of my ransacked home, trying to absorb the sheer magnitude of it. This wasn't just a sudden decision. It had been meticulously planned.

With shaking hands, I went to my study, where the ominous envelope sat on my desk. I tore it open and scanned its contents. It was a clinical declaration, stating that my wife was suing for divorce on the grounds of irretrievable breakdown and instructing me to provide my solicitor's details so proceedings could move forward.

That night, sleep was an elusive dream. My mind raced, replaying every moment, every argument, every sign I might have missed. By morning, I knew I needed to regain some control—starting with my finances.

I headed straight to the bank. Writing out a cheque, I handed it to the teller, expecting the transaction to go through without issue. Instead, a nervous young woman returned, her face pale. "I'm sorry, sir, but there aren't enough funds in your account to honour this cheque."

I laughed at the absurdity of it. "That's a mistake. There's over thirty thousand pounds in that account. Check again."

Moments later, she returned, now accompanied by her supervisor. The look on his face told me everything. "I'm afraid she's correct," he said gravely. "Your account was cleared out a few days ago, save for one pound."

The ground beneath me seemed to shift. "That's impossible," I whispered, though I knew it wasn't.

I demanded to see the bank manager, a man I had known for years and was on first-name terms with. He welcomed me into his office, his sympathy evident before I even spoke. I quickly explained the situation, and he nodded understandingly.

"Your wife, as a joint signatory, withdrew every penny," he said. "Additionally, three days ago, she cashed a cheque for twenty-seven thousand pounds from your business account, putting it into overdraft."

My stomach dropped.

"That's not all," he continued. "Your joint building society account was also emptied—another twenty thousand pounds."

Seventy-seven thousand pounds. Gone. Stolen in broad daylight. I clenched my fists, my nails digging into my palms.

I begged him to transfer a few hundred pounds from my business account to keep me afloat and to remove my wife's name from any remaining accounts. He agreed, but the damage was done. My wife had left me practically bankrupt.

I needed a solicitor immediately. My own solicitor, about to leave for the Christmas holidays, told me that divorce law wasn't his specialty. What I needed, he said, was a barracuda. Someone ruthless. He gave me a name—a specialist divorce lawyer in Harley Street, London—before wishing me luck, his voice laced with pity.

With nowhere else to turn, I called my sister, explaining everything in halting sentences. "Come up to the Midlands," she said without hesitation. "Spend Christmas with us."

I agreed.

That Christmas, my world collapsed. I won't bore you with the intricacies of divorce proceedings—the legal jargon designed to confound, the courtroom theatre where barristers pull you in with one breath and dismantle you with the next. But one thing was sure: my wife had planned her exit meticulously, and she had executed it flawlessly.

I was left to pick up the shattered pieces of my life alone.

Within twenty-four hours of contacting Simon Carter of Symons-Carter Solicitors, I found myself sitting in his office, recounting the entire saga of my marriage, its disintegration, and the latest brutal blow my wife had delivered. As I finished, he leaned back in his chair, fingers steepled, and studied me for a moment before speaking.

“I am going to ask you two questions. Your answers will determine whether I take your case or not,” he said. His tone was calm but authoritative, leaving no room for negotiation. “First, do you intend to seek any form of reconciliation with your wife? And second, would you ever consider giving in to her future demands? If I take the case, I demand that you agree with my strategy at all times."

The answer came easily. "To both questions, a firm no. As for agreeing to your strategy, I am no expert in law—that is why I am here. I need a professional to fight my case, and if I trust you to do that, then yes, I will follow your strategy."

Simon nodded. "Good. Then prepare yourself because no matter how wonderful a marriage once was, divorce is a vicious battle. Think of it like stepping into a boxing ring, untrained, against a prize fighter. The prize? Everything you own, now and in the future. Your opponent is going to hit you with everything they have until you submit. That is why you need me. I am your fighter, your defence, your retaliation."

His analogy was painfully accurate. What followed was a twelve-month war of attrition. The main battleground? My wife's outrageous demands. They were completely untenable—she wanted the house, a substantial lump sum, lifetime maintenance payments, her company pension fully covered, and, the biggest blow of all, fifty per cent of the company's annual gross profit. She justified this last demand because, on paper, she was a fifty per cent shareholder.

Simon laid out the brutal truth. "We can do nothing about the money she has already taken," he said matter-of-factly. "She was a joint signatory on the accounts, and as company secretary, she had the legal right to access the funds. That's a battle we cannot win. However, we can fight her on everything else."

We had no choice but to concede her share of the house. After paying off the mortgage, her half of the equity would amount to around sixty thousand pounds, which would form the lump sum payment. However, Simon was adamant that there would be no ongoing maintenance payments. "We will structure the lump sum as a clean break settlement," he explained. "The girls are past the age of child maintenance, so she has no claim there."

The pension was another non-negotiable point. She would either take it as a lump sum or take full ownership of it and be responsible for future payments. That was her choice, but it was not going to be my burden any longer.

Then came the most cunning move of all—the company profits. Simon knew the battle over this would be ferocious, so he devised a plan that left me momentarily speechless.

"We will offer her something that looks incredibly generous on paper," he said, leaning forward. "You will resign as Managing Director and sign over your shares to her. Legally, she will be handed full ownership of the company."

I shot up in my chair. "Absolutely not! There is no way I am handing my company over to her!"

Simon held up a hand. "Let me finish. You will purchase a shelf company and in the months leading up to the decree absolute, you will transfer every asset, contract, and employee over to this new entity. Advanced Relay Service Co. will officially cease trading the moment your divorce is finalised. On the day of the decree absolute, your wife will inherit an empty shell. It will look like an incredible concession in court, but in reality, she will have nothing."

It was a brilliant, albeit ruthless, strategy. It would require an immense amount of work on my part—relocating offices, altering contracts, switching employment agreements, even finding a new accountant to ensure no leaks—but it was the only way to stop her from bleeding me dry for years to come.

The day of the divorce hearing arrived, held in the Family Division of the Royal Courts of Justice in London. Everything had been set in motion exactly as Simon had planned. The negotiations between our solicitors in the preceding months had been nothing short of brutal, but now, it was time for the final verdict.

My wife sat with her solicitor, their barrister standing to present her case. He read out the petition, detailing the grounds for divorce and the financial arrangements they claimed had been "agreed upon," conveniently glossing over the main point of contention—the company profits. When he was done, our barrister rose. He spoke for thirty minutes, meticulously constructing an argument that painted me as the devoted husband who had sacrificed everything for his family, only to be betrayed. My wife, in contrast, was portrayed as a cold, calculating woman with an insatiable appetite for spending, unconcerned with the well-being of the man who had provided for her.

It was the final round of the fight, and I was about to see if Simon's strategy would deliver the knockout punch.

He was clearly playing on the judge's emotions, carefully framing my wife as a greedy and indifferent woman while painting me as the devoted husband who had done everything to salvage a broken marriage. Then, as if to drop a bombshell into the proceedings, he calmly revealed our supposed plan for the company's future, a decision he claimed had been made that very day. A murmur rippled through the courtroom at the revelation.

The judge turned his sharp gaze towards me.

"Mr West, do I understand correctly that you intend to sign over the company by officially transferring your shares to your wife through Companies House?"

I met his stare and nodded. "Yes, Your Honour."

He shifted his attention to my wife's barrister. "Would this arrangement satisfy your client's claim?"

Her barrister glanced towards my wife, who, with a smug expression of triumph, gave a small nod. "Yes, Your Honour," he confirmed.

The judge then turned back to me. "Mr West, this is a most magnanimous gesture. Are you certain this is what you wish to do?"

I maintained my composure. "Yes, Your Honour."

He gave a slow, thoughtful nod. "Then so be it. The details of what has been agreed will be finalised between the decree nisi and the decree absolute. Therefore, my judgment today is that the divorce is granted, and the decree nisi is issued from this date."

I chanced a glance towards my wife. She was deep in discussion with her solicitor, a self-satisfied smirk plastered across her face as though she had just walked away with the crown jewels. I looked to Simon, who gave me nothing more than a quick wink and a knowing smile before rising from his seat. We left the courtroom without another word.

Once outside, we hailed a taxi to his office. As soon as the door shut, Simon slapped my leg and burst into laughter. "Well, we did it! That smug cow is going to be in for the shock of her life when she realises she has been left with nothing but a worthless piece of paper and a company seal." His laughter filled the cab, and for the first time in months, I felt the weight on my chest lighten just a fraction.

But there was little time to celebrate. The following months were a whirlwind of upheaval. Setting up new offices, securing a yard for storage, relocating stock and vehicles—it was a logistical nightmare. Everything had to be done meticulously, from changing business addresses on all documentation to transferring client contracts under the new company name.

I had to find a new accountant, as I did not want my previous accountant involved in anything that might be deemed questionable. As far as he was concerned, Advanced Relay Service Co. had ceased trading, which, in a technical sense, was true. The process was exhausting, but it was a necessary evil to ensure a seamless transition and to prevent my ex-wife from getting her hands on a single penny more than what was lawfully hers.

Selling the house was the easiest part. Before completion, my ex-wife had arranged for a removal company to strip the house bare. Every single piece of furniture was taken, leaving only empty rooms. I had no idea where it all went, nor did I care. My possessions, reduced to a few suitcases, were crammed into my car. Homeless, I moved into my office for a while, sleeping on a makeshift bed in the back room.

During this time, I remained in close contact with Mike Mathews, who suggested I return to lecturing at Sandhurst Staff College. The income was not regular, but it was lucrative and helped sustain me as I rebuilt my life from the ground up.

Personally, I was a mess. The first year after the divorce felt like a slow-motion car crash. The emotional emptiness gnawed at me, and for a while, I felt like I was merely going through the motions. But in business, everything fell into place almost effortlessly. The company flourished, earning a solid reputation within the industry.

Alysha, my ever-efficient PA, kept everything running smoothly. My new accountant, Gill, was an absolute asset—sharp, no-nonsense, and more than capable of handling the company's finances. By autumn, I was astounded at the profit margins we had achieved. Feeling immensely grateful to my team, I decided to show my appreciation.

I booked a prestigious hotel's banquet hall for a grand celebration. A formal dinner was arranged, followed by a speech of gratitude from me. Everyone—engineers, clerical staff, and their spouses—was invited. It was a night of fine dining, music, and dancing, a well-earned reward for the hard work that had gone into building the company.

That evening, I let myself enjoy the moment. I danced with many of the ladies, chatted with the husbands, and for the first time in what felt like forever, I allowed myself to relax. Unfortunately, I also drank far too much. I dimly recall being driven home, my world swaying in a pleasant, alcohol-induced haze.

The next morning, I awoke feeling oddly comfortable. That was the first clue something was amiss. This was not my bed. Nor was this my room. As I shifted, I felt a warm arm draped over me. My breath caught as I turned to see a woman beside me.

Gill.

She lay there, dark hair cascading over the pillow, watching me with a sleepy, knowing smile. Before I could utter a word, she leaned in and kissed me softly. And just like that, my life took a turn I had never anticipated.

From that moment, I never left Gill, nor did she leave me. That morning marked the start of twenty-three years of happiness, companionship, and love. We later bought a quaint cottage nestled in a picturesque village, surrounded by an acre of lush land. Over the next decade, we made it our sanctuary, modernising it with great care, designing breathtaking gardens, and building extensions and garages to create a haven away from the pressures of business life.

The only thing I ever complained about was her love of cigarettes and her fondness for gin and wine, often in copious amounts. I never imagined those habits would one day take her away from me.

August 2001. The company was thriving, standing firmly on its own feet, yet I found myself more engrossed in work than ever before. My daily routine had become second nature. Mornings were spent making an appearance at the office, checking my diary, and then heading out to meet clients, negotiating deals over long lunches or on the golf course, where the casual atmosphere often sealed contracts more effectively than any boardroom discussion.

Meanwhile, back at home, the renovations were finally nearing completion. Our cottage had transformed into something truly special, a reflection of the life Gill and I had built together. Yet, despite my love for the home we had worked so hard to perfect, I spent little time there. Gill, having left her own practice to focus on managing both our home and the company's finances, often reminded me that the purpose of our success was to enjoy life, not be consumed by it.

It was a glorious summer's day when the first warning sign struck. I was outside, painting the lounge window, the sun beating down on my back when suddenly, a crushing pain gripped my chest. My breath shortened, and a strange sense of detachment washed over me. Something was wrong. I stumbled inside, clutching the doorframe, my vision blurring. Gill turned, instantly registering the pallor on my face. The colour had drained from my skin, leaving me clammy and shaken.

She wasted no time. "Sit down," she ordered, her voice calm yet laced with concern. I tried to brush it off, blaming indigestion, but she knew better. Without hesitation, she picked up the phone and dialled emergency services. I wanted to protest, to tell her not to overreact, but before I could utter a word, the distant sound of sirens filled the air. Moments later, the paramedics were inside, surrounding me, checking my vitals, voices murmuring in clipped tones.

Two days later, after endless tests, X-rays, and being poked and prodded, I found myself sitting on the edge of my hospital bed when the consultant approached. His expression was unreadable, his clipboard held firmly in his hands.

"You are a very lucky man," he began. "You have just suffered a pulmonary embolism. Looking at your medical history, I see you had major surgery on your legs some twenty-four years ago. Over time, a rather large blood clot has dislodged, travelled through your heart, and lodged itself in your lungs. Frankly, how you have not suffered a massive heart attack is beyond me."

I stared at him, his words sinking in like stones in water. "And what happens if the clot moves again?" I asked, my voice quieter than I had intended.

The consultant's response was blunt, almost too blunt. "The next place it will travel is your brain, and you will know nothing about it. You will be dead before you hit the floor."

For a long moment, silence stretched between us. It was a strange thing, facing mortality so candidly. My mind whirled with thoughts—not of my demise, but of the company, my employees, the engineers and their families who relied on me, and, of course, Gill. The life we had built; the plans we had made.

"What about work?" I finally asked, needing something to anchor myself. "Will I be able to carry on?"

The doctor sighed, clearly having had this conversation with stubborn men like me before. He folded his arms and studied me carefully before responding. "If you continue as you have been, pushing yourself to the limit, I can tell you with certainty that you will not see next Christmas. My professional recommendation is that you stop working altogether. Retire. Take a long break. No more stress, no more late nights, no more overexertion. Your body cannot sustain this pace any longer."

His words hit me harder than any blow I had taken in my life. Retirement. The very idea seemed alien to me. I had spent my entire life pushing forward, fighting, building, creating. How was I supposed to just stop?

I swallowed the lump in my throat, looked up at him, and asked, "Do I have any choice in this?"

The consultant's eyes met mine, unwavering. "No."

The following day, before I was discharged, Gill and I sat down with the consultant for a long, honest conversation. We talked through the reality of what lay ahead, the adjustments that needed to be made, and the future we had to build together—one that no longer involved me burning the candle at both ends. As much as it pained me, I knew we had no choice but to follow his recommendations.

And just like that, life as I had known it was about to change forever.

CHAPTER TWENTY-ONE
LETTING GO

Gill and I had decided to keep our plans confidential until we had a firm strategy in place for the future. Coincidentally, I had a scheduled lunch meeting with Julian Wright, the managing director of one of our competitors. We had always maintained a good working relationship with his company, often assisting each other by managing the overflow of work when necessary.

During lunch, Julian quickly noticed that I was not my usual self and asked if something was wrong. I confided in him about my recent hospitalisation and mentioned that Gill was organising a holiday to help me recuperate. I also requested that his company take on any excess work we might have in the foreseeable future.

Julian was perceptive. He sensed that my concerns ran deeper than what I had shared. With a sincere tone, he asked if there was anything more he could do to help. I hesitated, then realised I needed to unburden myself. I told him I was seriously considering closing the company and taking early retirement. We spent a long time discussing the pros and cons, weighing our options. Eventually, Julian asked whether I would consider a takeover rather than shutting the company down. If I was open to the idea, he wanted permission to discuss the possibility with his chairman.

I told him I was willing to explore any option and would be happy to discuss it further. With that, we parted ways, and I returned home to inform Gill of the conversation.

The following day, I received an invitation to meet Ken Randall, the chairman of Julian's company, later that afternoon to discuss our potential agreement. I accepted and travelled to his offices. It was my first time meeting Ken, and we got along well from the outset. Our conversation quickly turned to the health challenges that had prompted my decision. Ken expressed interest in acquiring the company as a going concern, provided his auditors could review our financial records for the past few years. If everything aligned with his expectations, we could move forward.

I assured him this would not be an issue and agreed to forward the necessary documents.

Gill retrieved the last three years' audited accounts at the same time, I compiled a concise report detailing our current contracts, future budgets, growth projections, and the company's intended trajectory had my circumstances been different. Once everything was assembled, we delivered the package to Ken Randall.

Rather than dwelling on whether the offer would materialise, Gill and I decided not to place ourselves under unnecessary stress. We booked a well-earned holiday, knowing that my service manager and PA were fully capable of handling the company's day-to-day operations in our absence. The next month passed blissfully in the Caribbean, filled with iced drinks, warm sunshine, and much-needed relaxation.

All too soon, it was time to return home. Upon arrival, we were greeted warmly by the team, eager to hear about our trip. I quickly settled back into work, tackling the messages that had piled up in my absence. Word spread that I was back, and before long, my phone rang incessantly. Eventually, I had to ask my PA to manage my calls while I worked through my backlog.

That afternoon, Alysha entered my office and informed me that Julian Wright had called, requesting to speak with me as soon as I was available. I returned his call, and after exchanging pleasantries, he got straight to the point.

His accountants, along with Ken and the board, had reviewed our financial records and held a meeting. The outcome was clear—Ken had been formally authorised to enter negotiations with me to secure an agreement for the takeover of my company. Julian asked if I would be available for a meeting on Thursday with Ken, himself, and our respective accountants to discuss the terms.

I agreed but requested an agenda outlining the topics for discussion so that I could prepare adequately. He assured me he would send one, and we ended our conversation.

That evening, Gill and I sat down for a long discussion about the forthcoming meeting. We developed a structured plan to ensure we covered every essential detail. This included stock valuations, vehicle leases, employee contracts, and ongoing pension contributions for the staff.

One point we were both adamant about was ensuring the new company retained all existing employees, including the service manager and engineers. We agreed that their new employment contracts should mirror their current terms and that these should be signed before the takeover was finalised. Additionally, for any employee unwilling or unable to transition due to location or other reasonable factors, we decided they would be provided with a redundancy package equivalent to at least three months' salary, along with professional references.

With our plan set, we felt prepared for the negotiations ahead.

Over the next two days, Gill and I meticulously went over every detail of the upcoming meeting. We carefully calculated the value of our stock, assessed the worth of our contracts, and projected the profit margins for the next five years. Additionally, we factored in pension payments, ensuring that everything was accounted for up to the standard retirement age. These figures would serve as the foundation for our negotiation, forming the backbone of our compensation takeover proposal.

We also made a crucial decision regarding confidentiality. The only person, aside from us, who would be privy to this possible transition would be my PA, Alysha. Her role in the company's daily operations was indispensable, and we would need her expertise to ensure that the necessary administrative groundwork was executed seamlessly. We made it clear that discretion was paramount; until the deal was finalised, no one else could know. With the final presentation reviewed and polished, there was nothing more to do but attend the meeting and see where the cards would fall.

The day before the meeting, Gill and I decided to bring Alysha into our confidence over lunch. Rather than discussing it in the office, where any whispers might raise suspicion, we invited her to a quiet, cosy pub just outside town. Over a light meal and coffee, Gill took the lead in explaining everything that had transpired over the past few weeks. She spoke about my health scare, the stark warnings from the doctors, and the difficult decision to step away from the company. Alysha listened intently, her face a mixture of concern and surprise.

When Gill finally mentioned the takeover discussions with Ken Randall, Alysha's eyes widened, but she quickly nodded in understanding. "I had a feeling something was going on," she admitted. "But I never imagined it was this serious." She assured us that she would do everything necessary to assist with the transition, keeping everything strictly confidential until we were ready to make an official announcement. With her on board, another major hurdle was overcome.

The following morning, Gill and I arrived at Ken Randall's offices. Although I had been there before, I was once again struck by its sheer scale and professionalism. The building itself was a sleek, modern glass-fronted structure, standing tall amidst a high-end business park. Inside, the reception area exuded an air of quiet efficiency, with polished floors, state-of-the-art furnishings, and a sense of corporate prestige. It was a stark contrast to our more modest setup, but it only reinforced the fact that this transition could take my company to a new level under the right leadership.

We were greeted warmly by Julian Wright, who escorted us to the boardroom, where Ken was waiting. Although I had met Ken previously, this was Gill's first introduction. He welcomed us with a firm handshake, his manner confident yet approachable. He was a man who exuded authority but also possessed an easy charm, making it clear why he was so successful in his field. His reputation preceded him, and within moments, it was evident that this meeting would be conducted in an atmosphere of professionalism and mutual respect.

The first hour of discussions revolved around our respective companies. Ken provided an insightful overview of his organisation's history and operations, and I did the same for ours. The conversation then shifted towards the logistics of merging the two businesses and how a unified venture would benefit both parties. We methodically worked through each point of the proposed itinerary. I was pleased to see that there were no major objections to my requirements, including those related to staff contracts and pension payments.

One particularly encouraging revelation was Ken's interest in my service manager. His company's project manager was due to retire in six months, and he saw an opportunity for my service manager to understudy him before taking over the role. It was an unexpected but welcome solution, ensuring job security for my most trusted employee.

After a brief break for lunch, we delved into the finer details of the takeover. Ken acknowledged the strength of my company's top four contracts, which, in terms of financial value, rivalled his own company's top eight. He expressed concern over whether these long-standing clients, many of whom had been with us for over eight years, would be willing to transfer their business under new ownership.

To address this, I proposed a proactive approach. I suggested that Julian and I visit each of these four clients to discuss the transition, reassuring them that their service would not be compromised and that their agreements would remain intact. Ken agreed that this was a sound strategy, and with that, we resolved the last significant point of contention. Now, it was up to the accountants to finalise the settlement figure.

As Ken's accountant and Gill retreated to another office to crunch the numbers, Ken invited me on a tour of his facilities. The efficiency and scale of his operations were impressive. Everything ran like a well-oiled machine, a testament to the level of organisation and precision his company maintained. It was reminiscent of my days in the military, where every inspection demanded an immaculate presentation.

After what felt like an eternity, we returned to the boardroom to find Gill and Ken's accountant in animated conversation, each holding a large glass of wine. I immediately wondered whether this was a good or bad sign. Either I had just been outmanoeuvred in negotiations, or Gill had simply found a kindred spirit over a bottle of red.

I quietly approached Gill and asked how things had gone. She assured me that everything had proceeded smoothly and the proposed settlement package was fair. Now, it was down to Ken to make the final call.

We all resumed our seats, and Ken summarised the key points of our agreement. He then presented the final takeover figure, which was contingent upon our four major clients agreeing to continue their contracts under his company's management. The final step was for his board to approve the motion, but from what he had gathered, there was overwhelming support for the acquisition.

With a firm handshake, the deal was set in motion. As we left the office, Gill and I exchanged glances, knowing that we had just taken a monumental step toward closing this chapter of our lives and beginning a new one. It was a day of significant change, but for the first time in a long while, I felt a sense of relief and clarity about the future.

It was late in the day, and returning to the office seemed pointless, so Gill and I went straight home. As we sat together that evening, we reflected on everything that had been discussed at the meeting and what the final figure would truly mean for us. For all intents and purposes, it was our long-term pension fund, a safety net for the rest of our lives, along with a lump sum to invest. It meant security, comfort, and the ability to live out our days without financial worries. When one looks at life from such a vantage point, it is, perhaps, the most satisfactory position to be in.

The next morning, I returned to the office with a renewed sense of purpose. I briefed Alysha in full detail about the meeting, making sure she was aware of everything that had transpired and what was to come. Her workload would increase significantly in the coming weeks, and I wanted her to be prepared. First on my list of tasks was contacting my solicitors, briefing them thoroughly on the takeover and providing them with Ken Randall's solicitor's details so they could liaise and finalise the contracts. Then, I reached out to the four longstanding clients whose contracts formed the backbone of the company. I scheduled meetings with them for the following week, ensuring Julian would be present as well. These meetings would be pivotal in securing a seamless transition.

As I went through the motions, I felt the weight of responsibility pressing down on me. My consultant's words from the hospital echoed in my mind with newfound clarity. The last thing I wanted was to end up on a hospital slab after everything I had been through, both in my military and civilian life. I thought back to Nick, a man who, like me, had believed himself invincible. He had built something substantial, considering himself at the peak of his career, only to be blindsided by the very pressure that came with success. I had not fully grasped the toll of responsibility until now.

When you are responsible for employees and their families, when their livelihoods depend on your leadership, you unknowingly carry an ever-growing burden. The bigger the company, the heavier that weight becomes. It was only now, standing at the precipice of retirement, that I could see how the years of stress had crept into my very being.

Realisation struck me with absolute clarity. This was the moment to let go, to walk away before I lost everything I had worked so hard to secure. Some moments in life demand to be seized, presenting themselves for only the briefest time before they are lost forever. I rose from my desk, closed my briefcase, and walked out of my office. As I passed Alysha's desk, I wished her goodnight and, with genuine gratitude, thanked her for her unwavering support over the years. She gave me a curious look before offering a small smile and simply saying, "You're a good boss." Those four words carried more weight than she could ever know. I drove home that evening and, for the first time in a long while, allowed myself to enjoy my weekend up to the fullest.

The following week, Julian and I met with the four longstanding clients. Each meeting was a success. Julian connected well with the key personnel, and every company reaffirmed its commitment to renewing their contracts with the new firm. Their confidence was bolstered by the assurance that the engineers, who knew the intricacies of their machinery, were transitioning seamlessly into the new company. One by one, the final pieces fell into place.

The legal side of things, as expected, dragged on. Solicitors worked at their usual sluggish pace, drafting the necessary takeover documents and employee contracts. Nevertheless, progress was steady, and the final date was set: the first of January. One month remained.

Two weeks before Christmas, Gill and I gathered the entire staff for a meeting. I stood before them, my heart heavy yet resolute, as I shared the news. The initial shock was palpable, but as I explained that the company was being taken over rather than shut down, relief washed over their faces. I assured them that their contracts remained unchanged, their jobs secure, and their pensions intact. I thanked them sincerely for their loyalty and hard work, emphasising that their well-being had been at the forefront of our discussions. Arrangements were made for them to visit the new premises that weekend and to meet Ken Randall, their soon-to-be employer. The transition would be smooth, and their futures remained stable.

As the meeting concluded, I lingered in my office, sorting through files and preparing for my departure. As I moved to leave, I noticed Alysha still at her desk, her eyes brimming with unshed tears. She quietly admitted that she would not be moving with the rest of the staff. The daily commute to the new office was too far, and she had made the decision to take early retirement to care for her grandchildren. Her voice trembled as she confessed that, after working with me, she could never imagine working for anyone else. The years she had spent at my side had been the most rewarding of her career.

I felt an unexpected lump rise in my throat. I thanked her for her years of dedication and for being the backbone of the company in ways few had ever realised. To show my appreciation, I assured her that her final pay cheque would include a six-month salary severance as a goodwill gesture. She wiped her eyes, smiled, and softly wished me a good weekend. We both understood that this was goodbye.

On the final Friday evening after Christmas, the entire team came together for one last farewell. One by one, I shook hands, exchanged words of gratitude, and wished them success in their new journey. As the last of them left, silence filled the office, a stark contrast to the years of bustling activity. I stood for a moment, taking in the space that had been my world for so long.

With a deep breath, I locked the yard for the final time and walked away, knowing that I had given everything I could. And that, at last, it was time to start anew.

Chapter Twenty-Two
Losses

As we journey through life, we inevitably lose things—money, possessions, jobs, arguments. Some losses are trivial and quickly forgotten. Others leave a permanent mark, reshaping our very existence. But nothing prepares you for the anguish of losing something truly irreplaceable: your health or that of someone you love.

Over the years, I witnessed the slow decline of not only my own health but, more painfully, that of my beloved partner. These losses, though deeply personal, set the stage for an experience I would not wish upon anyone—yet one I know too many will endure.

Gill, my ex-accountant turned wife, had always been a heavy smoker. The habit had caught up with her, leaving her with a weakened immune system and a deteriorating lung condition. Every winter became a battle. The slightest infection could turn lethal. Doctors urged us to escape the harsh British cold, warning that even a simple flu could spiral into pneumonia. So, each December, we packed our bags and fled to the Caribbean, renting a villa where the warmth offered her a fragile reprieve. We stayed until March, returning home only when the worst of the winter had passed. These annual escapes gave her a measure of stability, but as the years slipped by, her lungs failed her more and more. Eventually, she became tethered to oxygen cylinders, her once-vibrant life confined by the very breath she struggled to take.

The first real blow came in May 2002. My father, after a brief illness, was admitted to hospital. Within a week, he was gone. His death hit me like a brick, but grief had to wait. My mother and sister looked to me for strength, and I had no choice but to provide it. In the months that followed, I arranged for my mother to move back to the Midlands to be closer to my sister and her children. I sold their house in Surrey, found her a place in sheltered accommodation, and made sure she was settled. She was content with the arrangement, and my sister found comfort in having her nearby.

Life, as always, refused to stand still. The world had changed dramatically after the attack on the Twin Towers in 2001. Al-Qaeda had risen to infamy, unleashing terror on the Western world with a brutality that demanded attention. My expertise in counterterrorism did not go unnoticed. I was invited back to the Staff College in a casual role; my insights were highly respected. Soon, my knowledge was sought elsewhere—police training colleges, councils, and organisations tackling civil unrest. I accepted some of these engagements, finding satisfaction in sharing my experience, but I set firm boundaries. My marriage came first. I had learned, at great cost, that no professional duty should come before the things that truly matter.

Then, in October 2004, my mother passed away. I had always known she was never quite the same after losing my father, and in the end, I believe she simply couldn't go on without him. Once again, I had to be the steady hand, the unshaken pillar for my sister and her children. I handled the estate, ensuring her final wishes were met. I kept my grief private. Alone, in moments of quiet solitude, a single tear would escape—but never in front of others. Loss had become a familiar companion, but it did not grow easier to bear.

In August 2007, the foundation of my world collapsed once more. My sister had been battling pancreatic cancer, but she seemed to be holding her own. She was strong and resilient. I had convinced myself she was winning the fight. But by the time I arrived at her hospital bedside, the truth was inescapable. The doctors' words were grim: she wouldn't survive another 48 hours. She passed away within 24.

With her gone, my family had been reduced to ghosts and memories. My niece and nephew, though blood, were strangers to me. Only Gill remained—the one person left in my life. And yet, even she was slipping away. Her condition worsened, her lungs betraying her more with each passing day. I couldn't shake the question that haunted me: What had I done to deserve this relentless devastation?

The last five years took their toll on both of us. I masked my sorrow behind a brave face, but Gill saw through it. She always did. Still, she smiled as if to reassure me that despite everything, we had built a life worth cherishing. One evening, as she looked at me, her voice weak but steady, she said something that has never left me.

"I wouldn't have asked for anything more than the life we've had together."

Even as the weight of loss bore down on me, those words reminded me of what truly mattered.

CHAPTER TWENTY-THREE
ON MY KNEES

The Grim Reaper had not yet finished with my family.

In June 2010, after weeks of unbearable back pain, Gill insisted I see a doctor. My GP referred me to a prostate specialist, who, after several tests, delivered the devastating news: I had advanced prostate cancer. Chemotherapy followed by radiotherapy was the recommended course of action—if all went well, I'd make it through.

I won't dwell on the brutal side effects of those treatments, only to say those six months were pure agony. But even as my body weakened, I continued to care for Gill. Her greatest fear was not for herself but for our future.

At the end of the six months, I returned for my final check-up. The news was crushing. The cancer was still there. This time, the doctors proposed an alternative: brachytherapy. Under anaesthetic, they would inject forty radioactive isotope pellets directly into my prostate—targeted radiation without the torment of chemotherapy.

Another hospital visit. Another gruelling wait.

Christmas was approaching, and I refused to let cancer dictate our lives. Gill and I escaped to the Caribbean, just as we had always done. When we returned in March 2011, a letter from my specialist was waiting among the pile of posts. A follow-up appointment. More blood tests. And then—finally—some good news.

I was given the all-clear. I was over the moon.

But our joy was short-lived. That final trip had drained Gill more than I realised. Her breathing worsened to the point where she relied almost entirely on a wheelchair. Every step was an exhausting battle. I could only wonder how much longer we had left together.

Still, I had my own battles to fight. Every three months, I returned for routine check-ups. In September 2011, something changed. After my usual blood tests, the doctors ordered a full-body scan. I thought nothing of it at the time—just precaution, I assumed.

It wasn't.

My specialist sat me down, his face grave. The cancer was back. Worse, it had spread to my bladder. This time, it was aggressive and relentless. The only option was immediate surgery to remove both my bladder and prostate.

I asked him what the alternative was. His reply was one I'll never forget.

"If you don't have this operation, I doubt you'll see Christmas."

I sat there, stunned.

Then he added, "But if we do it, you'll have at least another ten years."

He went on to explain that I was an ideal candidate for a ground breaking new procedure—the Da Vinci Robotic surgery. A machine programmed with my medical scans and history would perform the operation under a surgeon's supervision. It was cutting-edge, precise, and far less invasive than traditional surgery. The alternative? Open surgery, which, he admitted, I likely wouldn't survive.

I had no choice. I couldn't leave Gill to suffer alone.

"When can you do it?" I asked.

"How about Thursday?"

I blinked. "It's Tuesday today. You don't mean this coming Thursday, do you?"

"Yes," he said simply.

And so, in October 2011, I went under the knife.

I remember the anaesthetist injecting my arm, telling me to relax. Then—nothing.

When I woke, it was chaos. Men were holding me down. I was fighting, gasping for breath. Terrorists were torturing me. I struggled to escape—until reality finally shattered the illusion.

My lungs had collapsed during surgery. They had revived me with a forced oxygen mask, inflating my lungs just enough to keep me alive. The lack of oxygen had induced hypoxia, triggering horrific hallucinations. In my mind, I was back in Ireland, trapped in a nightmare.

I spent three weeks in critical care. Another three in intensive care. Throughout it all, Gill visited in her wheelchair, offering the quiet strength I had always relied on.

By late November, I was finally discharged. Gill, determined to lift my spirits, booked another Caribbean trip.

"This is for your recovery," she said.

We soaked in every moment of that final holiday, though I didn't know then that it would be our last.

The return flight was brutal. Gill's breathing deteriorated rapidly. The pressurized cabin wreaked havoc on her fragile lungs. When we landed, her doctor delivered the final blow: she could never fly again.

It was a double-edged sword. Without our winter escapes, any respiratory infection could be fatal. And in April, that's exactly what happened.

A chest infection turned into pneumonia. Her doctor had her admitted to the hospital immediately. I visited every day, staying for hours, doing everything she could no longer do for herself. I watched as she fought a slow, agonising battle, struggling for every breath.

She could no longer speak, but she squeezed my hand—one last act of love.

Then, I watched her take her final breath.

Gill, the love of my life, was gone.

My world ended that day. I wanted to go with her. But life is not that kind. It forces you to go on, even when there's nothing left to live for. Life has a way of picking you up, dusting you off, and throwing you back into the fray, whether you're ready or not. Losing Gill was worse than losing my entire family combined. The void was unbearable. But I knew I couldn't keep drifting in grief, trapped in the past. So, I forced myself to reconnect with old friends, rekindling bonds with my former military comrades. I attended reunions, mess functions—immersing myself in the familiar world I once knew. Gill was always with me. I often asked myself, what would she do? And I always found the answer.

I threw myself into every possible endeavour, filling my time until I barely had any left for myself. The demand for my lectures on terrorism surged, and soon, I found myself speaking everywhere, offering insights into the growing threats of these organisations. The pinnacle came when I was invited to address foreign dignitaries at the UN headquarters in New York. It was in that moment—

standing in a room of world leaders—that I realised my life still had a purpose.

In June 2013, I made the painful decision to sell the cottage Gill, and I had poured our hearts into. Every inch of that home bore her presence, her touch. It became too much to bear. I moved north, purchasing a 17th-century farmhouse near the Scottish Borders—14 acres of grazing land and five acres of woodland. I envisioned a holiday retreat, building lodges for guests while restoring the farmhouse itself. For the first year, I focused on renovations, replacing electrical and water systems, modernising bathrooms, and bringing the old house back to life.

Then came the blow. My builder, while working in the loft, uncovered a devastating flaw—the entire flank wall was unstable. A structural survey confirmed the worst: it needed to be demolished and rebuilt. My insurance wouldn't cover the cost, and I faced an enormous financial burden. With no choice, I hired an architectural firm to oversee the reconstruction and moved into a rented bungalow while repairs were underway.

Around the same time, I received a letter from my oncologist in the south. I had chosen to stay under his care for regular cancer screenings. This time, after the usual tests, something felt off. A full-body scan. A next-day appointment. Then, the news: a tumour had wrapped itself around my spine. The specialist laid it out plainly—without intervention, paralysis was inevitable.

The surgery was beyond the capability of any UK surgeon. My oncologist knew of only one man who could attempt it—Professor Alexandre Mathieu, a French-Canadian spinal laser surgeon at the Lawrence University Cancer Health Centre in Quebec. But there was a catch. The British healthcare system wouldn't cover the cost. If I wanted to live, I had to fund it myself.

I agreed without hesitation. Days later, an email arrived. Professor Mathieu had reviewed my case. He believed he could remove the tumour but emphasised the complexity of the procedure. He needed me in Canada within two weeks, warning that after surgery, I'd require six months of recovery. The hospital stay would be expensive, but he suggested renting a cottage from "friends of the hospital" to save money. Then came the staggering cost breakdown. I wired his surgical fee and half the hospital expenses immediately.

Everything had to be set in order before I left. I informed my architects, depositing funds to cover the rebuild while I was away. I hired a removal company to pack and store my belongings for six months. My car went into long-term storage at the local Mercedes dealership. I even met with my bank manager, locking down my finances to prevent unauthorised transactions.

With my entire life in limbo—my home under reconstruction, my possessions in storage, my body at war with itself—I boarded a plane to Canada, placing my trust in a surgeon I had never met.

Chapter Twenty-Four
Canada

On July 10th, 2014, by 9:30 a.m., I boarded Air Canada Flight AC232, bound for Quebec. Ten hours later, at around 4 p.m. local time, I landed at Jean Lesage International Airport, exhausted but resolute. I went straight to the Lawrence University Cancer Health Centre, a sprawling facility on the outskirts of the city. After what felt like an endless series of forms, I was finally led to the office of Professor Louis Alexandre Mathieu.

He was a warm, engaging man, his French-Canadian accent giving his words a rhythmic cadence. "Call me Alex," he said with an easy smile, immediately putting me at ease. He reviewed the surgical plan and ordered additional tests for the following day. In the meantime, I was placed in the hospital's guest suite, with a promise that the "Friends of the Hospital" would soon reach out about long-term accommodations. A guide escorted me through the facility, showing me the restaurant, the lounge, and my suite. After a quick meal, exhaustion took over, and I collapsed into a deep sleep.

The next morning, after a light breakfast, I returned to Alex's office, where his secretary introduced me to a cheerful hospital porter. "I'll be with you all day," he said, holding up my itinerary. Then began a relentless battery of tests—bloodwork, X-rays in every uncomfortable position imaginable, CT and MRI scans. By the end of it, I felt like a human pincushion.

That evening, as I sat in the hospital restaurant, I noticed a man younger than me eating alone. I'd seen him earlier, moving from one test to another, mirroring my own routine. He looked like he could use some company. I introduced myself and asked if I could join him. He welcomed the gesture, and over a meal of lobster, we got to talking.

His name was Jimmy, an ex-American Ranger who had crushed spinal discs in a parachute accident. Alongside the damaged vertebrae, doctors had discovered a small cancerous growth. No other surgeon had dared to operate. Alex was his last hope. If left untreated, the fragments pressing against his spinal cord would soon leave him paralysed. I was struck by his resilience. Despite everything, he spoke about the future with unwavering determination. That night, a friendship was born—one that would soon grow into an unshakable bond.

The next morning, as Alex and I reviewed my procedure, I mentioned Jimmy and his incredible attitude. Alex nodded. "That's good to hear. You two will be seeing a lot of each other in the coming months."

After the consultation, I met Jimmy again in the hospital reception. We had both been scheduled to meet with a representative from the "Friends of the Hospital" to arrange accommodations. Jane, a lively woman with a warm, no-nonsense demeanour, greeted us. She explained that she'd be showing us two rental properties in Stoneham-Et-Tewksbury, about a 20-minute taxi ride from the hospital. Both were two-bedroom homes available at preferential rates.

"Would you prefer separate places, or are you open to sharing?" she asked.

I turned to Jimmy. "What do you think? Splitting the cost?"

"Absolutely," he replied without hesitation.

The second house sealed the deal—a quiet, single-story home with a garden nestled in a small neighbourhood. A short walk led to a shopping mall, and best of all, the owner, Helen, who was part of the "Friends of the Hospital," would handle cleaning and grocery runs at no extra cost. It was perfect.

That weekend, we settled in, getting to know each other better. Jimmy was easy going, full of stories about his hometown, Fort Morgan, Colorado. He spoke of climbing trips, fishing outings, and his family's thriving pharmaceutical business, which he was preparing to take over one day.

"You should visit sometime," he said, meaning it.

"I'd like that," I replied, and I truly would.

The weekend passed all too quickly. By Monday morning, I found myself outside Alex's office, nerves creeping in. When he called me in, his tone was direct yet reassuring. He wanted to admit me immediately, with the first part of my surgery scheduled for the following morning. The procedure would be performed in two stages using keyhole laser surgery. First, through a frontal approach, Alex would remove most of the tumour with a laser and separate the upper and lower discs from the affected vertebrae. I would remain under sedation for twelve hours to ensure the wound site stabilised. Then, through a rear incision, he would remove the remaining tumour and the damaged discs, replacing them with Polycarbonate Urethane Nucleus Discs encased in titanium alloy shells. These artificial discs, filled with saline, would compress naturally under pressure, mimicking the function of real spinal discs. Once the operation was complete, the extracted tissue would undergo pathology testing. Only then would we know if chemotherapy or radiotherapy was necessary.

I signed the consent forms, Alex covered a few final details, and I was taken to my hospital room. There, I met the anaesthetist and a team of medics who performed the necessary pre-op procedures. From that moment on, I was forbidden from eating or drinking. The rest of the day was an agonising wait. I distracted myself with magazines and television, telling myself I'd endured worse—but the anxiety never faded. At last, dawn arrived. I was wheeled into the operating theatre.

I have no memory of coming around from the anaesthesia, but I do recall waking up later to a gentle voice instructing me not to move suddenly—and then, remarkably, being asked to try standing. To my astonishment, within six hours, I was walking with the help of a physiotherapist. That evening, Alex visited my room. He was pleased with the results—the tumour was completely removed, the infected discs replaced, and the procedure had gone exactly as planned. He wanted me to remain in the hospital for observation for a few more days just to ensure everything settled well.

Not long after he left, I had a surprise visitor, Jimmy. His usual jovial demeanour was a welcome sight. He had me laughing in no time despite my soreness. He wasn't allowed to eat that night—his own surgery was scheduled for the next morning. I wished him the best, promising to be there when he came out of the operating room.

The next six weeks blurred into a routine of recovery and treatment. Alex recommended a course of radiotherapy as a precaution. Though exhausting, I agreed. Jimmy, however, refused any further treatment. He had heard too many horror stories about the side effects and decided to take his chances. I tried reasoning with him, but his mind was set. Thankfully, Jean and Helen took turns showing us around Quebec, giving us a much-needed escape from the hospital environment. The day finally arrived when we were both discharged.

In my final meeting with Alex, I thanked him for everything. Still, I admitted I was hesitant about flying home. His response was simple: "Why not take a holiday first? Give yourself time to recover properly." I told him I'd think about it. He assured me all my medical records would be sent back to my UK hospital, then wished me well.

When I returned to our house, I found Jimmy in deep thought. Over a long conversation, he revealed his plan—to see as much of the world as possible before settling down and taking over his father's business. Canada, South America, the Orient—he wanted to experience it all. Helen, our ever-thoughtful landlady, suggested a Canadian rail tour. She knew a travel agent in Quebec who could arrange everything, including accommodations and the famed Rocky Mountaineer journey through the mountains. It was perfect. Jimmy was all for it. "If we're passing through the States," he added, "I want to stop in Denver. You have to meet my parents." And so, our next adventure began.

After forwarding most of our belongings to Jimmy's home, we boarded a train that would carry us across Canada. We travelled light, our backpacks stocked for the two-week journey ahead. If you ever seek a once-in-a-lifetime experience, this trip should be at the top of your list. Canada unfolds before you like a masterpiece—vast, untamed, and breathtaking. From Quebec, we journeyed to Montreal, then on to Toronto, skirting immense lakes and towering mountains. The city welcomed us warmly, its people treating us as old friends. As the train pressed westward, we passed through Winnipeg, a land of endless forests and crystalline lakes. We crossed bridges that defied reason, marvelling at the sheer audacity of their engineering. Stopping for a few days in Jasper, we stood in awe of the towering mountain ranges, the roaring rivers, and the waterfalls that tumbled with relentless energy. Finally, we arrived in

Vancouver, where we spent time on Vancouver Island, gazing out over the Pacific and indulging in the freshest seafood imaginable.

Our next leg took us across the border via Amtrak, bound for Denver. Crossing into the U.S., we underwent a thorough customs check. Immigration officers combed through our bags, ensuring nothing illegal had slipped through. Satisfied, they cleared us for entry. We made a brief stop in Salt Lake City, then pressed on toward Denver, where Jimmy's father awaited our arrival. Our time in Canada had come to an end. But in many ways, the journey was just beginning.

CHAPTER TWENTY-FIVE
FINALITY

The drive from Denver to Fort Morgan was marked by a constant flow of conversation, part welcome-home chatter from Jim's father, Jeff, part reflection on our recent operations and hospital stay in Quebec, and part musings on life back in Stoneham. Jimmy joked fondly of our friends Jane and Helen, peppering the journey with anecdotes and laughter that made the long drive seem shorter than it was.

It took us a couple of hours to reach Fort Morgan, and when we finally pulled into Jimmy's home, I was taken aback. The property was impressive—grand, almost regal—with a long driveway that curled into a wide roundabout, flanked by a house that stood with quiet authority.

We stayed there for about a month, and during that time, I came to know Jeff and his wife, Rita, not just as Jimmy's parents but as dear friends. We shared long conversations about life's twists and turns, about past chapters we had lived and the ones still unwritten. Both Jeff and Rita thanked me, almost too warmly, for looking after Jimmy during our time in Canada. They said he had spoken often of my encouragement and how that support had meant more to him than they could ever express. Rita remarked that Jimmy had changed—matured—and credited me for his transformation. I shrugged it off at the time, not thinking much of it. But that gratitude would come back to me later in ways I could never have imagined.

With our sights set on adventure, we began meticulously planning our next journey. I still had access to my open-ended bank card—an invaluable tool for international travel. It allowed purchases and cash withdrawals without restriction, drawing from a reserve account if needed. Perfect for booking flights and hotels and navigating unexpected costs.

Our plan was bold: fly from Denver to Cancún, Mexico, then travel south by car, exploring the country as profoundly as time allowed. From there, on to Costa Rica, followed by the Bahamas for a brief sailing escape. Then, across the Pacific to Japan and finally to South Korea. From there, back to Denver—and eventually, I'd return to the UK. It would take us six months. This, I knew, would be my final great adventure before retiring for good. And I intended to savour every moment.

When the time came, I thanked Jeff and Rita for their kindness. We parted ways not just as guests and hosts but as lifelong friends.

Cancún welcomed us with a humidity that clung to the skin and the kind of vibrancy that only Mexico can deliver. We reached the Renaissance Hotel via a talkative local taxi driver and made it our base for a few days while settling in and sorting a hire car. We planned to drop it off in the south, allowing us maximum freedom to explore.

Mexico is a land of contrasts—old and new, rich and poor, tradition tightly interwoven with modernity. The people are warm, and the food is exceptional. The key to understanding Mexico lies in its local eateries—its Cantinas. That's where the heart of the culture lives. Skip the tourist traps; they're built to drain your wallet and offer little in return. The deeper south we went, the greener and more welcoming the country became, a vast shift from the dusty roads we'd left behind.

We hit our first snag when trying to travel to Costa Rica by train. What seemed a romantic idea turned quickly to disappointment when we learned the lines through Guatemala, Nicaragua, and Honduras were primarily defunct. Even if running, the journey would've taken fifty hours. We diverted to Querétaro Airport and booked a flight instead.

I won't labour over our time in Costa Rica or Bermuda—only to say both were revelations, filled with natural beauty and cultural richness. But Japan—Japan was something else entirely.

There is no parallel for the way Japan lives between two worlds: tradition and progress. We arrived at the height of cherry blossom season, and I'll never forget the surreal sensation of walking through a storm of fragrant petals as a breeze whispered through ancient gardens. Their landscape design, particularly in the Kyoto region, was more than aesthetic—it was spiritual. Over a month, we visited wonders from Mount Fuji to the Nachi Waterfalls, Hell Valley in Hokkaido, and the breathtaking Akiyoshido Caves. We glided between cities on the Shinkansen—the bullet train—each place we stopped revealing another layer of Japan's soul.

That chapter of our journey would stay with me forever.

Then came Seoul.

We checked into the Marriott Hotel, a sleek glass monolith in the heart of the city. Our suite was on the 12th floor—two rooms joined by a shared living space, modern and quiet. We planned to stay a month. But something about Korea felt… off. From the start, I sensed unease. People seemed distant, even suspicious. Their wariness of outsiders sat like a veil over every interaction. Jimmy told me I was being too British about it, too rigid. He advised me to relax and let it go. I tried.

We spent the first few days seeing the sights, including some of Jimmy's old haunts. But even he began to feel a chill in the air—"some form of resentment," he called it. Wanting a proper look at the city, we joined a coach tour, hoping for an organised route through the history and landmarks of Seoul. What we got was rushed, impersonal, and wholly disappointing. Crowded stops, barked instructions, and little chance to take in what we saw.

The hotel concierge listened to our complaints and suggested we hire a private guide, something the hotel arranged regularly. That night, we discussed it over drinks, trying to put our finger on what didn't sit right. Jimmy said the city was too packed and too fast-moving like New York, he said, but without the mindset to pull it off.

We agreed—something had to change.

A couple of days later, as we sat down to breakfast in the hotel lounge, the concierge approached us with a polite smile and a question.

"Would you be available this morning?" he asked. "Your tour guide will be arriving around mid-morning if that's convenient."

We exchanged a glance and nodded. "Of course," I replied. We were eager to begin a more personal exploration of Korea and looked forward to meeting this mysterious guide.

Sure enough, just after eleven, the suite bell rang. I opened the door to find a small, casually dressed young man standing there, no more than twenty-three, with an infectious grin stretching ear to ear. He greeted us with a firm handshake, one of those enthusiastic ones that instantly puts you at ease.

"I'm your guide," he announced brightly.

We invited him in, and it didn't take long to warm to the chap. Cheerful, quick-witted, and charming in a self-effacing way, he introduced himself as "Do-Hyun-Chung"—but insisted we call him "Joe."

Seated comfortably in our lounge, he leaned forward, eager. "So, what do you want to see? Where do you want to go? And how long have I got you for?"

We laid it out for him—our interest in Korean history, architecture, and culture. We wanted to see as much of the country as time would allow. We mentioned the DMZ as well, though we'd been warned that the official tours were overcrowded, sanitised, and didn't offer much insight into the reality of the place.

Joe laughed. "It'll take a week—maybe more—to show you everything you want to see," he said. "But I've got a 4x4. I'll take you wherever you want to go."

Then he paused, his tone shifting slightly.

"As for the DMZ... I'm probably the only guide in Korea who can actually take you into the Zone."

We looked at him, surprised.

"I was born there," he explained. "My family still lives in Taesung."

He told us about the village, nestled within the DMZ itself—an anomaly that had refused to die. When the Zone was first created, the villagers refused to leave. Both North and South, against all odds, honoured that decision. To this day, Taesung remained inhabited, its residents farming ancestral land as they always had. Joe visited often, bringing supplies they couldn't get from the tiny shop within the village.

“If you want,” he said, “we can visit. Stay overnight. I’m going up there soon anyway.”

He laid out the logistics. The border was manned by American servicemen and South Korean soldiers. Every visitor was registered on entry and exit, and entry was only permitted under the escort of a resident. Joe, of course, still counted.

We agreed on a fee for the week and shook hands. I still wasn’t thrilled at the idea of sleeping within the DMZ, but Jimmy was all for it. He had a familiarity with the place, and his confidence put me at ease—at least, momentarily.

The next seven days were nothing short of remarkable. We crisscrossed the country, ticking off temples, palaces, shrines, and ancient ruins, with Joe acting as a one-man encyclopaedia. He knew every corner, every backstreet, and every bit of local trivia that brought the history of each place to life.

He was equally savvy when it came to food, guiding us to the best restaurants and tucked-away cafés—places tourists rarely found. Nightlife, we politely declined. Joe offered suggestions, but we had no desire to tangle with Korea’s ever-present drug culture.

We stayed overnight in a few locations as we moved deeper into the south, and Joe was grateful for the hotel rooms we booked for him. When the week was nearly up, we extended our arrangement. He seemed genuinely pleased. I had the impression he’d never taken guests on such an extended tour before.

Eventually, we returned to Seoul for a brief rest at the hotel. But Joe was soon back, cheerful as ever, asking what we’d like to do next.

“How about we pack some overnight bags?” he said casually. “We’ll head up to the border tomorrow morning. Visit my family.”

We agreed.

That evening, Jimmy rang home. He recounted the highlights of our travels to his father and mentioned we'd be heading up to the DMZ in the morning. There was a pause on the other end. Clearly, Jeff wasn't keen on the idea. But Jimmy reassured him, said it was all safe and above board.

Then he passed me the phone.

Jeff's voice was calm but carried a familiar edge of concern. He thanked me again—for looking after Jimmy during his recovery—and asked me, once more, to keep an eye on him. I reassured him. We were strong again, back to full health, and had barely thought of the operation in weeks.

"Stop worrying," I said with a chuckle.

Jeff laughed and wished us well, promising to have something warm waiting when we got back.

As I put the phone down, I glanced at Jimmy and said quietly, "I think your dad wants us to go home."

Crossing into Taesung proved more of a challenge than expected. We passed through American security first, then South Korean, each checkpoint a deliberate reminder that we were entering one of the most sensitive strips of land on the planet. Joe had to present a series of documents to prove he was a resident and that he would be responsible for us during our stay. Only then were we waved through, allowed to continue on into the village.

It had rained heavily through the night, and by the time we arrived at Joe's parents' house, it was already past midday. The village was quiet, cloaked in the heavy damp of the storm that had only just begun to ease. We were cold, weary, and ready for warmth in every form—thankfully, we were not disappointed.

Inside the house, we were welcomed with an immense spread of food. The aromas alone lifted our spirits. At the centre was a dish called Chapchae—a stir-fry of pork and glass noodles with crisp vegetables, made using meat from Joe's father's own pigs. Surrounding it were numerous smaller dishes, each one colourful and fragrant, accompanied by bowls of rice. These were what the Koreans referred to as Bapsang, and the etiquette was clear: every dish was to be sampled.

Then came the formal introductions—Joe's father, Min-Jun; his mother, Ha-Un; his grandfather, Tae-Hyun; and his grandmother, Eun-Ji. They welcomed us so warmly, so wholeheartedly, that it was almost overwhelming. Later, Joe explained the reason for their generosity. We had helped give him a good living, he said. He sent money home throughout the year, and though they had heard stories of his 'tourist friends', we were the first they had actually met—hence the extra fuss.

That afternoon drifted into the evening with ease. Through Joe, who now doubled as our interpreter, we asked countless questions about what life was really like in a village trapped in such an unusual space—caught between two worlds, one foot in peace, the other inches from conflict.

Their answers were sobering. This had always been their home, and for the older generations, there was never a question of leaving. The younger villagers, however, dreamed of life in the South—never the North. Life there was, in their words, a matter of survival.

They spoke matter-of-factly about soldiers from the North crossing into the village to steal livestock. Chickens, pigs—anything they could take. Every night, the villagers secured their animals in sturdy pens. It wasn't fear that drove them, just hard-learned caution. The soldiers never came too close to the homes, but the fields were fair game.

Surprised, I asked how such incursions were possible. I had always imagined the border to be fenced, mined, a heavily guarded no-man's-land. But Min-Jun shook his head.

"There are no fences around this part," Joe translated. "No, mines. Not near the village."

According to him, the rest of the border was secured, but this area—barely a mile wide—was open land. Thick with trees and brush, it was easy to hide in, and the North Korean patrols used it freely. No one ever defected, he said. They came to steal. Cabbages, carrots, unripe or not—it didn't matter. Food was scarce in the North, and pilfering from Taesung was routine.

As night fell, there was a knock at the door. A local police patrol, clipboard in hand, came to check the resident register. Everyone had to be accounted for. A curfew was now in place, effective until dawn.

I was surprised—but not alarmed. This place operated by its own rules.

We turned in for the night, but sleep came hard. The storm had returned with a vengeance. Thunder rattled the windows, and near-monsoon rain hammered down upon the roof, turning gutters into waterfalls and sending wind whistling through every crack in the walls.

Then came the morning—and with it, chaos.

We were jolted awake by shouting and frantic movement. The whole house seemed in uproar. We dressed quickly and stepped out to find the family in a state of mild panic. Joe explained the situation. The storm had done more than disturb our sleep—it had weakened the animal pens, and the pigs and chickens had escaped.

Some of the chickens were still pecking about the yard, but the pigs had scattered. His father, clearly distressed, was preparing to search the surrounding fields.

We offered to help, and our offer was gladly accepted. Joe said he would go with his grandfather, while Jimmy and I were to join Min-Jun on the tractor and head out across the farmland.

And so we did—unaware that this innocent errand, triggered by a night of foul weather, would soon lead us across an invisible line… into a nightmare.

For two hours, we tramped through the sodden fields, soaked to the skin, slipping and sliding through mud as we tried to stay on our feet. The rain had turned everything into a treacherous quagmire. Eventually, we recovered one of the pigs and managed to secure it in the trailer.

Then Jimmy spotted two more on the edge of the field, half-hidden in the undergrowth. Without thinking, we ran towards them—an instinctive move and not a smart one. Spooked, the pigs bolted more profoundly into the brush.

Joe's father began shouting and waving his arms in desperation, trying to stop us. It took us a moment to realise what he meant: we were to approach slowly, or we'd lose them. We waved back, acknowledging him—but it was too late. The pigs had already vanished further into the thicket.

Still, we pressed on. Eventually, we caught them, wrestled them into sacks, and began to haul them back towards the tractor.

And then it happened.

A sharp, excruciating pain struck the back of my neck. My world collapsed in a blur of black.

When I came to, my hands were bound, my chest pinned by a heavy boot. I was being jostled violently in the back of what I assumed was a jeep. Jimmy lay beside me, unconscious. My head throbbed with the dull ache of trauma. My vision was hazy, but through the blur, I could make out the figure standing above us—brown uniform, red star on his hat.

We were in trouble.

We were in the North.

I tried to sit up, to speak, but my captor slammed his boot into my face. The blackness returned.

At some point, the vehicle stopped. We were shoved out of the back like sacks of grain, hitting the ground with a bone-rattling thud.

I didn't know where we were. Somewhere far from help, somewhere hostile. The treatment made one thing clear—any attempt at resistance or even speech would be met with violence. Every time we opened our mouths, we were silenced with a fist, a kick, or the butt of a rifle.

Silence, I realised, was our only defence—for now.

Instinct took over. My training kicked in. Years ago, I had drilled for this exact scenario—capture, isolation, interrogation. It had felt theoretical then. Now, it was all too real. I reminded myself of everything I'd been taught about evasion, survival, and endurance. Those lessons, buried for decades, surged back in sharp focus. They would be my only protection in the unknown hours ahead.

We were dragged into a cell. Calling it a cell was generous. It had barely enough headroom to stand upright. The doorway looked like it had been designed for children or midgets—deliberately demeaning.

Jimmy was dumped in beside me, groaning. Despite all his physical strength all his military background, I could see this was already taking its toll on him. I could tell he wasn't prepared for this—not mentally. And I feared it would get much, much worse.

"We're in a no-win situation," I told him quietly. "You need to man up. This isn't going to end quickly. We've got to keep our heads, stay alert, and watch everything they say and do."

Then the memory struck me—Joe's father shouting, waving, eyes wide with panic. He hadn't just been trying to stop us from chasing pigs. He'd been warning us. We were crossing the border. We had misread everything—and now we were paying the price.

We had fallen into the worst possible scenario. What we'd heard about the North Korean regime wasn't exaggerated—it was understated. We were now facing the very real prospect of torture, imprisonment, and even death.

I glanced at my watch. It was approaching midday. We had been in their hands for nearly five hours. Interrogation would be next. That much was certain.

An hour later, they came for us.

We were marched from the cell and into a dimly lit room. There, we were ordered to strip. Our clothing was taken, and we were issued rough smocks and loose-fitting trousers. All our possessions—wallets, watches, everything—were confiscated. Then, we were separated and placed under armed guard in adjoining rooms.

Two officers entered mine. One carried a clipboard; the other, I quickly determined, was the senior. One of them spoke English. They ordered me to sit at a desk and began their questioning.

For two long hours, I was interrogated. It was tense, deliberate. They wanted to know everything—why we were in Korea, why we had visited Taesung, where we had come from. I answered truthfully. I explained we had both undergone cancer operations in Canada and were travelling as part of our recuperation. We were exploring cultures, taking in the world while we still had the strength. I held nothing back. There was nothing to hide—or so I thought.

Then, a third officer entered.

He carried a sheet of paper—and, to my surprise, my wallet.

Without a word, the original interrogator took the list, opened my wallet, and laid my identification cards out on the table.

The moment he picked up one in particular, I saw his expression shift.

He had found my Sandhurst Staff College pass—also my ID card from the Sandhurst Military Academy. It identified me as a retired Major.

I felt my heart drop. The silence was deafening.

Then came the inevitable explosion.

"You have lied to me. You are not a tourist—you are a military spy!" he screamed, grabbing a cane from the table and lashing out.

The blows came fast and merciless. I tried to protest, but that only made it worse. In North Korea, you do not argue. You do not speak unless spoken to. And you never, under any circumstances, meet your interrogator's eyes.

I was beaten until I lost consciousness. When I came to, I was back in the cell, bloodied and bruised. Jimmy was lying beside me, unconscious, too. The nightmare was real, and it had only just begun.

I would later learn that he had also been labelled a spy. His mistake? A tattoo. A large US Army Ranger insignia was inked across his upper arm. It couldn't be hidden, and it didn't take a genius to draw conclusions.

We lay side by side, whispering in the dark, battered and aching. There was no strategy now—only survival.

Eventually, exhaustion overcame us, and with every muscle screaming, we drifted into an uneasy sleep, two soldiers lost in a war we hadn't meant to enter.

We were questioned again. Once more, we protested our innocence.

The officer who had previously beaten me seemed, surprisingly, a little more human that morning—his tone less harsh, his eyes no longer burning with hostility. He admitted to being confused about my background.

I gave him a brief account of my military history. I explained that I was in my late sixties now and that I had left the services over thirty-five years ago. During my time in the Army, I had studied terrorist organisations extensively, which led to me lecturing on the subject. After a bomb explosion—one that left me injured—I was forced into early retirement.

I told him plainly: I was not a spy, and neither was Jimmy. We were tourists. Our accidental crossing into North Korea had come about through sheer misfortune.

I explained how we had arrived in Taesung with our driver, Joe. Following a violent storm, some of the livestock had broken free, and in searching for them, we had inadvertently strayed across the border. There had been no intent—just a tragic misstep.

To my surprise, he seemed to accept my explanation. He nodded and said he would report his findings to his superiors. We would have to wait for a decision.

In the meantime, he informed me, we were to be sent to a foreigner's work camp.

Before being taken away, I asked for a moment.

He allowed it.

I told him about the cancer operation I had undergone, how it had left me with a pouch for a bladder, and that I had only a few remaining pouches in my jacket. I asked if I might retrieve them and whether further supplies could be arranged.

He agreed and said I would be seen by a doctor—an Indian man serving the republic who was familiar with such procedures. The officer assured me he would honour the doctor's recommendation.

That man was Ravi Patra.

Dr Patra was an Indian physician who oversaw the Indian community managing North Korea's counterfeit garment industry—factories that produced fake designer clothing and footwear for export to India and, eventually, the West.

It took several days to gain his trust, but he seemed to warm to us. He took a particular interest in my medical condition, frequently asking about the skin grafts I'd undergone. He was amazed at the intricacy of the surgical work on my hands and arms, often praising the surgeon's skill. I owe that man a great deal—not just for the care he provided but for saving my life on more than one occasion.

Dr Patra informed the camp administrator that I was to be given the pouches found in my jacket, and he would arrange to source more through medical suppliers in China. However, very few ever arrived, and the situation soon became one of recurring embarrassment and discomfort.

Ravi also requested to monitor our general health and, more surprisingly, recommended that we be placed into a re-education programme. He argued that we didn't understand the ways of the Korean regime and that such ignorance might prove dangerous.

Then came a comment that stunned both of us.

He asked whether we had relatives who might be willing to purchase our release. He explained that due to the dire state of the Korean economy, it was not uncommon for political prisoners and foreign captives to be sold back to their countries or families—if the cost could be met.

Without hesitation, Jimmy provided his father's name and contact information, assuring Ravi that Jeff would pay to secure his freedom.

I had no such option. There was no one who could do the same for me.

Soon after, we were relocated to another cell block—this one housing around ten other foreign prisoners, all in various stages of starvation and decay. It didn't take long to understand why.

There was no sanitation. We squatted over a rusting pail in the corner of the room. The stench was unbearable initially, but eventually, like everything else, we grew numb to it.

Washing was a luxury we no longer had. There was no running water. The only chance to bathe came when it rained—and then, you made the most of it.

Each morning, before the sun had even risen, we were woken—probably around 3:30 a.m.—and marched under armed guard to perform manual labour. There were no machines. We ploughed fields with mattocks, planted rice in endless paddy fields, bent double in cold mud. Those who failed to work fast enough or made errors were punished without hesitation. Canes across the backs of the legs. Fists to the face.

Many of the weaker prisoners didn't last long. I saw men beaten to death. I saw men shot.

There was one moment that will stay with me until my last breath.

A Swedish man in our group—thin as a rake, hollow-eyed—had an open wound on his chest where a rib protruded grotesquely through torn skin. He was in agony. That morning, he simply gave up. He dropped to his knees in the field, clutching his side.

A guard stormed over and kicked him twice in the ribs, shouting for him to get up. The man rolled over in the dirt, groaned, and—clearly delirious—swore in his native tongue. He picked up a clod of earth and threw it weakly in the guard's direction.

The guard didn't hesitate.

He drew his pistol and shot him in the head.

That was the level of terror we were under.

There were no trials. No second chances. Only survival—if you were strong enough to endure it.

During the first eighteen months of our internment, I learned to survive in ways I never thought possible.

My training came back to me—lessons from special operations selection, where we were taught how to survive in the wilderness. I remembered the grasses and weeds that could supply essential vitamins, the bitter-tasting leaves that offered protein, and the simple fact that anything alive could, in extremis, become food.

I ate cockroaches, black beetles, and spiders. I even caught rats—disembowelled them, skinned them, and ate their flesh raw when necessary. I know it turns your stomach just to think of it, but survival strips away your choices. A living thing becomes the food of life.

At first, Jimmy thought I had lost my mind. But he soon realised that, unlike the others, I wasn't wasting away. In fact, despite my age, I remained stronger than many of the younger men. He reluctantly adopted my methods, and his condition improved—at least for a while.

Still, I could see him fading. The illnesses became more frequent. Each bout made him weaker. The guards, of course, had no sympathy. They beat him more savagely than ever in an effort to keep him working. Time and again, I stepped in to shield him. Time and again, I paid for it with vicious beatings of my own.

Then, one day, it all changed.

After another ferocious assault on us both, Dr Ravi arrived at our cell, flanked by two guards. He ordered that Jimmy be taken out.

I panicked. I thought they were going to execute him.

I tried to intervene, but Ravi stepped close, holding me back. He leaned in and whispered, "Jimmy goes home. He will be looked after."

I froze.

I looked at him, too stunned to speak. Ravi gave me a small, almost imperceptible smile—the first true act of compassion I'd seen from him.

And then he was gone. And so was Jimmy.

I was alone. My friend, my companion, my comrade was gone.

And I think... my will to live went with him.

A fog of despair settled over me. For the first time since our capture, I came close to giving up.

That's when it hit me—what this regime indeed was. I had seen, felt, and endured its cruelty. But now I understood its purpose.

This was the endgame of terror. This was what happens when the terrorist wins.

This is what life becomes when state-sponsored terrorism is allowed to flourish—unchecked, unopposed. This wasn't just about one man's dictatorship. It was the realisation of every despotic fantasy that had ever been dreamt: Hitler's Reich, Genghis Khan's empire, Caesar's conquest of the known world. None of them succeeded.

But Kim Jong-Un had.

He had created a nation governed by absolute fear, where the people cowered in silent obedience, conditioned from birth to never question, never hope. The outside world was invisible to them. They lived and died in the only reality they had ever known: submission.

As for me, my feet were in ruins—shredded by repeated beatings. I could barely stand. Dr. Ravi intervened again, insisting I finally be transferred into the re-education programme he had advocated for years earlier.

Suddenly, I found myself being scrubbed, shaved, and dressed in clean clothes. I was moved into a dormitory and given a wooden pallet to sleep on. Compared to where I had been, it felt like paradise.

Each day, I was taken to a classroom where I was subjected to endless propaganda films and lectures—all in Korean, a language I barely understood. Still, I sat through it all, nodding when expected, never smiling. Smiling, I had learned, was dangerous—it could be interpreted as mockery, a form of dissent.

I learned how to worship "The Supreme Leader" and how he had allegedly given us a wonderful life filled with opportunity and abundance. It was laughable—except that no one was laughing.

Had I voiced my true thoughts, I would've been taken outside, hanged, or shot without hesitation. And probably made into an example.

So, I remained silent. I listened. I endured.

After eleven months of this indoctrination, I was taken to the Administrator's office. I was informed—coldly, without ceremony—that I had already been sentenced, in my absence, by the Provincial Special Courts.

My crimes?

Entering the Democratic People's Republic of Korea illegally. Failing to show respect to the authorities of the Republic. And theft—of a pig, deemed the property of the state.

For these offences, I was to serve five years of hard labour.

Without pause, I was returned to my dormitory, issued a new smock and trousers, and marched back to the foreigner cell block. Then, it was straight back to the fields.

And nothing had changed.

Not that I expected it to. But things soon took a turn—though not for the better.

People began dying.

At first, the deaths were attributed to heat exhaustion and dehydration. But even when we were given water, more and more fell. One by one, they collapsed where they stood. Within hours, they were gone.

I wrapped the dead in straw. There were no coffins. No body bags. I buried them in shallow graves, exactly where they dropped.

It was a grim, haunting task.

Eventually, the truth came out.

It wasn't the heat. It wasn't a lack of water. It was measles.

The infection had spread quickly and violently. When the authorities discovered the cause, an order was issued from above: the soldiers were to be inoculated immediately.

That's when Dr Ravi came to me again.

He needed help. I had been vaccinated as a child and was, therefore, immune. The guards wouldn't contract the virus from me. That made me valuable.

For the next several weeks, I accompanied Ravi across the region, helping treat the sick and administering inoculations—hundreds of them, all sourced from China. I moved among the soldiers, dispensing injections, following Ravi's lead.

But make no mistake—I was still a prisoner.

To the soldiers, I wasn't a medic. I wasn't even a man.

I was an animal.

Just another tool to be used until it broke.

I had lost a considerable amount of weight during my time at the re-education centre—nearly thirty kilos. The reason was simple: I no longer had access to the weeds and insects that had once supplemented my diet. My body, already battered, had begun to weaken rapidly. I told Dr Ravi that I was feeling light-headed and fatigued. His response was unusually sharp.

"Tomorrow," he said, "we visit the southern border posts to administer inoculations to the guards. That's the area where you were captured. You must be fit. You will need all your strength."

Then he looked at me—sternly, but with something else in his eyes. Something softer.

"You have been a great help," he added. "And I wish you well for the future."

It was a strange thing for him to say, out of character. But I let it pass, though it lingered in my mind like an echo.

That night, I barely slept. An hour or two, no more. I was eventually awakened by Ravi himself. He was quiet, almost gentle. As we drove south in the truck, he said nothing. Then, abruptly, he reached into his bag, pulled out an orange, peeled it slowly, and handed me two segments.

I stared at him in disbelief.

I hadn't seen fruit—real fruit—in over four years. It looked like a gem, glowing softly in the morning light.

"Eat it," he said. "You will need your strength today."

I didn't hesitate. I placed the segments in my mouth and savoured them like nectar from the gods. I could have wept. I could have kissed him.

He looked at me—calm, deliberate—and spoke in a voice I had never heard from him before. For the first time, he used my name.

"David," he said. "You have recently been sentenced to five years' labour. By asking for your assistance with this measles outbreak, I've kept you from being sent to Camp Fourteen in the

North. A Kwan-Li-So labour camp. No one ever leaves there. You will not survive five more years. There will be torture. Forced starvation. If you disobey, even once, you will be executed."

I was stunned. I told him I had already been in the country for over four years. How could they add another five?

"They have," he replied quietly.

Tears welled in my eyes and spilt down my cheeks.

Then he said firmly, "Today, I will give you an order. You will obey it without question or hesitation. Promise me this now."

I nodded. "Of course," I whispered. "I would never disobey you."

"Good," he said. "Because you must act the moment I tell you."

The day unfolded like all the others had. Inoculations. Border posts. Endless fatigue. The heat pressed down like a blanket.

By the afternoon, Ravi told me we had just one more outpost to visit before we returned to the camp. I nodded and followed.

We arrived. We did our work. I could see the border in the distance—so close it almost hurt to look at. The landscape beyond seemed to shimmer, just out of reach. Freedom.

Then, without warning, as we were driving back, Ravi veered off the main road onto a rough track. He didn't speak. He drove fast, the truck bouncing and jolting across the uneven ground.

Suddenly, he pulled to a halt.

To the left, I saw rows of cultivated land. Cabbages.

My heart stopped. I knew this place.

Taesung.

Ravi grabbed my hand and shook it firmly.

"I order you to run," he said. "Do not stop. Do not look back. Good luck. Go."

I didn't hesitate.

I leapt from the truck and ran with every ounce of strength I had left. I crashed through undergrowth, brambles tearing at my skin, ripping into my legs and thighs. But panic fuelled me. Adrenaline overrode exhaustion.

I ran. And ran. And ran.

Until finally, I collapsed—gasping, broken, trembling—on a patch of freshly ploughed land.

I don't know how long I lay there. Minutes? Hours? Time lost all meaning.

Then, through blurred vision, I saw two figures running toward me. I struggled to rise, staggering to my knees.

They seemed familiar. And I… to them.

"Ha-Un?" I said. "It's good to see you… after so long."

It was Joe's parents.

Recognition bloomed on their faces. They ran to me, tears streaming, and pulled me into their arms. I was held, hugged, supported. And then half-carried to their home.

They alerted the local police. I could barely speak, my mind still refusing to believe what had happened. They wanted statements—details—but I was too far gone. The weight of freedom, the shock of it, crushed my ability to think.

They would not allow me to leave until an ambulance arrived the following day.

That evening, they bathed me, spoon-fed me, cleaned my wounds, and wrapped me in comfort I hadn't known in years. It was tender. It was real.

As the mist of exhaustion settled over my eyes, I felt my mind cloud. But I welcomed it. I sank into the warmth of clean sheets, a quiet room, and the knowledge—fragile though it was—that I was finally free.

And I drifted into the deepest, most peaceful sleep I have ever known.

The following morning was a whirlwind of activity. The local police returned to the farm and informed me that I was to be transported to a hospital in Seoul, where I could receive treatment for my wounds and be medically assessed. The British Embassy had been notified of my situation and would be sending a representative to discuss arrangements for my return to the UK once I was deemed fit to travel.

But before they could get another word in, Ha-Un sprang into action.

She began shouting furiously at the officers, waving her arms with righteous indignation. "He will leave when he has regained his strength—not before!" she barked. "He has suffered enough in the North! I will not allow the same treatment from the South!" Her voice thundered through the modest home.

Min-Jun joined her, and between the two of them, they physically ushered the officers out of the house, pushing them back despite their protests. I watched, stunned—and then, for the first time in five years, I laughed. A genuine, unfiltered laugh. It felt alien and familiar all at once.

That morning, we spoke freely, and though I could only manage broken Korean, it felt good to have simple, heartfelt conversations again. They told me how they had cried when we were taken, how Min-Jun had tried to stop us—how we had crossed the North without realising. They were investigated by the authorities for weeks after, treated with suspicion, and subjected to intense scrutiny.

I apologised. They waved it away. "It was not you who treated us like criminals," they said.

Then came the news I hadn't expected.

Their mother, Eun-Ji, had passed away shortly after our disappearance. The stress, they said, had been too much. They didn't blame me. She had been ancient, and her time had come—but I could see the sadness in their eyes, still sharp and unresolved.

Later that day, Joe arrived.

It felt like reuniting with a long-lost brother. He launched himself at me, hugging me so tightly I thought he might crack my ribs.

"You're so thin!" he exclaimed. "So gaunt!"

That earned him a sharp rebuke from his mother. "Don't be so rude! If you had been through what he has, you'd look gaunt too!"

Despite myself, I chuckled again.

I doubted anything remained of my old belongings, but I asked anyway. They told me everything had been taken by the police and sent to the British Embassy.

Joe went to a cupboard and retrieved a mobile phone.

"It belonged to Jimmy," he said softly.

He explained that he had heard Jimmy was taken back to America after being released from a hospital in Seoul. He was puzzled—why had the Americans managed to secure Jimmy's release and not mine?

I told him the truth. "His father paid a ransom."

I asked if I could see him. Joe nodded, charged the phone, and handed it to me later that evening. I found Jeff's number in the contacts and dialled.

It rang.

And then I hung up.

I looked at Joe, despair flooding through me. "I can't speak to Jeff," I said. "I promised him I'd look after Jimmy. I failed."

Joe didn't argue. He took the phone and stepped out of the room. Five minutes later, he returned.

"I spoke to Jimmy's father," he said gently. "I told him what happened. He's coming to Korea… to take you home."

Tears welled again. I had no words.

I said a tearful farewell to my friends in Taesung. I will never forget them, nor the kindness they showed me. They had given everything they could in a world where so much had been taken from me.

The next few days were spent in Seoul Hospital. To my surprise, I was given a clean bill of health, though I was placed on a high-protein diet to help rebuild my strength. Embassy officials visited regularly, arranging a replacement passport and verifying my identity through my old credit card. They provided clothing and toiletries, helping me feel, at last, human again.

I was allowed visitors, though advised by the Embassy not to speak to the press—which I had no intention of doing.

Then, there was a sharp knock on the hospital door.

Jeff walked in, beaming, his face alight with relief. He slapped me on the back and wished me well, his warmth washing over me like sunlight.

We sat for hours, talking about all the places Jimmy and I had visited, the things we had done, the plans we'd made. But he avoided mentioning the North. And so did I.

Still, I sensed something was wrong. Something unspoken.

Eventually, I looked at him and said, "There's something you're not telling me. You haven't said how Jimmy is."

Jeff's smile faltered. Then he looked at me, steady and clear.

"Jimmy passed away last year."

The words hit like a sledgehammer. I brought my hands to my face and sobbed—deep, aching sobs that tore through my chest.

Jeff held me like a grieving child, arms wrapped around me as I wept uncontrollably. Another part of me was gone—my friend, brother, my soul mate.

Was it my fault?

"How did he die?" I whispered.

"Liver cancer," Jeff replied gently. "He had two years of happiness back home before it took him. Not a day went by when he didn't speak about you. He tried everything he could to get you out. He made me promise that if you ever came back, I would help you however I could."

He paused, then added, "That's why I'm here."

Jeff had already arranged a temporary visa for me to visit the United States. He and Rita had opened their home to me—for as long as I needed until I was ready to stand on my own again.

For the first time since my release, I felt something stir.

Not grief. Not hope.

But the faintest echo of peace.

Together with Jeff, I boarded the plane. I was trembling. Even then, I couldn't quite believe it—that I was free and returning to civilisation. Part of me still feared it was a cruel trick, that I would wake up back in the camp.

When we landed in America, the customs officials were remarkably kind. I'm sure they knew who I was and what I had been through. Not a single awkward question. Just a warm voice that said, "Have a nice stay, sir. Welcome to America."

I spent every day with Jeff and Rita. Their kindness helped me begin the long recovery journey—not just physical, but mental. Only then did I begin to understand how deeply wounded I had become in North Korea. To this day, I still wonder how I came through it at all.

Eventually, I contacted the architects overseeing the work on my house in the UK. The news was sobering. With no contact for over three years and no indication of my whereabouts, the unpaid builder's invoice had gone to court. A judgment had been made to sell the house. The proceeds were used to pay the builder, the architect, the solicitor's fees, and the considerable court costs. Whatever was left had been deposited with my solicitor.

Later, an official from the British Embassy revisited me. They requested that I attend a meeting at the Foreign Office once back in the UK to answer a few questions about my time in North Korea.

I declined.

I told them I had been gone for five years—five years without any contact, without a single inquiry, without one attempt by my government to find me. I wanted no contact now. I did, however, ask them to contact my solicitor to inform him of my return. That, they agreed to.

The time had come to leave the home that Jeff and Rita had so generously given me. A home of healing. A place of peace. I was leaving not just a place but a sanctuary—and with it, the memories etched into my mind, ones that would never fade. The beauty of Colorado, the extraordinary kindness of the people there, and the friends I had made—and lost—in both Korea and America.

I left with a heart full of sorrow and hope.

That final drive from Fort Morgan to Denver International Airport was quiet and heavy with unspoken words. Jeff and Rita had become like family to me. I realised they didn't want me to go, just as I struggled to leave. But my homeland was calling. I knew I wouldn't feel truly free until I was settled back in the land I was born to.

At the check-in desk, I handed over the few belongings I had packed and received my boarding pass. I could see the British Airways 747 resting on the flight apron through the glass.

When my flight was finally called over the address system, I turned to Jeff and Rita for the last time. It was an emotional goodbye. We kept our composure, but only just.

Tearing myself away, I turned and strolled toward the departure gate. I handed over my boarding pass, then turned back one final time and waved.

I haven't seen them since that day.

As the plane lifted off the runway and soared into the sky, I felt something stir inside me—something like wonder. For a fleeting second, it felt like the beginning of another adventure.

But I caught myself.

No more adventures. I'd had quite enough for one lifetime.

I chuckled under my breath and thought, Act your age.

Looking out the window, I watched the American landscape slip away beneath me. I knew, with quiet certainty, that it would be the last time I would ever see that country.

An air stewardess approached.

"Would you like a drink, sir?" "Yes," I replied. "Champagne, please."

The End

www.ingramcontent.com/pod-product-compliance
Ingram Content Group UK Ltd.
Pitfield, Milton Keynes, MK11 3LW, UK
UKHW020625070725
6753UKWH00003B/50

9 781917 640640